ALSO BY EILEEN DREYER

Brain Dead

Bad Medicine

Nothing Personal

If Looks Could Kill

A Man to Die For

With a
VENGEANCE

Eileen Dreyer

St. Martin's Paperbacks

WITH A VENGEANCE

Copyright © 2003 by Eileen Dreyer.
Excerpt from *Head Games* copyright © 2004 by Eileen Dreyer.

Library of Congress Catalog Card Number: 2002035885

ISBN: 0-312-99546-6

Printed in the United States of America

St. Martin's Press hardcover edition / March 2003
St. Martin's Paperbacks edition / March 2004

St. Martin's Paperbacks are published by St. Martin's Press, 175 Fifth Avenue, New York, NY 10010.

10 9 8 7 6 5 4 3 2 1

This book is dedicated to all the Tactical Medics, especially my classmates and teachers at the Tactical EMS School at Camp Ripley, Minnesota, who go out there and do it, while I only have to pretend now. As the world finally knows, you're the real heroes.

Because we're a team.

Stay safe.

Acknowledgments

Once again I relied on the best in the business for their help, advice, and wisdom. Thank you isn't nearly enough.

Dr. Mary Case and Mary Fran Ernst, St. Louis County Medical Examiner's Office; Mary Rose Psara, R.N., St. Louis City Medical Examiner's Office (see, Rose? I remembered); Michelle Podolak; Lt. John Podolak, Sergeant Zarrick, and Sergeant Richard Hudson of the St. Louis Police; Office Bob Duffin, St. Louis City SWAT Team; Lt. Jeffrey Bader and the St. Louis County Tactical Operations Unit; Paramedic Lt. Bob Ziffert, Creve Coeur Fire District.

Special and eternal thanks to Todd Burke and the entire, amazing, dedicated, excellent staff of the Tactical EMS School for gracious patience and unstinting encouragement, not to mention a vast wealth of knowledge and experience. And to the class of 1998, Camp Ripley, Minnesota, who made me welcome and got me through. Especially my red team. I couldn't have gotten up the walls without you guys. You're my heroes. I hope I got it right for you.

My most heartfelt thanks to Andrea Cirillo for her support and patience, to Jen Enderlin and Matthew Shear for believing in me and waiting for me. To Julie Garwood, who gave me the key to Maggie and Sean over coffee. To Kristin Hannah, who showed me another way up the hill. To all my friends and fans in the business who have been there, who've cheered and comforted and supported me through the last two years. And, of course, the Divas. 'Nough said.

To my family, especially my husband, Rick, who never knew just what he was getting into when he said "I do." I can only thank God you did. Because we're a team. And as my SWAT friends will tell you, that means everything.

With a
VENGEANCE

It is always with the best intentions that the worst work is done.

OSCAR WILDE

CHAPTER 1

It was the cicadas that pushed everything into critical mass.

The cicadas and a paranoid schizophrenic.

The cicadas, a paranoid schizophrenic, and a hat made of defective aluminum foil.

But mostly, it was the cicadas.

St. Louis in the summer is miserable enough. Hot, humid, and suffocatingly still, it resembles an anteroom to hell. Tempers shorten. Frustrations sharpen. What would be annoying any other time becomes unbearable.

But that summer was even worse. A cicada population of biblical proportions had awakened from two separate periods of dormancy to drive every person in the bistate region to violence. Breeding and eating at a ferocious rate in their hurry to mate and die, the insects whined out a satanic symphony of grinding dissonance that could incite a saint to suicide.

Within days, minor car accidents escalated to hostage situations, suburban soccer moms were arrested on felony weapons violations, and sporting events saw more action in the stands than on the field. The recently declining violent crime numbers swept right back up, police ran double shifts, and emergency departments started stockpiling antipsychotic drugs like nuclear arms.

Which meant that nobody was really surprised when the disturbance call went out at 11:32 A.M. on a late-July morning for the four hundred block of Ohio Avenue on the city's south side. A bare-bones kind of street, Ohio boasted faded brick multiple-family dwellings that housed the substrata of people hanging on to the fringes by their fingertips; new immigrants, ex–project inhabitants, chronic defaulters. In a word, the kind of block where disturbance calls were as common as bill collectors.

Usually, though, the calls came long after lunch, when the avenue's less wholesome tenants woke from their nightly revelries. Eleven-thirty was a little early, even on this kind of hot, still, muggy day.

But then, the cicadas were out.

The responding unit arrived on the scene at precisely 11:53 A.M. to be met by a young black woman up to her elbows in toddlers, and one teary-eyed ten-year-old in a pom-pom skirt. A baby on one hip and a hand on the other, the mother didn't bother to wait for the cops to get all the way out of the car before she started in on them.

"He crazy!" she shrieked, waving her free hand at the undersized cheerleader who slumped next to her. "He tried to boil my baby, say she a devil, and all she done was try and sell him some damn candy bars. You get in there and drag his skinny white ass down here 'fore I boil it myself, you hear? My Sherees, she gotta sell forty bars by tomorrow, and he got the whole box in there, that crazy fucker."

Busy slipping batons into belts and caps onto heads, the cops, a rare two-person ride that consisted of a young white male and a more mature black woman, nodded like synchronized swimmers.

"You know this man?" the female officer asked.

"He jus' moved in a coupla weeks ago," the mother said, following them up the sidewalk, the kids orbiting in place. "He in there with squirrels and bats and shit. I saw it when I grabbed my baby. Motherfucker's crazy!"

After a few more pertinent questions, the officers left the woman in the street and ambled into the unremarkable square brick building whose only ornamentation was a bouquet of blue plastic flowers stuck into the address, atop which several of the ubiquitous cicadas were mating.

Back on the street, the young mother raised her voice above the noise to regale gathering neighbors with her eyebrow-raised, neck-snapping rendition of Sherees's run-in with the new neighbor. She'd gotten to the point where she'd grabbed little Sherees out of the crazy motherfucker's arms when two quick pops brought the group to sudden silence.

Gunshots.

From the second floor of the apartment building.

Everybody turned that way. Little Sherees, her tears dried, looked up at her stunned mother. "Mama, you tell them 'bout the gun that man stuck up his pants?"

Which was about the time the crazy motherfucker started yelling about hostages.

Maggie O'Brien was still securing her medic vest when she opened the door to the command trailer at the corner of Ohio and Wyoming. A normally unprepossessing 120 pounds over a five-foot-five-inch frame, Maggie looked instead like an extra from a Chuck Norris movie. Her thick umber hair was tucked up under a blue kerchief, and her rather normal figure was rigged out in blue-dyed urban cammos, elbow and knee pads, jump boots, Eagle pack, CamelBak hydration system, body armor, overloaded medic vest, and gas mask. She carried her Kevlar helmet under her arm and her gloves in her helmet. SWATBabe, as her friends had dubbed her, was on duty.

The four hundred block of Ohio had been evacuated of all but police equipment and personnel. Two perimeters had been established, the interior perimeter two apartment houses wide, the exterior taking up the entire block. Strobes flashed, radios crackled, uniforms cluttered the street, and a smaller knot of like-camouflaged men clustered near the midnight blue trailer Maggie approached just beyond the interior perimeter.

Maggie had been beeped no more than fifty minutes earlier and had joined the rest of the newly minted St. Louis City/County Cooperative Special Weapons and Training Team only moments before. It was her third call as the team's Tactical Emergency Medic, the first that was still active by the time the team arrived. The very first in which she'd been called into the trailer. She hoped nobody noticed that her hands were shaking.

"You want me, Lieu?" she asked, stepping up into a tiny space containing way too many bodies and an overworked air-conditioner.

"Other side of the trailer, Mags," the scene commander said from where he was bent over a grease-pencil-marked schematic of the block. "We have a medical situation inside the negotiators need you to help with."

Maggie nodded and backed out. It was standard operating procedure that the command center stayed separate from the hostage negotiators. The negotiators needed to establish a positive relationship with the hostage taker, something that could be jeopardized if that negotiator looked up to see the commander sending in the troops on a "shoot to stop" order. The way the St. Louis team had set it up, a third person stationed himself with the negotiators to relay news to command by headset. When a hostage situation involved a possible medical problem, the medics were trained to evaluate and assist along with the negotiators.

So Maggie knocked on the back door of the divided trailer and waited for one of the extraneous personnel to decamp before climbing aboard.

"We've got a medical person coming to talk to you, Bob," one of the negotiators was saying into the phone, his voice low and calm and soothing. The kind of voice you'd use with a jittery horse or a crazy person. ". . . yeah, sure, sit back a second. Let me fill her in, and I'll let her talk to you."

The negotiator was a middle-aged, medium-sized black guy with old, soft eyes and fidgety hands who looked oddly out of place in jump boots and high-tech gear. Surreptitiously putting the caller on hold, he turned Maggie's way.

"Well, don't you look fine," he greeted her with a smile.

She grinned back. "I look like a click beetle on steroids." It wouldn't do to give her father's old partner the kiss she usually greeted him with. "Hi, Uncle John."

"Tommy would be so proud."

Maggie held on to her smile by force of will. She didn't need to know how proud her father would be right now.

"Oh, shit," the other guy in the trailer moaned. "I just knew it. If we have a crazoid, O'Brien can't be more than five feet away."

The other guy Maggie knew, too. A sergeant out in Manchester where Maggie played paramedic part-time, he was trim and slim and military-issue, right down to his blond buzz cut and snapping gray eyes. And he just loved being a cop.

"What do you mean?" John asked, forehead creased.

The other guy scowled. "Don't you know? Maggie here's not just a nut magnet. She's the pilgrimage destination for every psychotic, schizophrenic, and dome-headed geek in the Midwest."

"Slander, Flower," Maggie disagreed. "I'm sure I don't pull any more netjobs than anybody else."

Flower, nicknamed in an homage to *Bambi* because of his unfortunate preference for Mexican food, hooted in derision. "So you really think it's a coincidence that you're the medic called for a guy who tried to parboil a pom-pom girl because her candy bars were possessed?"

Maggie shot Flower a sheepish grin. "Could happen to anybody."

Maggie spent a moment wiping the sweat from her forehead. It was damn near a hundred degrees outside, she was carrying about seventy pounds of equipment on her, and the cicadas were driving her to distraction. And to top it off, she had to score her first negotiating gig with John, whom she respected more than almost anyone in the world. Even the meat locker air-conditioning in the trailer wasn't much help.

"I assume the medical condition is more than just little voices?" she asked.

John's smile was a bit tight. "Suspect and hostage have both suffered gunshot wounds. Suspect to the right arm, hostage to the right thigh. That's all he'll give us so far. The suspect's name is Montana Bob."

Maggie forgot about the humidity and sat down on the other chair. "Bob?" she asked, peeking out the window. "No kidding. And in an apartment, too. I'm so glad. He's been camped out beneath the Fourteenth Street overpass for years."

"You know him?" John asked.

"Didn't I tell you she would?" Flower retorted.

Maggie smiled. "Oh, sure. You've seen Bob, Uncle John. He hangs around the Toe Tag Saloon all the time. He's a regular at the Biltmore." The Biltmore being the nickname for Blymore Memorial, one of the big trauma hospitals in the area where Maggie served most of her time as a trauma nurse. "Brings me flowers. Bob's a paranoid schiz with delusions of U.N. invasions. Which means the candy bars aren't really satanic. Probably more along the line of a transmitter from 'them.' "

"Them?" John asked.

She smiled. "You know, John. 'Them.' CIA, FBI, aliens. The ones who are trying to take over. The ones who wire his head and try and get him to do bad things. The candy bars probably had a diabolical device planted in them—computer chips being the latest favorite—to control his mind."

"To kill him, actually," John said.

Maggie nodded. "He is kinda fun to play with, isn't he?"

"The hostage he shot," Flower snapped, "is an officer."

Maggie stopped cold. "We know who it is?"

Her Uncle John looked hard at her. "Yeah, Mags. It's Sean Delaney. He's fine right now. We want to keep him that way."

Maggie was real proud of herself. She didn't give herself away by any more than a blink or two.

"You know him, too, I'm assuming?" Flower asked.

Uncle John smiled gently. "Maggie knows everybody in the city. She grew up in the department."

Maggie did her best to smile back. "Delaney's dad and Tommy were asshole buddies," she said. "We kind of grew up together."

Then, before John could reassure her again, she set down her helmet and held out her hand for the headset. "Tell me what the status is."

"Delaney and Myla Parker answered a disturbance call. Evidently Montana Bob saw the uniforms and pulled out the .38 nobody knew he had. Sean got Myla out before Bob got him. That's been about. . . . oh, seventy-five or so minutes ago."

"Myla's okay?"

"Yeah."

"And Sean took a shot in the thigh?"

"Right. He says it's—"

"Just a scratch," Maggie answered along with him. "He said the same thing last year when we put a chest tube in him."

A breath. A quick close of the eyes to lock out Uncle John's distress.

"Okay." Maggie nodded and flipped the mike on. "Bob?" she greeted her longtime patient, her tone an instinctive echo of John's. "It's Maggie-o, Bob. Can you talk?"

There was a brief moment of silence, a scuffling sound on the line, and then the tremulous voice Maggie knew so well. "You bastards. You've taken her, too."

Maggie couldn't help but grin. Well, at least she was on familiar turf. "No, Bob, I swear, it's Maggie. Nobody's hurt me. You know I won't let 'em hurt you if you listen real close."

Nothing.

"Bob?"

"Prove it."

Maggie fought down the urge to scream and nodded.

"Okay, Bob, can you see the big blue van outside? I'm gonna step out the door and give you our sign. Now, I'm going to be dressed like them, Bob, but that's okay. They're here just to make sure nothing worse happens, you understand? If you listen to me, nobody else is going to get hurt. Okay?"

"I'll shoot you if you're lying."

John, on the other headset, twitched with distress. Maggie waved him off. "I hope you would, Bob. Now, watch out the window."

"Be advised," Flower was murmuring into his own headset to the command post. "Subject is approaching the front window. Believed to be nonhostile."

"C2 to A10," Maggie heard in the receiver taped to her free ear. "Make entry to building on my word."

Which meant that while they knew where Bob was, the entry team was going to sneak inside to get closer to Bob's apartment.

Maggie yanked off the headset and eased her way out the door. It was oddly quiet out there, even the cicadas hushed. Weapons had been raised a notch higher, all attention focused on that window.

Maggie saw a shadow in the apartment window, saw the blinds raised. She caught the sight of a lot of pale skin and the dull glint of metal and almost laughed.

"What the hell?" one of the guys demanded.

"C2 to A10, suspect is visible in side one number three window. Go now."

Maggie ignored the voice. She never acknowledged the dark snake of police that slipped toward the rear door. Lifting her arm as high as she could, she flipped the Longhorn salute. There was a pause, and then the odd figure in the window disappeared. Maggie squeezed back inside the van.

"Did I see what I thought I saw?" Flower demanded, lowering the binoculars he'd been using.

"A naked man wearing a steel pot on his head?" Maggie asked, reclaiming her chair. "Sure. His aluminum foil hat must have stopped working."

"What does that have to do with the Longhorn salute?"

"Bob went to University of Texas," she said, sliding the headset back on.

"Hence the moniker, 'Montana Bob,' obviously."

Maggie grinned. "The CIA took over Texas years ago."

"I'd heard that," John concurred.

"Bob?" she asked, back on line. "You there?"

"Thank you, Maggie," he whispered. "You walked the valley of death for me. Just for me, for me. But you have to get out. They know I know, and they're going to kill me. I don't want them to kill you, too."

"Well, they can't kill me," Maggie assured him, "because I *don't* know, so it's okay. I promise."

"Watch our brave Maggie boogie-board that big delusion pipeline," Flower murmured behind her. Maggie, sweating as she thought of the policeman on Bob's floor, ignored him.

"No, Maggie," Bob argued, "they will. They've killed Sancho and Urban and the dog and snake. They've killed them all, and I know. I know because I heard them whispering in the night, I saw them, I hear them now, with their radios in their wings just waiting for me to step outside. They're trying to get a message to me right now, can you hear 'em?"

Every crazy in the Mississippi Valley thought the cicadas were trying to get a message to them. Maggie wasn't the only one who wished the damn things wouldn't sound so much like radio static.

"I hear it, Bob, but that's not what I—"

"They're here, though, Maggie, killing and killing in their night angels suits, black as night, black as death—"

"Which is why we're dressed up this way today," Maggie assured him, wondering who his new imaginary playmates were. Bob was always imagining cabals. But he'd never imagined anybody named Sancho as a victim before. Maybe he'd been reading *Man of La Mancha*. Or *Doctor Dolittle*. "We're trying to fool them into getting you out safe. But we can't unless you help us, Bob. That officer you have, he's one of us. He's my friend. And we've got to get him treated, or they'll hurt you, Bob. They'll hurt us all, okay? They'll know."

"They already know, Maggie. All of them. It's why they tried to get me to take that phone. The one with the computer chip in it."

"No, that was just to talk to you, Bob. To try and figure out a way to get you out safe. But you figured out a way, didn't you? You used your own phone. You know your phone is safe, because you check it and wrap it in Saran wrap, just like I told you."

"That's it, Maggie. But I think they're listening anyway. I don't think I have much time."

"Then let's get you two taken care of, Bob, okay? I want you to tell me about the officer's injuries. You need to help him so I can sneak you away before they know. Please?"

"I can't, Maggie," he whined pathetically, the drone of the insects almost louder than his voice. "I can't think."

"Then look," she commanded. "Look at his leg. Come on, Bob. You can do this. Tell me what it looks like."

It took Maggie twenty minutes to get a good picture of what was going on inside and to talk Bob through basic first aid. It took another two hours for John to talk Montana Bob out of his apartment. By that time, the temperature had scaled up another fifteen degrees, the neighbors were arguing with the cops, and the news crews had grown more plentiful than the cicadas. Maggie spent the time out on the street making sure her team was hydrated and trying like hell not to think of what was going on in that apartment.

Bob had only suffered a superficial wound, one the team could safely dispatch back to the ambulance that was stationed beyond the outside perimeter. Officer Sean Delaney, though, who had pushed his partner back out the door before Bob could close it on them, had been bleeding for a good couple of hours, and nobody wanted him to try and make it out of the apartment. So when Bob opened his apartment door, the entry team that was by now positioned in his hallway would sweep him out like bad dirt, and Maggie and her partner would run in from where they waited alongside the gas team to treat the cop while the building was secured.

"A10 to C2, stand by," Maggie heard in her earpiece. "Subject door is opening."

Bob was coming out. Everybody outside suddenly went quiet as they watched the building entrance, as if they could see the drama unfolding. Tucked behind trees and hedges, the containment team kept their guns leveled on the field while watching the entire scene. Even the cicadas seemed to pause, until all Maggie heard was radios and the gas team guy's heavy breathing.

"Suspect secured!" she heard in her earpiece. "M1 and 2 enter."

Maggie struggled to redistribute all the weight she carried as she climbed to her feet. She was sweating like a horse, her heart rate was damn near red-lining, and Sean lay upstairs bleeding all over Montana Bob's floor. Good thing she was in shape for shit like this.

Maggie had made it halfway across the lawn in a bent-knee run when four of the entry team slammed back through the front door to send Montana Bob sprawling onto the sidewalk. Maggie saw him go down, saw the pot go skittering down the sidewalk as more cops piled on top like a rugby scrimmage.

In that moment she damn near forgot about Sean. Bob had shot a cop, and not one person on that pile was going to let him forget it.

"Maggie, run!" Bob was screaming, his cheek scraping into the sidewalk, his limbs sprawled and squashed like a frog on a driveway. "He's here, Maggie, get out! Get o-o-u-u-t!"

And Maggie, even knowing that her first priority was the wounded policeman, had to stop.

"Hey, you guys, go easy," she insisted, dropping into the fray. "It's not his fault. He's just crazy. Come on, let him breathe."

When she got past all the riot gear to where Bob lay

panting on the ground, she saw that there were tears on his sallow cheeks. "I'm sorry," he whispered, his eyes pleading. "I got you into this, Maggie. I'm so sorry . . ."

"Aw, c'mon, Bob," Maggie assured him, pushing his dingy hair back from his face as she surreptitiously checked to make sure that his injury was, indeed, superficial. "It's okay. I promise. They'll take care of you now."

"No," he countered sadly. "They'll kill me. You get out now, Maggie. Please . . ."

"Maggie," one of the team members said as he motioned everybody else to ease their holds on the suspect. "We have him."

Maggie nodded, wishing she could make Bob feel better, and patted him on the cheek. Then, leaving him in safe hands, she lumbered up the stairs to the front apartment.

"You asshole," she genially greeted the downed officer when she made it through the door.

Slouched against a wall decorated in right-wing newsprint, tacked-up roadkill, and marked-up news photos, Sean Delaney offered a whimsical smile and a halfhearted wave of the Hershey bar he'd been munching from the half-empty box on the floor. "Want some candy, little girl?"

Maggie smiled. "You're eating all that poor kid's profits."

"Hey, Bob and I had to keep our strength up. Paranoia's a high-energy sport, ya know. Besides, I knew I'd have to be at my best when you showed up." With a waggle of his eyebrows, he patted the stained carpet. "Come sit by me and make my pulse race, honey."

Maggie snorted unkindly and dropped to her knees alongside the second team medic. "You must be bad, Delaney," she said, pulling equipment from her vest. "That's the worst excuse for sexual harassment I've heard since Eddie Kawalksi snapped my bra in sixth grade."

Delaney just grinned, his eyes fever-bright and his forehead creased with discomfort. "I'm bleeding, O'Brien. That should get me some points."

"You've been bleeding before, Delaney. Doesn't get you anything but light-headed and wet."

"No, Maggie," he disagreed. "I got that from seeing you in cammos."

Maggie grinned as she checked his racing pulse. "You really have to try and hang around with some humanoids sometime, Delaney. By the way, are you hypovolemic, or are you just happy to see me?"

The other paramedic, a skinny guy named Jazz, had already secured Sean's Beretta and was busy pulling out fluids and lines for some volume replacement. Maggie did a quick assessment and reached for her scissors. Even with the pressure bandage she'd talked Bob through applying, Sean's pant leg was soaked and the floor beneath him sticky with old blood. The good news was that if the bullet had hit a major artery, Sean would have been dead an hour ago. So the bleeding wasn't critical. It was, however, enough to make Maggie want to puke. And Maggie wasn't a puker. At least about blood.

"I'm always happy to see you, honey," Delaney managed, a little late and a little too quietly. "Especially when I know you're about to have your way with me."

Maggie looked at the mischievous light in those usually sharp green eyes. She saw the sweat stains on his uniform shirt, the lank, sticky hair that was usually brushed to a mahogany gleam, and the fact that his face, normally so strong and tan, was a little slack and the color of putty. Sean Delaney prided himself on looking like a poster child for St. Louis's finest. Today, he looked like a fallen cop soufflé. And still, he had that gleam in his eyes. He was having a hell of a time.

Which really made Maggie mad. She wasn't the one who should have been shaking here.

"Don't honey me, you uncoordinated, hormone-happy bog-trotter," she snapped, not nearly as hotly as she'd intended. "Just shut up and let me get in your pants."

"I thought you'd never ask."

"You shouldn't talk to her like that," Jazz finally ob-

jected. Jazz, who didn't know either of them too well yet.
"It's not right."

A tall, thin, quiet guy with acne-pocked skin and hair
like a blond Brillo pad, Jazz saw his job as a mission and
all his patients holy. Jazz was never allowed near a phone
during hostage negotiations, because he kept trying to get
the hostage taker to take Christ instead. On the other hand,
Jazz was one of the best trauma paramedics in the bistate
area, with the plus that the sound of gunfire didn't spook
him. Even if it was directed at him while he worked. So
people overlooked his conversional tendencies.

"It's okay, Jazz," Maggie reassured him. "Delaney
knows I'll pay him back later."

Jazz just shook his head like a mournful dog. "Didn't
your father ever teach you that you deserve better than sexual taunts?"

Maggie stopped cold. Delaney whistled through his
teeth. "Now you've done it," he said.

Maggie couldn't quite take her eyes off the very sincere
medic. "Do you know who my father is?" she asked.

Jazz actually blushed. "It doesn't matter."

"Can I have my drugs now?" Sean asked on a deliberate
whine.

Maggie couldn't quite answer.

"How 'bout a donut?" he demanded, tugging at her arm.

She looked down, startled, and shook herself. "Eat another Hershey bar." Leaving Jazz quite out of it, she went
after Delaney's pants. "Asshole," she muttered, but it
wasn't quite clear whom she was addressing.

Maggie didn't get into the Emergency Department at Blymore to check on her patients for another hour. Technically
her responsibility for them only lasted until the moment she
delivered them into the paramedics' waiting arms. After
that she stayed with the team for cleanup and debriefing.

At today's debriefing she heard how she'd handled her
first hostage negotiation like a pro, and that if she ever

cared for a perp before an officer again, she was going to get her cute little ass kicked right back to Nightingaleville.

Maggie grinned at the first and ignored the second. According to her charter, the commander was perfectly right. A tactical medic followed the good principles of triage, in which the more serious injury was treated first. And her officer had certainly suffered the more serious injury. By checking on Bob first, she'd thumbed her nose at very important priorities. And considering how Maggie felt about her team, in any other situation, she wouldn't have hesitated.

But her intervention had helped the team control Bob. And Jazz had already been upstairs sharing the good news with Officer Delaney. Besides, Delaney didn't need to know how much he'd scared her.

Because of the relatively quick solution to the action today, debriefing only lasted through two boxes of donuts. Quick enough for Maggie to get to the ED before they shipped Delaney off somewhere, slow enough, she hoped, to avoid most of the Sturm und Drang.

Instead, she walked through the sliding doors of Blymore Medical Center to be greeted by pandemonium. The press had arrived en masse, every cop with a ride was cluttering up the hallway, and Bob, instead of settling down, showed every sign of blowing like Krakatoa. And that didn't even take into account that the waiting room was overflowing and mostly contagious.

This time, though, Maggie checked on Delaney first.

"Well, buy me slippers and call me Dorothy," she heard behind her as she checked out the chart that hung on Sean's door.

Maggie didn't even bother to turn around. "You've never even seen *Wizard of Oz,* and you know it."

A tall, leggy African-American man in salmon-colored scrubs and marcelled hair swung a deliberately limp wrist at her. "I know. I am *such* a disgrace to my stereotype."

Maggie looked up at her friend's horsey face and laughed. "Well, practice. The entire press corps is out there.

Think what you could do for the hospital if you went out there and did a few choruses of 'My Way.' "

"In feathers," her friend said. "It could change the face of medicine as we know it."

"Might do it some good, Martha."

Martha was her friend's club name. His real name was Dr. Allen Fitzmaurice, MD, FACS, trauma surgeon and Emergency Department director. Standing six-foot-four, he weighed in at about 170 and was probably the ugliest man Maggie had ever seen. He was an even uglier woman.

"Help!" Bob screamed down in room three. "Help! They're going to kill me!"

As was usual with crazies, Bob's outburst set off three more screamers, who were all, evidently, at risk from the FBI. The rest of the packed hall escalated right behind them.

"Is O'Brien here someplace?" one of the docs demanded farther down the worklane. "She snuck in, didn't she?"

Maggie ignored him, just as she always did. "Is the officer going to live?" she asked Allen instead.

She got an elegant shrug and a saucy grin. "That bullet hit any higher and he coulda been night watchman in a harem."

"Do me a favor and tell him that."

"You make it sound like he did it on purpose."

Maggie sighed. "He did. He does. This is the third time, ya know. I think he just does it to yank my chain."

"The same reason you joined the big, brawny boys in blue?" Allen countered with a barely lifted, carefully plucked eyebrow.

Maggie flushed a little. "You know why I joined. I grew up with these cops. I feel a . . . responsibility to them."

Allen laughed. "Rationalization will get you nowhere, my darling. We know all about sublimation in this state."

Maggie couldn't even manage much of a smile. "Oh, shut up."

"By the way," Allen assured her. "The outfit is *très*

butch. Do you know you swagger—just that much—when you wear it?"

Maggie looked down at the cammos and jump boots she still wore along with her black POLICE/PARAMEDIC T-shirt. She did, in fact, know she swaggered when she wore them. Ever since she'd first tried them on for Tactical EMS School at Camp Ripley, she'd been thinking of wearing them down to the ED for work. Maybe help keep some of the crazies in line. Or the doctors.

"Maggie," she heard behind her, "are you going to get in there and calm that crazy bastard down?"

Or, she thought with a halfhearted sigh, the nurses. Turning, she faced her newest inquisitor.

"His name is Bob, Carmen," she told the nurse who glared at her from five feet away. "You might try using it. He usually responds to it better than, 'Hey, you crazy bastard.' "

Carmen Peterson was a hot young postgrad nurse with the features of a spitz and the temperament of a corgi. Everything pissed her off, but most of all Maggie pissed her off because Maggie wouldn't get pissed off along with her. Carmen was standing there now, fists clenched on lean, overexercised hips, and small, thin mouth pursed in obvious impatience. Even her eyes were small and pursed, like raisins left too long in the sun.

"Listen, I have eight other patients, one of them a woman whose husband beat the crap out of her for burning the pot roast. Would you rather I hold your crazy bastard's hand or help her get the hell out of the house?"

"I'd rather you blow the house up with the husband in it."

Carmen twitched. "We're way past that. Now, what about that crazy bastard in three?"

This time Maggie found herself grinning. "That crazy bastard in three brings me flowers once a month and warns me when we're in danger of alien invasion. What have *you* done for me lately?"

For a split second, Carmen's pose held. Then her face

split into a grin wider than Maggie's. "All the crazies love
you best," she retorted in a six-year-old's whine. "Get him
off my hands?"

Maggie laughed. "Since you asked nicely."

Carmen spun on her heel, leaving Allen shaking his
head. Allen didn't understand why Maggie got along with
Carmen. There were days Maggie didn't either.

"Do I have to bring you flowers, too?" Delaney asked
from inside trauma room two.

Maggie shoved his door the rest of the way open to find
him pale and sweaty and supine on a trauma cart with a
unit of blood and a bag of saline already hooked up. Her
stomach heaved at the sight of him, but she knew better
than to retreat from the field.

"I don't want anything from you, you idiot," she retorted, handing Allen Sean's chart and stalking into the
room. "The only thing I ever did ask for you keep forgetting anyway."

He grinned. "A cop can't promise not to get shot, Mags.
Takes all the fun out of the job. How many people have
told you how proud Tommy would be of you?"

Maggie knew a deliberate topic change when she heard
it, but she couldn't refuse. In fact, she scowled. "At least a
dozen."

His smile this time was softer. "You *were* pretty amazing out there today."

Maggie didn't give an inch. "You just get off on tough
chicks."

"Tough chicks with balls."

"In that case, maybe you'd like to dance with Martha
over there."

"Only if he leads!" Allen called from the hallway.

Delaney laughed like a kid.

"Maggie!" Bob called from across the hall. "Maggie,
please save me!"

Sean's laughter died. "Go on over and see to poor Bob,"
he pleaded. "He needs your soothing hand more than I do."

"Everybody needs it more than you do, Delaney," she said.

"I'm not kidding," he said. "Take care of him. I, uh, really feel sorry for him. He's not a bad guy."

"High praise, coming from the hostage."

Delaney actually had the grace to look uncomfortable. "You know what I mean."

Maggie relented. "Yeah, I do. I'll go see him."

But first, she needed desperately to detour to the nurses' lounge. She hadn't been kidding earlier about puking. Delaney just didn't get how much it upset her to keep seeing him on one of her carts. And she wasn't about to let him know. So she ran off like a baby before he found out.

It took Maggie another fifteen minutes to face Bob, and even then she wasn't sure she was up to it. She found him strapped down in four-point restraints and all but frothing at the mouth, his eyes rolling, his face sweaty and ashen. One arm sported a bandage, the other an IV for antibiotics. His face was scraped and bruised, and his dirty, scrawny body was only half-covered by a sagging patient gown.

"Maggie, they didn't get you yet," he whispered, turning big washed-out blue eyes at her. Eyes that saw things nobody else did.

Maggie wet a washcloth and wiped the sweat and spittle away. "I'm just fine, Bob."

"It's too late, Maggie," he pleaded, closing his eyes. "They've injected me with bacteria. I can feel it weighing on my heart, Maggie, heavy on my heart where my sins live . . ."

"That's just antibiotics for your gunshot, Bob," she hushed.

But Bob wouldn't be settled. "No, no it isn't. You know. You know. Get my stash and run, Maggie. Get my stash, where my heart lived. You get it, okay?"

Maggie smiled as if she meant it. "Sure, Bob. I promise."

Tears filled his eyes, and for a moment, Bob was really there. Afraid, ashamed, appalled at what he knew the world thought of him. Of what Maggie thought of him. He tried to reach for her with a hand that was tied to the cart, and Maggie stretched over to meet him halfway.

"It'll be all right, Bob," she soothed, squeezing hard to get past the layers of delusion and terror and emptiness. "I promise."

Bob's smile, when it came, was infinitely sad. "Don't . . . promise . . ." He hiccupped, twitched, refocused. ". . . get it, Maggie—"

And that fast, his eyes rolled back and he began to convulse.

For a second, Maggie just stared. He wasn't even on a monitor, for God's sake. He'd just been shot in the arm. But if there was one thing Maggie could recognize, it was cardiac arrest.

"Call a code!" she yelled, vaulting right up onto the cart to punch on his chest. "Call a goddamn code!"

"What's O'Brien up to now?" somebody demanded.

But nobody ignored a code call. The announcement went out. Carmen scuttled in to crank up the monitor as Maggie bent down to breathe into that terrible, gaping mouth.

The team poured in like water over a dam. Patsy Levins, the medical resident on, choreographed the code like a chorus number from *Les Mis*. Maggie took over the drug position, shoving everything in the crash cart straight into Bob's bigger vessels. She pumped and exhorted and demanded answers, but right on the stroke of five o'clock, Patsy yanked off her gloves with a definite snap and walked from the room. Montana Bob, still strapped to the emergency room cart he'd so often called home, lay silent and staring.

"I guess he should have listened," Carmen said as she pulled out morgue sheet and toe tags.

Maggie couldn't quite move from the bottom of the bed, her hand on Bob's cold, waxy foot. "Listened?"

"The voices told him he was going to die," Carmen said. "I guess they were right."

But they shouldn't have been, was all Maggie could think. She'd been there. She'd seen his injury. It hadn't been fatal. Hell, it hadn't even been minor.

He shouldn't be dead, no matter what his voices had said. No matter what anybody said. As she stood looking down on that empty, wasted husk of a human body, Maggie wanted to know why the hell he was.

She couldn't quite say that, though. She couldn't tell the staff that she was terrified she'd let this sad little man down. So she patted his foot, as if he would know, and fought surprising tears for a homeless psychotic.

"He brought me flowers," she said, and turned away.

CHAPTER 2

"All hail the new SWATbastard!"

Maggie looked up from her whiskey and grimaced. "Is that like ratbastard?"

"No," the young cop said with a blush. "It's, you know, new SWAT member. But, uh, what do you call a, you know, woman?"

Maggie couldn't help a grin. "Ma'am?"

"SWATwoman," somebody suggested.

Maggie laughed. "Nah. Sounds like I wear tights."

"SWAT-Mamma."

"Don't even go there."

The Toe Tag was packed to the rafters, the music something country, and the smoke thick enough for an EPA alert. Everybody was here to cheer the first successful mission by the brand-new St. Louis City/County SWAT team.

Come to think of it, they were probably toasting down at City Hall and in the county council chambers in Clayton as well. The idea that the city and county, two separate entities in a highly political neck of the woods, would co-operate enough to mount a joint barbecue, much less a SWAT team, would have been considered harder to believe ten years ago than Mideast peace.

St. Louis had, after all, separated itself from its own county as far back as the late 1880s, when city fathers felt that county residents would be a drain on their rich coffers.

Now that the roles were reversed, the county was just as leery to take on the city's problems. Not only that, but pride on both sides preserved a rivalry more cherished than the one between the Cardinals and Cubs.

So the SWAT team headquarters was in the city, the equipment van kept in the county, and the assignments all down the line split evenly. And, astonishing to everybody in the metropolitan area except the SWAT members themselves, the team had proven effective, amiable, and fiercely loyal to each other. Which was the point of the party.

Or, more accurately, the open house. The Toe Tag, after all, was not only the favorite city cop bar, it was the favorite medical bar, and the favorite press bar. A bare bones, brick-and-Formica city watering hole that was so often found in the near south side, it boasted neon beer window decor, two pool tables, and glasses adorned with body outlines.

For the party it also included the entire SWAT team, still in urban BDUs and black POLICE T-shirts. Maggie and Jazz stood out only by the addition of the word PAR-AMEDIC on theirs.

"Tommy'd be real proud of you," one of the old-timers told Maggie not three inches from her face. "He here?"

Maggie did her best not to flinch from the blast of re-breathed beer. "Thanks, Mike. No, he's not here."

The cop, beefy and ruddy and white-haired, was jocular with everyone except Blacks, Jews, Hispanics, gays, and women cops. Except for Maggie, of course. Maggie was Tommy's kid.

"Okay," he said, patting her back. "I'll call him later. He should know."

Maggie just nodded and turned him in another direction.

One of her SWAT teammates shoved an ED doc off the stool next to Maggie and wagged a finger in her face. "Don't ever do that to me again," he warned.

Maggie saw the mischief in his eyes and grinned. "I promise," she said. "Do what?"

Paxton Barber wagged his finger again. Paxton was their best entry man, fearless and cold and deadly accurate. A five-foot-six-inch ex-paratrooper with precision-clipped rus-set goatee and shiny, shaved head, Paxton loved being right behind the shield, lining the rest of the team up behind his weapon like ducklings trying to stay dry in a storm. Even more he loved participating in the precision teamwork. Pax-ton missed the paratroopers. He had been the one to pull Montana Bob to his feet out on the sidewalk.

"Didn't your mama ever tell you not to break up a cat-fight?" Pax demanded, his voice only slurring a little.

"Cats don't bring me flowers."

"Nobody brings you flowers."

"Bob did. Every month. Flowers and the latest paranoia periodical. He didn't deserve the full-cop-shot-salute, Pax."

Paxton patted her hand like a grandfather. "Not your decision to make, Mag. I had it under control."

Maggie sighed. "If it was so under control, why is he dead?"

For just a moment, Paxton's easy manner disappeared. "You'd rather it be Delaney?"

"Don't ask stupid questions. I thought the purpose of the team was to keep casualties to a minimum."

"They were."

Maggie thought of those frightened eyes, that emaciated body stretched out on her cart like a captured animal.

"You took hold of him, Pax," she said, not even looking up from the black body outline on her shot glass. "Did I miss something?"

Paxton kept on patting. "You gonna be this way for all our perps?" he demanded quietly. "Might be a little coun-terproductive. You're gonna have to make the same choice again, ya know."

Maggie had long since considered that same very serious question. "Don't worry about my choices, Pax. I'm just trying to make sure I didn't screw up. Bob was my re-sponsibility, too."

Paxton sighed. "There was nothing more, Maggie. He just died. And you know the poor bastard's better off, so why make yourself nuts?"

"He might have wanted a chance to vote on the idea."

"Enough!" one of the team yelled, giving Maggie a shake. "We have a presentation to make."

A cheer went up, and Maggie had to set aside her preoccupation with Bob. It was time to celebrate. She'd worked harder for this moment than anything in her life, and her entire life had been work. She'd struggled to get her nursing degree on waitress wages, and then her paramedic license while nursing in the ED, and then, worked both jobs as diligently as possible until she was finally eligible to take the training at the Tactical EMS School that enabled her to apply to the brand-new SWAT team.

The SWAT team that had just had its first successful mission, which her friends wanted to celebrate with her. The last thing Maggie wanted was for something to diminish it. Even, she thought with a pang of guilt, Bob.

The self-appointed MC, a burly sergeant from County's Seventh District who was in charge of the equipment van, lined up the rest of the team on either side of Maggie and Paxton. Twenty-two of them, comprising the two answering squads, from a twenty-one-year-old alternative weapons expert to a fifty-year-old sniper, all grinning like game show contestants, half of them way past the legal limit. The other half—the evening team—stood with Cokes in hand instead of whiskey, and beepers in belts, since they were now on call.

Twenty-three guys and Maggie, already tight enough to die for each other, already good enough not to have to. Which was about what the announcer was saying as he placed cheap Burger King crowns on each team head to the bleary applause from the crowd. More eulogy than congratulations, his speech ended with rousing wishes for good health, good collars, and good pussy.

"Well, except for Maggie," he insisted with a salacious grin. "Unless she wants to, of course. I mean, after all, it is the new century. But if not, then good . . . uh, good . . ."

"You want good, baby?" one guy yelled, sloshing beer

over a hospital x-ray tech. "Come on over here, and I'll give good!"

"You have to know what good is first, McGill," Maggie retorted. "Besides, honey. Size *does* count."

She got a huge ovation, to which she bowed.

"We're not finished yet," the announcer objected. "There's one more presentation."

As if by magic, the crowd parted. Paul Trevor, one of their snipers, used his appropriately designed nose for a trumpet voluntary, and an honor guard appeared at the back. Cops, nurses, and barflies lined up to salute as six policemen marched forward in their formal blues, one reverentially carrying a big box in white-gloved hands.

"As you might have heard," the announcer intoned over the noise, "we kinda, well, weren't sure whether Maggie would fit into the team." The audience hooted. "Even though her nickname around town was Little Zen."

"There've been women on the teams before," Maggie protested.

"Yeah," the MC countered. "But not . . . uh . . ."

"Women medics."

All eyes lit and smiles were presented like rewards.

"Exactly," the MC allowed. "The SWAT team, you will admit, faces greater challenges than even the average Zenmeister would confront. So to reassure ourselves that she wouldn't, well, wash out at a bad time, we, uh, made sure her training was . . ." He grinned like a pirate, and even Maggie laughed. "Rigorous."

"I used to be five inches taller and twenty pounds heavier," Maggie agreed. And she'd almost grown back all the hair she'd lost from the stress.

"Well, this presentation is to settle the question once and for all," he answered grandly. Giving it enough flourish for a third-rate magician, he pulled open the box.

"For bravery above and beyond the line of duty," he intoned. "For brilliant negotiating with a lunatic in the line of fire. For the cutest ass in the Missouri SWAT Association . . ." He lifted his gifts and the place went wild. "To protect said ass."

"Not to mention the accompanying tits," somebody added.

Maggie was laughing so hard tears rolled down her face. They'd somehow found her a Kevlar bra and underpants.

"You sure it's big enough?" she demanded.

"I borrowed your bra from the locker room," Paxton assured her.

"How many times I gotta tell you, Pax?" Maggie demanded, donning her new attire over her T-shirt. "Wear your own damn bra."

"Speech! Speech!"

Thankfully, everybody was too involved with malt and hops to realize how difficult it was for Maggie to speak. Nobody noticed the tears that threatened or the wobble in her voice. But Maggie noticed. Maggie noticed that they were all beaming at her, every member of her team, as if she were their most precious friend. Their kid sister. And they were all proud of her.

It was just what she'd imagined, she realized. It was damn near everything she wanted. This, after all, was her religion, these people her creed. She'd tried other, darker churches that smelled of incense and beeswax instead of cigars and beer. She'd tried painted saints and omnipotent deities, and finally found her faith in these fragile, contradictory people who surrounded her. The frontline warriors who had raised her, the medical forces who had nurtured her.

Not the gods who sat silent and watched. The ones who waded right in and fought the good fight.

Maggie imagined her Kevlar bra and Burger King crown as sacramental vestments, and grinned like an idiot.

"You guys are too good to me," she finally managed, knowing perfectly well that they understood. "Now, if you could just manage some panty hose . . ."

Fifteen minutes later Maggie was still suffering hearty blows on the back and ribald commentary. Another round had been bought for the SWAT team, and Maggie was posing for her dozenth photo in her crown and underwear. In one corner of the room, a cop groupie was doing headstands in her sundress. In another, four guys were lining up imaginary shots on the wall photo of the mayor. Paul Trevor, he of the trumpet-sized nose, had just challenged Maggie to an undoubtedly lethal game of darts.

"Don't do it, boy," a gruff little voice said behind her. "She more likely to hit you than that board."

Forgetting all about the game, Maggie swung on her heels and laughed.

"Big Zen!"

Short, round, bright-eyed and soft-handed, the newcomer was African-American, grandmotherly, and benign. Possessed of the most legendary voice in the city, Big Zen was able to maintain a near-mythic composure in the face of chaos and disaster, which had earned her her nickname. She was the city's best dispatcher. She was also Dr. Allen Fitzmaurice's mother.

"Hi, baby," she greeted Maggie with a massive hug Maggie had to bend down for. "I'm proud of you."

Maggie had grown up literally at Big Zen's knee, which had earned Maggie her own nickname. Tommy had often considered Big Zen his own personal baby-sitter.

"Don't tell your son about my underwear," Maggie warned with a grin. "He'll just want some of his own."

Zen chuckled. "Not my Allen. Not flashy enough. Listen, girl, big brass asked me to introduce you to somebody. This is Susan Jacobsmeyer from the *Post-Dispatch*. She does those personality things in the weekend paper and wanted to meet you."

Maggie blinked a couple of times at the woman who had joined Zen. A tall girl, shapely enough to have six-foot-five-inch Paul pulling off his crown and holding it over his heart. Also blond, blue-eyed, and so young she still had baby fat in her cheeks. Maggie saw her eyes widen at the spectacle before her.

"Not a police reporter, huh?" Maggie asked.

The girl blinked like a baby rabbit. "My last story was on the history of Forest Park."

Maggie grabbed Paul's crown and put it where it would camouflage his bad manners. "Down, boy. She doesn't know the rules."

Paul sighed, and the baby reporter's eyes widened. "You're the new SWAT medic?" she asked Maggie in failing tones.

Maggie grinned. "The words 'police/paramedic' on my T-shirt probably gave me away, huh?"

Big Zen gave her a poke in the ribs. Maggie just slid an arm around the tiny woman's shoulders and sipped at her Jameson's.

"The paper would like to do a profile on you," the girl said, still almost in a whisper. "Your work, your life . . . that kind of thing."

Maggie was just drunk enough to be frivolous. "Sure."

The girl was nodding absently, her eyes still swiveling for action. "I'd really appreciate a chance to set up a time. You know, like, to talk. Get photos."

Maggie grinned, spread her arms to exhibit her newest attire. "You don't think this would work?"

"I gotta tell you to behave?" Big Zen chastised.

"She wants color, Zen," Maggie said with a big hug for her surrogate mom. "Between us we can manage that, don't you think?"

This time Zen just shook her head.

Maggie gave the reporter a half wave with her shot glass. "I'll be at, uh, Blymore ED tomorrow evening. Give me a call. In the meantime, hide behind the police reporter. It's safer over there."

Maybe if it had been earlier in the evening. Maybe if the reporter hadn't distracted her. Maggie should have at least heard the change in noise level in the room. She should have seen the warning in Big Zen's soft brown eyes.

"Maggie, girl, there you are!"

When the beefy hand hit her shoulder, Maggie had to

brace herself to keep from flinching. But instinct was too strong, and she knew he felt it.

"I hear you busted your cherry today, girl!"

Maggie didn't even realize she'd closed her eyes until she opened them to find that every person within a twenty-foot radius was watching for her reaction. The seas had parted, after all, to allow him access.

He was tall, a broad-shouldered, redheaded giant of a man with ruggedly handsome features, a bristling handlebar mustache, and a rather wicked scar displacing the corner of his lower lip. His smile was broad, his manner expansive, his attire military-pressed jeans and Police Academy T-shirt.

"Hi, Tommy," she greeted her father.

Big Zen, she realized, had slid off into the shadows. Maggie didn't blame her.

"Hi, Tommy?" he retorted, clapping her again on the shoulder like an avuncular uncle. "That's all I get from you on the day I've waited my whole fuckin' life to see? 'Hi, Tommy'?"

Maggie tried her best to give him a big smile as she swung her arms wide. "Like the duds?"

Tommy hooted. "I'd like 'em a hell of a lot better if they were on a real cop."

Maggie's arms fell. "Which means, I assume, that you don't think the health of your fellow officers is any concern?"

An old argument, one Tommy wouldn't succumb to. "Pussy job," he said just quietly enough that the team could only see his bright, wide smile. "But you've tasted the big show now. I'm waiting for you to say, 'It was great, Tommy. It made me want to grab a gun and wade right in. It made me want to—' "

Since Maggie knew exactly what it had made her father want to do, she interrupted him. "It made me glad that first aid was all I had to handle."

She saw his jaw tense, felt his fingers dig deeper into her shoulder. Saw the shadow of disgust skim those merry blue eyes. But Tommy "The Terminator" O'Brien, once the scourge of the St. Louis Police Department, merely laughed and shook her one more time, just for emphasis.

"Oh well," he said in that same, deceptively casual tone. "Guess I can't expect real balls on a girl."

Maggie was damned well not going to let her father know how those words affected her.

"I guess not, Tommy," she said instead, and watched him turn away.

"So that was Tommy 'The Terminator' O'Brien," the little reporter said, her eyes suddenly way sharper.

"Yeah," Maggie said. "That's Tommy."

"I'm amazed," the reporter said carefully as she watched his slow progress through the crowd of backslapping, laughing men and women. "Considering the reception, it's tough to remember that he was kicked off the force."

The Official SWATbastard Bus, which looked a lot like the lieutenant's Aerostar minivan, dropped Maggie off at her place along about 3 A.M. Not that she couldn't have driven herself, they all assured her from inside as the police escort waited behind, lights still shuddering against the brick walls of her sleeping neighborhood. It was just a celebratory precaution.

Maggie nodded sagely and forbore reminding them that she hadn't driven in the first place. She just wished they'd been cautious enough to help her remember how to get up to her loft.

Keys. Door. Stairs. Lots of stairs. Maggie giggled, then she sighed, still trying to figure out how to balance the euphoric high of the celebration with the keen distress she couldn't shake over Montana Bob.

They hadn't understood, any of them. Successful mission, they'd crowed. Perfect coordination, like a fuckin' ballet out there on the street. It was only Maggie who kept thinking of the analogy of successful operations and lost patients.

And being the nurse she was, she couldn't let it go until she knew whether she'd been at fault.

She didn't realize the lights were on in her loft until she'd been standing in her open door for about thirty seconds. It took another thirty to realize that her television was on. And her stereo. And her microwave. And that sitting in her favorite comfy chair—actually her only comfy chair—was an invader dressed in nothing more than official St. Louis city police boxer shorts, Kerlix bandage, snorkel mask, and flippers.

Maggie lived in a loft on the top floor of a renovated warehouse in the Soulard district. Bare brick, high ceilings, original scarred-wood floors. Echoes and space and clean surfaces over which to imprint herself. She'd done it with Van Gogh posters on the walls and swaths of bright fabric draped from the ceiling, mosquito netting over her old brass bed. A compilation of estate sale furniture, huge, brightly scattered pillows, and a faux mantel crowded with improbably painted ceramic animals.

And, evidently, Delaney. Sprawled all across her clean spaces, both in reality and imagination, his laughter banishing shadows and his perceptive eyes negating space.

"I imagine it would be too trite to say that you should still be in the hospital," she drawled, dropping her purse and crown on the trunk she used as a hall table and kicking the door shut behind her.

The clang of the door almost drowned out the sound of Insane Clown Posse on the stereo and what looked like old *Sea Hunt* reruns on cable.

Delaney just grinned. "You know modern medicine," he said, his voice nasal and alien-sounding beneath the mask. "They said I could leave if I found somebody to take care of me." He threw his arms out in punctuation. "Surprise."

Maggie didn't move any farther into the room. "And you explained your key to my place how?"

"I watch your cat when you leave town. Everybody knows that. The guys who carried me up here are dying to find out how pissed you're gonna be when you see me."

"Well, they should be happy. I saw you. I'm pissed."

She'd just done a little two-step off the hardwood step into her massive living area when he lifted the mask for her to see that he still wore the color of a cholera patient. Not only that, he'd been watching for her. Maggie knew, because the popcorn he'd obviously started was almost finished popping, and he knew damn well that other than fresh pasta, popcorn was her favorite tranquilizer. And Sean couldn't cook pasta.

"You didn't screw up," he said baldly.

Maggie stopped for a second not four feet short of the furniture cluster that included his chair. Then, shaking her head, she walked on past him to flip off the stereo and pull the popcorn out of the microwave so she could dump it into an old metal bedpan. "You've obviously been sent as the sacrificial soft shoulder."

Which just showed how worried the brass was, and how little they knew of Delaney's dislike of the position.

"There was some concern," he said. "There were reporters at that party tonight, and you did mention Bob more than once."

"He shouldn't have died."

"But he did, Mags. It happens. It was his day to be in the big book, that's all."

"Awfully complacent about it, Delaney," she retorted, suddenly hot all over again. "Especially since you were the one who asked me to watch over him."

Delaney again hid behind his goggles. "I found myself liking the guy, okay? Probably Stockholm Syndrome or something. You know. The hostage developing a dependent relationship with the hostage taker?"

"I know all about Stockholm Syndrome, Delaney."

Sean's smile was suddenly soft, suddenly old. "I know, Mags."

Shaking her head, Maggie wandered back into her living room. "There wasn't any reason for him to die."

"There will be. They'll find it in the postmortem. I promise."

Maggie couldn't quite look at him. "Was there something I missed? Was there?"

Sean reached out a hand and took hers, his fingers strong with conviction. "No, honey. There wasn't. Maybe meth or coke. He was pretty hyped. No other injury. You called it perfectly."

"Not drugs," she immediately disagreed. "The only drug Bob took was his Haldol. He was adamant about it."

"And you don't drink. But you sure did tonight, didn't you?" Giving her hand one more quick squeeze, Delaney let go, which showed how well he knew her. "Tell me about the party. I've been sitting up here all alone thinking of you in that bulletproof bra and damn near passing out."

For a second Maggie cradled that warm popcorn to her chest like a security blanket and thought about the terrible certainty that something had gone wrong. Something she hadn't caught. Something she'd have to find out about, no matter what her friends thought.

Then, catching the concern in Delaney's tired eyes, she grinned and plopped herself onto the big chintz sofa-sleeper alongside his chair. And she told him. She told him everything, from the first step into the bar to the cheers and siren squirts that had sent her up her own stairs not five minutes earlier. And Delaney laughed through it all.

"I suppose you expect to stay here for the next few days," she finally accused, out of popcorn, low on blood sugar, and lower on energy reserves.

His grin, more pulled than ever, brightened all over again. "I'll protect your cat from invaders."

"My cat *is* the invader," she said, climbing slowly to her feet. Her big day was over, and she had to get back to the real world. Sacraments again, she thought, as she remembered tucking her Communion veil away in a box, just like her new bra. "And you're not getting the bed."

Delaney tilted his head to the side to consider her edict. "Why? That's where I usually sleep."

If Maggie hadn't been raised with police, she would have blushed. "Well, there's the problem. When you're here, there's usually very little sleep involved. And that's what both of us need. So scoot over, and I'll pull out the couch."

She'd just about made it past him when he reached up with surprising strength and pulled her onto his good leg. The goggles were somehow gone, and Delaney's dangerous eyes were half-closed.

Maggie knew better. She'd always known better. But she gave in anyway, wrapping herself right into what Carmen would have called the kiss of the century. Which, with Delaney, was the kiss of the week. Which, Maggie admitted with a frustrated little sigh, was why she always gave in.

This time, it was also a bit of revenge. Delaney knew better than most that it took a full supply of blood to consider what he was trying to do. And he'd left a goodly amount of that back on that hardwood floor on Ohio.

He had no more than unsnapped Maggie's bra when she heard his breathing stutter. Sweat popped out on his upper lip, and his fingers started to tremble. Maggie smiled and counted to ten, still locked onto him like a suction cup. Sure enough, by nine and a half he twitched and went limp.

Climbing off his lap, Maggie wrapped a hand around the back of his neck and pushed his face into his crotch. All she got out of him was a flutter of ashen eyelids and a half-strangled whimper.

"And the Lord said unto man," she murmured in his ear with a sly grin, "I have good news and bad news. The good news is that I have given you both a penis and a brain."

"The bad news," he chanted back just as he had the last two times he'd been shot, eyes closed and hands not the only suddenly limp things in his lap, "is that I've only given you enough blood to work one at a time."

Maggie licked the shell of his ear and chuckled. "Usually a figurative joke. Aren't you the lucky boy to keep getting these literal demonstrations?"

His head was still in his shorts, and his skin was still the color of wallpaper paste, but he was grinning again. "Even better that you so enjoy giving them to me."

Maggie let him back up and kissed the top of his head before getting to her feet. "Exactly."

Maggie had just tossed the couch pillows onto the floor when Delaney stirred behind her. "You did good, Mags. No matter what Tommy said."

Finally, Maggie laughed. And said the only thing that covered the occasion. "Asshole."

At the western edge of St. Louis city in a neighborhood called The Hill, the city police were answering a domestic dispute call. The street was at the edge of The Hill's usually neatly kept blue-collar houses, a short block of mongrel dwellings decorated in empty beer cans and broken lawn mowers. The humidity was thick and the air heavy beneath a hazy moon. A porch light or two had flicked on in the last few minutes, and a dog barked as if he could smell dinner. Most of the neighborhood, though, was doing its best to slumber beneath the constant throb of cicada love.

Out on the lawn of 1276 Peabody Place, Jimmy Krebs swayed and screamed up at the single-story shingle box house that used to be his, where a woman peeked out at him from the partially opened door.

"You stupid bitch!" he howled. "This is my house! *My* house! And that's my kid you and your fuckin' lawyer are keepin' from me!"

Emboldened by a long night of beer and blustering with the boys, Jimmy stood his ground right there next to his flamingo lawn sprinkler, arms crossed over the Cardinals logo on his T-shirt, jeans sagging over his nonexistent ass. Unwashed and unpretty, he was a skinny man with pretensions of power and a chronic dissatisfaction at the disappointment his life had become.

"You get outta here!" the young woman screamed through her screen door, her attention flicking between him and the darkened car that had just slid to a stop at her gate. "I got a restraining order against you, Jimmy! You can't be here!"

"I can't be at my own goddamn house?"

"That's right," the police officer said as she stepped from her opened car door to stand just beyond Billy's reach. A second policeman stopped just out of Jimmy's sight on his other side.

Jimmy swung on the woman, who wore sergeant's stripes on her blue sleeves. "Who the fuck're you to tell me to get out? I got a right to be here, and you're nothin' but another useless, lyin' cunt!"

"Yeah," she said easily, her hand sliding toward her baton. "But I'm a useless lyin' cunt with a gun. And you violated a restraining order. Which means you get a free ride in my car."

Jimmy, never known for his control, lost it. He swung for the officer and ended up facedown on his own lawn, his hands cuffed and his nose bleeding.

"And now you have a resisting arrest violation," the sergeant purred in his ear. "Oh, it is going to be a good night."

Jimmy, his arms twisted and cuffed behind him as he was hauled to his feet, refused to push his luck any more with the police. Instead, he shot his final wad toward the soon-to-be-ex-wife, who huddled on the other side of his front door.

"I'll get you for this, you worthless bitch! I'll get you!"

He screamed it all the way into the car and down the block, no matter that the police pretty much ignored him.

"I'll get you!"

His wife, left behind in the thick, throbbing darkness, didn't ignore him. Curled up on the floor, she laid her head into her crossed arms and sobbed. Because she knew, curled in the darkness that had become infested with cicadas and despair, that he would do just that.

The Toe Tag was long closed and the downtown streets pretty empty. High humidity melted the streetlights into blurs, and the moon sank past the high-rises to the west. Tucked into a parking space behind the City Hall, two passengers sat in a silent dark sedan sharing a flask, a smoke, and a problem.

"I'm not in the mood for complications."

"Well, I think you have one anyway."

A perfect circle of smoke lifted toward the car's ceiling. "Why, because she got upset? It was her first mission. Give her time to get used to it."

"No, because she kept talking about it at the bar. I don't think she's gonna just let that death go without asking questions."

"I told you. She'll settle in. Give her a couple more missions, she'll forget all about it."

"The same woman who now works as a nurse, a paramedic, and a SWAT medic at the same time? You don't think she's just a little obsessive?"

"I think that she's doin' all that to impress her old man."

"She wanted to impress Tommy, she shoulda just been a cop and gotten it over with."

"Yeah, well, she didn't. So we wait her out."

"I'm telling you, it's not gonna be that easy. She doesn't seem like the kind of person who just gives up."

"And I'm tellin' you, she's Tommy's kid. Which means that no matter what, she's loyal. She won't do anything to hurt her friends."

"We better hope not."

This time, the smoke came out in a thin, faltering stream. "I know. I'd hate to have to see somethin' bad happen to Tommy's kid."

CHAPTER 3

"You better not be trying to pin this shit on me," Maggie heard from behind her.

Bent over one of the ED workstations where she'd been perusing Montana Bob's chart, Maggie straightened to face her latest challenge. Predictably enough, it came from Bob's nurse of the day before. Fists again propped on cachectic hips, Carmen stood in the middle of the worklane as if bracing for a wall of water, tiny raisin eyes even tinier, color high on her sallow cheeks.

Carmen was not going to be jollied out of her rage today, Maggie realized. And since Maggie's patient load had already hit double digits, and she was expecting a multivictim van accident any minute, Maggie didn't have time to appease Carmen *and* make sense of Bob's final moments.

"I'm not trying to pin anything on anybody," she said as easily as possible, her focus back on the lab results she'd been studying. "I'm trying to understand. Just like any other patient I had who died. Bob came in with a minor wound to the upper arm and left wrapped and tagged. It doesn't make sense."

"He shot a cop!" Carmen objected, much as all the cops had the night before, as if that was all that needed to be said.

Maggie already had a headache. This wasn't helping in the least. "I'm not trying to bring him back from the dead,

Carmen. Just make sure I didn't miss something."

"Or make sure *I* didn't miss something."

Well, yes, Maggie wanted to say.

"The qualitative drug screen was positive for cocaine," she said instead, "which doesn't make sense. He swore he never did drugs."

Carmen snorted unkindly. "He also swore he used to work for the FBI."

Maggie smiled. "Yeah, he did, didn't he?"

"Besides, if he was positive for cocaine, that would have accounted for the lot. You know how that stuff is."

Yes, if Bob had had a sizable load of cocaine on board, it would have accounted for the lot. Cocaine wasn't called bad shit for nothing. Unpredictable, resistant to tolerance, the drug could provoke everything from heart attacks to blindness to rages, morbid fevers and sudden death, even in people who seemed to be used to it. If Bob had *not* been, one good dose could easily have sent him straight into orbit.

"Well, nothing else looks wrong," Maggie admitted, scanning the lab results one final time. "I mean, his electrolytes are screwed up, but that's not unusual in a code."

"And his vital signs were compatible with cocaine ingestion," Carmen said. "Jesus, his BP was something like 200/100. That wasn't usual for him, was it?"

Following Carmen's accusing finger as it divined the unacceptable numbers on the vital signs flow sheet, Maggie shook her head. "No. No, he was usually a pretty mellow guy. But then, if I'd just tried to boil a cheerleader and shot a cop, my blood pressure might be a little high, too."

"Or if I had cocaine on board."

Maggie sighed. "Or if I had cocaine on board."

Which Bob had always sworn he'd never taken. Which Maggie couldn't imagine him scoring anyway. Bob had always been a Mad Dog and Marlboro kind of guy.

Maggie hated it that she couldn't find any better explanation in his chart. She guessed she was just going to have to cudgel information from the Medical Examiner's Office, where they'd be doing a more definitive quantitative drug screen during the postmortem later that day.

"You working today, O'Brien?" her supervisor asked from the doorway out to the triage. "Or aren't we flashy enough for you anymore?"

Maggie still looked down at numbers that refused to change merely for her peace of mind. "I live to anticipate your every command, Sarge."

"Well then, new patients in rooms five and six, and some reporter to see you."

Maggie's headache immediately worsened. She'd forgotten about the doe-eyed little Girl Scout who wanted to capture her life in staged photos and meaningless quotes. Somehow, now that she was sober, it didn't seem like such a good idea after all.

"Be nice to her," Maggie said anyway as she closed Bob's chart and reslung her stethoscope. "She might mention you in the paper."

Handing off two new charts, her super snorted. "Not when Allen already has her by the arm."

"Good. Maybe he'll talk her into investigating his life instead. The pictures'd sure be more interesting."

"Does this mean that a SWAT officer has to be a woman to make the papers?" a soft baritone asked behind her.

Maggie turned around to find her favorite SWAT nose-trumpeter slouching behind her, this time in his more usual St. Louis City police blues.

"Hi, Paul," she greeted him with a big grin. "What are you doing here, besides trying to steal my limelight?"

His answering smile was pure Paul, ear to ear, although beneath that nose it was tough to tell. And then there was the mustache he'd tacked on under it, like a skirt beneath eaves, in an effort to add years to his baby face.

Paul wasn't just a memorable nose, he was all nose, his forehead and chin sloping so alarmingly he looked like a mole in trousers. He said that it all helped his capabilities as a sniper. Nobody was quite sure how, but one simply didn't argue with a sniper.

"As a matter of fact, one of your new patients is mine," he admitted. "A guy we caught trying to chain an ATM machine to the back of his car. When we brought the matter to his attention, he suddenly needed emergency care."

Maggie nodded. "Felonious back pain, huh? Well, I hope you're not busy, 'cause he's gonna have to wait for this belly pain in room three."

"Be my guest." He grinned again, his mustache twitching like the skirt on a hula dancer. "I'll be talking to your reporter. What's her name again?"

Maggie took hold of her charts and stood. "Bambi. Barbie. Heather. Something dumb like that. Take her home with you. Better yet, bury her in your backyard."

Maggie left Paul and Carmen comparing notes and pushed on to room five, her eyes on the new chart. Mrs. Phyllis Maitland, possible alcohol ingestion, definite belly pain, undoubted pain in other anatomical regions. Maggie walked into the room scanning the vital information, her mind still back on those lab results at her workstation and the reporter who was dogging her heels.

Which was probably why Mrs. Maitland blindsided her.

Usually patients don't go after hospital staff until the staff has at least made contact. Said or acted in a way the person feels to be somehow offensive. Mrs. Maitland decided, evidently, to forgo the introductory phase of the interchange.

Maggie made it no more than four feet into the room before meeting the problem—literally—head-on. She'd just looked up to introduce herself when she caught sight of a giant, chapped fist headed straight for her nose.

Maggie's reflexes were very quick. They weren't quick enough. The charts clattered to the floor, and Maggie followed. But not before that fist connected with the side of her face and slammed her into the wall.

"Fuckin' bitch!" the bull-like woman screamed as she headed in for round two. "Fuckin' . . . fuckin' . . . fuckin' . . . !"

Damn cicadas, Maggie thought muzzily as she struggled

back to her feet. They were making people so darned impatient.

"Bitch!"

Mrs. Maitland charged again, only this time Maggie wasn't surprised. Instead of absorbing the punch, she grabbed hold of the woman's wrist and used Mrs. Maitland's own momentum to pull her past and trip her over Maggie's foot. Before Mrs. Maitland could complete her thought, she was the one on the floor, her arm twisted up behind her somewhere near her fourth cervical vertebra and her nose mashed into the tile.

"Hey! Hey, you bitch, what are you doing? I'm suing—"

Maggie had a knee at Mrs. Maitland's neck and another on her back, but the rest of the woman was threatening upheaval. And Mrs. Maitland was the size of the average sofa sleeper. There was no way Maggie was going to be able to maintain control and reach the security panic button across the room, so she did the next best thing.

"Help!" she yelled at the top of her lungs.

The effect was explosive. Doors at either end of the room slammed open and at least half a dozen people poured in. Somebody punched the panic button, somebody else grabbed riot cuffs, and a few more people just stood staring at a serene-looking Maggie as she knelt on her attacker's back. It was left to Allen to state the obvious.

"You'd make a fortune calf-wrestling, darling."

Maggie smiled. "Four-point-two-seconds flat, Allen. Is that a record?"

Then she realized that her big-eyed friend from the night before was standing right next to Allen in the doorway. Amber. Crystal. Dawn.

"You're bleeding," she greeted Maggie.

Maggie knew. She was beginning to shake, and the room tilted oddly as several of her techs pulled Mrs. Maitland to her feet. Maggie thought a tooth might be loose. She knew she'd bitten her lip. She was really afraid her knees were going to give out on her, a too-familiar reaction to violence that made her more angry than the original assault.

"I can't leave you alone for a minute," Paul mourned, helping her to her feet. "Wanna press charges?"

"I'm sorry," the patient was wailing, "I didn't mean it!"

"Press charges, please," Allen begged. "So I don't have to press that cow's head under a big rock for her atrocious whining."

Eyes closed to keep the room from spinning, Maggie let Paul keep her balanced. Still she smiled for Allen. "Yes, Allen," she said. "I'll press charges."

If she hadn't, Allen would have anyway. His father had died at the hands of a drunk. His compassion for the species wasn't exactly legendary.

"Brave girl."

"Only because I agree with you."

"Of course."

"You're on The List," Maggie heard one of her techs snarl to Mrs. Maitland as they scuffled out the door, leaving Maggie to the ministrations of Paul, Allen, and the reporter.

Susan. That was her name. Not even Summer or Shannon. Susan, like an adult with a brain, with whom Maggie was eventually going to have to talk.

And, Maggie realized when she opened her eyes to see the door slam open again, security.

Her reaction was classic. Hope, anxiety, fear. The breathless wait to see what he'd do. Twenty-six years old, and she was still waiting for him to be proud of her.

"Screwed up again, huh?" her father asked, and Maggie stopped waiting. Maggie all but stopped breathing.

He should have looked diminished in his security guard's uniform, she thought inconsequentially. Everybody else did. He should have looked faintly ridiculous, with his holster holding no more than a cell phone and a beeper. But he didn't. He looked threatening. Maggie saw him raise one great, bristling eyebrow and fought new shakes.

"She roped and branded a drunk in under five seconds," Paul said with a blithe grin.

Paul only heard Tommy's jocular voice, saw the big smile, heard the same rough banter Tommy applied to all his fellow cops. But Maggie heard the shorthand that for twenty-six years had been compressed like toxic gas into a dismal five-room house in west St. Louis.

I'm sorry, she wanted to say as she shook even harder. *I'm sorry, I'm sorry, I'm sorry.*

She really wasn't surprised at Tommy. She was disgusted with herself.

"Didn't get her hog-tied before you got your bell rung good, looks like," was all he said. "You pissed off?"

"She's drunk, Tommy," Maggie said with a stiff shrug. "I shouldn't have been surprised."

"Doesn't mean you're not mad."

She didn't bother to answer. She didn't want to give him what he wanted.

"You might remember this the next time you try and tell me nobody should have a gun," he said. "You had a gun, that bitch never would have gotten close."

"You're absolutely right," Maggie couldn't help but retort. "I've petitioned for months to be able to carry a sidearm into work."

Allen goggled at Maggie's unfamiliar asperity. Tommy stiffened, then smiled, as if he'd won. Maggie, knowing he had, kept her calm face before her like a shield.

"You know what I mean," he said. "You're putting yourself in jeopardy by taking on that job when you won't use a firearm."

"You won't use a gun?" Allen demanded, hand on skinny hip. "Doing what you do on that team? What are you, crazy?"

"I'm a medic," she retorted without looking away from the disdain in her father's eyes. "I made it clear to everybody I wouldn't use a gun."

"She won't use a gun," her father repeated, "even though she's got more medals in quick-shot competitions than even me."

Hour after hour spent on a pistol range, Tommy's voice ringing in her ears, even over the ear protectors. Shot after shot after shot, one eye squeezed shut, hands trembling, heart in her throat, suffocated by the noise and the smell of cordite and the unwavering threat of those targets.

"I have to get back to work, Tommy," Maggie said with every ounce of control she could muster. "We can talk about it later."

"You're a target shooter?" Paul demanded, looking as stunned as Allen. "But your qualification scores always suck."

Maggie didn't bother to answer him either.

"What do you use for protection?" Allen asked, still distracted.

"My brain," she said, straightening herself and walking out of the room.

She'd pay for it later, Maggie thought as she sat in the worklane with a bag of ice to her aching jaw. In big ways, in little ways. She'd defied her father in front of the people who respected him, and he wouldn't let that go unanswered.

Why couldn't he have gotten a job as security chief in any other of the fifty or so hospitals in the area? Shopping malls, industrial parks. The airport, for Christ's sake. But when he'd turned in his resignation from the force nine months earlier, he'd made a beeline for the hospital where Maggie had tenure and settled himself in. And Maggie had asked for her first prescription for Prilosec.

"Could I talk to you now?" Sue the reporter asked, notebook poised and eyes blinking like semaphores.

The girl was standing on one leg, a gawky teen move that irritated Maggie more than it should have. But then, Maggie figured she was going to be easily irritated for a while. Especially while she waited for the swelling to go down on her cheek and her father to choose her punishment.

"Sure," she said. "I'm just waiting for X-ray results so I can go back to work."

"You're going back to work?" Sue asked in awed tones.

"It's happened before. It'll happen again."

Sue perched on the edge of a stool as if balancing between good and evil. Maggie couldn't really blame her. The worklane was knee deep in chaos. The van accident had arrived, pulling along in its wake a host of cops, paramedics, and ED staff who were trying to save at least three out of the four people who'd survived long enough to make it through the doors.

Two parents and one child were already on the "won't make it" list. Carmen was ushering one of the youngest victims across the hallway to the bathroom. The tiniest victim who could walk because she'd been the only one of seven in the van wearing a seat belt.

If Tommy wanted to know what made Maggie mad, this was it. Drunks were drunks, but people should protect their children.

Carmen and the carrot-topped toddler had made it halfway across the hall when all hell broke loose again. And again, it was Mrs. Maitland. Mostly naked and dragging a rather short security guard in her wake like a kite tail, she slammed out of a patient room and barreled across the hall toward the exit sign. Unfortunately, Carmen and her tiny patient were in the way.

"Get me the fuck outta here!" the woman screeched and caromed off Carmen, who tripped over the little girl, who went sprawling.

Maggie popped off her chair and dived into the fray. Half a dozen staff members piled on to control Mrs. Maitland, and a couple more helped Carmen up. Maggie pulled the little girl free and curled her into a nest beneath her chin.

"It's okay, sugar," she crooned in the toddler's ear as she sat right down on the floor. "It's okay."

The baby sobbed, Mrs. Maitland tossed three of her guards into the wall, and Maggie rocked back and forth on the floor.

"You're on The List with clusters now, you asshole," one of the security guards growled as he leapt back onto the pile.

"The hell with lists," Carmen offered, rubbing her butt with both hands. "Let's just send her out with the accident re-creation team and stand her in the middle of the highway as a marker."

"An airport runway," somebody else offered.

"The Mississippi."

"Oh, for God's sake," came Tommy's voice like the judgment of God. "Can't you do anything right?"

Maggie flinched, curled herself more tightly around the little girl, and closed her eyes.

Mrs. Maitland didn't seem any more immune to Tommy than anybody else. Just his appearance shut her up. Maggie heard him bend over that untidy pile of security officers and ED techs that blanketed the woman and just lift her off the floor. She smelled him, Aqua Velva and mouthwash and the faint smoke of old malt. He snorted in derision and she stayed hidden behind closed eyes.

"Maybe Maggie's right and she doesn't need a gun after all," he said to his security guards, his voice hugely amused. "Seems she managed to wrastle this steer without all you other little girls. You want to take some time to teach these babies how to control a subject, Mags?"

Wrapped around the tiny girl in her arms, Maggie opened her eyes in astonishment to see her father share a huge, conspiratorial wink with her.

He'd done it again. Transformed in the twinkling of an eye like a biblical miracle. Even knowing better, Maggie found herself smiling back like a six-year-old. "No thanks, Tommy. My schedule's kinda full. And Tommy. Calling them 'little girls' is sexist."

Tommy bent over her then and ruffled her hair, just as if she were the baby. "Well, God forbid anybody calls me that, little girl."

And then, with unspeakable gentleness, he went on his knees before the tiny girl in Maggie's lap and cupped her face in his big square hands. "You okay, poppet?" he asked in a soft whisper, stroking her skin as if she were a precious gift.

The little girl blinked, smiled, and reached up to his magnificent mustache. And then, with all those people still tumbled around her like cast-off toys, she giggled.

Tommy never took his attention from the baby in Maggie's arms. "Mad yet, Mags?"

"She's still just drunk, Tommy."

For a second, he stared at her, hard. Maggie held. Giving a bemused, frustrated shake of his head, Tommy reached over to gather the little girl in his arms. "C'mon, honey. Let's blow this pop stand."

As everybody smiled after them, the huge security guard settled the toddler on his shoulders and loped off down the hall.

"Amazing," one of the nurses mused.

Maggie nodded. "Tommy's always considered his work to be performance art."

And then, like everybody else, Maggie creaked her way back to her feet and got back to business. When she made it back to her stool at the end of the hall, it was to find that Sue the reporter was still waiting for her.

"What's The List?" the girl asked without preamble.

Maggie picked her ice back up and reapplied it to her cheek. "The people who piss us off. Surely you guys have a List down at the paper."

Miss Wide-Blue-Eyed Susan shook her head.

Maggie sighed. Whoever had had the dubious sense of humor to send this infant down here for this story was going to find their own name immortalized on The List, if they weren't careful.

"We all have our image of what The List means. One friend thinks of it as the passenger list for the *Titanic II*, another the applications for hell. I like to imagine everybody on a bus headed for a big cliff. With rocks at the bottom." Maggie shrugged, watching the baby she'd held trying to find comfort in Tommy's arms. "A little harmless virtual revenge for people who have to deal with the kind of patients who'd trample a two-year-old."

Maggie thought the reporter would understand. Instead,

she seemed to sit straighter. "It sure seems to involve a lot of . . . well, violence," she said. "Like the cops last night. I heard a lot of talk of shooting people, hurting people. Convoluted revenge plots. Seems kinda bloodthirsty to me."

Maggie was quickly tiring of the line of questioning. "Steam valve," she said quietly. "We see a lot of awful things here. We can't make them better. We can't make them stop. So we settle for making ourselves feel better with a little harmless fictional justice. It doesn't mean anything."

The girl nodded, her attention on the words she scribbled. "And you never worry about losing your humanity?"

Every day, Maggie wanted to say, but it would have sounded like a cliché. "This can be a tough place to work."

"And yet you went to all that effort to join an even tougher place to work?"

Maggie heard an eerie, low howl set up from the quiet room down the hall where families waited for the worst news. The relatives of the van family must have gotten theirs, she guessed.

"The SWAT team?" Maggie asked, deliberately turning away from the sound, even as the reporter turned inevitably toward it. "I enjoy being part of it."

The reporter turned back. "Enjoy it? You're kidding."

"As my old mother used to say," Maggie offered with a dry grin, " ' "To each his own," said the old lady as she kissed the cow.' I grew up with cops. They're kind of my family. I can't be a cop, so I do the next best thing. I keep cops safe."

"But your dad was a cop. Why can't you be a cop?"

Maggie shrugged and gave the best answer she'd ever been able to. "Because I'm a nurse."

For a second the reporter just sat there, trying so hard to stay focused on Maggie, when Maggie could see she really wanted to look past at that terrible, keening sound Maggie seemed to ignore.

"No other family?" the reporter persisted. "Cousins or anything?"

Not unless you counted the Bimbos, Maggie thought. But that was something else she wouldn't share with the reporter. "No," she said simply. "Only child of only children."

The reporter nodded absently, refocused on her notes.

"Interesting relationships, don't you think?"

"What's that?" Maggie asked.

The eyes slid back and focused. "Oh, I guess the fact that you consider yourself part of the police family, yet those police tossed your father off the force, allegedly for brutality. And that, although you won't be a cop like he wants—tough not to tell—you'll work your butt off to risk your neck for those same cops."

"Careful of those some—all fallacies about Tommy," Maggie suggested. "Tommy wasn't fired, he resigned. He's also the recipient of more Meritorious Service Awards and Medals of Honor than any other cop in the history of the force."

And more civilian complaints.

But then, the reporter probably wouldn't ever be able to find out the truth behind Tommy's resignation. Only Tommy's fellow officers knew that story, and they weren't about to share it. No civilian would understand that Tommy had resigned to protect another officer.

A rookie. Tommy's rookie, a fresh-faced ex—Eagle Scout who had lost control and beaten the crap out of a guy who'd raped a ten-year-old.

Tommy was a company man. A true believer in the thin blue line. It had never occurred to him to sacrifice a promising kid because he hadn't caught him in time. As the supervising officer, that boy's mistake had been Tommy's responsibility. So he'd walked in, handed over his badge, and gotten assurances that no more would be asked, or said.

Which was why the reporter also would never understand why Tommy was still so welcome at the Toe Tag.

Sue scribbled, her eyes focused on her pad of paper. "And then," she went on as if Maggie hadn't interrupted, "when you not only make it on the elite SWAT team, but make quite a name for yourself in your first action, you spend the next week pissing everybody off."

Why hadn't Maggie noticed that feral glint in the reporter's eye before this? "I'm not pissing anybody off."

"That's not what I heard."

"She's pissing me off."

There were five people clustered to the side of the autopsy room down at the St. Louis City Medical Examiner's Office. Typical of its era, the room echoed with high ceilings and old tiled floors. Harsh fluorescent lights sapped the shadows from the carts that were lined up along a wall, new customers waiting their turn. Metal autopsy stations gleamed in the center of the room.

One of the tables was in use, its burden frail and yellowed and sere. The human body at its least romantic: waxy-looking skin, half-opened, fish-cloudy eyes and limp, wasted genitals. An empty frame deprived of its engine.

Montana Bob's organs were all in jars, his brain and lungs and liver weighed and dissected and dispatched, his heart tossed into the scale like a hunk of meat in a butcher's shop. His torso was laid open, chin to crotch, to show that nobody was left at home. And still the five people stood at his feet wondering.

"She won't tell you what she thinks?" one of them asked, a guy in civilian clothes and a cop haircut.

The homicide detective on the case shrugged. "No final report is going out until Dr. Harrison reviews it. Especially since this is a cop shooting. And she's in court. So, we should know tomorrow."

The civilian snorted. "He didn't die of that pissant cut on his arm."

"You know that and I know that. But we have to make sure the media knows that."

"Hospital chart says he was positive for cocaine. How soon before we can get the quantitative tox screen?"

Lounging over by the ceiling scales, the death investigator shrugged. "A week, maybe."

The civilian, the prosecutor's representative on the shooting board, checked his notes. "He was on medication?"

"Antipsychotics," the homicide cop said. "He was paranoid. Thought the CIA was after him."

"They all think the CIA's after them. That or the FBI."

The homicide guy grinned. "Not Bob. He thought he was in the FBI."

Another of the civilians over by the door gave a sad smile. "As a matter of fact," she said, eyes on the desiccated husk on the table, "he was."

Four pairs of astonished eyes swiveled her way. "What?"

"Bob used to be Special Agent in Charge out in Bozeman."

Everybody else followed her gaze.

"Jesus," the prosecutor's representative breathed. "Who'd guess?"

"Does this change anything?" the homicide cop asked.

"Nah," the woman answered, pushing herself away from the wall and closing her own notebook so that it showed the gold-stamped FBI seal on the leather cover. "I'm just here for old times' sake. Would you mind if I got all the results?"

She got a sea of shrugs.

"Barring surprises, we'll have the shooting review board in a couple of days," the prosecutor's guy said and closed his book, too. "But right now, you want my personal opinion, it looks like he died of crazy."

"Yeah," she said, eyes suddenly soft and sad. "It does."

It was a conclusion Maggie finally came to on her own. All the evidence pointed to the fact that Bob had died of cocaine storm, a condition that inexplicably happened when cocaine was mixed with anxiety and police. Unpredictable, devastating, instantly lethal, and virtually impossible to pre-

dict or prove, it caused more problems than just dead cocaine users, because the death usually happened under
restraint of some kind, which meant that the police were
often involved and blamed.

Maggie had seen it before. Sudden, terrifying madness.
Body temperatures soaring past 106, convulsions, sudden
death. What, in technical terminology could be most ade-
quately described as an "Oh, shit." One minute the patient
would be fighting and screaming, and the next he'd just be
. . . dead.

Like Bob.

Even though he'd said he never took cocaine.

The people down at the ME's Office had been very
sweet and called her when the complete tox screen had
come in. Bob had forgotten his Haldol and taken cocaine
instead. Or mixed up the two. Or just decided to go out
with a bang. He'd had enough coke in him to go out with
fireworks. And he hadn't had another thing wrong with him
that should have put him in a body bag.

Maggie, not sure what she'd wanted, knew she hadn't
wanted that. So she grieved in her own way for a guy
nobody missed, and she worked her shifts at the ED and
out on the ambulance and the team, and she came home to
grudgingly share her loft with Delaney until he could walk
down a flight of stairs and go home.

Slowly, guys on the force stopped asking her why she
was so interested in one crazy guy who shot a cop. Slowly,
she began to enjoy her jobs again, especially the SWAT
team, where they were beginning to pick up business by
handling the area's high-risk warrants. She was even en-
joying the ED more, because she knew what nobody else
did. She knew that once she overcame her own superstition
that she'd somehow lose her place on the team, she'd put
in her notice at the ED, tenure or no.

Just two days ago the fire captain out at Chesterfield had
offered her a full-time firefighter/paramedic position when
it came up in a few weeks, and Maggie thought she just
might take it. She thought she'd enjoy spending quieter

shifts out in less desperate neighborhoods. She thought she'd enjoy not having to juggle three jobs. She especially thought she'd like the chance to sleep more and see her father less.

But that was something to anticipate. For now she had to get through the next few weeks while the cicadas yet ruled. She had to balance the different demands on her time, fight off another marriage proposal from Delaney, and keep her sense of humor about Sue the reporter, who was still shadowing her as if she were a Junior Achievement project.

At least, Maggie thought with some delight as she clocked in for an evening shift at Blymore, she was a hero again.

Well, not exactly a hero. The most observant person among two SWAT squads and at least thirty uniforms, anyway.

"Hey, Maggie?" one of the nurses asked as Maggie walked into the nurses' lounge. "Why is your name on The List?"

Dropping her nursing bag on the floor next to the magazine stand, Maggie laughed. "Did that jerk put my name up? I'll shove snakes in his shorts for that."

Maggie didn't have to look far for her proof. The List, that magical incantation that made everybody feel better when they had a difficult patient needing payback, was actually the nursing lounge's wall decor. Better than sponge-painting or tole, the back wall of the dingy, dungeonlike lounge was decorated in tiny, carefully printed rows of names. Extending from floor to ceiling, added to by anybody who knew the rules, checked and commented on like a tickertape. Once the wall was filled up, it was simply painted over and The List continued.

The good news was that they'd managed to keep the reporter from discovering it. The bad news was that they knew that eventually they'd get caught and have to stop.

But not yet. For now, every cop, paramedic, nurse, and doctor in the city knew where to go to vent his frustration for posterity.

And there was Maggie's name right at the tail end.

"Son of a bitch," she huffed, turning away to pull her day's equipment from her bag. "I bet it was Paul Trevor, who will pay for this insult in ways he can't even imagine. And after I was a heroine, too."

The nurse, sprawled on the sadly eviscerated couch that hugged the far wall, lifted a corner of the damp cloth she had over her eyes. "You'll explain, of course."

Maggie dropped into the matching armchair somebody had bought down at Sal Army for ten bucks and added to the various plastic chairs and moth-eaten microwave that inhabited the windowless cell. The room looked even more inviting with the lights off, as they were now. Jeannie Mars, the other nurse, suffered migraines. She suffered them even more when her husband gambled away her paycheck and her workload was hard. So Maggie entertained her in the dark.

"I single-handedly saved the SWAT team about five hours of standing out in the heat last night waiting to see if a barricaded drunk with a gun would come out of his house or not."

It was their most common 1040 or hostage call; armed drunk on the wrong side of a locked door. Mostly they waited for them to answer the phone or fall asleep. More often than not they fell asleep. The night before, half the police force clustered out in the north county street trying to figure out why their subject wouldn't answer the damn phone after he'd gone to the trouble of shooting out every streetlight on the block. Maggie managed to bring it to an end simply because she found herself facing the wrong way.

She'd been escorting one of her guys past the TV news trucks at the exterior perimeter to the ambulance for some minor care, when she happened to notice a party at a neighboring house. Five guys in ball caps and muscle shirts sat clustered around a TV on somebody's deck. Empty beer cans cluttered the stained cedar, and high fives and arm punches were being shared as if they were ringside at a Lakers game.

"C2," she'd called the lieutenant on the mike she'd clipped to her helmet strap. "What's the description of the perp again?"

"White male, thirty-five, brown, and hazel. Marlins cap and Budweiser T-shirt. Why?"

"Wave. He's watching us all on the news."

"How long did it take for you to see him?" Jeannie asked now, hand over forehead as she chuckled.

"Three hours."

"And that got you on The List?"

"Nah. I got on The List because Paul had never met *Ted*."

That got a real laugh. "Bet he was surprised."

"Well, just because the whole damn team thinks they need to hold my hand now that they know I meant it about not using a gun. They decided they had to walk me to my car to keep me from being raped or pillaged. You can imagine how funny I thought it was when they got there to see old Ted sitting in the passenger seat, and all ten of them pulled guns. They almost shot out my stereo."

"But you introduced Ted."

"I did. Nobody else seemed quite as delighted as I was."

"Why? Because Ted has no legs?"

"I think it was the fedora. Ted's very formal, you know. I even bought him a tie last week."

"Who's Ted?" one of the techs demanded, overhearing the last exchange as she walked in for her shift. "You got a honey?"

Hitting the wall switch, the tech flooded the small room with typical hospital fluorescence, which won her more than a few curses from its current occupants.

"Maggie has a protector," Jeannie giggled.

"His full name is Techno-Teddy," Maggie said, reaching over to rifle through the catchall desk in the corner. "A practice dummy, kind of like Resusci Anne, but for tactical weapons practice. Ted's a bit worse for wear, so he drives around with me to make the bad guys think I have a big strapping man in the car."

"With no legs," Jen giggled again, the rag puffing off her face.

"Kind of like dating the Scarecrow," the tech offered.

"The perfect boyfriend," Maggie agreed as she found the bottle of Wite-Out and got up to erase her good name from the wall. "He's cute, always smiles, dresses well, and never says a word."

The tech grinned. "He got a brother?"

But Maggie forgot to answer. She'd reached the wall and was kneeling on one of the plastic chairs to get access to her name. With the light on, she saw the whole list, which currently covered at least half the wall. Hundreds of names printed in a dozen different hands and colors. The cops made it a practice to print a gang member's name in an opposite gang's colors, the ultimate insult. The nurses used whatever pen was left in their pocket. One of the techs, a high school senior looking for a career in theater, made little caricatures out of her capital letters.

Name after name after name in relentless succession, some repeated, some with clusters and stars after them. Gangbangers and drunks and thieves and lawyers. People from all over the metropolitan area who had made a reputation for themselves by being nasty or frustrating or unredeemable. People not necessarily seen at this hospital, or even in a professional capacity.

Maggie didn't use The List as much as others. But she knew a lot of the stories, recognized a lot of names. She couldn't help but think of all the frustration and anger that had been carried to this, the city's personal wailing wall. A safe place to deposit all the rage and disappointment and despair, where it wouldn't hurt anybody.

Just as she always did when she was near The List, she let her attention wander. Her mind mostly on the revenge she was planning to take out on Paul, Maggie absently checked other names as she carefully daubed out her own. She was eyeing a column about three over from where hers still resided, when she stopped, her attention snagged.

There was a name she recognized.

Urban McGinley.

Maggie's name was only half blotted out, her hand poised over the B as if waiting for the restart button. Her focus had stopped dead on that other name. A name with a cluster. A name not at all near hers, probably a few months back, only easily noticeable because it had been at an equal height. A name written in a light, possibly woman's hand in black.

Urban.

An odd name. Maggie just couldn't figure out why it was a name that bothered her.

Urban McGinley.

She skimmed farther as if it would help explain her sudden unease, her hand still poised and waiting, her own name half-camouflaged. She saw a lot of names. Names mostly of men, but some of women. Fancy names, sad names, worthless names.

And then, Maggie saw another name that stopped her.

Snake Pilson.

Snake, Snake. Written in heavy red. Blood colors, which meant that the owner might have been in a gang affiliated with the Crips, whose colors were blue.

Why did that seem to go with Urban?

"Maggie?" somebody said behind her.

But she didn't answer. Those names went together, and she was trying like hell to remember why.

And then she heard it. The names she'd just recognized, repeated in a breathy litany. Urban and Snake.

Sancho and Urban and the dog and snake.

Snake. Not as in reptile. As in Snake Pilson. A person.

Maybe Bob hadn't been reading *Doctor Dolittle* after all.

Perched there before that wall of futility, Maggie felt her stomach slide with a terrible thump of prescience. She knew darn well how reliable Bob was. She knew how he collected unrelated incidents like shiny rocks in his big basket of delusions until he could pronounce them related. She knew that two names on a wall of hundreds shouldn't bother her so much.

But they did.

Innocuous names. Coincidence, nothing more. And yet, Maggie was beset by the terrible conviction that these two names were portents of disaster. She knew it the same way she knew to call a code seconds before she needed to, even though the patient talking to her was no more than bemused, not able to tell her exactly why he'd come in. Unable to describe symptoms or define discomfort.

"Something," he would inevitably say, eyes sliding away, as if he could already see something she couldn't, "is wrong."

And without knowing why, except for the ballooning pressure in her chest that screamed disaster, Maggie would yell for help, or begin treatment, or just slam her hand against the code button so that the team erupted into the room just as the patient's eyes rolled back in his head.

She felt it now, seeing those names.

Urban and Snake.

Sancho and Urban and the dog and Snake.

They were the people Bob had told her were being killed. The proof he'd tried to give her that he was in danger.

That he was going to die.

And, oh God, he had.

The question was, had they?

CHAPTER 4

But Bob had been crazy, Maggie thought as she stood with the Wite-Out drying in her hand and her name only half-gone.

Certifiable. Mad, medicated to the eyeballs, and tagged like a wolf in the wild. He'd tried to turn a cheerleader into wonton soup, for God's sake.

And yet Maggie kept hearing his voice, frantic and frightened and so very sure of himself. *They've killed them*, he'd said. *Sancho and Urban and the dog and Snake*.

Maggie had thought he'd pulled conspiracies out of the ether, just like always, spinning his mad cabals from the sweat of paranoia. Except for the fact that at least two of the names he'd given her were on The List.

Unless, of course, paranoia was catching and Maggie was just seeing conspiracies where there were none.

Besides, who were the all-important *they*, and why would they go to the trouble? Especially for Bob. Bob was as harmless as an infant, as believable as a tabloid, and far too busy consigning himself to hell to bother anybody else.

For a second, Maggie closed her eyes. She listened to her heart accelerate, felt the air grow tight in the closed, cluttered little nurses' lounge.

She knew better. Hadn't she just been able to quiet all the clamor she'd caused by questioning Bob's death?

Hadn't she finally convinced herself that it had all been nothing more than bad karma on a hot day?

Deliberately sucking in a breath, as if that were the way to reset the machine, Maggie opened her eyes. She finished daubing out her name. She talked and laughed with her friends and walked out onto the hall to begin her shift. But just to make sure, to prove to herself that she shouldn't be infected by the ravings of a paranoid schizophrenic, she walked over to one of the computer stations and ran the name Urban McGinley for records.

There were none.

Breathing a sigh of relief, Maggie went off to get reports on her patients. She admitted two and dismissed three and helped sew a toddler who'd taken a tumble from a shopping cart.

And then, when she was inputting all the information from those patients, she took a moment to check up on Snake Pilson.

Who showed up.

Who had been seen in the ED for a gunshot wound to the head from a bad crack deal near Tower Grove Park. Who had been treated, admitted to SICU, and finally pronounced an organ donor ten days later.

It was simple, she told herself as she stuffed her equipment back into her battered old cloth bag at the end of the shift. Bob, good little paranoid that he was, saw sad stuff going on around him. Needing a reason for it besides the insupportable idea that bad shit just happened, Bob had created order through conspiracy. It was, after all, his job. And Bob had always been so very good at his job.

Maggie went home that night to an empty loft and echoing silence. She fed Ming, the Siamese cat she'd inherited from one of the Bimbos, put Loreena McKennitt on the CD player, and padded around her rooms in bare feet and silk pajamas. She thought of calling Delaney and decided against it. She missed his manic humor, but the price for it was still too high. So she watched old reruns, bad infomercials, and early-morning weather, ate reheated canneloni and thought how stupid it was that she was going to ask her friend in gang intelligence to look up the names Dog and the Snake and Sancho and Urban for her.

"Not dog, d-o-g," George Stein said two days later over a basket of nachos. "*The* Dawg. D-a-w-g. Also known as BD for Big Dawg. A.K.A. Dwayne Carver. OG for the Sixty-Six Rolling Crips."

Maggie sat quietly by as George wiped Velveeta from his chin and snapped up a couple more chips. Like anybody who knew cops, Maggie had offered to trade food for information. Of course, she didn't want to be obvious about it, so she did it at the weekly softball game in Forest Park, where George played shortstop for the Seventh District team and Maggie kept score.

It was another hot day, the grass brittle and dry beneath her feet, the dust puffing up from the diamond as a batter kicked at the plate. Forest Park sat at the western edge of the city, the second largest city park in the United States, which held among other things, a zoo, an outdoor theater, and an art museum.

The bare-bones athletic fields, complete with lights, benches, backstops, and all-purpose goals, were tucked between the Mounted Police stables and the highway, and saw just about every team sport but ice hockey played over them in the course of a year. Today, the Seventh District was playing the Third in a grudge match. Maggie's position was third base lawn chair, tucked right next to the bench, where she could keep a close eye on the action and talk to George.

And endure the other observer, she thought grimly as she pulled her wide-brim Jamaican straw hat a little farther over the freckles on her nose.

"Shouldn't you be playing, Maggie?" said observer was asking.

Maggie didn't bother to turn for her answer. She'd seen Sue the reporter arrive. Decked out in camp shorts and tank top, the girl glowed with perspiration and health, and carried mineral water around like Communion wine. Seventh District's third base coach took a look at her and suddenly had trouble remembering signals.

Well, Maggie thought with a wry grin as she watched the batter take an unsuccessful swing at a high, lofting pitch. At least nobody else would pay attention to her conversation with George.

"If you look closely," Maggie told Sue, bare arms briefly out to her sides, "you'll see that I am wearing my scorekeeping uniform. My ball uniform is completely different."

"Softball, anyway," George agreed with a waggle of his bushy eyebrows that relayed his opinion of the sandals and short fuchsia sundress Maggie wore. A squat, swarthy guy with more hair on his knuckles than his head, George was known to be bedding at least three dispatchers, and held the long-standing record for traffic arrests. Maggie patted his hand in gratitude for his friendly leer.

"I would have thought you'd play ball," the reporter insisted.

"Just because you've seen me in BDUs?" Maggie asked. "That's such a cliché. I've been the unchallenged police association scorekeeper since I was ten years old."

Scraping the bottom of his basket for cheese dregs before picking up the second helping that waited in his lap, George laughed. "Yeah, right after you threw the ball to the pitcher and knocked out the first base coach."

"Who happened to be my father."

"Doesn't look like it would matter much," Sue the reporter said, her attention on Allen, who was at that moment winding up to pitch with a decided flourish. For today's game, Allen had wisely chosen his attire and hairstyle from a J. Crew catalogue.

"More clichés, Sue," Maggie said. "Allen is probably the best softball pitcher in the state. Besides being a hell of a rugby player, soccer goalie, and my personal investment counselor."

"But he's not a cop."

"He's the police surgeon. Cops can always find a way to get a ringer in the game if it's important."

"I'm amazed they let him play. You know, because . . ."

"He's the single gayest man in four counties? Well, here's a home truth, Sue. If a man can play ball like Allen, other guys don't care what he does. Heck, if Oscar Wilde had played better cricket, there never would have been a poem from Reading Gaol."

The current batter, a watch commander with huge breasts and no balance, lobbed a pretty Texas leaguer into short center and trotted to first. Maggie marked the single in her book.

"You came up with those names awfully fast, George," she said, her attention ostensibly on the next batter. "You sure about the Dawg?"

His own attention on the length of leg exposed beneath the reporter's camp shorts, George nodded vaguely. "Sure. You asked about some of the big dicks in the south side gangs. I don't have to go far."

Which meant she probably hadn't needed to buy him his two hot dogs, either.

"Why you askin'?" he asked. "This something to do with the SWAT team?"

"Nah. The hospital. What can you tell me about them?"

"Sancho and Snake and the Dawg? Bad motherfuckers. The worst. Rap sheets that read like a copy of the penal code. Good little organizers, though. Sancho and the Dawg redesigned the Six-Sixes into one of the most efficient gangs on the block. Happy for us they got capped before they could do real damage."

"Capped?"

"Yeah, sure." Unconcerned, he shrugged. "Bound to happen sooner or later. A B-17 ball turret gunner has a longer life expectancy than a top gangbanger."

"So which of them is dead?"

George looked up and blinked. "Well, I thought you knew. All three."

Another thump, somewhere in the pit of her stomach.

"No. I mean, if they came through the ED, we'd just list given names, ya know? And we might not have been the ones to process them. I just heard there'd been quite a run on dead gangbangers lately and hadn't picked up on it." She smiled, knowing damn well George was susceptible. "Pretty embarrassing, ya know? Especially now that I'm on the SWAT team."

George licked a finger and patted Maggie's bare knee. "Yeah, but that's not stuff the medic needs to know. The medic just needs to know how to clean up after we take out the bad guys."

"That's me," Maggie said, marking a standing strikeout in her scorebook for one of the detectives. "The cleanup crew."

"Is that why the crime rate is down?" the reporter asked from George's other side. "Because the gangs are reorganizing?"

"Partly. The Six-Sixes and the North Grand Disciples were doing a little turf dance and took out some of their best and brightest. We'd give them posthumous awards if there weren't a bunch more snotnose kids getting ready to take their place."

"But Urban McGinley isn't one of them?" Maggie asked, snatching one of George's nachos.

"Nope. Name's familiar, but he's not one of our homeys."

Just as Maggie was going to ask something else, the field erupted in dust, tumbling bodies, and a spate of obscenities. By the time the dust cleared, there was a softball at Maggie's feet, four bodies piled up on third base, and Maggie, laughing so hard she was crying.

"You get that marked, O'Brien?" Delaney asked from the bottom of the pile.

"I did, Delaney," she assured him with a grin. "It was an error."

The pile heaved, and Delaney was on his feet. "It was not!"

"You dropped the ball," Maggie said, unperturbed.

"The wind knocked it out of my hand. A Santa Ana. A sirocco. A fuckin' act of God, O'Brien."

"Yeah, Sandy Koufax tried that same excuse out in Candlestick Park, where they really do have wind. They called an error on him, too, Delaney. Take it like a man."

Delaney's grin shone through the hovering dust like the Cheshire Cat. "Asshole."

Maggie wasn't at all sure why she wouldn't let it go. Three of the names Bob had given her were gangbangers. Gangbangers who had died of what, for gangbangers, were natural causes. Two gunshots and a knifing. She knew because with the names George had given her, she checked the records. She'd even snuck into Delaney's squad car and run them through his computer. And with all their names—sur, Christian, and otherwise—she'd found them after all.

Bad motherfuckers just about covered it. It seemed that the only thing those three hadn't been suspected of was the Lindbergh kidnapping. For three young men no older than twenty-five, they had sown misery and destruction over the city neighborhoods like dragons' teeth. No one but their mothers would miss them, and after reading a couple of the reports, Maggie wasn't sure even their mothers would be that desolate.

But she couldn't get them out of her mind.

Or, to be more precise, her gut. That indistinct region near her solar plexus that predicted disaster. Something wasn't right, and she didn't know what it was.

She thought of asking any of the cops, but cops tended only to respect cop guts for cop business. Nursing guts were reserved for issues of health and welfare.

Which was how she came to say something to Delaney three days later as they stood out on the police shooting range in far West County.

It was sweltering out, the air heavy and thick, the clouds stacking up heavier and thicker from the southwest. Every television set in the area was flashing thunderstorm warnings and tornado watches, which meant that the SWAT team had to get their practice rounds over as soon as possible. Delaney, who had been kept off the SWAT team by dint of his usually lousy scores, was there to try one more shot at qualification.

All of them were clad in a variation of sweat-stained T-shirt and jeans, with the obligatory ear protectors hanging around necks and goggles atop heads as they waited their turn. The rattle of gunshots was making Maggie sweat even harder.

"You really don't have to be here, ya know," Delaney told her quietly, for once not smiling.

Maggie's grin was not pretty. "It's part of maintaining qualification. Even if I never use a gun, I have to prove I can."

And put up with all the ribbing from the rest of the team, who had heard about her quick-shot medals.

"I'll lay you fifty Maggie's just making it up to look like a man," Paul insisted with a lifted eyebrow. "Her scores are always just passable. No way she'd do better emptying a clip that fast."

Maggie ignored him and waited her turn, perfectly comfortable with the fact that her earlier scores had been deliberate.

"Seems like there's a lot of gang activity lately," she said.

Delaney gave her a look. "You thinking of joining yet another new task force?"

Maggie shrugged. "Running down some rumors at work. I'm the official police force connection now, ya know."

"Anything the force should know in return?"

"Nah. We just found ourselves embarrassed at finding out from the news that our dead gang population has risen somewhat. Oddly enough, administration thinks we should know this stuff."

"Hey, Maggie," Paxton called over to her. "You go next. Show these pussies how to shoot!"

"You show 'em, Paxton. I'll watch right here."

"Heard you talking to George," Delaney said, slipping on his goggles and checking his rounds as he waited for a clean target. "He give you what you need?"

"That, two noogies, and one of his chips. One name we heard seems to have been a mistake. Urban McGinley. George didn't recognize it as a local. Must be something else."

Delaney nodded, distracted by his upcoming test. "Must be."

"Quick shot?" somebody else demanded farther down the line. "Maggie? I'd sooner believe she could pitch a no-hitter."

"So Urban McGinley doesn't ring any bells, huh?" Maggie asked Delaney.

Delaney didn't even look her way. "Nope."

"What is quick-shot competition?" Sue the ubiquitous reporter asked, looking like a kid playing dress-up in the oversize goggles as she waited with Maggie. "You mentioned it before."

Maggie stepped back from Delaney to give him room. "It's pistol target shooting, but you fire as fast as you can."

"And you've medaled?"

"Mmm-hmmm."

"But you won't use a gun on the SWAT team."

"Nope."

"Why not?"

"It's not in my job description," she said, her attention on Delaney as he took his two-handed stance and a deep breath. "I'm the team medic. I monitor them during the operation—make sure they're healthy, warm in the winter, cool in the summer, fed, watered, and walked on a regular basis. Position myself to rescue them if they're wounded and care for civilians or hostiles if my people are cared for."

"And if you're in a situation where you have to defend yourself or one of your men?"

"I have the rest of the team to do that."

She got a few more blinks from the reporter. "That's a lot of trust."

Maggie actually smiled. "You don't know much about SWAT teams, do you?"

Delaney fired, his attention complete, his movements more controlled than Maggie had ever seen them. She saw at least two rounds hit well and smiled.

"Why won't you use a gun?" the reporter asked Maggie.

"Because I'm scared of them."

Blink. Blink.

Delaney stood back, his round fired. The reporter wouldn't take her attention from Maggie.

Maggie couldn't stand it. "I've spent my life seeing the bad things a gun can do," she said. "I'm not comfortable around them. Discomfort causes hesitation, so I shouldn't be relied on with a gun in a tight situation. I rely on other skills and leave the guns to the guys who like 'em."

"Then why spend all that time perfecting the technique?"

Maggie decided the kid should have gone into homicide. She would have been a great interrogator. There was something about those big eyes that made you want to get the torment over with.

"It was my father's way of helping me get comfortable with the equipment."

"Come on, Maggie," another of her team members demanded. "Show us your shit. I got twenty on you."

"You're the only one," somebody else yelled with a laugh.

A veritable chorus of derision followed, which had all the makings of a long and serious game of "torment Maggie."

Delaney turned, lifted his goggles and held his gun toward her. Maggie saw the avid attention of her friends and knew they were forcing her hand. If she didn't shoot a target, she'd end up shooting one of them. Taking her own breath of surrender, she slipped on her ear protectors and reached for the gun.

Her movements brisk, professional, and neat, she

checked the weapon, accepted a clip from Delaney and slid it in. She tested the unfamiliar weight of Delaney's Beretta and took note of the fact that the nearing storm was pushing brief gusts of hot air across the range from left to right. Flicking off the safety she took her mark at the firing line, perfectly aware that silence had fallen over the whole range.

Another small gust of air ruffled the grass and set the body-shaped target to fluttering. Maggie measured it and lifted her arm straight before her. Then, one-handed and in blinding speed, she emptied the clip.

Reengaging the safety, she emptied the gun, secured it, and handed it back to Delaney, who was grinning. The range was silent as a tomb. Everybody out on that line could see that Maggie had put every round into a quarter-size cluster dead in the middle of the outline's groin.

Maggie didn't get any more information that day. She did, however, go out to her car after work the day after to find that beneath his good shirt and Marvin the Martian tie, Ted now sported a Kevlar jockstrap.

That weekend the Everyday section of the *St. Louis Post-Dispatch* ran a teaser entitled "Woman in a Man's World." The series, about the area's groundbreaking SWAT team medic, it said, would commence on Thursday. On Tuesday the series gained an added dimension when the St. Louis Police Department public relations officer called the *Post* with the news that the SWAT team was being dispatched to a hostage situation. If she was interested, Sue the reporter was officially invited to observe.

The Everyday senior editor held the layout in the hopes that this would provide Sue a snappier lead and action pictures to punch the story. The police department public relations officer was thanked, directions were taken, and Sue the reporter ran for the door with the *Post*'s best city desk photographer hot on her heels.

Maggie got her own notification just as she was returning to the Chesterfield #3 firehouse from an early-morning run to the hospital with an injured construction worker.

"Oh, hell," her partner complained when he heard the distinctive tones. "That's your bat beeper, isn't it?"

Maggie unclipped the iridescent blue device from her belt and nodded. The number 1040 flashed on the screen, the code for a SWAT call. "Hostage situation on . . . uh, Peabody Place," she said, reading the full message. "Is that in the city?"

"Beats me. You leaving?"

"Yep. Might as well get my backup in. I have a cape and boots to don."

Since a SWAT team member was technically on call all the time, the police worked their shifts backing up local districts. The medics worked their shifts with immediate backup available.

"I'll call," her partner said with a big, shit-eating grin. "You start cleaning the rig."

By the time Maggie's replacement arrived, the rest of the crew was watching the *Today* show and Maggie was clad in her BDUs. Since all the team kept their personal equipment locked in the trunks of their vehicles, Maggie checked her stash, then her map.

Peabody Place was on The Hill, an ethnic neighborhood that in pre-PC days had been known as Dago Hill, west off South Kingshighway, where Italian immigrants had settled, and the mostly Italian descendants still celebrated their heritage.

Family dispute with hostages.

Any 1040 call demanded that the full team respond. Maggie climbed in alongside Ted, who was looking particularly natty in a vague kind of way, slid her magnetic cherry light onto the roof, and turned the car east.

The outer perimeter of the hostage scene circled a short block of unmatched, disheveled-looking houses. Chain link ringed a few of the yards, and sagging porches emptied onto unkempt yards. Even the fire hydrants, all painted red, white, and green, seemed dingy and chipped.

The Hill was a mostly blue-collar neighborhood at the western edge of the city, traditionally proud and close-knit, packed with famous family restaurants and Italian markets, and cemented in its pride by the gothic lines of St. Ambrose Catholic Church. Peabody Place seemed a street that had lost its purpose.

Maggie slid her car in behind Paul Trevor's and climbed out to gather her gear. Another hot day, another close, storm-swollen sky. Another round of the Cicada Chorus that all but drowned out the chatter of police radios. The street itself was empty, the residents long since evacuated. Maggie saw the blue van tucked beyond a big, barnlike house and headed for it, zipping up and collecting her focus.

She'd been distracted the last few days. Gnawed at by a dead schizophrenic who'd left unanswerable questions. Now, though, Bob would have to wait back at the car with Ted. Maggie's heart rate had already picked up, her stomach and mouth dried out, her senses sharpened. Like all good tactical team members, Maggie had the ability to block out everything but the mission. As she joined the rest of the team beside the blue van, she did that very thing.

"What do we have?" she asked, clipping her hair up on her head and accepting a strip of electrical tape to secure her ear mike.

"Everybody's here now," the scene commander said, "so we'll set up the situation. The suspect is a thirty-four-year-old white male named Jimmy Krebs. At approximately 7:15 A.M. he barricaded himself in that white house over there with the flamingos on the lawn. The subject is under a restraining order during divorce proceedings, but showed up today and assaulted the wife. Just about the time he pulled out the gun, she managed to escape out a window for help."

"Which leaves?" Maggie asked.

"His four-year-old son, who was asleep in the back."

Maggie noted the creases of strain on the lieutenant's

face and knew that this wasn't going to be a typical situation. There was no drunk in there waiting to fall asleep. This guy was bad.

"He did fire off a few shots at the answering unit, but no other gunfire has been heard," the lieutenant went on. "Negotiator just got a throw phone in and talked to the boy, who seems healthy, but frightened. The impression we're getting from the suspect is that we're gonna be here a while."

And it was by then close to 9:30 A.M. Checking his notes and map, the lieutenant began pointing. "Okay. We have a single-story dwelling with four sides and ten openings."

To minimize confusion when discussing a structure, the team always numbered the sides, floors, and openings, such as windows and doors. Side one always faced the street, with all numbers climbing in a clockwise direction. The lieutenant pointed these out on the quickly drawn schematic he'd spread on a clipboard.

"Bill, go ahead and set out your squad in containment," he said. "Paxton's already at the residence at 1230, which is an almost identical layout to the target dwelling. Entry team join him there. We have permission to use it for entry assessment. Snipers, I'd like one of the positions to be on that garage by side three. Thermal imaging indicates subjects are in the kitchen. I want input on possible access and subject movement. Gas team, take up positions at side two, opening two, and side four, opening nine. One medic with gas team one, the other here to roam 'til you're needed. Questions?"

Every member of the twenty-four-person team turned a moment to assess the layout. The target house was a shingle-and-stone structure stuck in among neighbors of brick and siding like an untidy interloper. One story with detached garage and chain link fence, with a yard that was as much dirt as grass. A couple of toys lurked amid the weeds, and a bike leaned against the front wall.

The neighborhood was serviced by alleys that ran along the back of the houses instead of driveways, which meant that there wasn't a whole lot of open space between residences. Good cover, which was as much a liability as an asset.

Maggie the nurse noted that the Krebs house seemed dismal and sullen, with peeling paint and sagging screen door. Maggie the team medic considered access points and noted every opening she could see on the visible house sides. The windows on side one were shuttered, the door closed tight. Barricade face.

Maggie the pragmatist thought that if the commander turned off the utilities to the house, which was part of negotiations tactics, it was going to swelter like an oven on high. And if this guy was as pissed at his wife as he seemed, he wasn't coming out soon.

They were in serious trouble, and every person on the team knew it.

"Wife's at the ambulance," the lieutenant said to her. "Why don't you be my roving medic and get some medical info from her? I think she needs to see a female about now."

Wrapping her black sweatband over mike and hair so she could don her helmet, Maggie tucked her gloves into her belt and turned for the outer perimeter, where Mrs. Krebs waited with the ambulance.

The first person she saw when she arrived was Delaney. In uniform, but bareheaded, he was bent into a protective comma over a young woman perched on the back of the ambulance Maggie recognized by his stance and the woman's frail control. She was a dishwater blonde in hair and looks and demeanor. The kind of woman who had long since learned how to disappear into the background. Her features, her dress, her posture, were all vague and unthreatening, even her sobs silent so they didn't attract attention. If she'd been cast in bronze, her title would have been *Victim*.

Today, the statue was decorated in black and blue and old, sick green that marked the bruises she was trying to cover. And, of course, the rust of new blood. She clutched an ice pack to her jaw, and Delaney held her hand, murmuring to her as only Delaney knew how.

Maggie almost smiled. It was one of Delaney's gifts. Because he'd been born to a victimized mother, he understood what it took to comfort one.

"Mrs. Krebs?" Maggie greeted her, crouching at the woman's other knee. "My name's Maggie O'Brien. I'm a paramedic with the tactical team. How are you?"

Mrs. Krebs startled like a spooked horse. She had such pretty blue eyes, Maggie thought inconsequentially.

"Maggie O'Brien?" the woman asked with a quick, flinching smile that seemed to surprise her. "Like that big Irish bar downtown?"

Maggie smiled back. "Just like," she admitted. "My father named me after it."

Mrs. Krebs nodded a couple times. "I'm Annie."

Maggie reached out to lay a hand on Annie's nightgown-clad knee. Faded flowers and old cotton. As familiar a uniform to Maggie as to Sean.

"Annie," she said. "I hope this lout here told you how grateful we are you were able to get out that window. If you hadn't, we couldn't be here to help your boy."

Tears welled in those huge eyes. "His name is J.J. After . . . after . . ."

Maggie saw the brief flash of rage, quickly snuffed. Too dangerous for a woman in Annie's position.

"The asshole who broke into your house today?" Maggie asked with a soft smile.

Annie startled again, then smiled, the tears still falling. "Yeah."

Maggie patted. "Would you mind helping us again?" She only waited for a hesitant nod. "I need to know if there's anything you can tell us about your son's health to help him be comfortable in there. Also . . . I know this sounds bass-ackwards, but anything about his dad's health, too. Are either of them on any medications they might need? Do they suffer anything like asthma that might get worse in a situation like this?"

"No . . . no, neither of them. Except that Jimmy drinks. He's been drinking more lately . . . and then this morning . . ."

Maggie didn't wait for the rest of the sentence. She just patted that sad, thin little knee and climbed to her feet. "If you think of anything, anything at all, you let one of the paramedics here know, and they'll come get me. Okay?"

Another sheen of tears, a sobbing breath. "You're not going to make me leave?"

"With your baby in the house?" Delaney asked with a patented Delaney smile. "Never."

"Oh . . . oh, thank you . . ." Her face crumbled into misery; her hands clutched at each other as if seeking purchase. "My baby, he's never been a-away from me. And his dad . . ." Another sob, louder, less controlled, the kind that once let loose couldn't be contained. She raised those sad eyes to Maggie and lost the rest of her fragile control. "Oh, please . . ."

Maggie wrapped her arms around the woman and rocked her like a child. Held her, knowing that just then that was all she could do. "We will," she promised, even knowing better. "We'll get him out."

When she finally couldn't do anything else, Maggie handed Annie Krebs over to the paramedics, and she and Delaney walked away.

"You're good at that," he said to her.

"Comes from living with the Bimbos."

"I'm good, too."

Maggie's smile was soft, since it was nothing but the truth. "Yes, Delaney. You're good at it, too."

"We're good together," he insisted, leaning a little closer. "So you want to tell me again why won't you marry me?"

Maggie ignored him as she threaded her way through perimeter officers toward the Italian fire hydrant that marked the interior perimeter, her attention focused on her team. It was already ninety out, and at least one of her snipers was stretched out on a tar paper garage roof. Those guys were going to have a long day in the sun.

Besides, she'd had this argument so many times, she didn't need to waste her concentration on it. "Because, as I tell you every time you ask," she said, pulling on her sunglasses to cut the glare, "I like a little stability in my life."

A hand went over his heart. "I'm stable. I have a job. I have a car. I even have a house."

"Maggie!" a woman's voice called from beyond the police barricades. "Hey, Maggie, over here."

Maggie ignored her. She preferred laughing with Delaney. "You have a broken-down '71 Goat, you live in the part of the house your father didn't trash before he died, and as for your job, you've been busted so many times your sleeve has Velcro strips. Hell, Delaney, if you were stable, you wouldn't have been tossed back onto the streets for the fifth time in four years."

"That wasn't because I wasn't stable. It was because I couldn't keep my mouth shut."

His grin was pure mischief, as if just because he was cute and funny, she should forgive him anything. Which most times she did.

"Then, there are the women," she goaded him. "All those cute dispatchers and cop groupies and Rams cheerleaders you simply can't keep your hands off."

"Aw, c'mon, Mags. That's ancient history."

"How ancient?"

"I don't know. Months. Years. I'm a reformed man, Mags."

"Just like you're a reliable cop."

Suddenly that little-boy grin disappeared. "I'm a *good* cop."

Maggie stopped and sighed. "I didn't say that, Sean. Now, go away and let me do my job. And you do yours."

Sean retreated straight to that lady-killer grin that worked on everybody but Maggie. "If you weren't in the middle of an operation, I'd kiss your cute little upturned nose."

"And I'd break yours."

"Maggie!" the voice came again. "Can I talk to you?"

"You can't keep ignoring her," Sean said.

Maggie squeezed her eyes shut. "I'll horsewhip the person who told her where we were."

"All she had to do was listen to a police scanner."

"Tell her to go away."

"Tell me you'll marry me."

Maggie opened her eyes to let him know how funny he was. Unfortunately while she was doing that, some idiot let the baby reporter through the lines.

"Maggie, I'd like to get a couple of shots of you here if I could," she panted as if she'd climbed a hill to get there.

Maggie sucked in a slow breath, and Delaney scuttled away like a pickpocket. She'd get him later.

"I can't talk to you now, Sue," Maggie said. "I'm a little preoccupied. See me when this is over."

"Well, my deadline is in about an hour. Is that time enough?"

Maggie considered the tableau out on the shimmering street. "No. Nowhere near."

She started walking. Sue followed her, and Maggie stopped again. "I don't think you understand," she said, trying to listen to the chatter in her ear as she spoke. "You can't distract me when I have a four-year-old in that house and all my men positioned to enter. I'll talk to you later, okay? For now, get behind the perimeter where you'll be safe."

Maggie turned again. Sue didn't follow. She didn't have to.

"Before you go," the reporter said. "I thought I'd ask. Did you ever find out about Urban McGinley?"

Maggie stopped. For a second, she couldn't connect the name. When she did, it was like being yanked back by a bungee cord.

"No. No, I didn't. It's not important."

"It's just that I was surprised none of the police remembered the other day. I mean, you know, who he was. Father McGinley was pretty notorious."

Maggie lost forward momentum a second time. "*Father McGinley?*" she asked, turning.

Was the reporter gloating? "Yeah, don't you remember? He was the priest who diddled all those altar boys. Geez, the archdiocese had kittens over it."

"A10 this is C2, be advised," the cop said in her ear. "We're now on standby."

Maggie's heart raced. With all the listening devices out there, the lieutenant had devised personal codes. This one meant that negotiations were going south. They were on alert to go.

"Where is he now?" Maggie asked, yanking on her gloves. "Father McGinley."

The reporter laughed, as if Maggie were the most out-of-touch person on the planet. "You really didn't know? The father of one of the altar boys got hold of him. Beat him into Jell-O."

Maggie closed her eyes, wishing like hell she wasn't going to hear the rest.

"A10, prepare team to advance . . ." her lieutenant murmured in her ear.

"Father McGinley's dead," the reporter concluded.

Maggie opened her eyes. But she didn't face the reporter. She turned instead for the Krebs house. She slid her helmet back on. She hiked up her vest and eyeballed the position of her team and thanked Jimmy Krebs for providing such a perfect distraction. And just briefly, before she got down to business, she thought how ashamed she should have been for the thought.

CHAPTER 5

One of the most surprising facts Maggie had learned in Tactical EMS School was that the average hostage negotiation lasted eight hours. The bad news on this sweltering August afternoon in St. Louis was that the eighth hour had come and gone. And like the golden hour in trauma medicine, the minutes past eight hours climbed quickly to a crisis point.

Maggie had been on standby four times so far, moments when Jimmy Krebs had become so volatile that the negotiators were sure the team was going to have to storm the house and take him out. The entry team had curled itself around the garage, waiting to access their primary entry point, the kitchen. The containment team was sprinkled over lawns and porches, tucked out of sight like bad news to protect the field, and Maggie had shadowed the gas man by the corner of the next-door neighbor's house, waiting for word to follow in.

But the negotiators had persevered, Jimmy had been placated, and everybody had backed down from an intervention position to simple alert. As the minutes stretched to hours, anxiety ratcheted up another notch, patience wore a little thinner, and every eye and ear strained to catch proof that the little towheaded boy in the kitchen was safe.

Maggie had seen him. Once during one of her rounds to check on her team, she'd climbed up to lie alongside Paul

and his spotter on their sweltering tar paper roof and borrowed the Zeiss binoculars to get a peek into the dingy,
untidy kitchen Jimmy Krebs had commandeered. She'd
seen little J.J. right away, a still, pale little boy slumped in
a kitchen chair over a bowl of untouched cereal. Dressed
in oversize Sesame Street pajamas, he'd filled the window,
as if Jimmy Sr. had deliberately placed him in the way of
the snipers. Taunting them with their inability to get at him
past his own child.

Maggie had seen Jimmy, too, flashes of sagging jeans
and restless hands as he'd paced beyond his son, obviously
in intense conversation with the negotiators. Maggie had
seen the curl of cigarette smoke and the litter of beer cans
on the floor and knew, just like everybody else, that their
chances of getting a good outcome from this situation were
waning by the minute.

The sun passed zenith and began to set. The heat gathered and weighed. Tempers flared and throats grew dry. By
six that evening, which was the ten-hour mark, everybody
was walking a razor's edge.

Maggie had had to recall one sniper because of heat
exhaustion, and continued to pass out power bars, bananas,
apples, and half-strength sports drinks. Shifts changed and
new uniform police showed up, but the day shift refused to
leave. The sun was settling over the highway. The containment team grabbed quick sandwiches where they crouched
in the bushes. The entry team stayed curled around the back
side of the house, and Jimmy Krebs began to demand
money to leave. His son, still in his pajamas, hadn't yet
eaten his cereal. Maggie was exhausted, tense, and irritable.

And worse, distracted.

She had Jimmy and her team spread out in front of her
and Urban McGinley lurking within.

Urban McGinley.

Father McGinley.

Pedophile. Dead pedophile. The fourth dead person out
of a list of four Bob had given her.

Coincidence.

Maggie wanted to believe that. Pacing the perimeter of a hostage situation brought on by a drunken, self-absorbed asshole, she couldn't quite find it in her heart to feel anything for four other self-absorbed assholes. And the four men Bob had warned her about had definitely fit that description.

Then why did those deaths bother her so much?

Maggie checked her watch, listened to the empty static on her earpiece, and headed over toward the ambulance to check once more on Annie Krebs.

Those deaths bothered her because her gut was aching again. Because something didn't fit, and she didn't know why. Because deep down she'd never quite believed that Bob had dosed himself with cocaine and then tried to boil a pom-pom girl.

But if Bob was right, and those four guys were dead because of more than just shared bad habits, then what? Could somebody really have gone to all the trouble to kill a crazy guy like Bob because he connected the deaths of four pretty worthless individuals who had been taken off the active roster?

Why?

That was the question. Why?

No, Maggie thought. The question was, did she really want to ask that again when the furor had finally died down from the last time?

Another day, she told herself with a severe shake. Right now she had more immediate things that needed her attention.

But after ten hours of very intense concentration in hundred-plus-degree heat, she was having trouble holding her focus.

Until she saw the forlorn figure sitting between the open back doors of the ambulance.

"Annie?" Maggie asked, palming her helmet off onto the ground and squatting on her haunches. "How are you?"

Annie barely reacted. She was hunched over, just like

her son, with nothing to hold on to. Nothing in front of her but cracked pavement and weeds.

"Honey, they're still talking in there," Maggie said, laying careful hands on Annie's. Feeling the instinctive flinch she knew so well. "I saw J.J. again about twenty minutes ago, and he's eating cereal."

"Captain Crunch," Annie muttered.

Maggie smiled. "Captain Crunch. Have you had anything to eat lately? Any water? You need to take care of yourself so you can take care of J.J., ya know."

Annie didn't respond, so Maggie stood up to talk to the paramedics, who not only promised Annie nourishment, but offered Maggie ice water. Maggie dumped a styrofoam cup of it over her sunburned neck and headed back to her team.

She was halfway back to the house when the earpiece crackled to life.

"Be advised . . ." the lieutenant murmured.

"Lieu, hey, Lieu, he's . . ." It was Paul, his voice tight and urgent.

Maggie stopped, looked toward the house. Saw the containment team toss their sandwiches in the dirt.

"He's pouring something on the floor," Paul insisted.

"Entry team stand by," the lieutenant snapped. "Tell me what you see, sniper one. Gas team one, can you put one through the kitchen window?"

It had been ten hours and twenty minutes. Maggie began to run. She had to get to her position by the other gas team.

"Affirmative on that," the gas guy answered quietly. "Just give me the word."

"Oh, Jesus, Lieu!" Paul. Frantic. "It's kerosene. Stop them! He's pouring kerosene!"

"Gas team hold!" the lieutenant all but howled in Maggie's ear. "Sniper, green light! You have the ball!"

Maggie skidded on the sticky blacktop and whirled back for the ambulance. She could see Annie come upright, as if she'd heard, even this far away, the tinny little voices in Maggie's ear. Ashen, eyes wide as she caught the sudden action. Eyes the same color as her baby's.

Maggie heard the report of a high-power rifle.

"Entry team, go! Go!" the lieu called.

"No . . . oh no, oh no, oh no!" a howl, a moan, a plea. Paul's young voice cracking in agony. "Oh, Jesus!"

Maggie thought she heard the whoof of an explosion back in that untidy wood house just as she reached the ambulance.

"Get me your turn-out gear!" she screamed at the paramedics.

"What?"

"Give it to me!"

Annie stepped in front of her. "What's happening?"

The paramedics pulled a slick yellow bundle from a side locker and ran for her. Maggie threw them her protective helmet and pulled on a fire coat and helmet.

"Wait here," she said to Annie and spun away.

"The breathing apparatus!" somebody yelled.

Maggie didn't have time. She ran hard for that unpretty house, heavy in her equipment, ungainly, sweating, and terrified. She saw a couple of the containment guys scrambling like cockroaches across the untidy lawn, pink flamingo tumbling over before the assault. She heard over her earpiece that the suspect had lit the kitchen. She saw the smoke puff from a window as she slammed through the front gate and heard the cursing, jostling noises as entry team one swung the battering ram at the back door. She was no more than two steps from the porch when the gas man tackled her like a linebacker and pulled her right to the grass of that miserable front yard.

She heard the pops of a handgun and knew that the father was trying to keep them out. Four of the entry team barreled around the side of the house toward the porch, the bulletproof shield held before them like a jousting shield. Maggie fought like an animal against the urge to get to them, to get into that house. To get that towheaded little boy safely away. Maggie knew about burns. She knew, and she didn't want that son of a bitch to do that to his child.

She'd promised Annie. She'd promised to bring her little boy back.

"The kitchen is fully involved!" Paxton's voice cried in her ear from where he was stationed at the back, by the kitchen door. "We have no access!"

Maggie pulled free just as the side windows exploded outward and flames licked the eaves.

"No-o-o-o-o!" she heard Annie wail out on the street.

"I can get in!" she yelled over her mike. "Just give me access!"

"Suspect's exiting side three!" somebody yelled.

"Where's the hostage?"

"Not with him!"

The entry team exploded into action. Maggie lurched to her feet and ran for the front door just as it splintered behind the weight of the ram. She followed her team in at a dead run.

Maggie found J.J. on the bubbling green tile kitchen floor. She smothered the flames and curled him into her coat and carried him back out the front door. She breathed into his charred mouth and pumped his stricken heart. She tasted the kerosene on his stiff, gaping lips and smelled it in the exhaled wisps of air that brushed her cheek as she ran. She tried so hard to ignore the raw, slick patches where there used to be white-blond hair, the claws that had been hands, the scatter of brittle leaves that had once been Sesame Street pajamas.

"Get his mother away," she rasped into her mike as her team guided her back out through the smoke. "Do it now."

Maggie saw, as she ran the baby to the ambulance, that Delaney had walked Annie away. She saw his shoulder curve around the woman, saw the other police form a barricade to protect her, heard her high, wild grief.

Maggie would remember it all at odd times later, but now she ran that little boy to the paramedics, even knowing that they couldn't help. That the hospital couldn't help. That his father, in a rage because he couldn't control his own life, had poured kerosene on his child and lit him.

"Maggie?"

She looked up to see the paramedics waiting to take little J.J. out of her arms. She saw that they knew, too. She knew that they would try anyway, so she handed the child off and slammed the ambulance doors behind them as they climbed inside.

The siren screamed. The lights shuddered. The ambulance jerked to a dead run that would have flattened anyone in its way. Left behind, the cops and reporters and neighbors stood in untidy clumps over the streets, their silence sudden and stricken.

And Maggie stood with them, her hands empty, her neck burned, her lungs tight with smoke and tears and fury.

"The son of a bitch just surrendered," somebody said in her ear.

Maggie turned back to see the holocaust that consumed J.J.'s house. She saw a neighboring house begin to char. She heard the ambulance fade away and the air horns of fire trucks approach. She saw the team manhandle somebody around the corner from the alley and knew that it was J.J.'s father.

"Subject has suffered a gunshot wound to the thigh," somebody said in her ear mike. She couldn't discern voices anymore. They all sounded tight, terrible, grief-stricken. Later they'd all blame it on smoke. Now they didn't care.

"They should have let *you* at him, Little Zen," one of the team said as Maggie approached. "You would have at least made it a good groin shot."

"Fuck that," she said in her own tight, quiet voice. "I say we just kill this fucker."

And then she stepped forward to help treat him.

Maggie walked into her loft at midnight, drunk, singed, and smelling like a barbecue. She didn't bother with the lights or the cat or the sound system. She walked down the steps and started ripping off her BDUs.

She had spent the evening debriefing the Krebs situation

as if its outcome hadn't mattered, then held Paul as he'd vomited up what he'd seen into the toilet at the Toe Tag for four straight hours. She had stood Tommy's praise and the reporter's stunned disbelief and all the sharp fury of her fellow teammates at the bar and never said a word except in Paul's ear as he'd hunched over that dingy, unwashed toilet.

She'd gotten the news from the hospital that little J.J. Krebs had officially died just as the bar was ready for closing. Then, knowing perfectly well how drunk she was, she'd walked out and driven home.

Maggie made it down the two steps into her echoing living room before she realized she wasn't alone. For the flash of an instant she was frightened. Someone was there in the dark with her. Someone panting and sweaty and radiating rage like heat off a summer street.

Maggie stopped dead in her tracks, her hands wrapped in the hem of her shirt, her breath raspy and ragged in her throat. She looked into the corners where the shadows dominated and heard him. Smelled him. Recognized the same sounds and smells and struggle in herself.

She didn't move. She just waited as if she deserved what would come. He didn't say a word. He just walked up to her and pulled the shirt out of her hands to tear it straight off her head. He ripped her tank top and yanked at her belt, and suddenly she answered. Fought as hard as he to shed clothing that suddenly seemed to reek of smoke. BDUs and blues both, discarded with angry, hungry hands and mouths fused in fury. Punishing, frenzied movements, a dance of darkness across Maggie's hardwood floor. From one end of the loft to the other, over couches and cushions and bed, they coupled in perfect, deadly silence. Ignoring fresh burns and old injuries, in white-hot rage. He pushed her against the wall and heaved her up. She locked her legs around his waist and her arms around his neck. He pounded into her as if he could purge himself. She pulled him inside her as if he could scrape it all away.

They stumbled to the bed and battered each other all

over again. Then again on the floor. Maggie didn't know how long. She didn't really care. She knew he didn't. Sometimes it was just too much, and there was nothing else to do but scourge it away. And never, there in the high emptiness of that loft, was a word said by either one of them.

Maggie woke to hear the phone ringing. She woke alone. She wasn't surprised. More relieved, actually. Especially considering the state of her head and her stale, aching body.

The bed was a disaster, sheets and blankets tangled and sagging and damp. Her skin was raw and hot and salt-rimed like a Margarita, even with the ceiling fan cooling her. Maggie saw the faint light slicing through the blinds and thought it was nearing dawn.

The phone kept ringing.

Maggie lifted up on her elbows and rubbed at gritty eyes. She pushed a tangle of hair off her face. She looked around and saw that the rest of the loft was in even worse condition than she or the bed. Shards of ceramic littered the floor. Her answering machine, its guts spilled like confetti. Two glass tumblers, a teapot, the contents of her mantel, and at least one cat food dish scattered in pieces across the floor like a shattered mosaic. Good thing Ming knew enough to hide, or he might have landed on the floor right after his food.

Maggie had to clean it all up. She had to do it before she answered the phone or her beeper or the wake-up call of the sun. She damn near climbed out for the broom in her bare feet before she realized that she'd just end up with soles studded in ceramic shards. The patchy burns that ringed her neck and wrists were quite uncomfortable enough on their own.

The phone kept ringing.

The hell with them, Maggie thought, searching for clothing to replace the musty sheet she was wearing. Let 'em wait 'til I'm ready. She had to clean up the mess in her loft. She had to strip the bed and scrub the floor. Besides, the way she was feeling, she didn't think she was going to be ready for the rest of the world anytime soon. Maybe another month or so.

Damn that Delaney anyway.

All she wanted to do was to brush her teeth. Wash away the taste of him, and beneath him, the taste of kerosene.

But the phone kept ringing.

Groaning, Maggie gave up. She lurched to her feet and gingerly stepped over to the phone, which had somehow survived. She already had it to her ear before it occurred to her it might be Tommy. She almost hung up.

It wasn't.

"It's okay," the quiet voice said.

Maggie actually shivered. "What's okay?" she asked, her own voice still raspy and sore.

"The fucker's dead. It's taken care of. It's okay now."

And then, a click.

Maggie stood there a few minutes staring at the phone. She heard the automated operator click on to tell her to do something, but she couldn't quite pay attention to what. She kept thinking of that quiet voice. That odd, sad message.

It's okay now.

What was okay? Who was dead?

Maggie sucked in a dreadful breath.

The fucker's dead.

She remembered, even through everything. Because of everything. She hung up the phone, just like the recording said, and then picked it back up and dialed.

"Four west," one of the night nurses answered in a hurry from the prison ward.

"Doris," Maggie said. "This is Maggie O'Brien from ED checking on a new patient you got last night. Jimmy Krebs."

"How did you know?" Doris demanded.

Maggie shut her eyes. "Know what?"

"He just died."

Maggie didn't even respond. She just hung the phone

up and stood there in the middle of her littered floor, naked and shivering and afraid.

She had her answer. *The fucker's dead.* And, oh God, she wasn't sorry.

Which was why, she suddenly realized with terrible clarity, the other four fuckers were dead as well.

CHAPTER 6

"What do you mean, she found out what's going on?"

The car this night was tucked away in a side street by Union Station, the lights off and the air-conditioning humming almost as loudly as the cicadas who thrived in the trees.

"I mean she called the hospital before anybody else knew Krebs was dead. You haven't heard that she's psychic, have you?"

The second man rubbed a weary face. "Shit."

The smoke ring that drifted toward the ceiling of the Crown Victoria was imperfect, impatiently formed. "I don't suppose we can just trust her not to figure out what's going on."

"Not if people keep talking to her."

"Will she keep her nose out of it?"

A sigh, a shuffling in the cocoon of silence in a night throbbing with cicada love. "We'll have to watch her more closely, I guess."

Another silence, longer, more uncomfortable. "She *was* pretty upset about that kid . . ."

"Said things in the street I've never heard her say before. Actually sat on the father and told him he was a worthless sack of shit."

The smoker grinned. "Did she really? Nice to know she has it in her."

"She *is* Tommy's kid."

"I guess so."

"So what do we do?"

Another smoke ring's worth of consideration. Another half dozen bars of the cicada symphony. "For now, we let her be famous. Should take up most of her time, anyway."

He got a chuckle from his compatriot. "She'll hate it."

"Good. That'll keep her busy."

She did hate it. What Maggie most needed in the days following the death of that little boy was a normal course of events. Debriefing, recovery, resettlement into familiar patterns. Delaney to amuse her and the SWAT team to comfort her. To comfort each other. Quiet and order and routine. Instead she got chaos, and she got it full in the face.

It seemed that Susan the reporter had brought a photographer along to Jimmy Krebs's house. The photographer, obviously hearing the clarion call of the Pulitzer committee, had managed to get off a good roll and a half of film of Maggie stumbling out of the house with the baby in her arms. In the process, he'd produced the kind of picture that newspapers thrive on, firefighter heroically breathing life into stricken child with smoke billowing in background, the supporting cast clustered around her like a dark chorus choreographed to highlight her frantic, yellow-coated escape.

AP and UPI picked it up. National news featured it. Political and religious leaders commended the determination obvious in all those stricken faces. Mothers and talk-show hosts eulogized that bright little boy in the Sesame Street pajamas.

Worst of all, where the picture went, so went the accompanying article in which Susan Jacobsmeyer had succeeded in transmuting Maggie into some terrifying Florence Nightingale/Rambo hybrid. Suddenly *everyone* wanted to know all about Maggie O'Brien, as if she were the first explorer or the last virgin.

And so Maggie couldn't retreat to the haven of her loft,

where the silence would wash her like a warm bath. She couldn't disappear with her team to the Toe Tag for group therapy or with Delaney to the woods for some mindless, macho, athletic challenge to work off the frustration. Instead, Maggie found herself caught in a web of bright lies, artificial smiles, and uninformed praise.

Maggie had nightmares. She smelled kerosene at the worst moments and heard a child screaming in her sleep. And none of her sudden fan club understood the fact that she wasn't being coy when she refused to talk about how she'd felt stumbling out of that house with a dying child in her arms.

Even worse, she didn't just have that dead child on her conscience. She had his father. She had Bob's list of four within her own List. She had a secret that effectively ate away whatever peace was left to her.

One of the people at her hospital was committing murder.

And Maggie wasn't at all sure she should do anything about it.

"Oprah?" Sean chortled from where he lay on his back on the weight bench in the Police Academy workout room.

Spotting him as he did his reps, Maggie sighed in disgust. "Like they say, one picture is worth a thousand fundraisers. The hospital's excited, the fire department is excited, and God bless them, the twin governments of St. Louis are creaming their shorts. The county exec actually thanked me for having the foresight to have a photographer handy to snap that picture, since it's done so much to quiet complaints about a joint SWAT team."

"Thoughtful of you."

Maggie considered telling Sean about that voice at the back of her head, about the one on the phone the other morning. But she wasn't ready. She hadn't even had the guts to take another look at The List. The memory of that little boy still dragged at her arms and stopped her sleep.

The circus surrounding her was still too frantic to allow introspection. The official cause of death for Jimmy Sr. had been listed as post-op air embolism. The officer had been cleared of the shooting and the case closed.

Much as Montana Bob's had been closed. And, Maggie suspected, Urban and Sancho and the Dawg and Snake.

But if Maggie couldn't manage to ask questions yet about Jimmy Krebs, she sure as hell couldn't do it about the others.

So she changed places with Sean on the weight bench and let him spot her while she did her own reps.

At least she was getting to the gym every day. If she didn't work off at least that much pressure, God knows what she'd do the next time Tommy clapped her on the back and told her he'd never been so proud as when he'd heard what she'd said to that perp who'd ashed his kid.

"Aw, you can handle Oprah," Sean assured her with a noogie to her sweaty horizontal head. "Hell, maybe the National SWAT Association should make you their poster child. You're cute, you can string sentences together without embarrassing yourself, and you've never been photographed aiming a gun at a kid in a closet."

"Your support overwhelms me, Delaney," she grunted.

"Well, you know I think you're cute."

"I know you think I'm easy."

"Nah," he said with a brash grin. "Nothin' about you's easy, Mags."

Resettling the bar onto the rack, Maggie let Sean haul her up off the bench. "Something to remember the next time you think of proposing," she suggested with a pat to his sweat-streaked cheek.

Sean's expression didn't change a bit. "I'm just glad the asshole had the good sense to die."

Maggie froze on the spot. "Why?"

Sean shook his head like a pastor before an unrepentant sinner. "We've had these discussions before, O'Brien. You can't still try and tell me that sometimes tit for tat isn't enough of an argument. Worked for the Old Testament. Works even better for capital punishment."

"The old basic sixth-grade boys' playground morality, huh?"

"The rest is just semantics, Mag, and you know it. Besides," he said, tweaking her nose, as if she were just the cutest thing on earth, "by taking care of it himself, he saved you pinko liberals all that effort of trying to believe he deserved a fair trial and a life lifting weights in prison. Hell, he even saved space for another worthy on The List."

And that was that. Sean walked off to try his luck on the leg machine, and Maggie stood there, left behind like a stray thought. For a second she could have sworn she'd heard something more than usual banter from Sean. For a second, she thought she heard an odd echo from the voice on the telephone.

But only for a second. And only, she realized, because she was suddenly listening for it.

But that was ridiculous. Flipping her towel over her shoulder, she shoved her secret away again and headed off to work the kinks out of her shoulders.

On Tuesday she did an interview with the *Today* show and the local noon news. On Wednesday she found out that Oprah had discovered a diet guru more interesting than she and bumped her. Maggie spent the day wading through a high tide of sick and injured at the ED instead. Unfortunately, every third person not only knew who she was but wanted to kiss her cheek to say thank you, even though she hadn't saved the baby after all.

On Friday she was back helping the SWAT team serve high-risk warrants in North County.

" 'A woman of peace in a violent profession,' " the gas guy intoned reverently as Maggie took up her position with him alongside a shabby duplex in Overland, where the county narcotics guys were using the much-better-equipped SWAT team to serve up their incarceration invitations.

Only one squad went out to serve warrants, and it was usually fast and easy. Maggie spent most of her time scratching at the prickly heat around her neck and ignoring the cicadas, who still spent an inordinate amount of time mating on her helmet.

"One more person quotes those damn articles to me," she calmly threatened through the glove she held in her teeth so she could get her fingernails at her collarbone, "and I will show you how violent this peaceful girl can be."

"Oh, but it's poetry, O'Brien. It's immortal."

"It's about thirteen minutes away from extinction, I hope. Maybe after the news lights switch off I can go buy my Tampax without somebody calling me 'SWAT Angel.' " She closed her eyes in ecstasy at the brief relief brought on by sharp fingernails. "I'm thinking about getting it tattooed on my ass."

"Don't tell me that if you don't mean to show me."

"I'll tattoo it on Ted instead. Then everybody can see it."

One unkempt front yard away, the entry team gathered in an untidy knot just to the left of the front door. Maggie transferred her glove from mouth to hand. Dennis Arnold, the gas guy, lifted his shotgun to his shoulder.

"Dennis, put a few through the bathroom window," Pax said in Maggie's ear.

Two shotgun-shell-size canisters of CS gas in a small bathroom went a long way toward discouraging drug dealers from dumping their supplies down the toilet when they heard the words "Police! Open up!" Dennis pumped and fired the Remington 870 in quick succession. Glass shattered, and sudden, surprised shouts could be heard from the house. Flower swung the battering ram at the front door.

"Police! Open up!" Pax yelled, and the entire team shoved right through the shattered front door. Maggie waited through five minutes of shouting and bodies crashing against flat surfaces to hear her name called.

It wasn't. The raid went smooth as silk, netting three

T-shirted and jeaned suspects who were hauled out into the front yard to finish coughing out the gas.

"Just another day at the office," Dennis said, securing his weapon.

Maggie scratched again and pulled out her riot cuffs to help secure the now-submissive perps. "Not even a good excuse to play Drain the Gene Pool."

Which brought her to a halt no more than four feet from the party. Lord, she thought in disgust. If I'm going to suspect everybody who mentions vengeance, I'm going to have to add my own name to the top of the list. Drain the Gene Pool indeed.

As if on cue, Dennis chuckled, his attention on breaking down his weapon. "At least that asshole of yours took himself out for us."

Maggie stopped, wishing he hadn't said that. "Which asshole of mine would that be?"

Dennis looked a bit startled. "You know, that father. Krebs." Then he grinned. "The way we're piling up names out here, you're gonna start running out of room on The List. And I know you had a special place for *that* fucker."

Maggie blinked. Shook her head as if she could clear it of the little voice that was just ruining her relationship with everybody she knew. Walking again, she nodded. "Yeah," she said, bending over the prone, sweaty bodies in the dirt. "But I wish he had gotten there without any help."

It was probably a good thing nobody heard her.

"I always wondered what it would take to make Little Zen lose her cool," Allen Fitzmaurice said the next day when he caught Maggie in the back hall cutting up the waiting room copy of *Newsweek* with her bandage scissors. Tiny, even, colorful pieces of Maggie's photographed face fluttered into the wastebasket like confetti at a parade.

Maggie looked up to see Allen in his trademark salmon scrubs and shot him a complacent grin. "Newsprint," she said evenly. "Reporters. Talk-show hosts. Hospital public relations officers."

"Attention." He grinned with a lofty wave of his hand that took in all the various annoyances of Maggie's recent life. "You're the flavor of the day, my darling, and everyone's taking a lick."

Maggie climbed to her feet and dropped the rest of the magazine in the trash like a dead rat. "Why, Allen, thank you. Now I feel not only overused and violated, but vaguely unhygienic."

"Well, at least the asshole paid for his sins. It certainly makes all this . . . disruption worthwhile for the rest of us poor peasants."

Maggie stood there at the end of her hall and sighed. "Not you, too."

"You'd rather he'd have lived to frolic through the jurisprudence system for the next thirty years or so?"

She scowled this time. "I'd rather that every person who recognized me didn't congratulate me on his demise, as if it was my own personal accomplishment."

But hadn't it been? Hadn't his death been for her? An answer to her anguish out on the street?

The fucker's dead. It's all right now.

Somebody had done that terrible thing, and they'd done it for her. And maybe, no matter how outraged Maggie should feel about those other people who might have been murdered, she hadn't really felt betrayed until this.

That one of her friends had tried to do her a favor.

That she had asked for a man's murder without even knowing it, and she had been obliged.

And now, she couldn't look at her friends without feeling betrayed, that even though she'd certainly asked it, they should have known she hadn't really meant it.

How could she want somebody dead?

Even Jimmy Krebs.

Even though, out on that terrible street, she had.

No, she thought with even greater sadness. It wasn't that her friend had killed for her. It was that her friend had felt so overwhelmed that he or she had felt the need to kill at all. And then made Maggie responsible for it.

"Oh, my darling, you're overreacting," Allen assured her with another Judy Garland wave as he started down the hall.

It took a second for Maggie to realize that Allen wasn't answering the question about her murderous friend. Just the more annoying one of her notoriety. It took her another to yank herself back and follow him.

"It's that common bond thing, you know," he continued, as Maggie caught up with him by room twenty, where one of the techs was trying to decimate the lice population of two homeless guys. "Put one hurt kid in a picture and everybody thinks they own him . . . unless there are flies on his face, of course. Then they just think they have to send him money."

Maggie almost laughed. Leave it to Allen to put everything into perspective.

"I'll remember that," she assured him. "Better yet, I'll make sure you're the one in the picture. See if you're still so philosophical."

Allen snorted like a draft horse. "Don't be absurd. I only wear turn-out gear to Village People parties. Now, wade back into the tide and make me proud."

Allen disappeared into the control desk, leaving Maggie slowing to a halt in the middle of the worklane. Ten feet away Carmen sat cross-legged on the floor, chin in hands, quietly talking with Mr. Petra, who thought he was an egg. Jeannie Mars was bouncing an abused baby on her hip as she updated the flowboard and wiped drool from her neck. In room seventeen Rashad, one of the techs, was trying to dodge the liquid charcoal he'd just helped shove down an overdose.

The hall was crowded, noisy, and dingy with the detritus of destruction of every kind. Phones rang, a dozen different alarm buzzers sounded, and out in the driveway another ambulance was cutting its siren on approach. It wasn't even that busy a day, and yet Maggie could see the wear and tear on everybody and everything around her.

They were just doing their best, the people Maggie knew. Trying their hardest with the tools they had to make things better. Day after day, year after year, they treated victim and perpetrator with the same care and tried to survive the fact that only the victims seemed to keep coming back.

Only the vulnerable, the lost: bruised women, silent children, the shattered and stunned, who ate away at the facade of distance caregivers wore like cheap party masks. Picking at the soft places with trembling hands and needy eyes, with hopelessness and despair, as if these people who worked in the halls of a hospital or the back of an ambulance or the front seat of a police cruiser were impervious to all that pain.

Oh, there were assholes out there. Maggie wouldn't deny it. But on the whole, the people she worked with were only doing their best. Trying to get by. Trying to keep up. Trying, in the face of overwhelming odds, to make a difference.

Maggie stood frozen at the edge of the worklane that had encompassed so much of her life and weighed the decision she knew it was time to make.

She considered what it would do to these people if she went forward. If she really sought out the murderer among them.

It could be Carmen doing this. Sharp, impatient Carmen, who could tap dance through a code like Fred Astaire on speed. Or Jeannie, who cared so much she drove herself to blinding headaches. Maybe Allen, who neatly camouflaged his oversize heart in greasepaint and shtick. It could be any one of the people she worked with, and she didn't want it to be.

She didn't want to hurt any of them. She didn't want to expose them by ferreting out that person who had succumbed to the temptation to strike back. She didn't want to admit that the rest of them would resent her need to do it.

Maggie belonged so few places, but she belonged here. She belonged to her SWAT team and her fire squad at Chesterfield. She'd spent twenty-six years working toward no goal but that, no matter what it had cost her.

She didn't want to lose them.

She didn't want to lose the people who filled them.

But if she started asking questions again, she would. Not just the murderer. Every other friend who knew the terrible temptation of such an act. Each fallible, frightened person who meant so much to her.

By exposing the murderer, Maggie would expose them all.

And she, in exposing them, would be their betrayer.

Down at the end of the hall, Carmen, edgy, impatient Carmen, leaned forward and brushed a bit of hair off Mr. Petra's forehead. Then, as gently as if he were an infant, she began to croon to him.

"Hey, aren't you the gal I seen in the paper?" a voice asked at Maggie's elbow. "The one with the baby?"

Maggie turned, bracing herself for the inevitable congratulations. "Yes, ma'am."

The lady was tiny, a sparrow in peacock's raiment. White lamé-looking sweat suit and orange baseball cap with NASHVILLE in sequins. Green-sequined tennis shoes. An Irish flag by Andy Warhol.

Maggie really dreaded this one.

The lady just smiled and patted her arm. "I'm sorry," she said. "I know you tried your damnedest." Then, with a little smile and a shake of her head, she looked over at the man Carmen was crooning to. "He ain't much," she said, "but he's mine."

And then she walked back to the room that was supposed to be Mr. Petra's.

"Crazy fuck."

Maggie's heart damn near halted in place. It said something about how distracted she was that she hadn't even smelled Tommy on the wind.

"Mr. Petra's nice," Maggie said.

"He's nuts."

"That's the technical term, Tommy, yes."

Tommy gave an impatient huff. "Waste of fucking protoplasm." And then he stalked on down the hall, never once acknowledging the little man who watched him pass.

But Maggie watched Tommy. And Maggie realized that she'd made her decision. She was going to find out who killed those people. And she knew why.

Because of Tommy.

Because if she just walked away from what was wrong, she'd become what he wanted her to be. She'd finally, after fighting him for twenty-six years, agree with him. Tommy didn't believe in justice. Tommy believed in being right. In being in control. It was more important than being kind or empathetic.

Hell, Tommy didn't know what the word *empathetic* meant.

But Maggie did. Maggie had nurtured it in herself like a withered seedling in Tommy's wasteland for too many years, and she damn well wasn't going to let it die of starvation now.

Maggie did believe in justice. She believed in the possibility of redemption, no matter what she faced on a daily basis. And she believed that she'd condemn herself to hell if she succumbed to the seduction of revenge.

Maybe Jimmy Krebs deserved to die. She'd sure thought so the minute she'd shut the door on that ambulance. But it wasn't her right to ask for it. Or anybody else's to give it to her. Because if she'd meant to ask for Jimmy to die, she might just ask next for Tommy or Carmen or even some idiot who just pissed her off for no apparent reason. And she didn't know if somebody wouldn't just answer her request.

So she'd begin this investigation because of Tommy. And then she'd continue it for Montana Bob.

The other five men who had died had been malevolent. Dregs of the gene pool, without a doubt. Sometimes, in the empty, silent moments of night when everything weighed a little too heavily, being human, she could understand the wish for their deaths. But Bob had been harmless. Bob had simply been inconvenient. And inconvenience was no reason for murder.

Which meant that no matter what was going on, or who was doing it, Maggie had to stop it.

She didn't know, honestly, how long it had been going on already. She just knew that she couldn't let it go on any longer.

Damn it.

Sighing once more, Maggie plastered on her work face and headed on up the hall. She had no choice. She had to find out who was murdering people and stop him. The problem was, she knew for sure that what she was doing was the right thing to do. She still wasn't sure it was the best thing to do.

Not two miles away at the *Post-Dispatch* city room on Tucker Boulevard, Susan Jacobsmeyer was also thinking of lists. Not just the one she'd heard about at Blymore Medical Center—the one she'd actually seen on the dingy nurses' lounge wall. She was thinking of the list she'd compiled of things Maggie O'Brien had not told her. Facts and figures that skewed the nurse's unemotional rendition of her life just enough to make an intelligent person question it.

Susan was thinking of the fact that Maggie, who had told her about that list dedicated to revenge, had, before witnesses, expressed a desire to kill the father of that little boy. The father who was now dead. Who had died unexpectedly at Maggie O'Brien's hospital.

Maggie, whose father had been kicked off the police force for allegedly trying to kick somebody's face in. Who had come from a family of five stepmothers, each appreciably younger and drunker then the one before. Who attacked her career like a mission and considered men with MP5s her heroes.

Susan sat there at her cubbyhole workstation with her

research material spread and stacked before her. The background information on Maggie O'Brien before her, and the copy of the coroner's report on Jimmy Krebs in her hand, Susan considered the puff piece she'd written on Maggie O'Brien. Then she thought about the article she wanted to write instead.

Settling Maggie's head against his shoulder, Sean nuzzled her cheek with his own. "All better now?"

Maggie knew that Sean couldn't give her stability. He couldn't give her security or peace. Most days she wasn't even sure he could give her the benefit of a fully working brain. But what Sean could give her was brief, bright bursts of joy. It was his gift, a whimsy that touched everybody around him. An odd talent for a tough cop, but one that had saved his very cute ass on more than one occasion, not all of them in the field. In fact, one memorable time had been right here in Maggie's loft.

But that wasn't what Maggie was thinking of as she savored her latest taste of delight, her sweaty head nestled against Sean's even sweatier shoulder, her arm thrown across his chest.

God, but he could make her scream like an air raid siren. He even made her grin like a kid, which she'd been able to do only around him since she'd been a very small girl.

She was grinning now. And curling her toes, which still tingled, quite nicely.

"You could take that act on the road," she admitted to his chest hair.

"I have," he assured her, then laughed when she swatted him. "And what's your count up to so far tonight, my girl?"

"Six." She sighed lustily and wiggled her toes again. "I'm beginning to feel like a home run derby."

"It has everything to do with clever hands and a bat that can swing for the fences. And a generous heart. After all, my count is only two."

She was giggling now. "I guess I just have more drive."

"That's what I love about you," he said, creating brand-new delights with his hand. "Your single-mindedness."

"If you love that so much about me, maybe you could help me with a problem."

"Your single-mindedness," he retorted a little sharply, as if he knew where this conversation was going. "Not your obsessiveness."

Maggie lifted her head off his chest and glared eyeball-to-eyeball. "Much as I hate to dispel the myth, Delaney, woman does not live by orgasm alone."

His grin was pure Delaney. "Wouldn't you like to try?"

"God, no. There'd be no time for pasta." She waited for the inevitable pulled face, then patted him like a toddler. "Now, come on, even you'll need a little time to . . . uh, suit up again. I need to talk to you."

"No you don't." He proved it by taking her breath away with another of those patented kisses of his. "Take some time off, for God's sake, girl. That's what I'm doing. Taking time off. No work. No bad guys. No bosses or suits or rules . . . well, except the ones involving physics and thermodynamics." Another kiss, and the proof that Sean didn't need as much warm-up time as most batters.

Which was another reason Maggie kept their relationship to duplicate keys and a few camping trips. She needed to share what she did. Sean needed to ignore it. Not that he didn't enjoy what he did, immensely. But when he got home, he shut the streets outside. And most days, that was that.

Maggie had waited all day to talk to Sean about her suspicions. To ask him the first tough questions. She didn't want to ask anybody at the force how to proceed, for the simple reason that it would take one loose word at the Toe Tag for her suspect to find out. And Sean, for all his madness, had a fine sense of duty and an ironclad oath of confidentiality.

But Sean didn't want to deal with duty when he had her naked and ready to play. And more fool she, Maggie kept losing her clothes around him.

"You really don't want to know that I think Montana Bob was right?" she asked in a very breathy voice as Sean nibbled at the base of her throat.

"No, I don't. I want to know what you intend to do with that chocolate sauce in the microwave."

"You won't find out 'til you talk to me. I think Bob was murdered, Sean. I think Jimmy Krebs was, too."

Sean sighed like a six-year-old being denied McDonald's. "I think you'd much rather have a chocolate-covered Delaneysickle."

"Sean . . ."

He was using his mouth to distract her. This time, it worked.

The next morning Maggie woke up in her bed alone, achy, and depressed, because she still couldn't figure out how to proceed, and once again, Sean hadn't helped.

Well, except to really take her mind off her problems by upping her personal home run count nicely into double digits.

The problem was, she needed some advice. Badly. She might be a good nurse and exemplary paramedic. She might even have absorbed quite a bit of cop lore over her years at Big Zen's proverbial knee. But Maggie wasn't at all sure how to go about an investigation—a *quiet* investigation—on her own. And there wasn't anyone at the hospital or the police department she could go to, who could help her. Everyone at work was a suspect, and every one of her cop friends would distrust her curiosity even more than her gut instinct, and immediately alert her friends in the ED.

Maggie had three choices. Sean, who couldn't get unwrapped from his hormones long enough to engage his brain. And Big Zen, who had decided this was the perfect time to visit her grandbabies in Georgia.

And one more

One more.

If she was very lucky, and very, *very* careful.

Maggie sighed and got dressed. The day before her had just gotten a lot longer.

An hour later Maggie stopped before one of Dogtown's ubiquitous chain-link gates. She didn't want to be here. The last place on earth Maggie ever wanted to be was the house she'd walked out of at seventeen.

Not that she'd been very successful at staying away. Not with Tommy as a father. But still, it took a hell of a lot to bring her back to the house on Tamm.

Dogtown. Not that far geographically from where Jimmy Krebs had barbecued his four-year-old. Differentiated in the city by the immigrant populations who had lived there, the Italians on The Hill, the Irish in Dogtown. No surprise that an Irish cop would be found there.

The neighborhoods weren't that different, but the two houses were. Where Jimmy Krebs's house was just this side of derelict, Tommy O'Brien's house could have doubled for a military barracks. Surgically neat, the two-story building was all precision and military-style order. There were no dandelions in Tommy's grass, no mud within his chain-link perimeter. Not so much as a paint chip on his white-sided, American-flag-highlighted house.

For just a second, Maggie viewed it just as she had Jimmy Krebs's house that day. Jimmy's house might have been sullen, but Tommy's was closed off. Shut up and battened down, like the lid of Pandora's box.

The inside was even worse, although Maggie knew that Tommy's latest wife, Cheri the Cheerleader or Bimbo number six, had at least tried to soften the martial decor with stuffed animals. The wife before her, Betty the Barfly, had tried it with the live variety. That had lasted until a four-month-old Ming had gone airborne over the back alley. Ming now spent her time hiding in Maggie's loft.

Maggie paused a moment, her hand on the front gate, to take a fortifying breath. God, she hated having to rely on

Tommy. But Sean hadn't helped, and Big Zen wasn't in town.

So she'd have to sound out Tommy.

Not that Tommy would care that Jimmy Krebs was dead. Heck, he probably wouldn't even care that Montana Bob was dead. But Tommy cared about his force. His men. It was why he was so famous, and so retired. He cared about loyalty. And if Maggie could put this problem in the lap of loyalty, she might just have a chance at Tommy's help.

If she was very lucky, Maggie would be able to whip up a little outrage in him that somebody in the ED was putting everybody in the area—including his beloved force—in jeopardy by acting alone. And in such a cowardly manner.

If the murders had been cop-related, Maggie might have been afraid of Tommy's involvement. Tommy, after all, believed in justice. At just about any price.

But cop justice. Justice served up with boots and nightsticks and maybe a little planted evidence so that a known perp would be a sure con.

But this was hospital justice. Justice served with drugs and sleight of hand and a vast knowledge of physiology. None of which Tommy had. None of which Tommy wanted.

Tommy was a cop. Tommy took pride in acting like a cop. If a cop had murdered these people, Maggie would have seen cop fingerprints all over them. She saw no fingerprints at all. Which meant, in a hospital, that the perpetrator had to be somebody familiar with hospitals.

So, one of two things would happen when she presented her suspicions to her father. He would either offer the sharp investigative intelligence he was famed for, or he'd let her know that he knew exactly what was going on and wouldn't help her. Because Tommy still kept those big Irish ears of his flat to the St. Louis ground.

But whether he helped or simply stayed silent, Tommy wouldn't interfere with her. List members were dying. Police had access to The List. At best they could be considered complicit. At worst . . .

Well, Tommy wasn't going to stand by and let the worst happen to his force.

Maggie kept telling herself that.

The day was another hot one, exacerbating the never-dying prickly heat and threatening Maggie's temper. The cicadas seemed to have all jammed themselves into Tommy's two maples, throbbing and whining at their psychosis-inducing pitch, and Maggie was sweating. And she hadn't even said what she'd come to say yet.

But Tommy O'Brien's kid had never learned how to avoid unpleasantness, so she walked on up the surgically edged sidewalk and climbed the concrete steps to the scrubbed front porch. She was just about to knock on the front door when she heard Tommy's voice.

"You either do it or I will."

Maggie stopped dead, her hand raised to the door. Oh, hell, she thought. I'm not going to get my help after all.

She dropped her hand. For a second she just stood there, getting herself oriented. Listening. Waiting. Dragging in a couple of calming breaths so she could face the scene inside the house.

Another growl, soft, menacing. "What the fuck you waitin' for, you stupid bitch?"

Before she could change her mind, Maggie pulled open the front door and walked in.

The house was shadowy, all the blinds closed against the heat. The refrigerator hummed in the background. Not a cushion or bowling trophy lay so much as a millimeter out of place. The day's newspapers were folded like napkins on Tommy's battered old Naugahyde recliner, and on the far wall Tommy's service photo hung so it reflected from three different mirrors. Maggie smelled Pine-Sol and cigarettes like incense and beeswax in a church and knew she was home.

She instinctively turned to the left, where an archway led to the dining nook. She knew it would be occupied, and she knew what the occupants would be doing.

Neither person acknowledged her. Maggie didn't expect

them to. Tommy sat at an oak, early-American dining set Maggie's mother had originally tried to soften the house with. Susie the Slut hadn't lasted long past the corresponding bill from JCPenney.

Across from Tommy sat Cheri, nineteen, rail thin, cheaply blond, and ponytailed like an old carhop. Tommy loomed over her like retribution. Cheri kept her head bent and her attention fixed on the table in front of her, her skinny frame trembling like a tree in high wind.

A gun lay on the table in front of her. Shiny and black and deadly, it sat in her shadow like sin. A Beretta nine millimeter, the duplicate of Tommy's service revolver.

Cheri's hands were clenched in her lap, and her shoulders were hunched in a protective posture, as if Tommy were beating her.

Tommy hadn't touched her. Maggie knew. He didn't have to.

Because Tommy had a gun, too. Only Tommy's gun was in his hand, and it was pointed squarely at Cheri's chest.

CHAPTER 7

It was his backup gun, a chrome-plated Smith & Wesson .357 that Tommy buffed like a cherished phallus. He only brought it out for special occasions.

Like this one.

"You shoot me, or by God I'll just shoot you, you worthless whore," he snarled, the expression on his face one only the nastiest perps had ever seen. Those and Tommy's six wives. The collective Bimbos. And, after this little trick, probably wife number seven, whom Maggie was sure he had waiting in the wings for the outcome of this little scene.

It didn't occur to Cheri, of course, that this was Tommy's version of passive-aggression. Tommy hated calling the lawyer. So he called his wife's hand. To the end-game. To the place where he proved to them in the most horrific way that they didn't even have the courage left to save their own lives.

That he was, irrevocably, in charge. In control. In power.

After that, he could leave.

"You can't do it, can you? You can't even pull the trigger. You can't even save your own worthless life."

It was his personal mantra. He'd chanted it with every wife, and he'd done it with Maggie the day she threatened to walk out of his house. The day she *had* walked out of his house.

Which was why, she was sure, she was the only woman in his life he couldn't let go.

"Aw, Tommy," she mourned, seeing the pathetic cast of Cheri's features and slipping her own hands carefully into her own jeans pockets to show lack of aggression. "Couldn't you at least fight up to weight?"

"You get out of here," he threatened her without lifting his glare from his wife. "I'm busy teaching this cunt a lesson."

Maggie had warned Cheri. She'd warned them all, at one time or another. But when Tommy courted, he was enchanting. And by the time the relationship reached this stage, he'd so sapped any personality or self-respect from his wives, they felt they deserved whatever they got.

Even this. Even his harsh, hypnotic voice shredding the very last vestiges of self-worth they clung to.

Maggie kept her voice carefully even as she stood in the arched doorway and played out the rest of the script. "You know I can't leave, Tommy."

Tommy didn't move, a cat focused on a tasty mouse. A power player toying with a particularly contemptible victim. Cheri, still unable to get her eyes up from her lap, sobbed once, then quit.

"This is between her and me."

"It's between you, her, and the St. Louis police when I call them," Maggie retorted in her same careful voice.

Tommy's laugh was deliberately brutal. "That never makes a difference, and you know it. Go right ahead. Nothin's gonna save this bitch now. Certainly not you."

"The laws have changed since last time, Tommy," Maggie said in neutral tones. "And the uniforms aren't all your old buddies who can code the complaint out. Think about it, please."

"Bullshit. You don't think you'd actually stop me, do you?"

"No, Tommy, I think you'll stop you. Just like you always do."

But it *had* been Maggie who'd stopped him. Who'd gotten hold of the gun a couple of times, and called the police when she could, and once shot out the porch light to distract him long enough to get Sally the Stripper out of the house.

Maggie had stopped him every time, which she thought, maybe, he wanted her to. But she wasn't so sure that one of these times he wasn't going to take this little power game of his one step too far.

Not that he'd shoot on purpose. That would put too quick an end to Tommy's game. No, Maggie was afraid that one of the wives would finally have enough backbone left to give as good as she got. Or that one of them would actually talk back and surprise him into pulling the trigger.

Maggie had thought of making him promise never to do this again, but it was a promise Tommy would never make. Tommy never made promises he knew he'd break.

"Cheri?" Maggie said.

There was a pause. "Uh-huh?"

"Honey, I'm going to come up and put my hand on your arm. I want you to get up and go with me."

Another pause. Tommy watching, his gun unwavering.

"I got noplace"—sob—"to go."

"Oh, we'll find someplace, honey." Probably with one of the other Bimbos. By now they had quite the support group going. "Tommy, this will all be over a lot sooner if you can just let Cheri walk. You know that. Then you can get on with business."

Business undoubtedly being wife number seven. Who would she be? Maggie wondered. Ellen the Eighth-Grader?

"What if I don't want it to be over? What if I want to see if this mouse is actually going to have the guts *once* in her fucking life to stand up for herself?"

"How long you been sitting here so far, Tommy?"

"Hour. Maybe more."

Maggie nodded, not moving, making sure that her posture was completely passive. Her voice, when it came, never lifted beyond the almost hypnotic quiet she used with crazies and hostage takers. The tone of voice she'd perfected by the time she was twelve.

"Then I think you win, okay? It's about time for a beer. The Cards game is on, and I need to ask your advice on something."

She almost got his undivided attention. "You haven't asked my advice in your life."

"You think I just came over here on the off chance you had a pistol aimed at Cheri?"

"Yeah. Yeah, damn it, I do."

Actually, she should have thought to do just that. She'd seen Tommy around Cheri lately at the Toe Tag and known that they were at the end of their joint tether.

"Sean wants to marry me," she said to distract him.

"Still?"

"Yeah. He won't let up."

Still Cheri didn't move. She didn't breathe. Smart victim.

"You want me to tell you what I think?" Tommy barked.

"After I get Cheri someplace beyond pistol range. I don't want her blowing out your brains before I can tap into them. Nobody has an ear for what's going on in the force like you, and I want an idea of what the hell's up with Sean. He's bouncing around like a bad check."

The time was not right to talk about Montana Bob when Maggie could smell Tommy's animosity like thick soup in the small room. So she threw Sean at him.

Well, at least if nothing else, Tommy had single-handedly cemented her resolve to act with honor about the murders.

Tommy held his pose for long moments. Cheri and Maggie held theirs.

Then, with a lurch, he slammed to his feet. "Oh, what the hell," he snarled, scooping up the other gun and heading for his room. "Waste of time anyway, worthless cunt like her."

Cheri curled tighter. Maggie wondered if all the women in the world knew that instinctive posture. While Tommy was lovingly securing his weapons, Maggie hustled Cheri out the front door and into her car. One call got temporary lodgings at Wanda the Whore's apartment on Flad. An hour with Tommy while he alternately vilified Sean and the Cardinals, was enough to save Cheri's precious stuffed animals and gain Maggie answers she didn't want.

Tommy never even noticed that her hands were shaking.

Two hours later Maggie's hands were still shaking. She'd made the domestic abuse complaint, just as she'd promised. The uniform who had answered had been one of Tommy's cronies. First complaint for this wife. No charges filed.

Son of a bitch.

Both of them. Sons of bitches.

No, three sons of bitches. Tommy had also been more than happy to fill Maggie in on the various and sundry complaints against Sean that had sent him bouncing around districts like a bad minor league pitcher. Sean, who had so recently tried to prove to Maggie that he was stable and dependable, suddenly couldn't seem to pass a week without arguing with a superior, cutting one too many unacceptable corners, or just blowing off procedure entirely. And that evidently didn't even take into account his party behavior.

Maggie reached her loft and found herself unable to stay put. Unable to think past the smell of that rigid, airless house on Tamm and the frustration of broken promises. Pacing every clear inch of her hardwood floor, she fought her way past the last three hours.

Fine. She couldn't do anything about Tommy or Sean. There were plenty of other things she could do something about. Plenty of things to do. She'd just damn well do them.

She had to come up with some kind of idea on how to accomplish this friggin' investigation on her own, since it looked like that was how it was going to happen.

She had to calm down and think rationally enough to do it.

She had to have pasta.

That brought her skidding to a halt in the middle of her living room. What a great idea. Massive doses of carbohydrates always made her think better. Food and being on her feet. All she had to do was think about what it would take to find Bob's murderer while she collected supplies for pasta.

If there was, indeed, a murderer.

Please don't let there be a murderer. Let it be a massive misunderstanding.

Spaghetti alla puttanesca. Maybe Tuscan spring vegetable sauce. Some minestrone, a little Caesar salad. A lot of work and patience, fresh ingredients and mountains of helpless vegetables to chop in an orgy of transference. Of course, Maggie would probably just be sitting down to eat when she got a call for the team.

What the hell. She'd just serve it up in the back of the command trailer. She'd sure done it before.

So Maggie did what she always did when she had to outdistance Tommy. She moved. Exchanging jeans and sandals for T-shirt, shorts, and tennis shoes, Maggie took up her shopping list and headed for the Farmers Market.

The Soulard district, a ten-square-block area of brick row houses and converted warehouses on the river just south of downtown, had grown up around the Farmers Market in the 1800s. The market itself, the second oldest extant farmers' market in the U.S., had opened in 1779, and still drew people from all over the bistate area, especially on weekends, to sample fresh produce within its open brick walls.

Maggie loved the neighborhood, where Mardi Gras and Bastille Day were celebrated with all the fervor of St. Patrick's Day, where jazz and blues fluttered through the air at night and the myriad aromas of fresh flowers and cooking food mingled with the thick brew of hops that hovered along the streets that ran close to the Anheuser-Busch Brewery on Pestalozzi.

It was a great place for a single woman to live. Good neighbors fought to cement a marginal neighborhood while protecting the historical value of an area that had housed first French, then German immigrants, and finally urban survivalists in its tidy, red-brick row houses. Maggie cherished the postage-stamp-sized gardens and neighborhood taverns that collected for the IRA on one corner and Farm Aid on another.

Today, she couldn't be bothered to spare it all any more than a glance. She spent the seven blocks to the market trying to walk past her morning, and the time shuffling through the market trying to figure out how she should move forward.

Maggie stopped first at Mr. Capelli's stall. Mr. Capelli had been selling fruit and vegetables since Christ served fish, and his son was a detective in sex crimes. Mr. Capelli, gnarled and smiling, patted Maggie's hand and snuck her free damson plums.

"Tomatoes, Mr. C," she said, thinking that the cicadas outside the open-air brick building sounded particularly alien this morning as she sank her teeth into the soft fruit. "Lots and lots of tomatoes. An artichoke, a few zucchini, some celery, carrots . . . oh, and garlic."

Lots and *lots* of garlic.

"Ya got vampires?" Mr. Capelli demanded with a raspy cough when he saw how many.

"Big ones," Maggie assured him.

A plan. She needed a plan. She needed to figure out how those people died, why they died, and who killed them.

"You got stress," Mr. Capelli announced with a nod of his furry gray head as he loaded the tomatoes she picked into a paper bag. "What kind?"

"Tuscan spring vegetable sauce kind."

He whistled. "That bad. It don't got no garlic, that sauce."

"It does today."

He just nodded and packed.

Okay, Maggie thought as she added potatoes and chard to the cache. You don't need Tommy. You don't even need Sean, the horny bastard. You can come up with a plan all on your own. Think of it as a medical problem. Pretend it's an epidemic instead of a rash of murders.

Parsley. She needed parsley.

She needed charts. First from Jimmy Krebs and Montana Bob, and then the four guys on Bob's list: OG Big Dawg Dwayne Carver, Urban McGinley, Sancho Martinez, and Snake Pilson. She needed to double- and triple-check all those lab values, search through medical double-talk and acronym hash to find the action that didn't fit. The glitch in the time line that shouldn't be there. The pattern that couldn't be explained away.

She needed to see if she could get a whiff of just how those people were dying.

"String beans, Mr. Capelli. I need string beans for the minestrone."

And names. Maggie needed names off The List in the nurses' lounge. Names of people who might be dead just because they'd made a staff member unhappy. She needed to see if she could find out just how many might have died, and maybe get an idea why. She needed to know how long this had been going on.

She needed access to the newspaper morgue to get more background on possible victims than just what she found on the charts and the wall.

She needed a common denominator. A name that might show up frequently enough on the charts that she might be able to track the killer by his or her footprints.

She needed a goddamn miracle so that nobody would notice what she was doing.

By the time she'd made it back out into the afternoon sun with an armload of vegetable sacrifices, Maggie was no calmer. She was clearer. She thought.

So she walked off the rest of her doubt on her way back home.

She went over the plan in her head to look for loopholes. To look for a way out. She marked off the seven blocks to her loft like a soldier on a quick march, so absorbed by her problem she didn't notice the clusters of people who scattered before her bent-headed determination. It took her four blocks to realize she was being followed.

She ran over her plan one last time and couldn't fault it. Charts, names and names. She thought. She hoped.

She sighed. She still had to have somebody help her put it together. She had to talk to somebody, and she was going to have to do it soon. Maybe Big Zen would come home in time.

It was right about that point, when she ran out of half-decent ideas about what to do, that Maggie finally heard the footsteps.

Quick, skittering feet. Familiar, as if they'd been behind her for a while.

One of her neighbors grinned suddenly as he headed her way, then shook his head.

Maggie knew that look. She never so much as bothered to stop.

"Oh, no you don't," she all but snarled without turning around. "I have done my good deed for the week. Go away."

Her warning startled a family of four into scurrying around the far side of the minivan they were trying to unlock. The footsteps behind her never hesitated.

"You are *so* not following me," Maggie insisted, hefting the bag in her arms, as if it could better communicate her priorities. "I have had *enough*. So go. Find somebody else to torment."

A gay couple crossed the street rather than face her down on the narrow sidewalk. Maggie didn't really blame them. She would have run from her, too.

Without warning, she swung on her heels.

Maggie took one look at what had been on her heels and burst out laughing. She was being followed by a dog. Well, at least she took it on faith that it was a dog. It looked more like what happened when a weasel had carnal knowledge of a bullfrog. Perched on its haunches, it was starving, fly-laden, mangy and bright-eyed, as if it were there at her personal request.

Maggie shook her head. "I must have a sign on my ass."

Her follower just thumped his too-large tail on the sidewalk.

Maggie couldn't manage more than a sad shake of her head. "Oh, why the hell not? It seems to be that kind of day." And turning back onto her original course, she headed for her building. Just as she'd suspected, the dog followed right along.

Ming was not going to be happy. Oh well, Ming had survived before. And Maggie could do with something else to keep her from violence.

"Oh, not again," Allen mourned when he saw her pin the notice on the bulletin board the next day.

Maggie shrugged. "You play sports. I find puppies."

"You act as clearinghouse for every misbegotten non-humanoid orphan in the city. What is it this time?"

She managed a smile. "Either the runt of ET's litter or a nuclear experiment gone horribly wrong. I'm not perfectly sure."

Allen pulled a face. "And you expect some sucker to take it off your hands."

"I've placed all the others."

This time it was Carmen who chose to comment. "A dog?" she asked, looking up from where she was printing a new name at the end of The List. "Well, at least it isn't a rat this time."

"A vole," Maggie corrected, trying hard not to notice what Carmen was doing. "It was a vole."

Maggie allowed fleeting regret for her lovely day yesterday. After cleaning her loft, she'd amassed a staggering pile of decimated vegetables. She'd chopped, she'd diced, she'd pureed. She'd decontaminated the dog, then shared her pasta with him and Ming, who particularly loved minestrone. She'd written her list of things she needed to do for this investigation as if that would keep her in perfect control, then gone to sleep to the heady aroma of fresh garlic, tomatoes, and oregano filling her room along with the angst and drama of *Tosca*.

But now she was back to reality. The names she'd included on her own list last night were her friends, and Maggie didn't want any of them to be there. But she couldn't help wanting to ask Carmen about the addition she'd just made on the nurses' lounge wall. About any other names Carmen might have scrawled.

Any names that might also be on Montana Bob's list.

Maggie had managed to get hold of the charts from both Montana Bob and Jimmy Krebs. Before stashing them in her bag for later perusal, she'd done a quick scan to see if she could find a familiar name.

She had, of course. She'd seen Carmen's name on both. Carmen, who was at least as outspoken as Allen about who went on The List. Carmen, who was impatient, intolerant, and temperamental. Carmen, who had, in fact, created the ED's infamous party favorite, the Drain the Gene Pool board game.

Of course, Maggie's name had shown up on those charts, too, so maybe it didn't mean anything.

Maggie was also the all-hospital Drain the Gene Pool champ. She had the feeling she was about to abdicate her throne.

"And you insist that this . . . mammal . . . followed you home," Carmen said.

Another shrug. A pat at the very imaginative description of the animal that was undoubtedly cowering beneath her couch to keep out of Ming's orbit. Ming, Maggie had discovered, seemed to have very definite ideas about just what constituted a life-form worthy of her association.

"They all follow me home. I think there's an abandoned animal Web site out there with my address on it."

"Yeah," Carmen snorted unkindly. "Www.sucker.com."

"*You* took one," Maggie reminded her.

"Yeah, well, I log on frequently."

Carmen had taken a three-legged Chihuahua with a nervous tic. But then, Allen had adopted the obscene, bent-winged parrot that had somehow managed to land on Maggie's third-story window.

"Well, my darling," Allen offered with a pat to Maggie's head. "Considering the other creatures who could follow you home, dogs are probably the least problematic."

Maggie laughed. "At least they don't leave the toilet seat up."

"Oh," Jeannie greeted them all when she saw the note. "Another animal. Maybe this time I could—"

"No!" the other three retorted.

Jeannie raised an eyebrow. "You don't think I'm good enough to adopt one of Maggie's pets?"

"I think you've adopted too many," Maggie told her.

Every time Jeannie's husband abandoned her for the gambling boats, she adopted another child substitute. Her house was beginning to smell like the St. Louis Zoo.

"Fine," she said with a hurt little nod. "Just fine."

Maggie didn't know what to say, except that Jeannie's name hadn't been on either chart. But that wasn't something she could share. It probably wouldn't make Jeannie feel better, either.

"Maggie," Allen said, "are you joining the singles for group therapy tonight?"

Group therapy being the after-shift congregating of ED personnel. The singles crowd hit the Toe Tag. The married ones usually ended up at Denny's breakfast bar. It was usually a toss-up which Allen and Maggie hit.

This time she just shook her head. "Not tonight," she said. "I'm in the middle of painting the loft."

She was in the middle of hospital charts.

She started them that night. She continued them in her spare time for three days. She read them over popcorn in the loft and Frappacino at Starbucks. She read them under hushed fluorescence at the library and natural sunlight at the Botanical Gardens. She went through those two charts as if they held the true secret to permanent weight loss.

She found nothing.

Bob had died just the way they'd said, suddenly and inexplicably. He'd had a load of cocaine aboard and no Haldol, which Maggie still questioned. But no time discrepancies, no IV drugs pushed right before his arrest. Nothing suspicious at all, except for the fact that he'd died of a superficial wound to the upper arm.

Jimmy Krebs had been under police watch and suicide watch, and had been dosed with nothing more than a little Demerol and potassium in his Ringer's lactate, like all good surgery patients. Nobody had been in his room for at least twenty minutes before he'd suddenly arrested. Carmen had treated him in the ED, but that shouldn't have made a difference, since he'd been up on the prison ward a good ten hours before dying.

Anybody really interested in killing a patient wouldn't have had to wait that long to do it. Nor would they have had to work too hard. With all the quick-acting drugs available, it would be foolish to administer something that would take so long to work that the symptoms could not only be treated, but the cause discovered.

No, the way to go was insulin. Digitalis. Pavulon. Fast. Silent. Efficient. Easy to obtain. Tough as hell to prove.

Given within minutes—if not seconds—of the anticipated death. Nothing that would take ten hours.

Which left Carmen off the program. And so far Maggie couldn't find another name common to both charts who might have had the opportunity.

Except hers, of course. And she knew damn well where she'd been when Jimmy Krebs had died.

Even so, Maggie carefully listed all the names of the caregivers in both charts. It made her feel as if, working hard enough, she might discover a pattern.

It made her feel as if she might be getting somewhere. At least it did until two days later when she hit her first roadblock.

It was at the end of her shift, and she was waiting for Snake Pilson's chart to come up in the tube system. Her shoes off, as if all she had in mind was a good post-shift rest in the nurses' lounge, Maggie passed her wait surreptitiously copying the next batch of names off the wall.

She'd just jotted her thirtieth name down on the inside cover of a romance paperback when Allen swept in the doorway. Close on his heels stalked Shara the supervisor and two of the more surly hospital maintenance guys.

"What, no pumpkin to take you away to the real fun?" Allen demanded.

Easing her book closed, as if she didn't feel like an exposed spy, Maggie managed a smile. She glanced at the assembled crowd and noticed that Shara had on her company face, which meant that somebody was in trouble.

"You clocked out, didn't you?" the woman demanded, ignoring Allen's soaring eyebrows. Shara was born for middle management. Medium size, medium build, medium coloring, medium weight. Most days, she blended right into the institutional walls.

"I'm trying to get up enough energy to drive home," Maggie assured her.

Shara huffed, as if Maggie were a delinquent fourth-grader. "Well, wait somewhere else. The painters have to get in."

Maggie's stomach clenched. "Painters?"

"We are *so* busted," Allen sighed, hands fluttering like dying moths. "Your little newsgirl has *Seen. The. List.*"

But Maggie hadn't been able to copy down more than a fifth of the names.

"Well, if newsgirl's already seen it," she said almost on a whine as she tried her damnedest to memorize even a few more names. "It's a little late to wipe it off."

Mary Anne Gregory
Tomarris Wilson

"*Just* what I said," Allen agreed. "After all, it gives the places such a retro Ellis Island look. But the philistines rule."

Iceman Williams

Maggie sighed. "The good national press about SWAT-girl wasn't enough, huh?"

Morris Vaughan

"Not when SWATgirl keeps a list of people she'd like to filter from the gene pool, it didn't," Shara snapped.

Maggie held a hand to her chest. "You won't recognize *my* handwriting on that wall," she protested.

Martin Abromowitz

"That's because you write with the other hand," Allen admonished. "I've seen you."

"And I've seen you use lipstick."

"Coral," Allen admitted. "What could be a bigger insult?"

Peter Burgan

Well, at least that name was safe. Maggie knew Burgan was alive. He was the CEO of the hospital.

"Can we get this done?" one of the painters demanded with a telling scowl toward Allen. "I got a whole waitin' room on four needs trim."

"Come on," Shara demanded. "Out. Let the men work."

And that fast, Maggie's best chance of really finding out how bad the situation was, literally disappeared.

Maggie collected her gear as she watched the names vanish in large swaths of uninspired hospital green. She snuck out to the desk to snatch Snake Pilson's chart from the tube and trotted out to her beat-up little Volkswagen so she could finish jotting down the names she could still remember, all the while beset by growing panic.

There was very possibly a murderer working her hospital, and Maggie didn't think he planned to stop anytime soon. And she was not an inch closer to stopping him than the moment she'd first recognized those four names.

By the time she finished reading Snake's chart, Maggie felt even worse. Snake had managed to survive for ten days before becoming donor organs. He'd done it in the SICU, where the treatment was fast and furious, the staff plentiful, and the interventions massive. It took Maggie two more days to compile a list of caregivers' names that was only a little longer than the passenger list for the *Titanic*, a lot of questions about head injury care at the Biltmore, and no further clues on how Snake Pilson died except for the obvious. Snake had succumbed to a massive head injury.

Snake didn't, however, have Carmen's name anywhere on his chart.

Maggie was back to square one.

She was, that is, until Mr. Glaven came into the Emergency Department with a self-inflicted arrow wound to the head.

CHAPTER 8

Half the ED staff stood clustered around the patient in room ten like New Guinea natives sighting their first Coke bottle.

"He looks like Steve Martin in *Saturday Night Live*," Bob Thomas said.

Bob, the neurosurgical resident on call, was the one who had to figure out what to do. The patient, a forty-four-year-old bricklayer with sparse mud-colored hair, no upper lip, and less neck, lay in his smiley-face boxers and black socks with an arrow sticking out of his head from left to right like a Halloween prop.

Jeannie Mars bent herself into a geometric figure of amazing angles. "How'd he do it?"

"Is he right handed or left handed?" Maggie wanted to know. But then, Maggie was the clinical forensic nurse on that night. Details like that mattered to the clinical forensic nurse.

"He did it," the paramedic assured her. "Crossbow."

The whole room seemed to sigh and straighten. "Ah."

"Aren't the arrows smaller?" somebody asked.

"Only your arrows," somebody else answered.

"He left a note," the paramedic said.

"A note?" asked a voice from the doorway.

Maggie looked up to see at least two ICU nurses and a kitchen aide peering in. News like this always traveled fast.

"Yeah," the paramedic answered with another slow nod.

"Something about wild turkeys and the millennium."

The crowd further considered in silence. Several nodded, as if it all made sense.

"Maybe he meant Wild Turkey and the millennium," the chief of cardiology suggested.

The respiratory therapists shook his head. "Wild Turkey's for deer hunting and football. You want Korbel for the millennium."

"Dom Pérignon," somebody else offered.

"You want," came from across the room, "to celebrate on time. Didn't anybody tell him it's over?"

"Musta been too busy with the wildlife."

"Hunting it or drinking it?"

"Maybe he should have considered a good spa and a massage," Jeannie said, but that was just because that was what Jeannie wanted.

The crowd at the door got into a discussion on the comparative therapeutic values of spas versus Wild Turkey for stress until Bob Thomas brought the focus back where it belonged.

"Maybe we should consider how to get the damn thing out."

It took fourteen phone calls and a priest to come up with something. Unfortunately, Mr. Glaven had done an only almost good enough job of doing away with himself. He took out enough brain cells to cease being Mr. Glaven. He retained enough to be a biological function. So, they had to get him to ICU, and the only way to do that comfortably was to get the arrow out.

Maggie wrapped her arms around Bob Thomas, who braced his foot against the side of the bed, and they both tugged. A rubber tourniquet attached to the clipped end of the arrow was pulled through after to provide access for irrigation and antibiotics. An IV line and NG tube provided nutrients, and a variety of catheters, drainage. Mr. Glaven's uninjured medulla provided the stimulus for breathing and heartbeat, so Mr. Glaven went upstairs to the ICU to wait for further progress or a Do Not Resuscitate order.

It was Maggie's job to transport. Since word had gotten out about Mr. Glaven, all the ICU staff who hadn't made it downstairs, managed to be in his room to greet him. Report was brief, the jokes bad, and the crowd disappointed that all they had to look at anymore were two small holes and limp rubber. Maggie'd already heard the jokes, so she left them to it.

She'd just made it to the other end of the ICU when she heard the call for help from bed one.

"Hey, out there! Somebody get me some more Pavulon! Hey!"

The ICU was top-of-the-line. Brand-new everything from a government grant so that the metal gleamed and the equipment worked. Unfortunately, the architect in charge of rehabbing had evidently made his name designing racetracks. The majority of the staff was at the other end of a five-furlong hall ogling Mr. Glaven's parietal lobes, which left only Maggie close enough to hear the disaster brewing in bed one.

"Hey, c'mon!" the voice screeched.

Maggie didn't even think about it. Nothing was more important in a medical crisis than getting and maintaining a good airway. Few things were dicier than quickly placing the endotracheal tube that provided it. The task was tricky, the pathway dark, and if the patient at all conscious, the tube had to get past spasming vocal cords.

The longer it took, the more chance the patient would lose brain cells. So to bypass problems, the team paralyzed the patient.

Everybody in the units and ED knew where the paralytics were kept. Everybody knew how quickly they were needed. It never occurred to Maggie not to trot over to the drug cabinet, dig out a bottle of Pavulon, and run into the code. Nor did she think to turn down the request from the harried doc to draw up and push the drug herself.

"Thanks," the doc said without looking up from where he was reinserting the ET tube.

"I'll record it," one of the nurses said, marking the time on the patient's bedsheet.

Maggie was already back out the door before it dawned on her what she'd done.

She had given a potentially life-threatening drug to a patient, and not one person had so much as looked at her. No one had questioned her or checked her actions. Her name wouldn't show up on the chart. Which, in a hospital that was chronically short-staffed, happened all the time.

If it could be called a positive side to this, that meant Carmen had certainly had the chance to get to Snake Pilson without her name showing up anywhere. On the downside, anybody else could have done it just as easily.

Maggie stood before the elevators as the doors opened and closed, and she didn't move.

She could check every chart until her eyes crumbled, and she still might not find that common denominator she was looking for. Because if what Maggie had on her hands was a smart common denominator, he or she would find the chance to act in just the way Maggie had. Commit an act that went unrecorded and probably unremembered. A quick sneak into somebody's room after bringing up another patient that kept the crowds busy, and the perpetrator would remain unconnected with the crime.

Especially if the perpetrator hadn't officially seen the victim for ten hours before he died.

Which made Maggie realize that she'd have to work very hard just to get back to square one. She pushed the down button again and missed the doors again, and just stood there.

"You sure there isn't any other way?"

This time the cigarette smoke drifted into the late-afternoon air. Just two more fans at a pickup softball game in the park. "She isn't just suspicious anymore, is she?"

For a moment, the first person just stood there. Stared

into the sun where it set across the highway. "No. I'm sure she's probably looking."

A nod. A quick circle of smoke, dissipating into the thick summer air. "Then we have to make sure she knows she should stop."

"If that's what you think."

"It is."

Maggie worked the rest of her shift and then did her twenty-four at the fire station. When she got home again, she fed Ming and Wheezer, reheated her vegetable sauce, and sat down with pasta to pore once more over her notes.

She needed more charts, of course. She would try and get OG Big Dawg Dwayne Carver's next, so she could continue her search. She would begin to check out the new names she'd pulled off the wall. But until then, she tried like hell to see a pattern.

And didn't.

Maggie checked every name, every time, every treatment, every lab result she'd copied like the Dead Sea Scrolls, and couldn't find a surprise at anybody's end.

What she needed, Maggie realized, were postmortem reports. A hospital staff could make no more than an educated guess at the cause of a death. Only the medical examiner could know for certain, since she could dig places doctors couldn't while the patient was alive. Sudden death caused biological and chemical changes that might show up only after death. Lab values might reveal something more suspicious. Drug- or poison-related deaths might be caught.

But only if there was reason to suspect them.

The ME usually only ran two types of drug screens: the standard one for barbiturates, opiates, and stimulants, and the screen for any drugs the patient might have been prescribed. An over- or underdose of therapeutic medication, after all, could be just as much a cause of death as a bullet to the brain.

On a normal day, however, nobody would think to look

for the breakdown products from Pavulon or unprescribed digitoxin. Potassium levels rose precipitously postmortem. Any number of things could be injected, and nobody would notice.

Maggie was screwed, and she knew it. So far, she not only didn't know who was committing the crimes, she didn't know how they'd been committed.

She needed some new ideas.

It was probably the Jameson's that made her think that Sean should be one of them.

She'd gone to the Toe Tag to commiserate with herself over her continued failures as Nancy Drew. A couple of the team were there, and a few of the nurses from the Biltmore, which led to some bawdy singing and a darts tournament. Maggie won both, her award being Jameson shots from each of the other contestants. She was sitting alone at the bar keeping careful eye on her progress when Sean joined her.

"It would have been unsportsmanlike to refuse," she reasoned before he had a chance to comment.

He was looking particularly Sean-like tonight, clad in his black POLICE T-shirt and jeans, with his hair still wet from washing, and his best little-boy grin firmly in place. Unfortunately, he'd donned his best Maggie-seduction apparel a few days too late.

"I haven't seen you around much lately, Mags," he said, sliding onto the stool next to her as if that, in itself, were a sexual act.

Still grinning. Wanting Maggie to notice.

Maggie blinked like an owl and carefully lined up the four shot glasses before her. "Sorry, Delaney. The song's nice, but I'm not in the mood to dance."

Sean bravely maintained his air of superior sexual prowess. "I'll bring the chocolate."

She just shook her head and went back to considering the wonderful tawny depths of the whiskey that remained in her second-to-last glass.

"I seem to be drinking more than usual lately," she told it.

Sean answered instead. "I think it'll take a lot more than this for you to be confessing into the fire irons."

Maggie couldn't help but chuckle. It was one of the bonds that tied her to Sean. Most kids grew up playing baseball or house. She and Sean had played AA. Sean's dad had been just as big a boozer as Tommy. The difference was that Patrick Delaney hadn't been a violent drunk. He'd been a teary drunk. So when it was too dangerous for Maggie to be in her father's house, Patrick and Helen had always concocted some excuse for her to spend time with them.

Weekend entertainment consisted of the Sunday afternoon AA picnic. Sunday evening, while Patrick and Helen watched television in the family room, Sean and Maggie held their pretend meetings in the living room. One would play supportive audience ("Welcome, Sean"), and the other would stand by the front windows, a fire poker in hand as the microphone, and tell their story ("My name is Maggie, and I'm an alcoholic"). Funny how the movie *A Man Named Bill* still gave her a feeling of security.

"I haven't been much help lately," Sean said suddenly. "Have I?"

Maggie gave him a considered look. "Not really."

His shrug was deprecating and regretful. "Well, we can't have sex on the bar. Wanna talk instead?"

Maggie snorted. "Now there's a heartfelt offer if I've ever heard one."

Sean gave her that killer grin of his. "I'm just being honest here, Mags. You always say you value that."

"Maybe not as much as you think."

The rest of her third shot disappeared down a suddenly thirsty gullet.

"So what has you reaching for Sweet Baby James?" he asked.

He was doing it on purpose, Maggie thought. Digging up every private joke nobody else would understand. Sweet

Baby James had been Patrick's fond nickname for his whiskey. They'd always known he was aching for a toot when he began humming James Taylor.

"Frustration," she said, deliberately setting away old memories.

Sean didn't even have to order his tequila. The bartender just dropped down two shots in front of him like clockwork and left. Sean downed one as if he were heading off for dawn patrol and turned back to Maggie.

"We can still go to my place, if that's all you need."

"If it were, I would have been there five days ago. No, I need an adult, and there are precious few of those in my life."

Sean downed the other tequila and grimaced. "Ouch. I hear a lecture coming on."

"No point in that. I've given up wasting my time."

"What are you doing instead?"

"Trying to figure out who killed Jimmy Krebs."

Maggie wasn't stupid. She didn't say it until she knew she wouldn't be overheard. Sean only drank two tequilas a night, and he'd gotten them. The darts competition was back in swing, and the bartender was down at the end of the bar where everybody was arguing over the baseball game on TV. Nobody was listening to Maggie but Sean.

"Good God," he said, stunned. "You were serious the other night, weren't you?"

"I was, ex-detective Delaney. Somebody killed Jimmy Krebs, and I think they killed Montana Bob, and I don't think those are the only ones."

"Why?"

"Why do I think it? Because somebody called me after Jimmy died. Why are they doing it? Because they've decided that writing names on a list isn't enough anymore, I guess. I'll probably have a much better idea after I've had a chance to talk to them."

"Somebody called you and said they'd killed Jimmy Krebs?"

Maggie ran a finger around the rim of the shot glass, as

if it could create music. "No. They only told me that it was okay now. That the fucker was dead."

"The fucker you said you wanted dead out on the street." She looked up at him. "You know."

"Everybody knows, honey. That was a little out of character for Little Zen. You amazed some folks."

Maggie just shook her head and went back to making her glass squeak.

"So nobody really said they killed anybody," Sean prompted.

"Montana Bob thought people were being killed. He gave me four names. Those names were all on The List. They were all guys who are now dead."

"They were given to you by a guy who got his lunch from the trash Dumpster in back of the Toe Tag. You don't really mean to say you took him seriously."

Maggie considered her fourth shot, still full and golden, and sighed. "I did, Delaney. I do."

"And so you're. . . ."

Maggie shrugged. "Going over charts. Getting some names of other List members. Trying to figure out who might be so burned-out they'd think extra insulin is an answer to the city's problems."

For a long few moments silence reigned at their end of the bar. Maggie finally gave up considering her whiskey and sipped at it. Sean tapped the bar top like a Morse code key. The Cardinals scored two runs and went ahead of the Marlins, provoking a round of cheers from the other end of the bar.

Finally, Sean sighed, as if the task before him was a weighty one. Maggie sabotaged his effort.

"You don't believe me."

It took a second for Sean to answer. "I think *you* believe it."

Maggie's laugh was not pretty. "That's what I say to people who think Mars is transmitting invasion messages through their teeth."

"Bob was a paranoid schiz, Mags. Shit, he thought Michael Jordan was behind the Kennedy assassinations. Sometimes coincidences actually do happen, ya know."

Maggie stared him down, right into his baby blues. "And what if I just don't think this is one of those times, Sean?"

Sean looked sad. He looked penitent. He looked like he was going to tell her no. "I think that if that's the case, you're going to ruin every friendship you have chasing ghosts."

He was right. Maggie knew that better than anyone. It made the whiskey burn in her stomach, because she'd actually thought Sean would believe her. But like she'd known all along, cops trusted cops for crime instincts. Sean didn't feel in his gut what Maggie felt in hers, and even Sean wouldn't listen to her.

"I guess this means you won't score a few postmortem reports from the ME for me, huh?"

"And if I do and you don't find anything? What will you do then?"

Maggie shrugged. "Score a few more."

Sean just shook his head. "There are a lot of people on that list, Maggie."

"I know that, Sean."

"I think you're wrong."

"I know that, too."

"Can I ask you one thing? Who do you think's doing it?"

"Somebody with a grudge and access to lethal drugs." She shrugged, as if it didn't hurt. "Somebody at my hospital."

He looked at her for a long time. Maggie thought he was just about to say something, when the front door opened.

"Oh, hell," Maggie sighed, noticing. "What's she doing here?"

And with Paul the sniper.

Sean turned to see, too. Susan the reporter was walking in from the street two steps ahead of Paul and laughing with him as if he were a prom date. Maggie felt as if she'd been betrayed.

"Nice to see you," Sean greeted the woman.

Another traitor.

Susan caught sight of them and lit up like a cheerleader, which she'd probably been. "Hi, Maggie, how are you?"

Maggie managed a smile. "Just fine, thanks. I thought you'd graduated from cop detail."

Susan's shrug was deferential. "Oh, after all the noise we got from that great shot Mike took, the paper asked for a follow-up. More in-depth of the team, you know."

Maggie nodded and wondered if she could throw another round of darts, so she could get another shot. Hell, forget the whiskey. She just wanted the darts.

She did notice that Paul was blushing. On him, it wasn't pretty. Too bad The List was temporarily down.

"What do you think she's up to?" Sean asked in Maggie's ear as Paul settled Susan at one of the Formica tables.

Maggie turned back to him, perfectly aware that Paul was about to join them so he could order.

"Hey, Brian!" the sniper yelled down to where the bartender was focused on the game. "Longneck Bud and a . . . uh, cosmopolitan."

"We don't do that shit," the bartender groused without moving.

"Beer's fine," Susan assured them all from that cheap little Formica table as if she were at the Ritz. Hell, she was even wearing a dress, some little black number. The cops in the back of the room were climbing to their feet like a hunting pack who'd just spotted a very tasty fox. Susan passed around a bland smile.

Paul got the drinks without once looking at Maggie.

"You know you're going to pay for this," Maggie said.

"I'd never let a teammate down, Mags," he assured her, even though there was sweat on his nose.

"Hormones beat good sense every time, Paul."

Paul looked sincerely affronted. "Not when a team member's involved."

Maggie's anger wilted. "Yeah, I know. I'm sorry."

Paul actually sniffed. "Well, you should be. Besides,"

he said, a big shit-eating grin splitting his homely features, "she wants to know all about *me*."

Maggie chuckled. "Probably because I told her you were hung like a pony. You can pay me next week."

Paul kissed her cheek instead and headed back to his table.

"Would it bother you, Paul," Susan asked, a hand to his arm, "to talk a little more about your mother's murder?"

Delaney looked over his shoulder at them. "Was she?" he asked Maggie.

"Sure," she said. "It's why he became a cop. Didn't you know?"

His grin was dry. "No. But then, I'm not every city cop's kid sister."

Maggie snorted. "She doesn't look like anybody's kid sister, and I bet our Susan's going to find out all about it."

"Take a good look over there," Sean advised. "You make one wrong move, and that woman's going to spread your suspicions all over the *Post*. You want that?"

"You trying to talk me out of this, Delaney?"

"I'm trying to tell you to think about it. Hard. You take every death to heart, as if it was your personal failure. You've always done that. Don't turn it into something it isn't."

"But Jimmy Krebs died."

"And the ME is comfortable with the cause of death. You think Dr. Harrison is covering up suspicious deaths, Mags? Do you?"

Maggie hadn't considered that. She'd known the medical examiner since Dr. Harrison had taken the job. The woman might be arrogant as hell, but she was more honest than Ralph Nader. And much more intelligent. This wasn't like trying to sneak one by the sheriff on *Dukes of Hazzard*.

"But what did he die of?" she demanded. "Nobody seems to know."

"And you're just going to waltz in and ask?"

"Yeah," she said. "If I have to."

But maybe, Maggie thought, maybe she was wrong.

Maybe she was spinning her own paranoia out of thin air. Maybe Dr. Harrison would ease all her fears with one quick final diagnosis that made sense.

Just to be sure, though, she decided to go through the other charts on Bob's list. Big Dawg Dwayne Carver and Urban McGinley.

Maggie remembered Big Dawg the minute she opened his chart. Crazy, fighting, cursing Big Dawg. She'd been sore for a week after that code. She'd stayed two hours overtime trying to calm his hysterical mother. But she hadn't suspected anything wrong at the time, and she didn't find anything now that would change her mind.

Big Dawg had come in with a couple of big holes in his chest, and he'd died from all the fluids that had poured out. The only person surprised by Big Dawg's death had been his mama, but that was just because she had refused to believe that her little Dwayne was a big-time gangbanger.

No, the only flag Maggie could raise from Big Dawg's chart was the fact that, once again, Carmen had been on.

But maybe, she thought wearily, that only meant that Carmen liked to do trauma. Just like Maggie. Her own name was probably on as disproportionate a number of trauma charts as Carmen's. And Maggie sure as hell wasn't killing anybody.

But somebody was. She just couldn't find out who.

Still, she couldn't stop. So she went in search of Father McGinley.

And had no luck.

Not anywhere in Blymore Memorial.

Maggie spent almost two hours with the medical records staff, made calls to three other hospitals, and finally took a trip to the library to check out newspaper files before she finally found him.

And when she did, she discovered what could have put a stop to this fiasco at the start.

"Son of a bitch," she breathed to the annoyance of the

woman working the next computer station. "Son of a bitch."

Urban McGinley, the pedophile priest, who had served his penance at the hands of a victim's father, had served in a private Catholic boys' high school in West County. He had been arrested by the Creve Coeur police and released on bond. He'd been brought in a week later to St. Isidore's ED by ambulance and died of injuries suffered at the hands of one Peter Clark, the father of one of his victims.

What he had not been, ever, was a patient in Blymore Memorial Hospital.

What was more, from what Maggie could tell, he had never made it anywhere near Montana Bob's radar range.

Montana Bob was a city psycho, his migratory range a total of about twenty blocks, from Salvation Army on Washington to the Toe Tag on South Broadway to Blymore on Jefferson. The good priest, on the other hand, had been strictly a county denizen, start to last. Which meant that in his once tidy, upscale, circumscribed life, he would have had no contact with Maggie's pet paranoid.

City dwellers considered themselves inherently separate from those of the county, and vice versa. County people were more likely to fly to Chicago than drive east of Kingshighway or north of Interstate 70, depending on where they'd been born.

County residents especially stayed away from everything in the city but the ballpark and, on a nice day, the zoo. A priest from an upscale school in Creve Coeur would have no more reason to know Bob than he would to spend time in a Medicaid-catchment hospital like the Biltmore.

Whatever Montana Bob had thought, the priest couldn't have died at the hands of any of Maggie's friends. He'd never been within ten miles of them.

Shiny rocks and a basket of paranoia, and Maggie had stumbled right into it.

Sitting in the library, the report of Father McGinley's death still displayed before her, Maggie thought of one of the last times she'd seen Bob upright. He'd sidled into the

ED on a late-spring day, his overcoat pockets spilling out socks and string, and his battered Old Marine ball cap lined in aluminum foil. He'd clutched flowers in his hand, just like always. This time it had been a couple of dandelions, a handful of white vinca, and a bright red geranium. Bob considered the city's Brightside flower planters as his personal hothouse.

"It's a beautiful day, Maggie-o," he greeted her, his gaze skimming her, as if the sight of her cost too much.

"Oh, Bob," she said with a smile as she accepted her regular tribute. "How lovely. The street crew's been working hard this year, haven't they?"

He looked around, wary of eavesdroppers. He leaned close enough for Maggie to smell the street on him. "Arabs, Maggie," he whispered. "Here at the hospital."

Maggie leaned toward him. "Doctors," she whispered back.

"Terrorists," he insisted.

Knowing some of the docs Maggie worked with, a valid assumption. But only on a personal level. There were no anthrax vendors at Blymore. No point in terrifying the people who already knew terror.

"No terrorists," she'd said.

"I *saw* them. Planting bombs. In patients."

Ah.

"But nobody's blown up."

"They're waiting 'til they fly."

"I'll alert everybody," Maggie assured him, because, in the end, that was all she could do.

"Remember," he said with a knowing nod. "Don't fly with any person who's had surgery."

"I will."

And he'd patted her arm, like always, happy that he'd saved at least her from the true horrors of the world. The phantoms that crept through his fragmented, frightened mind.

And Maggie, who knew better, had taken Bob's last

words to her as fact, when he'd only wanted her to be safe from his specters.

Shutting down the computer, Maggie collected her bag and purse and headed out of the library. There were new ornaments to buy for her mantel and pasta to make. There was life to be lived, and she meant to do it.

Maggie would never know how close she came to simply folding her investigative tents and gratefully stealing back into the night, relieved that none of her friends overheard her accusations.

But then, Wednesday happened. And though it took a while to realize the full impact of what occurred that day, one thing became quickly clear. On Wednesday, Maggie lost her last chance to believe Montana Bob was wrong.

She lost her last chance of all to stay safe and walk away.

CHAPTER 9

Wednesday was the day the SWAT team was scheduled to take down a methamphetamine lab outside Valley Park. With the temperature and humidity well into the nineties, the raid was going to be a sheer delight. Because meth labs were as volatile as the people who ran them, the full SWAT team would be called out. Because the chemicals used in a meth lab were toxic and combustible, not only would the West County Fire Department and Haz Mat team respond, but each SWAT team member would be fully covered in Level B encapsulating suits and wearing SCBA gear. Maggie figured she'd probably drop ten pounds by dinner.

The team was scheduled to meet at the McDonald's parking lot on Highway 141 at 3:00 P.M. Until then, Maggie had to pull at least six hours at the hospital. Which meant, of course, that Maggie would be pulled from a shift that would be bursting at the seams.

It was probably just Murphy's Law, but the heat didn't help. Nor the fact that school was scheduled to start next week and parents wanted their children's afflictions cured in time to clear the house. Nor, of course, the cicadas, which ensured that Maggie was served up a full dose of crazies. By the time she crammed down a sandwich at eleven, she'd shepherded one Virgin Queen to the Stress Center, given two Korean vets directions to the Choisin Valley—also known as the VA psych hospital—and reassured a lovely old man that rose dust really couldn't make him fly.

Even worse was the violence. A rape, two abused children, an aggravated assault, and a seventy-year-old man killed by a hit-and-run driver. And then, just when Maggie thought she'd get by with nothing more hostile and paranoid to deal with than meth dealers, she got in the Varners and Rennets.

The Varners and Rennets were South St. Louis's very own Hatfields and McCoys. Originally from Arkansas, the family had managed to get some seriously debilitated jalopies all the way up Highway 55 into the State Streets south of the brewery, where they continued their long-standing blood feud with every weapon known to man, and a few the ever-enterprising families had created just for the occasion.

A Varner never came in, but a Rennet didn't land in the next room. If a Varner shot a Rennet, a Rennet clubbed a Varner with a frozen leg of beef. If a Varner stole a wife, a Rennet stole a car. Any type of intercourse at all between the families ended up with one of each being treated and the rest brawling in the waiting room. The Varners and Rennets took up more space on The List than Smiths in a St. Louis phone book.

Maggie had the Varner. Virgil Varner, an easy player to spot, since Virgil had a huge scar across his forehead from the time he'd tried to shoot himself and missed. Now, Virgil had a matching slash that damn near bisected his nose.

Virgil, it seemed, had hit on Sam Rennet's hugely pregnant wife. Sam threw a couple of punches. Virgil countered with a pool cue, and Sam answered with a broken beer bottle. Virgil brought the discussion to a close with automatic weapon fire.

That alone wouldn't have necessarily caused much of a problem. Virgil, after all, had missed his own head. But when Virgil fired, Sam pulled his young wife in front to shield him. Myra Rennet took two rounds in the abdomen and was "looking to die real soon," as her thirty-six-year-old mother so aptly put it.

"This is not the time to lose our List," Jeannie growled, as a group of them stood behind in a littered trauma room watching Team One hustle Myra down to OR in a desperate attempt to save either her or her twenty-eight-week fetus, whoever got luckier.

"List?" Maggie retorted a little too sharply. "We don't need no stinkin' List."

"True," Carmen agreed, massaging the rage from the back of her neck. "What we really need is Virgil's MAC 10."

Jeannie's laugh was ghostly, a sure sign that it was migraine time. "A small room, a match, and a quart of kerosene."

Maggie nodded. "A smaller room and a machete."

For a second, the three of them just stood there amid the litter and blood and watched the empty doorway. Then, shoulders sagging, Jeannie sighed.

"There's just got to be a better way of making a living."

Maggie was all set to answer, when the three of them were interrupted by a thud and crash from the Varner side of the wall.

"Shit." Maggie sighed and spun out of the room.

Paul was coming to pick her up in no more than forty minutes for the SWAT action, and Maggie had five patients to hand off. Suddenly, she wasn't at all sure she'd last that long.

"Fuck! Aw, fuck!"

Maggie made it into Virgil Varner's room first to find him out of bed and trailing patient gown, IV line, and blood across the floor. Carmen skidded into her, and then Jeannie. And then, for a minute, the three of them just stood there staring. Virgil had the Anheuser-Busch eagle tattooed on his ass.

"Where's the fucking nurse?" he howled, his very unstable legs giving out on him.

Maggie headed over to pick him up. "Wishing she were."

"Hey, there's an idea," Carmen offered as she grabbed Virgil's opposite arm and helped lift. "What do you think?"

Val grabbed the IV bag and followed. "About what?"

"A better way to make a living. It'd sure pay more."

"We could work our own schedule," Maggie agreed.

"Wouldn't be on our feet as much," Jeannie added.

"Wouldn't have to deal with Rennets or Varners," Maggie concluded. "On the other hand, have you ever sat down in fishnets?"

She got two halfhearted smiles. It was a reflection of how close to the edge they all were. The patter was there. The tone was brittle as old bones. Even Maggie was having trouble keeping a quiet face.

Maggie slid Virgil's butt back onto the cart and headed for the IV bag she'd left on the sink. "Plumbing," she said. "Now there's an occupation."

Carmen headed for the door. "True. Also better pay . . ."

"Better clientele," Jeannie agreed.

"Better hours," Maggie finished the age-old joke as she rehung the IVs. "And just think. What's the worst thing we'd have to stick our hands in?"

"What the fuck's that for?" Virgil demanded, the esses whistling through his four missing teeth as he pointed to the bags.

Maggie readjusted Virgil's patient gown to cover as much as it could. "Antibiotics, Virgil. You don't know where that beer bottle's been."

Virgil's smile was equal parts delight and pride. "Same place that pool stick was gonna land. Up Rennet's skinny ass."

Maggie's answer was a brief, taut silence. She found her hand tightening the material around Virgil's throat and had to consciously ease up before she made a mistake.

Finally, expelling a harsh breath, Carmen turned and pushed Jeannie out the door ahead of her. "Plumbing it is."

Virgil and Myra came in at 2:06. By 2:25 Myra was

undergoing an emergency C-section and laparotomy, and
Virgil was waiting for the plastic surgery resident. He'd
been cleaned up, looked over, and started on IV antibiotics.
Security had all but corralled the twelve or so Varners and
nineteen Rennets down in the waiting room, and Sam Rennet had been dismissed into their loving care.

At 2:45 while Maggie was in the bathroom changing
into her SWAT identity, word came down that Sam Rennet's baby boy was dead. Maggie walked back out into a
full-fledged Varner/Rennet riot.

There seemed to be a hundred of them, all wanting the
others to fuck something impossible and swarming along
the hallway as if they were being chased by the bulls at
Pamplona. Which was probably close to the truth, since
Tommy came charging in right on their heels.

Jeannie went down in a tangle of equipment. Carmen
slid behind an equipment cart and stayed there. Women
screeched. Men howled. Visitors and staff ran for their
lives, and the equipment cart Carmen was hiding under
tipped over, tumbling urinals and Kerlix bandages across
the terrazzo like marbles.

Maggie'd had enough. Grabbing an IV pole, she waded
into the crowd swinging it like a quarterstaff. Rennets and
Varners screeched. Several tripped over several others. The
wave of wrestling white trash fell back before her wrath.
The only thing that made Maggie feel better was that one
of the first people she smacked was Tommy.

"Get the fuck outta the way!" he snarled, picking a couple Rennets up and tossing them against an equal number
of Varners.

"Help!" Maggie heard Virgil Varner howl over the
noise. "Fuck! Help!"

There were times Maggie was convinced those were the
only two words the Varners and Rennets knew. The problem was, she didn't think anybody else had heard him. And
if Maggie knew Virgil Varner, he was about to up the trouble ante a truckload.

Shoving her way through the melee—which had shaken

down to Tommy versus everybody—Maggie reached Virgil
Varner's room in time to run right into Jeannie.

Who was standing stock-still in the doorway staring at
Virgil as if his hair were on fire.

"Jesus shittin' Christ!" he was screaming, trying like hell
to get off the bed. "What're you doin' to me? Jesus! it
hurts!"

Maggie came to a screeching halt. Right on her heels,
Carmen bumped into her. "Your ride's here. He just helped
Tommy lasso the last of the Rennets."

Maggie nodded without taking her eyes off Virgil Varner, who was sweating like a pig and clawing at his chest
and neck as if he'd just been shot. "Help!" he screamed.
"Help me!"

Now Carmen took notice. "Oh, God," she breathed.

Then they all moved.

"You ready, Mags?" Paul asked in the doorway behind
her.

Maggie barely heard him. Her stomach was doing a sudden drop. "What hurts, Virgil?" she asked, already at his
side.

"Help!" he screamed, panting. Clutching.

But Virgil should have no reason to clutch. He only had
a couple of big cuts to his face. If he needed to clutch
anything, it should have been his nose.

"Maggie?" Paul prompted behind her.

She yanked the head of the bed straight up and reached
for the oxygen. Jeannie was going for the monitor. Maggie
heard Carmen calling for EKG, radiology, and a doctor
right now, goddammit.

"Maggie, we have to go," Paul insisted.

Slapping on EKG leads to show sudden PVCs, Carmen
sighed. "You always leave this shit behind for us to clean
up."

"What are we cleaning up?" Allen asked as he sa-
shayed in.

One look at Virgil shut down his smile like a bad hard
drive. Virgil was turning purple.

Paul strode into the room and grabbed Maggie by the arm. "We have to go *now*," he insisted.

Maggie knew they did. They had a tight window to make if they were to surprise the meth dealers. But she didn't want to leave. She wanted to know why Virgil was purple.

Virgil should not have been purple.

Allen patted her on the shoulder. "Go, my Nazi princess. You have much mayhem to inflict."

"Yeah, what the hell," Carmen snapped. "Looks like you've done about all the damage you could do here."

"Remind me to take you off my Christmas card list," Maggie snapped back.

She gave up, though, and followed Paul out the door.

"I really wish that for once they'd place the paramedics *upwind* of the meth labs," Maggie groused ninety minutes later as she crouched in the woods between the gas guy and Paul.

They had all gathered out here by the Meramec River, where old river houses crouched at the edge of the woods. Most of the houses had originally been summer retreats, plywood and tar paper affairs on tall stilts to weather the floods. River rats lived here too, the people who had no place better to go, no matter what the water did to them. The people who were close kin to the Varners and the Rennets, these clustered just a floodplain away from the more affluent of the county's population.

Today's raid was being made on one of the less lovely of the river dwellings, a dilapidated two-story house that had cannibalized autos in the yard and old watermarks halfway up the side of the wall. And, if the reports—and the pungent, ammonia smell—were any indication, a thriving meth lab inside.

Maggie was still amazed that nobody in the house realized that justice had come to call. The county police had closed the access road, on which waited an ambulance, a fire truck, and the Haz Mat unit. Twenty people in space suits had crept up the driveway in full sunlight and set up shop beneath the first-floor windows.

The containment team was tucked into the tall grass and bushes and trees that surrounded the house, their camouflage so complete even the birds were confused. The entry team, clustered together like virgins at a Viking feast, hovered at the right side of the two-story house ten feet from the river waiting for word to go in. At one edge of the perimeter, the lieutenant did his best to communicate quietly past the nerve-shattering whine of the cicadas, and at another the snipers waited in perfect stillness and sweated.

The gas man was pointless when taking down a meth lab. As explosive as the materials were in that house, no incendiary device of any kind could be used. So Dennis Arnold crouched behind a tree with a standard M16, and Maggie took up her position by Paul, because Paul could see what was going on. Paul would give her enough warning to act quickly if she was needed. Which was a good idea, because right now, Maggie was just a bit preoccupied.

Maybe she could call Blymore when she got out of here, she thought. Find out how Virgil Varner was doing. Find out what was going on.

Find out what had gone wrong.

Myra Rennet had died in surgery, which meant old Virgil would be up on murder two. Sam should have been up on something more than assault, but it was tough to prove that he'd deliberately caused his seventeen-year-old-wife harm. Virgil, in the end, would get the fuzzy end of the legal lollipop.

If he hadn't already gotten the fuzzy end of the ED lollipop.

Maggie thought of how she'd left Virgil, screaming, his hands clawing at his arm and neck, and she thought of another patient she'd had who'd looked just like that. A little old lady one of the interns had wanted just to get out the door. The problem was, that old lady had been getting IV potassium. The intern, thinking he was doing an expedient thing, had just dialed that IV wide open. And sent that little old lady screaming straight for the roof.

Potassium burned. It burned like a mother in high concentrations. It burned straight up your arm and neck and down your chest if you got high concentrations in an IV.

High enough concentrations to possibly kill.

And Virgil had sure looked as if he was thinking about succumbing to that very thing.

Maggie's stomach did another tight roll and dropped.

"We're a go," she heard in her ear.

The cicadas had reached the perfect resonance of a dentist's drill, reverberating right through Maggie's brain. She swiped at the sweat that trickled beneath her sweatband and tried her damnedest to focus on the mission.

"This is the police! Open up!"

There went Pax, right at the front. Flower on the ram, slamming into that door as if his last meal were on the other side. The team tumbled in behind like clowns out of a Volkswagen.

Maggie could hear the distant shouting, the commands in her ear, the thunder of boots on hardwood floors. Since the house had two stories, the team would separate at the stairs and sweep accordingly. Somewhere within those two stories, intelligence reported spotting some seven, possibly eight meth elves. And, of course, a bathtub full of combustibles. It was going to be a very chaotic scene for a few minutes.

Gunshots. Maggie heard gunshots. Beside her, Paul went rigid. His spotter moved his binoculars across the visible front of the house to catch activity. Maggie crouched alongside a sycamore and held her breath.

"First floor contained," she heard through her earpiece.

"S1 to C2. Two hostiles floor one," Paul snapped. "Side one, window three. Dropping from the ceiling."

More shouting. Boots, maybe a body thump or two.

"Got 'em. Second floor?"

"Three hostiles. Hold one."

"Officer down!"

Well, that was a call that got a person's attention. Maggie settled her breathing apparatus in place and climbed to her feet, ready to run.

"Where? Can we send in the medics?"

"Top of the stairs. Injury, no wound." Maggie could have sworn she heard a collective sigh of relief. "Second floor contained. Send in M1."

Which was Maggie. Her problems back at Blymore completely forgotten, Maggie bolted out of the trees at a crouching run.

"How many hostiles total?" they asked in her ear.

A couple of the team were hauling muscle-shirted perpetrators out the front door. Jazz, as the redundant medic, stepped forward to help handcuff. Pax met Maggie at the front door and pointed up the steps.

Maggie could still see a lot of activity. She heard lots and lots of obscenities. Taking a second to note where everybody was, she clomped straight up the steps to where Flower was reclining against the wall massaging his ankle.

"You're kidding," Maggie greeted him, her voice tinny and distant behind her mask. Darth Vader, she wasn't. "The county spends all those millions of dollars to have medics handy, and all you can come up with for us is a sprained ankle?"

"It hurts," Flower whined.

"Holster your weapon," she snapped, because it was, after all, her first priority. As if, made crazed with pain from a twisted foot, he'd start shooting.

He did so, his moves quick and slick so that the Beretta was secured. Only then did Maggie quickly bend to assess Flower's foot.

"Can you hop down the steps with help?" she asked, unlacing his boot.

"As opposed to humiliating myself by being carried down on a stretcher?" he asked. "Oh, yeah. I think so."

Maggie grinned. Ignoring the traffic that stepped over and around her, she completed her exam with expediency.

"Call up narcotics and the Haz Mat team," the lieu called from outside.

"Time for a drink," Flower agreed.

"Time for a lot of drinks," Maggie retorted. "You scared me, you jerk."

"No. Don't move. You can't go anywhere."

It actually took the two of them a second to realize that the voice wasn't one of their own. Maggie whipped around to find that they'd been flanked. The upstairs team had finished, all its perpetrators spread-eagled out on the lawn. The downstairs team was waiting back in the lab for the Haz Mat and narcotics team to dismantle it.

And there, two feet from where Maggie was bent over Flower, stood a bloated, bare-chested teenager with greasy brown hair, refrigerator repairman jeans, and, most importantly, a lighter. Held up in his hand as if he were about to ask for encores at an Eric Clapton concert.

"Who the hell are you?" Flower demanded, instinctively reaching for his gun.

"Fuck me," Maggie breathed, her eyes locked on the lighter.

"Get out!" the newcomer yelled.

His thumb was going for the flint. He made any kind of spark, and Maggie'd travel the ten miles back to Blymore airborne.

"Don't move!" somebody yelled from downstairs. "Put it down put it down put it *down*!"

The kid didn't move. Didn't take his eyes off Maggie. "Get out!" he insisted.

"Where the hell'd he come from?" somebody demanded. "Who missed him?"

"Might be another ceiling rat."

"A10, check the goddamn ceilings!"

"You son of a bitch—!" Flower grunted, trying to move.

"Sniper, can you take him out?"

"S1, negative."

"S2, negative."

Guns rose. The lighter rose. The kid was sweating like a pregnant woman, and Maggie suddenly didn't want him shot.

"Everybody hold up!" she yelled into her mike. "Don't move!"

Then she reached out her hand, because she could see the boy's eyes. She could see that there was no light there. No malice. No real understanding at all. Somebody had told him to do this, and she didn't want him killed for it.

"You need to give that to me," she said, sounding as alien as one of Montana Bob's delusions. "Please, it's okay."

"No!"

"Stop him!"

Maggie had no choice. Before that kid lit them all like a space shuttle, she had to stop him. She'd watched football since she was a kid. She didn't think she'd ever seen a more illegal tackle. She took the kid right around the knees and sent them both cartwheeling down the stairs.

"Maggie!" she heard in her ear as she thumped to a stop.

"Maggie?" she heard over her head as she lay there, on top of the poor kid, who probably had no idea of what he'd almost done.

"Did you do that just to be amusing?" Pax demanded from over her head.

"She's been practicing for weeks," somebody offered.

Maggie shot them all a silly grin. "Three Stooges School of Silly Pratfalls. Like it?"

"Yeah, you think you're so goddamn funny," Pax groused as he lifted her to her feet. "See how you like this. You're getting checked over with your patients at St. Isidore's."

Maggie lost her grin. "Hey, I got rid of the lighter."

Pax just stalked off. One of the mopes out on the lawn started laughing, a mean laugh, like the joke was on the cops. The kid started to cry. Maggie stretched out the aches she'd just acquired and bent to check him over.

"He almost fried us!" somebody huffed.

"We wouldn't have been around long enough to fry," somebody else answered.

"Fuckin' idiot," somebody else said with a shake of his head. "He woulda gone up, too."

"Musta thought he was a terrorist."

"Thought he was a fuckin' cherry bomb."

Maggie patted the boy's hand and started a head-to-toe assessment. She made it as far as his right arm, which had one acute angle too many. Great.

"I need an air splint and a stretcher," she announced, patting the teary boy all over again.

"Hey!" Flower complained, all alone now on the second-floor landing. "What about me? I almost saved you, ya know."

Maggie started laughing. Everybody started laughing, sharp bursts of relieved tension. Maggie settled her patient more comfortably until they could get him a splint and a ride to the ambulance, then headed upstairs to do the same for Flower.

She didn't really mind riding in to the hospital with the injured. When she could, she much preferred following them through to treatment. She knew, too, that once she was able to get the respirator off, her presence would calm the boy, whose name was Yancy Bill Butler. The Fourth. Maggie started the IV for his open fracture and patted his hand, then patted Flower's hand when he began to pout. And Terry Brown, the West County paramedic driving the ambulance, let her run the siren.

What Maggie objected to was being checked over. She hurt from stem to stern, had collected a bouquet of bruises on her right thigh and shoulder, and would limp for a week. But she didn't want x-rays. She didn't want blood studies. She wanted to get back to Blymore and find out about Virgil Varner.

The need to concentrate on the mission over, Maggie had an inordinate amount of time to worry about what she'd find when she got back to her own hospital. She should just call and get it over with, but she didn't have the guts.

She didn't want to know from that far away. Hell, she didn't want to know at all, but she had the most terrible feeling that she was about to prove Sean wrong.

So she politely strong-armed the ED resident into denying the need for x-rays, promised a visit to her private doc for blood studies if needed, and escaped in a county cruiser after making sure that Flower's x-rays were negative and that poor Yancy was still doing all right.

All right being a relative term for Yancy. Yancy's entire extended family was in jail, not that they would have done him any good if they hadn't been. Yancy might have been slow, but his family was mean. Besides which, meth dealing didn't provide health insurance. Yancy's long-term care would be iffy at best.

But Yancy was at least smiling at the face somebody had drawn him on an inflated rubber glove, so Maggie left without feeling she was deserting him, and she got herself back home.

Back to Blymore. Back to the bad news. She walked in holding her breath and didn't let it go until Allen grinned at her.

"Oh dear God, somebody put her up a tree."

Maggie looked down and saw her rural cammos. Then she remembered the matching face paint and grinned back. "It's my back-to-nature look. Like it?"

"My darling, L.L. Bean is back to nature. This is back to *Soldier of Fortune*. I *love* it."

There hadn't been a Varner or Rennet in the waiting room, which monumental sign Maggie didn't know how to interpret. Nothing to do but ask.

"Uh, Allen, how's Virgil? Last I saw him, he was looking for a truck ride to that great coonhunt in the sky."

Allen waved her off like a bad landing. "Please, I'm still trying to bathe that evolutionary mistake off my hands . . . no, come to think of it, that was Sam, wasn't it? Husband of the year. It's all right, though. We don't need to put him on The List. His own mama whupped him around like a ten-cent whore. I tell you, applause was heard three floors up. Oh, and the police managed to find a statute or two. He is now the ugliest man in lockup."

"Allen," Maggie interrupted, wishing for once Allen didn't practice the Broadway musical style of fact-giving. "What about Virgil?"

Allen's grin was suddenly bright as a child's, no artifice at all. "Massive MI. For his many sins, our boy blew out half of his left ventricle, and is even now screaming obscenities at the cardiac team." He frowned, persona solidly back in place. "Who deserve it, if you ask me. They all dress like accountants."

"An MI?" Maggie asked, suddenly breathless. "Really?"

Allen's smile was absolutely predatory. "What? You think you cast an evil spell on him? You think he ate some bad cephalosporin? Pork rinds, my darling. Nothing but pork rinds and hog fat. The man is a genetic wasteland. No one should be surprised."

Maggie's grin was surely too bright. She didn't care. Sean was right. She *had* been cooking up delusions. After all, if Virgil wasn't nailed after the day they'd all had today, then Hitler could have walked the Blymore halls with impunity.

"Couldn't have happened to a nicer guy," she agreed. "Or a nicer unit."

The contention between the ED and CCU had been longstanding and often vitriolic. Small revenges were greatly enjoyed on both sides.

Allen patted Maggie on the shoulder and bent to kiss her forehead, one of his Good Witch tendencies. He stopped a millimeter away and grimaced, the impulse obviously not strong enough to overcome all the greasy paint and sweat on Maggie's forehead.

"I'll consider myself kissed, Glinda," Maggie giggled.

He patted again. "Good girl."

And Maggie left for home, feeling better than she had all day.

She felt better until she checked her answering machine

to find a message from the St. Louis County Medical Examiner's Office. Yancy Bill Butler the Fourth had died in St. Isidore's ED. The death investigator wanted to know if Maggie had any idea why.

CHAPTER 10

"What do you mean he's dead?" Maggie demanded the minute she got the death investigator on the line.

On the other end of the line, the investigator named Jim Light sighed. "I mean he died. For no apparent reason. I've talked to the staff, but they said that they hadn't really had a chance to get in there and see him except to share glove art. Evidently you were the only one who treated him. Got any ideas?"

The tone of Jim's voice was professional, impersonal. No accusation implied. Still, Maggie felt it. She felt the sudden, shifting weight of Yancy's death dump her half-formed hopes straight into the dust.

She'd known it. Damn it, she'd known it all along, no matter how hard she'd tried not to. She'd actually almost made herself believe that if the murders weren't a figment of her imagination, at least maybe they were a past occurrence. Something that had happened, but had stopped once she'd noticed it.

But they hadn't.

Yancy Bill Butler the Fourth had tried to torch half a dozen cops at a meth lab, enough to piss off anybody in a uniform.

And now Yancy was dead.

He was dead in a hospital twelve miles away from Blymore, where Maggie's suspect pool lived. He was dead in the same hospital where Fr. Urban McGinley had taken the same celestial train ride.

Oh, Jesus God. Her suspect pool had just doubled.

Worse, it had expanded from the city out into the county, which geometrically increased her jurisdictional problems.

But she wouldn't think about that right now. Right now, she had to concentrate on Yancy.

Poor little boy. Poor retarded man, who'd only been doing what he'd been told. Who'd been put down like an unwanted dog after Maggie had tossed herself down a flight of stairs to save him.

Somebody had killed him, and this time Maggie couldn't tell herself she understood.

"What does your ME think?" she finally asked.

"He thinks I should talk to you. Which is what I'm doing."

In the city and county jurisdictions, a medical examiner, in these cases, forensic pathologists, were in charge of causes of death. These doctors mostly stayed in the morgue and court. Death investigators, often ex-cops, ex-nurses, or ex-agents, handled most death scenes and screened most calls. They also did much of the case organization, which was why this one was on the phone to Maggie.

"Maggie?"

"Uh, yeah. I'm here." Maggie collapsed onto one of her kitchenette chairs and rested her forehead on the table. "I'm just . . . uh, surprised. The only thing I found was a compound fracture of the right humerus. We splinted it, started a hep lock in his left forearm so he'd have an IV, and patted his hand a lot. Yancy was about a hammer shy of a tool belt, but I understood that to be a chronic kind of thing."

"Yeah. I heard. He fell down the steps?"

"On top of me. Yeah. I didn't find any other injuries. Just the fracture."

I swear.

There was a silence on the line.

Then why is he dead? Maggie heard in her head. It was sure as hell what she wanted to know. Maggie couldn't imagine that Jim Light hadn't asked it. She knew Jim, an ex-cop who was meticulous and decent. She didn't know him well enough to say what she wanted.

"Any known medical history?" he asked.

"Like, did he have chronic heart disease, or metastatic CA that just happened to reach critical mass at 4 P.M. today? No. Nothing I heard of. Of course, the family wasn't in the mood to be cooperative, and Yancy was hard-pressed to remember his own name."

"Allergies?"

"No known."

Another silence. An almost imperceptible sigh. At least Jim had tried his damnedest to find a likely cause.

"Could be a fat embolism," Maggie suggested, as if the Medical Examiner's office wouldn't consider that possibility. Fat emboli were a common complication of fractures of any kind. If the embolus reached the lungs, the person could die quickly.

Usually not without symptoms, though.

"Could be," her caller quietly agreed.

Maggie sucked in a breath. "Autopsy tomorrow?"

Unless there was a crying need, autopsies were scheduled from eight to five. It prevented rush jobs and emotional decisions. It also fomented the acid that ate away at tender stomach linings, because Maggie wouldn't know for at least another twenty-four hours what had caused Yancy Bill Butler the Fourth to go toes-up for no apparent reason.

"I'm sure."

Maggie nodded to herself, her forehead scraping against the unpolished oak of her tabletop. "Uh, when he died. Can you tell me what happened? What anybody noticed?"

Another silence. A short, telling one. "Nothing, evidently. The assigned nurse just walked in to find him asystole and that glove balloon still clutched in his left hand."

"Uh-huh."

"I can talk to you again?"

"Sure. Would you mind letting me know what you guys find out tomorrow?"

"If I can, sure."

Maggie didn't know what else to do. She said good-bye and hung up and thought about Yancy Bill Butler the Fourth laughing over a glove balloon.

Damn it. It was one thing to kill bad guys. Really bad guys. Gangbangers, child molesters, bottom feeders. But Yancy Bill had been an innocent. Like Montana Bob had been an innocent.

Which meant that if house was being cleaned, it wasn't just being cleaned of bad guys anymore. It was being cleaned of inconvenient guys and irritating guys. And that shit just had to stop.

God, she wanted to go to the police. Sit her little butt down on a homicide chair and fan her charts across a homicide desk like a poker deck.

But right now, that would be pointless. Maggie had nothing. No proof, no pattern, no name. She had a feeling. A suspicion. And as much as she loved her cop friends, Sean had shown her how they'd react to her dumping her questions on their desks.

There was something more, something that made Maggie edgy when she even thought about going to cops. But right now she had more than enough on her plate without adding more.

So she would have to wait. Collect more information. Consider what it meant that Yancy had died way out in the county, where Blymore people didn't play.

She just wished like hell she knew what that was going to be.

Realizing that she was never going to get any work done the way she felt right now, Maggie turned to assess the current animal collection on her mantelpiece. Ming, catching the look in Maggie's eye, hissed and escaped to a safe spot underneath the couch.

By five the next morning, Maggie sat before a kitchen table strewn with every note she'd ever made. She had diagrams and lists and one paper filled with nothing but names.

She still had nothing.

No proof. No pattern that would give her a name. Carmen had worked on several of the patients, but not all of them. The same was true for Jeannie and for Maggie herself. Not to mention at least six other people.

There was no longer any question, though. Somebody was killing List members.

No, not somebody. More than one somebody. More than one somebody who worked in more than one hospital.

More than one hospital in more than one municipality. In another city, that might not have meant much, but St. Louis was like the Balkans without land mines. Carved into neighborhoods by immigration and migration, the hundred-mile-square area was separated by hundreds of clear lines that just weren't crossed. The ninety-plus municipalities in the county shared information with their brother municipalities even more rarely than lottery winners, and with the city itself even less.

Maggie wasn't just looking into social separations, but legislative, police, and death investigation systems. Blymore was a city hospital, and Isidore's a county hospital, and never the twain usually met, unless an Isidore patient ran out of insurance and found himself summarily exiled to Blymore in the city.

Which meant that the chances of one person being involved in both hospitals was virtually zero. A lot of people in medicine worked more than one job, but usually failed to cross that all-important city-county line to do it. Maggie was one of the few she could think of who did.

Which meant that her one existing suspect had probably somehow communicated with another suspect. Had talked over frustrations, futility, and the fine art of revenge one too many times. Across city lines. Across county borders.

Did they still communicate, or had they just both agreed on what a good idea this was and gone their separate ways?

Was she expecting too much of them, or suspecting too little?

Maggie hoped she was expecting too much. She didn't even want to contemplate what it would mean if she suspected too little.

Because at least six people had died for no apparent reason in different places, and not one red flag had been raised. Which wasn't just wrong, it was damn near impossible.

Someone should have commented. Eyebrows should have been raised, whispers started.

She should have noticed, damn it.

But there had been nothing. No hint that somebody was meting out personal justice.

No hint except from one paranoid schizophrenic nobody listened to.

A paranoid schizophrenic who was dead himself.

Maggie wanted to vomit. Instead, she sat at her table with her worthless notes that couldn't prove anything, and wondered what it was Montana Bob had seen. She wondered whom he'd suspected.

Out of nowhere, Ming jumped up on Maggie's lap and began kneading her jeans. Maggie rubbed the cat's head and thought back to the day Bob had died. She tried her best to remember it, moment by moment.

She remembered that wasted face. Those huge, frightened eyes, the whites showing. The spittle at the corners of his mouth.

"I'm sorry, Maggie," she heard again. "I got you into this, Maggie. I'm so sorry. . . ."

She fell asleep there at the table knowing that something important waited just outside her reach.

Jim Light called Maggie back about Yancy Bill Butler while she was on duty at the Chesterfield firehouse.

"We're still waiting for quantitative drug screens and microscopics, of course," the death investigator said.

"Of course."

"But barring any surprises there, we'd have to say that

Mr. Butler didn't have a very good reason to die."

Maggie wished like hell she was surprised. "What are you going to list for manner of death?"

The Medical Examiner's Office determined two things. Cause of death, as in the agent of death—exsanguination from a gunshot wound, heart attack, etc.—and manner of death. Manner was confined to four categories: natural, suicide, homicide, and accident. The medical examiner could also leave the line open pending further investigation.

"Probably accidental," Jim said.

Probably. Meaning the file was still open.

"Thanks."

"Sure. I can . . ."

"Call me later if something comes up? Please do. Do me a favor if you can."

"If I can."

"His glucose was normal?"

"In the low hundreds."

Normal. Which meant that nobody had shot him up with insulin, a personal favorite among suicidal medical personnel.

Maggie sucked in a big breath and said what she needed to in a rush before she chickened out. "Recheck his potassium, and run digoxin levels."

A pause. A big pause. "Do I get a reason why?"

"I think you'll figure it out on your own. Especially if they're abnormal."

"You're not going to say anything else?"

Maggie pulled in another breath, trying like hell to trust the investigator with her phantoms. "Not yet."

A huffed breath could be heard. "Okay. I'll ask."

"Thanks."

Which left Maggie with a definite "died for no apparent reason" and nowhere else to look for answers. What was worse, she had the terrible feeling she'd be hearing that particular refrain again soon.

She just didn't think she'd hear it no more than two hours later.

The call was for a woman with chest pain. Maggie knew her well. An eighty-two-year-old woman with coronary artery disease, Mrs. Quinn was a gomer of epic proportions. Never better, never dead. Just slowly rotting away, one organ at a time. Maggie and her paramedic partner carried Mrs. Quinn into the ED on an average of fourteen times a year.

Exactly like every other time, Maggie ignored Mrs. Quinn's earsplitting whine to start an IV of D5/W with 20 meq of potassium, pop another nitro under her tongue for the pain, and inject a bolus of 100mg of lidocaine to stop the arrhythmias Mrs. Quinn was already exhibiting. Maggie had just pulled out a piggyback IV with maintenance lidocaine in it when Mrs. Quinn presented the universal symptom of imminent death.

"I'm going to die," she said in a quite reasonable voice. And then, she did just that.

Maggie worked furiously on her. The code team at Midwestern Med Center worked another forty minutes while the family screamed like paid mourners and the chaplain prayed. Mrs. Quinn turned relentlessly blue, and her heart deteriorated into stillness until the team finally shut off the equipment to let her die in peace.

For a minute, Maggie just stood and looked at Mrs. Quinn where she lay naked and flaccid on the littered cart. Maggie understood that people died. She knew perfectly well that it sometimes just happened. She couldn't get over the feeling that it shouldn't have happened this time.

"What the hell went wrong?" she demanded of the ED doc.

"I was about to ask you the same question."

Maggie shrugged, not able to take her eyes off Mrs. Quinn, whom she'd known longer than her own grandmother. "We were doing great 'til I gave her that lidocaine. Then she crashed like a Concorde."

"I don't get it," the doc said. "She's always liked lidocaine before."

"And lidocaine's always liked her."

His final judgment was an offhand shrug. "Oh well, considering the fact that this should have happened about ten years and three million dollars ago, no harm no foul."

Maggie stared at him. She stared at him long after he'd walked off. Then she stared at Mrs. Quinn.

No.

It couldn't be.

Mrs. Quinn had never hurt a soul.

Even so, Maggie's gut was clenching hard, and she was beginning to sweat. For no apparent reason at all.

Mrs. Quinn had been a pain in the ass, but then, so had most of Maggie's patient load and at least half her friends. Nobody would do this for no reason at all.

Would they?

Besides, the only person who had treated Mrs. Quinn had been Maggie. Who else could have interfered?

Maggie rechecked her notes and drugs. She actually thought to collect the empty IV and drug packages she'd used, but the debris had already been cleaned up and cleared out. She talked to Jim Light at the county Medical Examiner's Office all over again, and suggested he have the ME do a postmortem.

She was turned down. Mrs. Quinn had a long history of chronic heart disease, kidney failure, and Alzheimer's. She had a private doc who wasn't in the least surprised that she was dead, suddenly or otherwise. She had the bad luck to be over fifty-five, which put her out of automatic autopsy range. The ME's Office released her to the funeral home, and Maggie was left with terrible suspicions nobody would let her prove.

Suspicions that worsened when she reached her loft to find a short message on her answering machine.

"Leave it alone, Ms. O'Brien."

That was all. Nothing more. Just a whisper that didn't

sound like the one she'd heard before. Lower, more terrible, more certain.

More terrifying.

A week later, it was a patient at Blymore. A wife beater named Culpepper who came in with a butcher knife wound to the groin from a wife who'd finally had enough and gone straight for Mr. Happy. The Ever-Screaming Tyrant, she'd called it in the squad car. Unfortunately, at least in her eyes, she made the mistake of letting her emotions rule over her aim. She'd hit a little to the left and nicked the femoral artery instead.

Maggie had Mr. Culpepper all ready to swing down for his blood flow studies when all hell broke loose. Suddenly, the blood they were supposed to measure started spurting everywhere. It flowed. It dripped. It oozed from every orifice Mr. Culpepper owned.

Maggie pressed on everything she could find and yelled for help. She skated around the ensuing code like a one-woman hockey team.

It didn't matter. The man who had come in cursing, went out exsanguinated.

For no apparent reason.

Once again Maggie found herself standing alone in a silent, littered trauma room, soaked to her knees in blood, her goggles hanging around her neck, staring at a fishy white corpse. Her hands were shaking this time, because she'd seen the emergency clotting studies they'd done on Mr. Culpepper.

Anticoagulants, she thought as she scratched her nose with her gowned forearm. Somebody shot the bastard up with anticoagulants, and I didn't know it. How didn't I know it?

She saw Allen sashay past the door and thought to tell him. To demand he listen to her about what she suspected. In her head she went over every person who'd been in that room with her before Mr. Culpepper had crumped.

Carmen, of course. Carmen loved the smell of spilt blood in the morning. Jeannie, Rashad, Allen, two city paramedics, a supervisor, and a half dozen surgical residents.

Until Mr. Culpepper had started to bleed, Maggie hadn't even spent her entire time in his room. She hadn't thought she needed to. Which meant that anybody could have slipped in behind her and shot up Mr. Culpepper with enough heparin to do the job.

This time, though, Maggie was ahead of them.

She called the St. Louis City death investigator and told a story about suspiciously elevated coagulation studies. Mr. Culpepper would get an automatic autopsy, since his injury had been the result of a crime. But Mr. Culpepper would now also get drug levels for major anticoagulants, since Maggie couldn't understand why Mr. Culpepper could have bled out so fast.

"DIC," the investigator said with a certain amount of patronization.

As if Maggie hadn't thought of that first. Disseminated intravascular clotting, a syndrome associated with shock, by which the patient both clotted and bled to death at the same time. Devastating and difficult to treat.

"Did you guys try heparin for DIC?" he asked.

Maggie sighed. "Yeah."

Which made levels almost a moot point.

"Call me anyway with results, okay?"

"Oh yeah. Sure."

Maggie knew this investigator, too. A lazy asshole named Mort Gorman who must have had pictures of the mayor with a goat to keep his job. Maybe, she thought, it was time to try the cops.

She stood there in the noisy, echoing hallway, her hand on the phone, and couldn't pick it up.

She was afraid. Not just because another of her patients had died. Not because he'd died right under her nose, and she knew damn well that he'd been murdered.

She was afraid of something she couldn't name. That something that had surfaced the last time she'd considered calling the police. Something she couldn't name.

She couldn't call, either.

She just stood there, her eyes squeezed shut to close off her mounting panic, and tried not to think of who would have killed that man and put her fingerprints on it.

Maggie was walking back into the room to finish out the charting, when a uniform leaned in to check on Mr. Culpepper.

"Wow," he said with a big, shit-eating grin. "They were right. You really don't need no stinkin' List, do you?"

Maggie stared him right back out the door.

The nightmare woke her from a sound sleep. Montana Bob, screaming. Splayed out on a sidewalk like a stricken animal, spittle at the corners of his mouth, his eyes rolling and white-rimmed.

"He's here, Maggie! Get out!"

Maggie sat straight up in bed, scaring the hell out of her cat.

"Jesus."

He's here.

Not *they're* here. Not *they're everywhere*.

He.

Bob hadn't been afraid with Sean. He hadn't feared her, even in her cammos. But as the team had wrestled him to the sidewalk, he'd seen something that convinced him that he was going to die.

Someone.

Someone he'd recognized and been terrified of.

Maggie had thought then that he'd been his usual delusional self. Now she knew better.

And the only people who'd been close enough to see on that sidewalk had been other cops.

It wasn't just a friend in the hospital after all. Even two friends in two hospitals.

Bob had tried to tell her. Hell, Sean had tried to tell her. It wasn't just the medical people he hadn't wanted her to go to. He hadn't wanted her to go to anybody.

Cops might not have drugs, but they had grudges. They

felt just as protective of that list as the medical people. And they could involve themselves a hundred ways to make sure a perp ended up in the hospital and wasn't missed when he was suddenly dead.

Maggie should have listened better. She should have respected her own gut fear.

She couldn't go to the cops.

Which meant that even the people she trusted most in the world, her friends, her family, the men and women who had saved her from Tommy, weren't to be trusted anymore.

Where should she go?

Whom did she trust?

How could she ever replace the faith it had taken twenty-six years to find?

This time it only took Jim Light another day to call Maggie back about Yancy Butler.

"Normal ranges for both potassium and digoxin on Yancy," he said.

Maggie sighed. The other easy option was an air embolism, nothing more fancy than shooting about 50ccs or so of air straight into a vein. Favorite of TV murderers everywhere. Virtually impossible to prove.

"Oh, well," was all Maggie could think to answer.

"You got a reason to think Mr. Butler didn't just die?" Jim said.

"I have a feeling. Right now, though, I have no proof."

"If it'd been there, we would have found it."

"Is the ME closing the case?"

"Uh, no. Not yet."

Maggie just nodded. "If I get anything else, I promise to call."

For two days Maggie spent her free time tracking down names she'd copied from The List. On the third day, she got another hit.

Mary Ann McGregor.

Mary Ann, it seemed, had decided to drive herself home

from the country club with a blood alcohol level of .32. Mary Ann only made it as far as the off-ramp of Highway 270, which she tried to enter the wrong way. She took out a van of children on their way to camp. Three of the children had been killed at the scene. Mary Ann had been pronounced dead in the St. Isidore's ED.

Nothing suspicious in that, on first look. But follow-up newspaper articles claimed that Mary Ann's husband had questioned the cause of Mary Ann's death. A suit had been filed against the hospital. The cause of death, according to the newspaper, had been listed as cardiac arrest.

Which made Maggie understand why Mary Ann's husband had raised questions.

Cardiac arrest is the cause of everyone's death. The pertinent question would be why the cardiac had arrested in the first place. The county ME had never given Mr. McGuire an answer that satisfied him. Not something that surprised Maggie, either. What did surprise her, was that Mary Ann McGregor had died twelve months ago.

Not only did Maggie have a growing suspect pool, she had a lengthening time line. People had been dying without reason for at least twelve months, and Maggie hadn't even suspected it.

She'd felt two weeks ago that she was running out of time. Now, she felt as if she'd been asleep on her feet. Stupid, blind and lethal.

She had to get some answers, and she had to get them soon.

She checked her notes, trying to find anything she could follow up on before she headed in for her shift.

Heparin.

It jumped out like a message. Mr. Culpepper.

Before she thought about it, Maggie dialed the St. Louis ME's Office and asked for her least favorite investigator.

"I don't have the file with me right now," Mort Gorman whined when Maggie asked.

She swore she could hear scratching in the background and didn't even want to think about it.

"Did you tell Dr. Harrison about my suspicions?"

"Sure."

Too quick. Too slick. She didn't believe him.

But then, all Dr. Harrison had to do was look at the hospital lab work and she'd see that the Screaming Tyrant's owner hadn't died on his own.

Maggie suddenly felt she couldn't take the chance.

If anybody in this good world would be considered impartial, it would be Dr. Winnifred Harrison. Maggie might come out of the woman's office without any hair or eyebrows, but she'd come out with the truth.

"You tell Dr. Harrison I'm coming in to see her. We need to talk."

Now Maggie was sure she heard a gulp. "No you don't."

"You just tell her. In two days. That should give her plenty of time to get her test results back. I need to talk to her."

"She has a phone line of her own."

"I'll call that, too. But you're the one who's going to have to have the Culpepper file all in order, aren't you?"

This time Maggie swore she heard a soft, "Bitch" as he hung up.

She didn't much care. Presenting herself before the legendary Dr. Harrison might be the most self-destructive act she'd ever performed in her life, but at least it was that. An act. She couldn't just sit there anymore.

Especially when people were now dying at her hands.

At *her* hands.

And she didn't even know how.

CHAPTER 11

Susan Jacobsmeyer sat perched on the edge of a plastic-shrouded floral couch in far West County and rechecked the information she'd scrawled from her answering machine.

"So you're not satisfied with the care your mother received, Mr. Quinn?"

The couple that sat across from her was too earnest, too carefully dressed and too alike. Holding hands across a glossy faux Chippendale end table as if holding each other up, while a bad print of a rather grim Sacred Heart peered over their shoulders.

Susan didn't like them. Given enough time, she just knew they'd ask her if she'd found Jesus, or want her to watch their little Crystal sing "Tomorrow."

It didn't mean they had nothing to say.

Not surprising, it was the wife who spoke up. "Mother Quinn shouldn't have died," she insisted, her helmeted ash hair not so much as dipping with her furious nod. "She was such a fighter, wasn't she, Phillip?"

Phillip dutifully nodded. "Every time we had to call the paramedics to care for her, she got better. She was able to be sent back to Calmrest. Her home, you know."

Her nursing home, they meant.

Susan nodded carefully. "She was how old?"

"Eighty-two," the Missus said, patting her husband's

hand. "And, well, she hadn't been well, you know. Not for years."

"Not since my father passed."

Passed what? Susan wanted to ask.

"But if your mother was so ill, why do you think that this time there was some problem with her treatment?" she asked, then nodded her exception. "Besides her dying, I mean."

The Missus blanched and patted away. "Passed. We say passed. Because she's surely gone to our savior's reward, hasn't she?"

"Passed," Susan agreed before she got the rest of the pamphlet. "What made you feel you needed to speak to me?"

"Well," Mrs. Quinn said, "you wrote that article, after all."

Susan waited a moment, but it was obvious that Mrs. Quinn thought Susan should know which article she meant. "And that would be about . . . ?"

"That woman. That SWAT person. You know, who held the baby."

Susan forgot the flowers and the cheesy starving artists paintings on the wall and the fact that Mrs. Quinn smelled like the air freshener used in public toilets. She put on her best sympathetic listening pose and let the woman take over.

"Well, I mean, you made her out to be some kind of heroine, you know. And, well, when Mother died, and that person at the hospital mentioned that there was some question about, well, other people dying under that woman's care. You know?"

"No." Susan was very quiet now. Very focused. "I don't."

Mrs. Quinn flushed, as if wondering if she'd gone too far. But evidently her faith restored her, because she straightened her plump shoulders and threw back her head. Susan was overcome by the feeling that if Maggie O'Brien were in the room, Mrs. Quinn would have shot an accusing finger at her and cried, "That's the woman!"

"Somebody talked about that man who killed his child. The child in that photo. So sad, don't you think? So sad. But that suddenly he died, too, right after she took care of him. And that there might have been, well, others."

"Do you remember who might have mentioned this to you?" Susan asked, almost light-headed with excitement.

"Well, no. We were so distraught, you understand. One of the nurses, I think. Somebody in those outfits they wear on *ER*, anyway."

Which could have been anybody from a brain surgeon to the cleaning lady.

In the ED at Midwestern. Well, it was a place to start. If Susan got a real whiff of questionable behavior on the part of their Female SWAT Medic of the Year out there where she rode ambulances, Susan could then go with impunity to the source and start questioning people at Blymore, where Maggie O'Brien spent most of her quality medical time.

And if what the tight-lipped Mrs. Quinn suspected proved to be true, Susan had herself a hell of a story.

"And you want me to look into it?" she asked, trying not to clutch her notebook like a press award.

"Well, the police wouldn't listen to us. What else could we do?"

Maggie's third unexplained death came on Tuesday. This one was a chronic screwup who had just beaten a little old lady into a coma for the twelve dollars in her purse. After the neighborhood had caught up to him and pummeled him into unconsciousness, the police had made sure Levon Repton made it to the ED.

Levon woke surly and spitting to find himself cuffed and unpopular. He promptly spit in Allen's face. Allen promptly spit back.

Maggie made it a point to keep an eye on Levon. She made sure she knew who was in the room. She watched every procedure and double-checked the orders she got for his multiple contusions, two fractured ribs, and fractured right orbit. She even made sure she was the only one who gave him any medications.

She still saw him seize and die. Right after she injected his IV with normal saline.

"Oh, no you don't, you scum-sucking little son of a bitch," she growled, giving his chest a good thump. "Hit the button, Jeannie! He's coding!"

Jeannie hit the button. The code team tumbled in, with Allen leading the troupe like the Lord of the Dance, and Maggie turned to check the monitor. By the time she turned back around again, the syringe she'd used to inject Mr. Repton with was gone.

Maggie didn't have time to search for it. With a terrible sense of inevitability, she watched his perfectly normal sinus rhythm dump straight to asystole with only a brief visit to fine v-fibrillation on the way by.

"You seem to be having a run of bad luck, my little praetorian princess," Allen informed her, gloving up and calling for the intubation kit that was already being laid out.

"Everybody has slumps, Allen."

He snapped the blade on and tilted Levon's head back, his movements quick, efficient, and graceful. "Ah, baseball. One of the true aesthetic sports."

The tube was slid in and respiratory hooked on the Ambu bag.

"That's just 'cause they have the best butts," she said.

"And arms," Allen rhapsodized. "Oh, my darling, don't forget those arms."

The conversation continued in a desultory fashion, as it always did in an Allen code, and everybody smiled.

Everybody except Maggie.

They never managed to get Mr. Repton farther than fine ventricular fibrillation. They inserted lines everywhere there was an entrance, filled him with fluids, shot him with enough chemicals to jump-start a jeep, and bounced on his chest like a trampoline. They x-rayed him, tapped him like a keg, and scanned his head for a surprise bleed. Nothing worked. Levon died, and his mother could be heard doing the gang mother's lament in the waiting room.

Maggie spent forty minutes recording the event. She searched for twenty minutes more for that damn vial of normal saline, or even the spent syringe. She found nothing. She jotted down the name of everybody who'd first answered that code, who might have thought it necessary to steal that vial, and she fought tears at the names she'd listed. Allen, Jeannie, Carmen, Rashad, Patsy Levine the medical resident. Shara the head nurse.

Her list of suspects had just gotten shorter. One of her friends at Blymore had murdered Levon Repton, as sure as Maggie breathed. Her friend had also taken the trouble to implicate Maggie in Levon Repton's death.

Her friend.

She wondered if she really did have any friends.

Because what they'd done today hadn't been done to comfort her. It had been done to indict her for murder.

By the time she left for home, Maggie could hardly see. Her head was pounding, and her stomach was in turmoil. She'd had to call the asshole Mort Gorman, who seemed to think it was pretty funny that Maggie couldn't keep anybody alive. It was up to Maggie to remind him that none of this was funny, that she suspected foul play in Levon's death, and that she was coming in to see his medical examiner at the end of the day whether he liked it or not. She also copied Levon's chart so she could take it home.

"Maggie, my militant madonna," Allen said, waylaying her by the door. "Are you okay?"

Maggie looked up at him, her calm face on. "Just tired."

His pencil-thin eyebrow did a swooping lift. "Tired or anorexic? You seem to be getting sharper angles to your face. Not that it isn't attractive, in a heroin-chic kind of way. But I wonder if you're eating enough for all this breaking and entering you've taken up."

Maggie managed a smile. "Isn't the lounge refrigerator at this minute filled with pappardelle sulla pecora? You know when I'm stressed I cook pasta."

"Of course I know." Allen patted her on the head like a child. "I'm just not sure you eat it."

Maggie patted him back and headed out the door.

And ran right into Sean, who had been conspicuously absent from her life the last week or so. Apparently because he'd been spending his time sharing cigarettes with cops and paramedics in the ambulance garage.

Maggie was suddenly furious. Not that Sean was here. Not even that he hadn't noticed her. That he'd deserted her when she needed him.

That she'd missed him.

Not just the patented Delaney kiss. His humor. His baiting. The comforting pressure of his back against hers as she slept.

The son of a bitch.

The last thing Maggie needed was for him to know exactly what seeing him did to her. So she tried to walk right by him.

"What are you doing here?" he demanded, dismayingly startled.

Maggie really didn't like it that Sean wasn't happy to see her.

"Well," she said, shifting her nursing bag to her shoulder, "unless I've been sucked into an alternate universe without knowing it, I work here."

Sean covered well, but Maggie knew him well enough to catch his discomfort. Hands in pockets, he rocked on his heels, so that not only his change jangled, but his whole damn utility belt. Typical Sean.

Then he smiled, like lightning. Incandescent enough to make most people overlook the fact that he missed eye contact by just that much. Protective distance, his dad had always called it. Sean preferred the handle "dog and drunk protection." Never make complete eye contact if you know you're gonna make 'em mad.

He wasn't making eye contact now, and Maggie knew she was going to be mad.

"I didn't mean that, O'Brien," he said. "I meant, I didn't think you'd be here today."

"Checking my schedule so you'll know when it's safe to come out and play?"

Sean went very still, which meant that now he was mad. Usually Maggie respected that, but not today. Today she needed to know who was killing her patients. She needed to know how. She needed to find someplace where there was safety and logic and sanity. And she knew damn well it wasn't going to be here.

So she smiled stiffly back at Sean and turned to leave. Before she could reach the garage doors to the driveway, though, one of the cops spoke up. "Aw, don't be hard on the guy, O'Brien," he said. "He was just telling us how you were doing some List cleaning for us."

Maggie stopped dead, her heart stuttering. "What?"

Sean was suddenly as still as she. The paramedic, a sly, undependable guy with a huge ego, grinned along. "Oh, come on. Everybody knows you hate thugs and wife beaters. So does everybody else. What's the problem?"

Another rock landed on Maggie's chest. They knew. She looked from the cop to the paramedic and saw satisfaction in those eyes.

Oh, God, they knew.

Stepping carefully over to stand eyeball-to-eyeball with the paramedic, Maggie gave him her best trauma nurse stare. "The problem is that I didn't clean off anything. More than that, it only takes one loose-mouthed moron spreading that around to sink my nursing license. I'm sure you wouldn't want that to happen, would you, Harris? If that happened, then we'd never have the chance to work together again."

Her words were almost painfully quiet. Her eyes, she knew, were glowing like a nuclear meltdown.

Harris, who'd never faced them at full voltage, actually paled. "You got no sense of humor, O'Brien."

Maggie smiled and patted his cheek. "None at all."

Harris flinched and backed away.

Maggie turned back to Sean for a parting glance. "Besides, I know Sean wouldn't think somebody had killed a wife beater. Sean doesn't think that kind of thing goes on at all."

Maggie knew she should have kept her mouth shut. She should have sidled up to the knot of assholes and smiled and sucked all the information she could out of them. She should have played up to them, gotten them to believe she thought this was all a great inside joke. Because as she slammed out the door onto the front drive, she was overwhelmed by the feeling that what she'd just seen had been some kind of test. A good-old-boy, arm-punching, wink-and-a-nodding attempt to see if she were one of them.

To see if they had to yank the leash they'd just wrapped around her neck.

Instead, she'd dumped all the tension and fear of the last few weeks loose right on Harris's head. In one fell swoop, she'd failed their little test. She'd locked the only door that would have allowed her access into their tight little circle.

Maggie made it all the way around the corner of the driveway and out of sight of the ambulance garage before her legs gave out on her. She just folded right there on the curb as cars whizzed past her along the hospital drive and laid her head into her hands.

She had so wanted to be wrong. She'd even prayed, curling into a well-waxed pew in the cool dimness of St. Peter and Paul, trying to reclaim the god she'd given away so long ago. The one she'd prayed to before she'd found him to not be enough for her. To not be anywhere in those whispering, shadowed aisles that smelled like incense and secrets.

She'd been so sure she'd found a better god. A more perfect faith.

The whispers had been gone from the old church when

she'd gone back, though. Her faith had shattered along with all those ugly little ornaments on her mantelpiece.

She couldn't pretend anymore, and it was taking her apart piece by piece.

Maggie had been sitting there on the ground for five minutes when her cell phone started to trill. She considered not answering it. It would only bring her more bad news. She kept her head in her hands and listened to the cars instead and wondered what they thought of her sitting there curled over the drive in her scrubs.

But the damn phone was playing the Mexican Hat Dance, and Maggie found that she didn't have as much patience as she thought.

"Hello?"

"They're going to think it was you."

How lovely. A whispered voice. At least it wasn't the dead of night. Maggie hunched farther over, a penitent on the asphalt.

Well, she might as well get it over with.

"Simplify this for me," she suggested, her voice eerily flat even to her as she focused on the constellation of dandelions that had pushed through the curb at her feet. "If it's a threat, make it. If not, let me get home to my dinner."

"See how easy it is to blame the wrong person for somebody's untimely death? Why would you want it to be you?"

At least I don't recognize the voice, she thought in desperation. Please tell me I don't recognize the voice.

"Ah, I see. And it wouldn't be me if I'd only go back to wrapping ankles and leave the really tough questions alone."

Nothing. No answer. Which was answer enough.

Maggie simply hung up.

For a long moment she just sat there. Just let the wash of traffic noise soothe her. She should have been thinking about what to do next. She should have been trying to figure out how to get proof. How to get herself out of the net that was slowly strangling her.

But for the moment, all she could really grasp was that

she'd just been threatened. Somebody had made sure that
three of her patients had died suspiciously. In her care.

And then made sure she knew about it.

Somehow, not only had someone found out she was asking questions, they had found a way to tell her in no uncertain terms to stop. Just as Sean had told her. As he'd
warned her at the Toe Tag.

Don't tell anybody, he'd told her, his eyes so anxious,
his hand on her arm familiar and comforting.

Well, she hadn't told anyone her suspicions.

Anyone but Sean.

And now people were being killed for the sole purpose
of intimidating her. And Sean had been laughing with them
out in the garage.

He had been right after all. She shouldn't have told anybody.

Especially not him.

CHAPTER 12

Maggie was still sitting hunched over the driveway when the city police car skidded to a stop before her. She didn't bother to look up even when the passenger door swung open against her shins.

"Get in."

Sean.

Of course.

Maggie didn't move. She was shaking too hard to face him. There was going to be no game face today, no Zen of any kind. She'd had enough.

"Goddamn it, Mags," he snarled from the driver's seat, "Tommy just came out to jaw with those assholes in the ambulance bay. In another two minutes he's going to come walking this way. You really want him to see you like this?"

It was the single argument that would have propelled Maggie into a car with Sean Delaney at that moment. Yanking her purse and nursing bag over her arm, she climbed in and slammed the door shut. He didn't even wait for her to buckle her seat belt before hitting the gas.

"There have been known to be pedestrians in this area," Maggie snapped.

"I'm in a police car," he retorted just as sharply. "It gives me a certain amount of license."

"Yeah," she said with a sigh. "So I finally figured."

They swung out of the driveway and Sean hit his lights. Maggie flinched. "Taking some now, are you?"

"Speeding and free lunches are about the only perks I get on this job. Roll down your window. You need some air on your face to help you calm down. Your cheeks are all mottled."

Maggie stared at her hands as if they had a life of their own. They were certainly busy, winding in among *her* bag straps like burrowing animals. She wanted to wring something. She wanted to strangle someone. Oh hell, she wanted to break something, and she couldn't do it in a squad car packed to the light racks with about ten thousand dollars' worth of equipment.

"Come on, Mags," Sean nudged. "The window."

Maggie finally looked up to see that they were swinging north and west onto I-70. Sean added a siren to his flashing lights and punched the accelerator.

"Isn't this kidnapping?" Maggie asked.

Sean didn't bother to answer.

Maggie knew where Sean was going. It was where he always went to think. Considering it was close to the confluence of the Missouri and the Mississippi Rivers, which was a good half hour away, she could wish he'd head for Forest Park or the Arch instead.

"You and I need to have a little talk," he said. "I'm going where we can have it."

"Why not? I always have my cell phone if your friends need to reach me again."

"What friends?"

Maggie snorted unkindly. "Don't tell me they bothered to leave before calling me."

He still professed an air of confusion.

"Did you know they were going to call me, Sean?" she asked.

Maggie saw him flinch. Not much. Enough. She saw him draw in a pretty deep breath. "Did I know *who* was going to call?"

Maggie gave him a glare. He looked back, but his eyes

slid to a halt just a millimeter south of contact. Dog and drunk territory.

What did he know? What wasn't he going to tell her?

Maggie wanted to puke. With that one, sliding nonlook, Sean had taken her last place of refuge from her. Her hope of sanctuary. But she wasn't capable of telling that to him.

So she turned her attention back out the window. The wind snaked in, hot and thick and ripe. The scenery changed as Sean pulled off 70 at North Broadway at O'Fallon Park and headed up along the eastern borders of Bellefountain and Calvary Cemeteries.

Neighborhoods gave way to the huge parks of death, landscaped in gothic tombstones and lush foliage and wrapped in local lore. General Sherman and Pierre Laclede rested beneath these shaded hills. Cities of hodgepodged monuments stretched out silent and unvisited and walled away from some of the most virulent gang activity in the bistate area. A piece of the most prime landscape in the area, shared only by the dead and dying.

Sean flipped off the siren as they passed into the county and slowed by about three miles an hour, except at intersections, which he negotiated like a Grand Prix driver at Monaco. Broadway became Bellefountain Road and they kept speeding north. Maggie wondered if she was going to have the energy to get through this. She saw Sean digging into his breast pocket with long-practiced efficiency and frowned.

"When did you start smoking again?"

Sean didn't bother to look over. "It's nothing. I'll stop when things settle down again."

"What things?"

Which was when Maggie saw the new lines around his eyes. A tighter edge to his jaw. Being caught on the horns of a dilemma could do that to a person. Nobody knew better than Maggie.

She instinctively wanted to make it okay, and decided she'd had much too much practice at that over the years. A compulsion much like smoking, she guessed. Tough to stop once you really got started, no matter how bad an idea it was.

"Talk to me," he said, throwing the ball untidily into her court.

Maggie kept her attention out the window and sighed. "No. I don't think I will."

She knew he looked her way. "Why?"

"Besides the fact that the last time I told you anything all hell broke loose?"

Another quick look. Another lie of omission.

"All hell broke loose? What are you talking about?"

Maggie looked away again, fighting that ground-glass feeling betrayal always left in her chest.

"All right, how 'bout this?" she asked, unable to stop. Wanting to dig until he gave her a truth. One, lousy, god-damn truth. She deserved that from Sean, of all people. "Why couldn't you at least have told me that some of the police were involved?"

"You didn't—?" He clamped his mouth shut. Much too quickly. "What police?"

"No," she said, as if he'd finished the first thought. "I didn't know. I thought it was just my friends at the hospital. I thought it was just *one* friend at the hospital. Just one, unhappy, overstressed friend who needed to be helped. But I was wrong, huh?"

"Maggie, you're screwing yourself into the ground with this. What's the quote? 'Don't assume conspiracy if stupidity is answer enough'?"

"After all these years we've known each other, Delaney, this is not the best moment to start patronizing me."

"Aw, c'mon, Mags . . ."

Maggie sighed. "Drive, Delaney." That glass was in her throat now. "I want to see the river."

He drove. The wind rocketed through Maggie's hair and raised sweat on her forehead. The neighborhoods of North County passed, fast food and car shops and duplexes. Maggie fought tears and knew it was a losing proposition. If only she didn't have to give them to Delaney.

Fifteen minutes later, Maggie walked out onto Sean's place of meditation and found herself forced to admit that it was just what she needed. Separated from the city by a generous swath of farmland, the St. Louis County Juvenile Correctional Facility was a collection of brick Arts-and-Crafts-styled buildings that must have seemed elegant and enlightened back in the twenties when they were built. Now, they simply looked worn and lonely out there beyond the empty fields. Isolated, institutionalized, and battered by generations of troubled children, the compound spread itself out on a spectacular ridge of natural beauty overlooking the Missouri River, water and woods and sky stretching away like a taunt to the incarcerated.

Perfect for Maggie's mood, for Sean's personal philosophy, for the discoveries of the day.

Sean signed in at the gate, swept along the drive to the lookout point over the Missouri, and pulled off the road. The lane was empty, the nearest buildings boarded and deserted, and the stillness of the panorama soothing. Maggie climbed out into the humidity and the rising song of the cicadas and hopped over the stone wall to climb down toward the river.

She only walked a third of the way down. Far enough to obscure the misery behind and ignore the muck below, comfortably perched atop the illusion of a magical natural sight. There she climbed over onto one of the stone walls that made up the terracing and sat facing the water.

Maybe what she needed was another church. A place nobody could yank out from under her feet. Maybe Sean was right to come here for his solace. No people involved in a river. No greed or apathy or selfishness in distant trees. Just the hum of nature and the sweep of the wind.

But, of course, Sean caught up with her.

For a long few minutes, the two of them just sat there, Sean pulling on his cigarette as if it were nourishment, Maggie folding her hands in her lap as if she were at tea. A soft, warm wind tugged at Maggie's hair and whispered in the trees. A plane droned high overhead. Squirrels chattered, and the river glinted molten in the hard sunlight. And all Maggie could think was that there was nothing here on which she could vent her fury.

"Hawks," Sean announced, and pointed toward the north.

Maggie saw the birds circling lazily in the warm updrafts and almost smiled. As kids, Maggie had sought her solace in the cool shadows of St. Peter and Paul. Sean had headed straight for the river bluffs, where he could watch the birds fly. Even now he spent a week every winter up at Grafton counting migrating bald eagles.

Each to his own freedom, Maggie thought. Sean had picked more wisely though. Birds, it seemed, were more dependable than gods or humans.

"You gonna tell me now?" he asked.

"I don't have much choice, unless I want to walk back."

Still, it took her a minute. She knew Sean wouldn't mind. He'd be watching the birds and smoking, just as he had when he was sixteen. Maggie settled her breathing, tried her damnedest to clear her head, so she could put this all in perspective. So she could get some kind of response from Sean she could believe.

She sucked in a breath and followed the flight of Sean's hawks. "Did you know that I've killed three people, Sean?"

Sean stopped in the middle of a drag. "What makes you say that?"

"Because I'm the only one who took care of them, and at least two died immediately after I'd injected them with what should not have been lethal substances."

Her thumb pushing the plunger, her only desire to stop a deadly arrhythmia. Causing a worse one with the poison in her syringe.

Sean followed the flight of his birds. "Give it to me in order."

She did. Mrs. Quinn, Mr. Culpepper. Finally, Levon Repton, who was probably still waiting for his ride down from Blymore to the city morgue.

Levon Repton, who she could still feel seizing under her hands.

"Okay," Sean said, reaching for his fourth or fifth cigarette. "I'll trust you that the deaths were unexpected, and they happened while you were on the clock. Any reason to think they were homicide?"

"People don't go into asystole from a bolus of normal saline, Delaney. Not only that, all evidence of possible foul play disappeared right after each incident."

Sean shrugged. "Stranger coincidences have happened."

"Stranger than getting involved in that little test in the garage right after Levon did the dirt nap?"

"Stranger than that. All those guys said was they were glad some mopes were dead. We've all said it. Hell, *you* said it out on a street on The Hill not too long ago. It doesn't mean anything."

"How much does it mean that right after I walked out of my little tête-à-tête with you guys, I got a call on my cell phone telling me that if I didn't stop looking into what was going on I would be blamed for the new deaths?"

That finally got a reaction out of him.

"Jesus. Who was stupid enough to think that kind of threat would make you stop? It'd just piss you off more."

Maggie gave him a long, hard look. He was busy squashing his cigarette into oblivion and missed it. "Which is precisely what's happening."

Sean snorted. "I could have told them that."

"Then why didn't you?"

This time Sean met her eyes, and she saw outrage. "You think I had anything to do with that?"

"You tell me, Sean. Did you?"

Suddenly, Sean's eyes shifted. Jesus, Maggie thought.

"No, Maggie," he said, pulling out his last cigarette. "I didn't. Now, what have you found out?"

Maggie sucked in a slow breath and told him the truth. "I've found out that I don't think I trust you anymore."

He looked as if she'd gut-punched him. "You think I ratted on you to a group of people committing murder so they could terrorize you? Weren't you paying attention? I'm the one who knows that threatening you wouldn't do any good."

"I'm not sure you had any say in the matter, Sean."

He huffed and rubbed his hand through his hair. "You make this sound like a cabal, Mags."

"How do I know it isn't? Hell, two weeks ago I was upset when I thought one person was so overwhelmed that they'd taken to killing people. The more I look into this, the more I feel like I'm the only one in the bistate area without a copy of The List and a syringe full of insulin."

This time Sean met her gaze full and hard. "I am not killing anybody, Maggie. I am not trying to get you indicted for murder. And you know damn well I wouldn't try and use a lame-ass threat like that to stop you if I were."

"Then what are you doing, Sean? What do you know about this?"

Back to the cigarette and the hawks, now a ballet of them, circling and dipping and soaring over the silver river.

He shrugged. "Nothing, really. Oh, I've heard people talk. Shit, who hasn't? But who'd figure they were serious, ya know? I blew it off, just like everybody does."

"You expect me to believe that?"

"How long have you known me, O'Brien? You think that I'd drag you all the way up here to lie to you?"

She didn't know anymore, and that was the truth. But she'd said that already, and out of habit, she couldn't beat Sean over the head with it.

"What exactly have you heard, Sean? From whom?"

"Right now, I couldn't really tell you. I didn't pay that much attention; I told you that."

"Well, will you help me now? Talk to people, pull records, that kind of thing?"

He went so still Maggie almost thought he'd stopped breathing.

"Ah, well, that might be a bit of a problem, Mags."

As still as Sean had gone, Maggie went stiffer. "Why would that be a problem exactly, Sean?"

He shrugged, refusing to look her way, his hands shoved deep in his pockets. "Probably because I've just been put on suspension from the force."

Susan Jacobsmeyer decided that she'd died and gone to heaven.

"You mean to tell me you actually saw her kill somebody?"

The woman looked away a minute, then back. They were sitting in the Uncle Bill's Pancake House on Lemay Ferry, just two women sharing an afternoon muffin. Susan's interview wore an uninspiring flower print dress and bone heels and blue eye shadow. A nurse. Susan could spot 'em a mile away. They spent most of their lives in uniforms and couldn't figure out how to dress the rest. Kind of like nuns.

"Did you actually see it?" she asked.

"You mean, did I see her draw up potassium or digitalis from a labeled bottle and inject it? No. Did I see her inject something into the guy and then see him seize and die? Then, yes, I did."

"Why are you telling me and not her supervisors?"

A sigh, a tight frown on perfectly bland features. A pair of fingers rubbing distractedly at temples. If I were playing medical Deep Throat, I'd probably have a headache too, Susan thought.

"I'd heard you were asking around," the nurse admitted. "And sometimes in medicine, it's just more . . . um, expedient to make your charges through the press. Do you understand?"

As in, nobody at the hospital wanted to risk the bad publicity enough to ask the questions themselves. Susan smiled kindly and opened her notebook. "You've seen this happen before?"

Another pause. Another frown. "No, to be honest, I haven't. But there's been some talk lately. You know, since that man killed his little boy. And then the man died so suddenly afterward. She said right out on the street that she wanted him dead, didn't she?"

Susan shrugged. "I've heard lots of people in your business make the same kind of statement and nobody's died."

The silence was all but electric. "You sure about that?"

"You might as well tell me why you're suspended," Maggie said again, as Sean pulled up alongside her car in the hospital parking lot. "I'll find out anyway."

"Find out some other way," he said easily. "I still have some pride."

Maggie gathered her gear, trying her best to stifle the disappointment. Sean had admitted nothing and promised nothing. And she'd let him get away with it. Again.

"You can still keep an ear to the ground, even if you're suspended," she tried. "I mean, heck, how suspended can you be? You're still driving a unit."

He scowled. "That's a special consideration from a friend. It goes back right now."

Maggie nodded. "Fine. But you could spend some time at the Toe Tag, have beers on the morgue parking lot. Visit a couple of those hot-tub-baptism parties the Third District's so fond of throwing."

Sean lifted his gaze to the sky. "Oh, I already did that."

Maggie flinched. "So that was it. I take it the girls were just a tad shy of legal?"

"How was I supposed to know? Nobody looks their age anymore."

"You blame it on Britney Spears. I know."

As if she could be more disappointed. But she was. He'd promised her. He knew what he was doing to her.

Apparently, he didn't care enough to stop.

Which was why she kept turning him down.

"Will you keep your eyes open for me?" she asked finally.

"Yeah," he said, not facing her. "Sure. See you later?"

"Maybe."

Opening the door, Maggie climbed out, suddenly exhausted. Her gut had begun to trouble her again, that same stomach clutch she'd felt when she'd recognized those names on The List. Disaster was looming, worse disaster than finding murder in her own Emergency Department, worse than losing her best friend. Worse than being responsible herself for at least three deaths. Worse than that, and she didn't know where from. Or, for that matter, how to stop it. And she still had the medical examiner to face. Which, she thought with trepidation, was disaster enough for any day.

If a wall of African tribal masks didn't warn a person, she had no excuse for what she got. At least, that was what Maggie decided after facing the decor that graced the personal office of Dr. Winnifred Jemimah Sweet Harrison while she waited for her appointment.

She'd made this appointment with some trepidation. Now, she was close to outright fear. Howling wooden mouths and tufts of wild human hair tended to do that.

And that was before Dr. Harrison even stepped into the room.

The simple truth of the matter was that no matter how brilliant a scientist or unimpeachable a civil servant she was, Dr. Winnifred Jemimah Sweet Harrison was the most frightening person in the city and its three surrounding counties.

Maggie had seen Dr. Harrison a couple times at the ED. At a distance. Where it was safe. She'd never been personally introduced to the city medical examiner. And she'd certainly never had to suffer a visit to the doctor's office.

Maggie was sure Dr. Harrison chose the masks for their intimidation value. They weren't nearly as intimidating, though, as the six-foot, mocha-skinned, Armani-clad woman who stalked into the room and settled herself at the desk in front of them.

Heck, even good old Mort Gorman, with whom Maggie

had been arguing for the last two weeks, refused to step over the doorway.

"You want to tell me *what*?" Dr. Harrison demanded in scathing tones the minute Maggie finished introducing herself and the reason for her visit.

Maggie had known she was going to have to overcome Dr. Harrison's arrogance to press her case. But she'd thought the ME's scrupulous honesty would see her through. Suddenly she wasn't so sure.

Maggie still did her best to maintain eye contact as she gathered herself into Zen mode. "I want to tell you that I believe that some deaths this office cleared in the past months were actually homicides."

Maggie saw the fury rise in those spectacular chocolate eyes. "If you'll bear with me a minute," she insisted, trying very hard not to sound frantic, "I can explain why I've come to that conclusion."

Then, without waiting for so much as a nod, she did. She spoke of The List, about the discoveries she'd made, about the fact that she'd been trying to get in to see Dr. Harrison about the recent case of Mr. Culpepper she thought they could easily prove. She mentioned Mr. Repton, who was probably signing in downstairs even as they spoke.

"How dare you?" was Dr. Harrison's reaction.

Maggie wasn't surprised. After all, nobody questioned Dr. Harrison's judgment. But then, usually nobody had to.

"I have a list—"

"You have a list," the doctor snarled, suddenly more ferocious than the lineup on her wall. "*You* have a *list*!"

Maggie tried to clear her throat. "If you could just bear with me, Dr. Harrison—"

"Get out."

Maggie all but shut her eyes. "Please, ma'am."

"I said get out!"

Dr. Harrison, it seemed, wasn't in the mood to have her assumptions questioned. But then, Maggie had had hostage training. She knew how to negotiate her way out of life-threatening situations.

"If I could just look at the case files," she suggested calmly. "Match my information."

"Because you think I missed how many—?"

Maggie took a fortifying breath. "In the city? Seven."

Dr. Harrison was on her feet, and Maggie was really afraid. "Seven murders. *Seven.* That I, a board-certified forensic pathologist with more initials behind my name than the Surgeon General and twenty years' experience in urban violence passed over *seven* homicides because I'm what? Stupid? Crooked? *Vengeful?*"

Maggie straightened even farther. Nobody need know how terrified she was.

Disaster, she kept thinking, her gut clenched tighter than a prizefighter's fist.

"I didn't notice it either, and I was there when many of them died. How could you have possibly known that these deaths were anything but what they seemed to be? You would have had no reason to suspect digitalis or potassium overdoses to even test for them. And except for Mr. Culpepper and Levon Repton, every other person looked like they died of their initial injuries. I'm just wondering—"

But Dr. Harrison had already heard the magic words. "Mr. Culpepper," she cooed, eyes like granite. "The gentleman we called you about regarding suspicious heparin levels? The one *you* cared for?"

"The man I called your investigator about first to alert him to suspicious heparin levels."

Dr. Harrison's eyes briefly lit on the hapless investigator, who flinched in the doorway as if she'd wielded a whip. "No investigator of mine would fail to pass information of a suspicious death. Would he, Mr. Gorman?"

"Never," the suddenly sweaty Mr. Gorman said.

"Except this time," Maggie said in a perfectly equitable voice. "I talked to him three times, the last no more than a couple hours ago. That and the first, after Mr. Culpepper, are documented."

Maggie had just made Mort Gorman one of her worst enemies. Right now, she had to press home her point. "Dr. Harrison, can you tell me what James Krebs died of? It was never in the paper."

"Who? Krebs? The one who killed his baby?" The ME didn't so much as pause. "We're waiting for final tox reports. His ETOH was over two hundred at time of death, and he had Vicodin and marijuana on board. He could have reacted to anything."

Maggie's eyes raised. "Twelve hours after admission? His ETOH was only .190 on admission ten hours earlier."

And alcohol levels didn't go up from abstinence.

Harrison scowled. "Evidently, his family stayed late. And helped *ease* his pain."

"Makes you wonder what the cop at the door was for." Maggie anchored her hands on her knees. Sat up straight. "May I also suggest dij levels? Maybe some of the paralytics?"

Dr. Harrison's scowl grew ferocious as the seconds stretched out in appalling silence.

"Leave me your list," she snapped, manicured hand out.

Maggie blinked, barely able to hope. She handed over the list she'd made. Dr. Harrison didn't bother to look at it. "I wouldn't miss one homicide," she said with steely certainty. "It is inconceivable I would miss seven."

Maggie decided that this wasn't the moment to tell her there might be more.

"*I* will look at the records," Dr. Harrison stated, eyes narrowed on Maggie in disdain. "And I'll tell you now that I won't find anything. Do you understand?"

Maggie couldn't say anything more constructive than, "Thank you."

By the time Maggie made it back outside into the smoggy sunshine, she wondered whether she'd just done a good thing or made her life geometrically worse. There was nothing for it but to do what she always did when she needed a little unconditional comfort. She went looking for Big Zen.

The good news was that Zen was to be found no more than a couple parking lots away. The bad news was that within forty-two seconds of walking into the City Dispatch Center, Maggie discovered that she'd finally been completely busted. And that being busted was a much more terrifying problem than facing the medical examiner.

Her sense of impending disaster blossomed like a mushroom cloud.

The Police Communications Department lay no more than a parking lot away from the Police Academy, which sat a couple of blocks east of the morgue. A modern glass-and-concrete structure, it housed the people who answered and dispatched all police calls in the city in a glassed-off enclosure that took up the entire second floor. Maggie had spent enough time there to know most of the staff. Hell, she knew their families, their problems, and the internecine pattern of their sexual liaisons. It usually took Maggie at least fifteen minutes to wade through all the updates before she reached Zen's console. Today it was as if she'd walked in ringing a leper bell.

"I think loyalty's underrated these days," somebody muttered as she walked by.

"Don't see it as much as you used to," somebody else answered. "That's for damn sure."

Not one person made eye contact. Not one person said hello.

Maggie was being shunned as neatly as a Mennonite on meth.

"How was the ME, O'Brien?" a staffer actually asked.

Ah, Maggie thought, her stomach sinking precipitously. The weaselly Mort Gorman had dropped the dime on her. The word would be around the city faster than an anthrax scare.

"Which other poor stressed-out jerk you planning on turning in? How 'bout you? Wanted that asshole out on The Hill as dead as anybody else."

She could handle this, Maggie kept thinking. She'd expected it, after all. She'd known all along she'd have to face it.

Besides, she still had Zen. She always had Zen, who had all but raised her, tucked into the corners of various dispatch offices around town. Who had listened and advised and comforted in a score and more of crises Maggie had brought to her. Who never judged, never disapproved, never denied.

She had Zen.

Maggie reached Zen's console and realized that she could be wrong about that, too.

Maggie never said hello when she met up with Zen at the center. She just sat herself down on the adjacent chair at the console and smiled. Zen was in charge of dispatching officers of the Sixth and Seventh District, which demanded complete concentration and devotion, at least according to Zen. Without fail, though, when Maggie arrived, Zen would reach over without looking away from her screen and pat Maggie's knee until she had a moment to talk. Maggie hadn't realized how much she counted on that gentle ritual until it disappeared.

Zen didn't scowl. That sweet, tiny, round black woman didn't frown or freeze Maggie out with her eyes. But neither did she look at her. Neither did she touch her. She just kept working her screen and her keyboard as if Maggie weren't there.

Maggie waited.

She smiled.

She began to forget to breathe, waiting for that pudgy, ringless hand to flutter over her knee.

It never did. And Maggie was devastated.

Not Zen.

Oh, please, Jesus. Not Zen.

Not this woman without prejudice, without rancor, without fury, even after surviving the years she'd worked here, after losing her beloved husband in a drunk-driving accident and having to raise her children alone. After adopting all those children of all those cops who hadn't been as good fathers as they had police officers.

After everything, still Zen had kept her optimism. Her pure spirit.

She had always patted Maggie's knee, no matter what Maggie had done, or not done.

Please, Zen, Maggie begged in her head, as if it were the only thing keeping her alive. *Please don't turn away from me.*

Don't be part of this.

But Zen didn't look at her. She looked at her screen. And Maggie saw that Zen's eyes were sad.

Maggie could have taken angry. She could have taken resentful. She couldn't take the feeling that she'd somehow disappointed the woman who'd given her more maternal comfort than any of the five women who'd been temporarily housed with her.

She couldn't believe that Zen would hear what was going on and side against Maggie.

"How were your grandkids, Zen?" Maggie asked, knowing damn well she was pleading for forgiveness for something she had no business repenting.

Zen nodded. "Fine. Little Shandra's walkin'. Bobby was baptized."

No pictures, no grins. No contact at all.

Maggie felt as if she were withering, collapsing in on herself. "I imagine you've been hearing things," she said.

Those eyes just got sadder. "A lot of people wonderin' what you got against your own to turn on them."

"You don't think I have a responsibility to stop murder?"

"You really think that's what's goin' on? You sure enough that you said it right there in front of that white-faced rat in the ME's office? You know Mort Gorman's already let everybody in town know that you think we all murderers. You know what that means, girl."

"Somebody is a murderer, Zen. Somebody definitely is. I just can't prove it yet."

This time Zen actually closed her eyes, as if she were simply too uncomfortable to be discussing this with Maggie. "I think you're gonna hurt a lot of people, honey. A lot of people."

Maggie sucked in a shuddery breath and got to her feet. "Then I'm just going to have to hurt them."

Zen was already on another call when Maggie walked out.

Over the next thirty-six hours, the people in Maggie's life made their judgment known. Conversation stopped when she walked into the worklane at the ED. Requests were brusque and comments sharp. No patient suffered, but the extra help Maggie had always been able to count on simply wasn't there. She was a pariah.

No surprise she should feel so doomed, she thought as she trudged up the stairs to her loft at seven in the morning after a hard night shift. She'd effectively cut the cord to every person in her life with the exception of Sean, who only seemed to want sex and food from her. She'd even lost Zen's anchor, which hurt more than all the other losses combined.

She couldn't sleep, her chest was perpetually on fire, and she couldn't fit another carton of pasta sauce in any refrigerator in the bistate area. And she still had not a shred of evidence to back up the allegations that had set off this firestorm in the first place.

Well, Maggie thought, at least Jim Light in the county ME's office had agreed to talk to her again. Maybe he'd listen. If Maggie was going to destroy her life completely, at least let it be because she was right.

Disaster was still coming, though, she thought, fitting her keys into her door. Big disaster. Bigger disaster than the yawning black pit of disaster she'd been living these last days.

Really, really big disaster, and there wasn't a damn thing she could do to prevent it.

If Maggie hadn't been so distracted by that thought, she would have anticipated what happened next. She should have anyway, she thought as she opened her door to find that, once again, she didn't have her home to herself. For a minute she just stood there in the open doorway, the knob still clutched in her hand, her keys hanging from the lock.

It only needed this.

"Where the fuck you been?" Tommy demanded from her one good armchair.

He'd evidently been waiting a while. The chair was ringed in empty Busch longnecks, and his city police ball cap was askew.

"Brushing up on your breaking and entering skills?" Maggie asked, sweaty with both relief and sudden terror. Relief that she'd kept her precious files on her person instead of her loft so that Tommy hadn't been able to get to them. Terror, because Tommy was here. And Maggie knew better than anyone what it meant when Tommy suddenly showed up.

He was already climbing out of his chair. Maggie could see that he'd passed his own judgment on her. She could see that punishment was about to be meted out. Hell, his eyes seemed to glow with the anticipation of it.

Instinctively, Maggie grabbed her keys and closed the door to keep the confrontation between the two of them. She dropped her bag, her purse, her keys. She sidled away along the wall, curling just a little into herself to protect the greatest amount of vulnerable body mass.

"I don't know why I'm still disappointed," he hissed, stalking her. "I should fucking know better by now."

Maggie controlled her breathing. She forced calm on herself. She knew better than to try and defend herself. She'd just have to take what he'd decided she deserved and hope he left on his own. After all, she'd learned this dance well. Deliberately relaxing her joints, tightening her belly, she slid a bit farther away from the end table with the sharp edges.

Tommy's fists were balled, his shoulders rigid. "Who

the fuck do you think you are? Didn't you ever listen to a goddamn thing I said?"

No answer to that.

"I didn't expect much from you," he continued, backing her around the room. "Not when you were too pussy to be even a fucking meter maid. But I *did* expect you to understand the concept of loyalty! I did expect that you wouldn't sell out your fuckin' *family* just to make yourself famous!"

"People are being murdered, Tommy," she said, unable to keep quiet. "It used to be your job to stop that kind of thing."

He jumped so fast she didn't have a chance to duck the swing. "What the fuck do you know?" he screamed, backhanding her like a pimp on the street.

Maggie hit the wall and then the floor, her face on fire. This was going to be bad. She had to get back up. It would be worse if she didn't get back up. Tommy hated cringers.

"Do you go out there risking your life day after day having to deal with those mopes, knowing they're just going to be let back out to do it all over again?" he demanded. "Do you know what it feels like to be *laughed* at because you can't stop it? Because you can't control any of those assholes?"

"Yes," she said, regaining her feet, her voice quiet, her eyes quiet. "I do know."

"Aw, bullshit you know. You know nothin'! You hear me?"

She heard him. He was screaming six inches from her face, spittle hitting her like rain. And she was shaking and hating herself for it.

"You disgust me!" he snarled, and swung again. "You think you're better than them? Or do you care? Do you give a crap for anybody but you?"

Maggie didn't back up anymore. She huddled against the wall, trying to clear her head. Trying to answer him without inciting him. Trying not to play his game.

"How long have you known?" she asked, not able to make any better eye contact than Sean had the day before.

"How long have you known this has been going on?"

"Known?" he gasped in startled laughter. "I been fuckin' applauding!"

Well, that answered the question of whether he ever would have helped her.

"Stand up for yourself!" he screamed, punching now, chest and belly, crouched before her like a street thug. "You're such a coward you only hit a person behind his back? You only sneak around in corners and accuse good people who got more guts than you ever will? Your friends, you bitch! You may not be a cop, but you should understand how to stand by the brothers you work with. I taught you that. I *taught* you that, goddamn it!"

He was winding up for a belt that would knock her head into the hallway. Maggie couldn't help flinching. She must have closed her eyes, because the next thing she knew, Tommy was yelping in surprise.

"What the fuck is *this*?" he screeched.

Maggie opened her eyes to find Wheezer, her newest rescuee, firmly attached to the thigh of Tommy's pants.

Maggie damn near laughed. The dog wasn't making a sound. Just chewing frantically, his feet inches from the floor.

"My protector, I guess," she muttered through a swollen lip.

And Tommy, who had been threatening her just seconds ago, who thought nothing of battering his child, his wives and any cat within a six-state radius, burst out laughing.

Gently, he picked up the dog. "You're quite the mighty man, aren't you?" he demanded.

Wheezer grimaced and snapped at his hand.

Tommy just laughed again and set him down like fine bone china.

Then he pointed at Maggie.

"I don't want to hear another word about this. Not one more fuckin' word. You're finished."

Maggie didn't bother to answer. Tommy didn't expect her to anyway. He kicked his way out of her loft and stomped down the stairs. Wheezer trotted over to where Maggie lay against the wall and curled up into her lap.

"I guess that means I have to keep you, huh?" she said with a small smile that hurt. Then she sighed, nauseous and trembling. "Well, I guess as disasters go, this one was survivable."

She should have known better.

She was still crouched on the floor testing sore ribs when the phone rang. At seven-thirty in the morning. Nobody called at seven-thirty in the morning. Except unidentified voices and emergencies.

And, evidently, her fire captain. Maggie let her answering machine pick it up. The cap needed her out at the station ASAP.

Maggie went. She applied ice to swellings and cover-up to bruises, the first art of makeup she'd ever learned, and she headed out the door. When she walked into the captain's office half an hour later, she knew for sure she'd badly underestimated the scope of her disasters.

The captain took a quick look at her face, then simply handed her a copy of the morning *Post-Dispatch*. There, circled with the captain's own kelly green pen, was the reason for all that aching in her gut. She'd made her first appearance in Sarah Eagle's widely read local gossip column.

Whispers have reached this columnist that a certain young woman recently dubbed a heroine may very well be under investigation concerning some suspicious deaths on her watch. Nobody's talking yet, but Dr. Harrison, the city's beloved and bemusing ME, was seen ranting, and the heroine's name was definitely invoked.

Maggie kept looking at the paper, as if the words would change. So, they'd moved right past innuendo and straight to attack. And she had nobody to help her prove the truth.

"I think it might be best if you took a few shifts of vacation, Maggie," the captain was saying.

Which would only prove their case. Maggie fought to

keep a quiet face. "You immediately assume this is about me?"

"We heard from the county ME yesterday. He was asking about you, too."

Maggie just nodded. Stood. Precisely refolded the paper and placed it carefully on the captain's plywood desk right between his kids' pictures and his service award. "All right, Cap. If you think so."

Maggie was halfway out the door before the captain spoke. "Maggie? I'm sorry."

She wasn't about to be so banal as to tell him that she was too.

This time the two men weren't sitting. They were walking. Pacing actually, their steps taking them back and forth in front of the sculpture of King Louis IX that crowned Art Hill in Forest Park. Behind them rose the classic lines of the art museum the city had built for the World's Fair. Before and below them spread the misty meadows of the early-morning park.

The humidity hung like smoke close to the ground, muting the green and nestling the birds. Off in the distance, traffic hummed along the highways and feeder streets as the city went to work. But here, the park still held its peace.

"Who the hell's responsible for this?" the older man demanded, waving a copy of the same page Maggie O'Brien had just set back on her captain's desk some twelve miles away.

"I don't know," the other said, following as the other man turned a lap and returned the same way.

"You don't know. You don't know. Do you know who called her with that threat?"

"Probably somebody at the hospital."

"And you don't think it'll work. That the threat and the newspaper won't keep her quiet."

"It'll just piss her off. Maggie's sense of justice is stronger than her instinct for self-preservation. If only real criminals had died, she might not have started digging. But Montana Bob is somebody she couldn't ignore. And whoever thought of trying to scare her with these new deaths really screwed up."

"I know. I know. We should have stopped this a long time ago. We have to do it soon. Soon."

"Can't be soon enough for me."

That fast, the first man skidded to a halt and turned on his partner. "Then why the hell did you tell her you were suspended? How are you supposed to manage outside the system?"

"I told her I'm suspended from the force. Not from seeing her. I figured that would make it easier for me not to have to share . . . delicate information with her. If she thought I were still active, she'd damn well be asking to share my computer and the file room. You know that."

He got a nod, a sigh of capitulation. "Whatever you do, keep her away from us. And get ahold of what she knows."

"We're running out of time."

"By five tonight, every news service in North America is going to be on to this. The good thing is that we have her to offer up."

There was a silence.

The older man turned. "You have a problem with that?"

"You know I do."

"Well, the alternative is unthinkable. So you better get over your problem."

"Yes, sir."

The older man smiled, a knowing, hard smile that most of the public would never have recognized. "I thought you'd see it that way."

And then he left Sean Delaney alone to look out over the mists, where there weren't even any hawks to comfort him.

CHAPTER 13

The thing Maggie most wanted to do after leaving the fire station was find a dark, close place, just like Ming, and curl up into a ball. What she did instead was stop by a Starbucks for a cafe mocha and a *Post-Dispatch*. Then she drove back into the city to face her nursing supervisor.

"Yes," Shara said, tossing the folded paper back across her desk. "I've seen it."

Maggie reached around one of the myriad Precious Moments nurse statues on Shara's desk to retrieve the paper. Precious Moments and a Glamour Shot of Shara's twelve-year-old that made her look like a slut from Jerry Springer. Interesting. More terrifying, Maggie decided, than all those masks in Dr. Harrison's office.

Come to think of it, she thought, considering the offices she was destined to visit in a forty-eight-hour period, she could well do a comprehensive study of office desks. When Sean had been in Homicide, his desk had held a Christmas tree fashioned from shotgun cartridges and glitter. Zen's console carried one picture of Jesus and one of all her grandkids. The SWAT lieutenant's, if she remembered, held his kids' drawings and a statue of St. Michael, patron saint of police.

"What's your point?" her supervisor demanded in that petulant tone that declared she was overworked and under-appreciated.

Maggie blinked, doing her best to refocus on the issue at hand. "I want to know how that's going to affect my work here."

She wasn't even sure she wanted to work right now. If she didn't come in, she'd lose her access to what was going on. But if she didn't come in, she wouldn't have the chance to be involved in any more murders, either. She already wasn't sleeping. She certainly didn't need more help down the road to self-destruction.

"Well, since I know that none of my staff would deliberately hurt a *patient*," Shara demurred, "I don't see that there would be any point in asking you to leave right now."

Maggie nodded, not sure what else she wanted to say.

"Of course," Shara continued, "Legal is looking into the matter. Until I get word from them, I expect you to behave yourself."

Maggie wanted to laugh. Behave herself how? "I won't kill anybody, if that's what you mean."

From the color on Shara's face, it obviously wasn't. "I mean don't spread around your own slander about Blymore."

Ah. That behave herself.

Maggie got to her feet. "Thanks for seeing me."

"I'm not doing you any favors by letting you work. Nobody wants you out on that hall."

"I know that, too."

"Just so you do."

Maggie turned for the door, even more tired than before.

"And Maggie."

She stopped just shy of the door. Shara still wasn't looking at her. She was stroking that porcelain nurse like a talisman.

"Your time on the computers and in medical records will be strictly monitored." Now, she looked up, and Maggie saw the steel her supervisor hid beneath that perfectly bland exterior. "Understood?"

Maggie nodded. "Understood." Maybe she could get Sean to hack into something for her. Or maybe she could move to Wyoming and start all over again where nobody knew her.

And she didn't know any murderers.

Maggie was right. The lieutenant's desk in the SWAT offices held framed crayon drawings and St. Michael holding a police hat in his hands. Maggie sat before him, thinking that it was the most comfortable desk she'd faced in several days.

"This is all about your friend Montana Bob, isn't it?" the lieutenant asked, giving her puffy face that quick, nervous look that betrayed embarrassment.

"It started with him," Maggie admitted, now scratchy and impatient with exhaustion. She needed some sleep, and all she was getting was coffee. It didn't make for a calm interview, especially when it was the most important one of the morning. "But I've started looking around on my own, and I'm convinced that he was right. People are being murdered, Lieu."

"Do you have proof?"

"I have a collection of coincidences that are just too fantastic to be ignored."

"But no proof."

"No."

"Tell me about them."

She did, knowing he would listen without prejudice. Knowing she could count on his discretion.

He sat very still, a pencil caught in his hand, the light seeming to sink clear through his light eyes. And he kept his silence until she was finished.

Then he shook his head. "I don't know, Maggie. It seems a little far-fetched to me."

Maggie didn't realize how much she'd counted on his support until he said that. She damn near slumped to the floor.

"And the phone calls?"

He shrugged. "Might just as easily been somebody

showing you how easy it is to suspect an innocent person."

Maggie nodded, almost ready to get to her feet.

"I have to agree, sweetheart."

Maggie turned to see her uncle John leaning against the door. Broad, solid, sweet, his white hair softening the sharp, mahogany lines of his face. Maggie wanted to smile. She wanted to curl up on his lap just as she had when she'd been a girl and hold on to his shirt with both hands.

"Hi, Uncle John."

He frowned. "What happened to you, honey?"

Leave it to Uncle John to be the first to speak out about the patch job she'd done on her face. "Loyalty is much prized in certain places," she said.

His expression darkened. "And you don't want to say anything?"

Maggie felt even worse. After all the years she'd protected the Bimbos, protected the abused women in her care, coercing, jimmying, pleading them into taking the first step to stopping their abuse, she couldn't call Tommy on her own. He was still her daddy. He still made her feel small and needy.

"Do you?" the lieutenant asked, knowing better than Maggie'd imagined what they were discussing.

Maggie turned back to him with a small smile. "Family business, Lieu. It's okay."

For a second, he just watched her. "What do you want to do, Maggie?"

She sucked in a breath. "About what?"

"The team."

She went very still. "I *want* to stay on the team. Do you want me to?"

"Of course. Do you think any of them are involved?"

That she didn't even have to think about. "No."

"Do you trust them?"

"Of course. Do they trust me?"

"Yes." His grin was quick and telling. "I already asked. If you hadn't come in on your own, I would have called you."

She nodded. "You know how I feel about the team, Lieu. I'd never do anything to jeopardize it. If you want me off, I'll go."

She saw him consult Uncle John with his eyes. She saw the answer before he gave it. She was able to breathe for the first time since walking into her loft that morning.

"Tell you what," he said. "If we get a 1040, you be my secondary medic. Otherwise, business as usual. Next training session is at Northeast City High School next week. We're doing that school shooting mock-up." Shrugging, he grinned. "Hell, we'll all be camouflaged. Who's gonna see you?"

She scowled. "Every reporter in the Midwest, once that column gets out."

He shrugged. "We'll deal with it."

Maggie climbed slowly to her feet, altogether too familiar with masking the discomfort. "Thanks, Lieu. I owe you."

"You owe me, hand this off to IA or Homicide."

She shook her head. "As soon as I have something concrete. 'Til then, I think I'd be wasting time and paperwork."

There wasn't a whole lot he could say to it.

There wasn't a whole lot Maggie could do about it. If she got dropped from the ED, she would lose her access to patients. If she didn't come up with some kind of slam dunk on evidence, she'd go down without a ripple. If she didn't do it all soon, she'd lose every friend she ever had.

Well, the two or three still left to her.

Which was why she held out such hope for that county death investigator. He'd seemed so levelheaded. So willing to listen to her. Maybe when she saw him the next day, she'd get some cooperation. But 'til then, she was going home to bed.

She got as far as her answering machine.

"Who the fuck do you think you are?" the first voice demanded.

The rest of the messages were much in the same vein. Except for the threats. Some vague, some perfectly specific.

Some Maggie even believed enough to save on tape. Then she rerecorded her own message.

"This is Maggie O'Brien. I'm not answering the phone right now. If this is about an interview, no. If this is about a great opportunity, still no. If this is about a threat, you should know that I have caller ID. Thanks. Have a good day."

Then she went to bed.

She didn't get very much sleep. On the other hand, there weren't many messages left on her machine.

Another desk, Maggie thought. She was damn well getting tired of desks. This one had a red coffee mug that had LAST RESPONDER printed on it, and an ugly gray ceramic ashtray filled with jelly beans. Maggie snatched a green one and prepared to face the county death investigator.

"You were going to tell me your theory," Jim Light said, snatching his own as he settled his comfortable bulk into a chair.

Maggie would have preferred to talk to the medical examiner, but he was out of town at a trial. Hell, she would have preferred that the death investigation systems of city and county had been combined like the SWAT team, so she only had to humiliate herself once. But that wasn't going to happen in this politically neolithic town during her lifetime. So she sat down with her new friend and prepared to repeat her routine.

A nice, solid, ex-cop kind of guy was Jim Light, with a square head and a toothy smile. Strong grip and receding steel gray hair. The kind of look that belonged on a film priest.

"You really want to hear it? So far, it's been a hard sell."

He shrugged. "Well, I'll like anything better than what I have now. You realize, of course, that if you hadn't called us first on Yancy Butler, your name would have been at the top of the list I'd have given to Homicide?"

Maggie stopped chewing. In fact, she damn near choked. "What did you find?"

He sighed. "Nothing definite. But Yancy didn't die of that insignificant fracture. His potassium was way up, but so are most postmortem potassiums."

"But you believe he was murdered."

Jim took in a breath. "Proving it is an entirely different matter."

Maggie knew that her smile wasn't pretty. "You're talking to the queen of entirely different matters."

"So tell me," he said, grabbing another jelly bean, "what you think."

So Maggie did. Chapter and verse, with readings from her purloined charts and references to arrest reports. Hell, after this many recitations, she was thinking of typing it all up and passing it around like handouts.

But through it all, the investigator just listened. Quietly. Passively. Silently. And then he shook his head.

"And you haven't found any proof."

"I haven't even found a decent pattern, except for the fact that they were all on The List and my gut says they shouldn't have died. I was hoping that ME's reports might give me some better answers." Maggie let her gaze slip away, just that much. "I was also hoping if you agreed to help, you'd get in touch with the city ME's office and share information to come up with a better pattern than I could."

"Did you make that proposition to Dr. Harrison?"

Maggie had to grin. "I'm not that brave."

Again, he shook his head.

Maggie deflated. "You don't believe me."

"Do I think there's some great cabal of city and county police and emergency medical personnel bent on ridding us of nefarious citizens?" Jim asked. "Then no, I can't say that I do. But there has to be a better explanation for Yancy Butler's death than 'oops.' So I'm willing to listen. Just how many of those names you've collected belong on our doorstep?"

"Four so far. Urban McGinley, Mary Ann McGregor, Yancy, and Mrs. Edna Quinn."

Jim did a quick look up. "Who you also called me about."

Maggie nodded. "Whom I also called you about."

"Well, what the hell did she do that was so bad?"

Maggie couldn't quite look at him. "She was handy when I needed to be taught a lesson."

The investigator sucked in a startled breath. "You're kidding."

"I told you. There aren't just bad people dying anymore."

Jim shook his head again, really troubled. "Do you know that Mrs. Quinn's family has talked about disinterring her and getting a fresh opinion?"

"I hope they do."

"Do you know that they also have your name?"

"I imagine that since that little item in yesterday's paper, everybody has my name."

For a long second, he just stared at her. Then, evidently his favorite move, he shook his head again. "Are you really willing to put your own neck in the noose to prove your theory?"

Maggie shrugged. "If I can find proof of one murder, maybe I can get the rest of the cases reopened. And remember, I called you first about Mrs. Quinn and Yancy."

"Something not unheard of from past murderers."

Maggie waited. She watched as he wrote down the names. As he doodled. As he shook his head a couple more times.

"I can't promise you a thing. But I'll sure check our files."

"And have your boss call Dr. Harrison in the city?"

"Don't push your luck."

Well, at least he hadn't thrown her out on her ass. Maggie climbed yet again to her feet and made her aching way out the door, nursing bag and purse in hand. She'd been there over an hour, which meant that by the time she made it out to the parking lot, dusk was just beginning to settle. Distracted by the fact that she was in dire need of aspirin, cold packs, and a fresh angle at her evidence, Maggie didn't notice who was waiting for her until she reached her car.

"Any luck with the death investigator?"

Maggie skidded to an ungainly halt, her nursing bag swinging like a pendulum at her side. Sitting on the hood of the Camry next to Maggie's Volkswagen like a kid waiting for the drive-in was her favorite reporter, Susan Jacobsmeyer. This time, Susan was wearing jeans and a T-shirt. Loafers. Straight hair. No makeup.

No bullshit.

Maggie tilted her head in consideration. "Ah. I see that you've decided the little girl lost look wouldn't work this time."

Susan's smile was bright and sharp. "I do whatever it takes. I figured a woman like you would understand."

Oddly enough, Maggie did. Especially when she saw the sharp brain the reporter finally betrayed in her gaze.

"I'm sorry about the leak this morning," Susan said, sliding off her hood.

"Because she scooped your scoop?"

A shrug. "Partly. Mostly because I wanted the chance to talk to you first. You know that there are people out there who are howling for your blood."

Maggie shrugged. "And?"

"And there are two theories currently circulating. One, that you're blaming somebody else for your own acts, and two, that some enterprising soul accused you of your crimes to pay you back for turning on your own for no reason. Either way, there are some unexplained deaths that belong to somebody, and that's making people very nervous."

"And you want a piece of the action."

"Why not? I can get information you can't. I can go places you can't."

"You can be there when I confess that theory A is accurate, and I was only laying a smoke screen to camouflage my own nefarious activities."

"If I'm lucky."

Maggie's smile was genuine now. She liked this sharp-tongued Susan a hell of a lot better than Reporter Barbie Susan.

"I'll think about it."

"Think fast. I've already got some stuff. And more questions—"

"I'm questioned out for today."

"—like how the daughter of a man who got bounced off the force not nine months ago for brutality should make cracking dirty cops such a crusade."

"Or whether she's just carrying on her father's work?" Another bright, saucy grin. "Or that."

"Dig a little deeper about that charge against Tommy," Maggie said. "When you find out the real story, let me know."

"And then?"

Maggie shook her head. "I'll let you know."

"What happened to your face?"

Maggie unlocked her car and opened the door. "Acne."

Then she left the reporter with one raised eyebrow and no answers.

Maggie did drive away, though, with something niggling at her. Something she couldn't quite pull up to the front, something the reporter had stirred up. Maggie kept thinking about patterns. About the fact that she was sure she was missing something important right in front of her.

She thought about it so much that when she reached her loft twenty minutes later, she pulled out her charts yet one more time. She copied again the names, the dates, the causes of death. The reasons for their being on The List.

Mary Ann McGregor—drunk driver,
killed teenager
cardiac arrest.
Sancho Martinez—gangbanger deluxe
gunshot wound to the head.
Snake Pilson—gangbanger deluxe the second

exsanguination from knife wound to heart
Urban McGinley — prolific pedophile
beating, closed head injury
OG "Big Dawg" Dwayne Carver — gangbanger boss
multiple gunshot wounds exsanguination
Montana Bob — psychotic with inconvenient knowledge
cocaine poisoning
Jimmy Krebs — child abuse, murder
no final diagnosis

She added the people who had died since she'd started
looking, the people who hadn't had time to make it to The
List, or who hadn't deserved a place.

Yancy Bill Butler IV — methmaker
no final diagnosis
Edna Quinn — chronic body failure
cardiac arrhythmia
Hugh Culpepper — wife beater
exsanguination from knife wound, possible OD
anticoagulants
Levon Repton — assault and murder
sudden arrhythmia

Eleven possible deaths. Four hospitals, two death investigator systems, three police departments, and at least a
thousand combined health-care workers. And no one name
with the decency to jump out for her benefit.

Maggie considered her list. She considered every bit of
information she'd gleaned from every chart, arrest report,
and logbook. She realized that without even one final diagnosis from an ME's office, she was stumped.

The proof, as they said, was in the pudding. Or in this
case, the autopsy. There was nothing else for her to find in
the material she had.

She still had some List names to check. She could pile
up more coincidences, more unanswered questions, more
theory. But only the MEs had a shot of giving her answers.

If they believed her.

In the meantime, though, whatever pattern she thought she should see, eluded her.

Maggie was getting to her feet with a mind toward pasta, when she stopped.

Halfway up. Frozen. Her attention still on the list before her.

Like a gift from God, it was there.

Not the pattern she'd wanted. Something else. Some one thing she should have seen all along. Something she could, indeed, investigate.

Montana Bob.

Cocaine.

Good God, Maggie thought, plopping back down into her chair. *How could I have missed it?*

How the hell did a homeless guy afford enough of that kind of shit to die from it?

Jesus, it had been there all along. She'd kept saying she couldn't find solid proof that any of the deaths had been suspicious. And every time, she'd thought how odd it was that Montana Bob had died of cocaine abuse, when he swore he never touched drugs. When the Haldol he'd always been religious about taking hadn't been in his bloodstream.

For just a second, Maggie hoped. She stared at Montana Bob's name, willing the information to change, so she couldn't be disappointed again.

But it didn't. She should have at least looked. At least asked somebody besides the death investigators who had never known Bob, or the police, who hadn't cared.

Quickly Maggie pulled over the copy of Bob's chart. For the first time, she didn't flip back to the lab results. She scanned the personal information sheet. The data kept in their computer for all Bob's visits. Address, Medicare information, history.

Telephone number of nearest kin.

The kind of kin who might have had some consistent

contact with Bob. Who might even have cleaned out his apartment and have his meager possessions.

Including a Haldol bottle. Or some evidence of cocaine.

Maggie would start there. Then she'd call the VA, where Bob got his psych treatment, and ask about his medical compliance. Then she'd head down to Harbor Light, where the homeless guys lined up for lunch, and ask if anybody remembered Bob getting into cocaine. And how he'd managed it.

Betty Wilson. Bob's daughter. Maggie checked the name and address and found that Betty lived in St. Louis. Damn near holding her breath, Maggie placed the call.

And got Betty.

"Sure, I have my dad's stuff," she said when asked. "Why?"

Maggie finally breathed. "I'm having trouble understanding how he died."

She was met with a pause. "You, too? Did you know him?"

"Very well. And I can't imagine him taking cocaine."

Betty's laugh was dry. "I can't imagine him wasting his Night Train money. Daddy was a drinker. It's what got him tossed out of the FBI."

Maggie stopped breathing again. "He really was an FBI agent?"

"Sure. I have the citations. But Daddy . . . well . . ."

"I know. Could I come by and look at his things?"

"Sure. I'll be here all day tomorrow."

Maggie hung up and smiled. Patted Montana Bob's chart as if it were a particularly bright child. Or if she were.

Then she decided it was time to celebrate. Considering she lived in Soulard, that shouldn't be too hard. She couldn't swing a dead cat without hitting some kind of music. Blues, jazz, rock, bagpipes.

Bagpipes. An accordion and a fiddle. Skirling minor keys of loss and redemption. Maybe, Maggie thought, I'll just take a while to regroup and plan.

It was a sure bet she wouldn't be welcomed down at the

Toe Tag. Maybe she'd lift one with her neighbors at McGurk's instead. Grabbing her keys, her purse, and her new close and personal friend, the bag full of evidence, Maggie headed for her car.

As she parked a couple minutes later on Russell, Maggie heard the musicians tuning up across the street. Just what she needed. Guinness and angst. Closing up the car, she stepped out into the darkening street.

Humidity softened the streets. Music drifted from open doorways. The air lay heavy with hops from the Brewery. Maggie was busy thinking about how she could wheedle confidential information out of the VA the next day and didn't pay attention to the traffic.

She'd made it a third of the way across Russell when she heard an engine rev. She hadn't noticed a car. Hadn't even thought of the traffic on a sleepy Monday evening. She stopped at the curb, thinking that would be enough. She turned toward the sound to see that the car wasn't just approaching. It was accelerating.

Toward her.

A sedan.

A dark, late-model Chevy Cavalier sedan.

Maggie turned and jumped. She felt the glancing impact at her hip and knew what it was to fly.

Bricks, streetlight, concrete. Asphalt. A sweeping arc of it, and Maggie saw it in an instant.

Tuck and roll, she thought desperately. Tuck and roll. She tucked and rolled. Asphalt scraped her face. Her hands and knees. Her sore, sore ribs. But she rolled neatly out of it and landed curled against a streetlamp and decided not to move.

Maggie heard the car zoom past and knew that nobody had seen her get hit. She knew, in a moment of instinctive lucidity, that this hadn't been a planned attack. After all, who could figure she'd be there right then, when she hadn't known herself?

An impulse, she decided. A cop sitting incognito in the neighborhood, as they often did to keep an eye on things, who recognized her in the dying late-summer light.

Probably just like the first murder. A moment of desperation when it all seemed so unfair. When it seemed that, just this once, the person wanted theirs back.

And so some gangbanger who'd murdered children was now dead, and the neighborhood was a little more safe.

And Maggie, who'd had the nerve to point fingers at the people who acted out their frustrations, lay on the sidewalk aching and alone.

CHAPTER 14

Out in Chesterfield at the offices of Mardick, Inc., Sam Mardick blew his nose and shut off his computer. It was long past time to go home. He wasn't getting anything done, and he wanted to get a good stiff drink and lie down. He had to be the only sorry asshole in St. Louis who could catch a cold in August. Not only that, he had to catch it the day before the big company picnic at Tower Grove Park.

Sam loved the picnic. Softball and beer and volleyball with the women wearing short shorts and halters, like his own personal company team uniform.

Sam loved to look at women. He loved to drink beer. He fucking hated Mardick, Inc. He hated being the dumpy, balding son of a charismatic business giant. A six-foot-tall, granite-fucking-chinned business giant.

Not that Sam quite knew what he wanted to be instead. After all, he really didn't do much work. His old man had seen to that. Sam had a wife in Wildwood to take care of the house and the kids. He had a mistress tucked away in Clayton who told him he was a real man. He had a key to every private club in town, which he wouldn't have if he'd been born to a family of welders. He had no worries.

It didn't make him any happier.

He blew his nose again, thinking that not one of the company women would let him get close tomorrow when he was sneezing like a pig. Didn't matter. The beer man'd sure as hell let him get close.

Down in Soulard, Maggie joined the crowd in McGurk's. Pushed herself off the ground, brushed off her ripped jeans and T-shirt with shaking, scraped hands, gathered her purse and bag to her like unhappy chicks, and finished her aborted walk across the street in an ungainly limp. There was alcohol inside to deaden the pain. Soap and water to clean the scrapes. A fiddle and some pipes inviting her to share their misery and joy.

She accepted.

It was where Sean found her a couple hours or so later, nursing her fourth or fifth half-and-half and thinking that, dammit, maybe what would be fun would be a one-night stand with an Irish musician. That piper looked sweet and sad and sexy as hell in his black clothes and long black hair. Maggie bet he didn't know any city cops. Well, not in a good way, anyway. She bet he could talk about something other than perps and mopes and gomers. She bet he could talk about freedom and ghosts and sheep and green fields. Even if he was only from Chicago.

"Maggie?"

She really didn't want Sean interrupting her first decent fantasy in years. Not with that, "I've come to make sure you're okay" look on his face. After all, even though she'd had a rough evening of it, she'd also made her first real progress in a while.

She'd protected her place on the SWAT team. She'd talked two separate medical examiners into taking a second look at some of the deaths on her list. She'd discovered a new angle on Montana Bob's death and made an appointment to see his daughter. She'd even arranged a ride over to the Wilsons' with Susan Jacobsmeyer, whom she'd called right after getting out of the bathroom and twenty minutes of scraping gravel out of her elbows and palms.

"Susan?" she'd greeted the reporter, the phone tucked

against her shoulder as she used her hands to apply the Neosporin she kept in her purse for occasions just like this. "Maggie O'Brien."

There was no hesitation in the reporter's answer. "So your old man really took a dive for a kid who'd only been on the force for three weeks?"

"Yep."

"Well. I guess I take back at least five or six of the misconceptions I've been laboring under these last few weeks."

"In that case, I accept your offer of help. Be at my loft at ten tomorrow, and you can help me go through the personal effects of a paranoid schizophrenic who just might have stumbled over a conspiracy we sane people never saw coming."

"I'll be there."

And so Maggie had hung up and ordered her first pint. And taken her first look at that piper. Who was making her happy, too.

Unlike Sean.

"Go away," she said to her best friend when he slid onto the stool next to her.

Sean caught hold of her chin and tried to turn her his way. She refused to let him.

"What happened to you?" he asked, suddenly stormy. "Tommy?"

Sean was the only person who'd ever successfully sucker-punched Tommy O'Brien. It had been once when Maggie had shown up at the Delaneys' looking just like she did tonight. Before she'd learned to manage better on her own. Which she'd done because after that sucker punch, Tommy had put Sean in the hospital.

Maggie squinted through the smoke. "Why are you here? Come to think of it, you've been showing up a lot lately. Usually I have to find you. Are you following me?"

"I heard about the article in the paper and came to talk to you. Saw your car here and took a chance. Now, what happened?"

Maggie turned her attention back to the music and shrugged. "I met with a wee bit of an accident on the way across the street."

See? she thought. I'm even beginning to sound Irish. Real Irish. Not that sentimental crap Tommy listened to about taking back the country with guns. With Tommy, everything was about taking something with guns.

"What accident?" Sean asked, looking around, as if he could see it.

Maggie shrugged, wondering why she wasn't more upset. Wondering if she would be later. "The accident that happened when somebody who didn't think that the newspaper piece was punishment enough tried to run me down."

For that she got a long silence from Sean and a wink from the piper. Maggie grinned and winked back.

"Is this what it's like?" she asked.

Sean stared at her. "What?"

"Your flings. Is this what it feels like to decide to screw other women for no apparent reason?"

"You want to screw other women?"

"No. I want to screw *him.*"

Sean took one look at the piper and lifted the almost finished pint from Maggie's hand. "I think you're more upset than you think."

Maggie sighed. "Probably."

She didn't bother to interfere when Sean paid her shot and guided her out the door. She didn't even apologize to the musician, who was bent back over his pipes and didn't see her leave. It was okay. The bands here played six-week gigs. She could always change her mind later.

"Maggie," Sean said, "you have to stop this."

Maggie blinked at the fully dark night outside. The cicadas were softer, she thought. Probably dying of exhaustion. "Stop what?"

He kept her guided down the street. "This investigation. Give it to somebody else. Anybody. You're gonna get hurt."

She forbore telling him she was already hurt. In more

ways than ribs and elbows. "Who?" she asked. "I've talked
to two separate Medical Examiners' Offices, my supervisor,
my lieutenant, and you, and so far none of you have been
a big help. Where do you think I'd have better luck?"

"City Internal Affairs."

"That's what the lieu suggested. But cops aren't the ones
committing the murders."

"But they're the ones making sure the victims get into
the hands of the murderers."

Maggie skidded to a halt right in the middle of a cross-
walk. Sean dragged her along as if he didn't notice.

"I knew that," she mused, trying to work past the fog
left by the last few days and the last few beers. "I *knew*
that."

Something important lurked beneath that knowledge.
Something she'd let go in the glare of finding Montana
Bob's daughter. Something that lived in those notes she'd
been so carefully gathering.

But tonight wasn't the night she was going to un-
earth it.

"All right," she said to Sean. "I'll go. If you go with
me."

"Done."

Even she wasn't drunk enough to miss the fact that Sean
had just done a personal one-eighty.

"Why?" she asked. "Why do you think suddenly they
might help? You didn't even want me to talk to *you* before."

She saw the lie in his eyes long before he said it. Because they'd blow her off long enough to make her happy,
was what he wanted to say. Because he was throwing her
a lifeline that was attached to air.

Why did he keep disappointing her?

Why did she stay with him anyway?

"You have to start somewhere," was what he said instead, as if he didn't know she'd already recognized the
dodge.

A week ago, Maggie might have told Sean about her

appointment with Betty Wilson and her deal with Susan Jacobsmeyer. Tonight she sucked in enough air to make her dizzy and stayed silent.

After all, she'd kept things from Sean before. She'd just never kept everything from him.

It was only fair, though. She didn't even want to contemplate what he was keeping from her.

So she followed him down the street and up the stairs to her loft, and she prayed that at least for a while, they could pretend that everything was all right between them. Just like old times.

Maggie had actually found a smile, albeit a wry one, at the thought, when she got the door open to her loft. The smile died. Behind her, Sean cursed. Quietly, foully, and succinctly.

There would be no pretending tonight.

All the beer in Maggie's stomach threatened revolt. Her eyes watered. Her hands shook.

The car out on Russell had been an impulse. A stupid, angry mistake. This, though, was an act of cold deliberation. This was a violation.

"Motherfuckin' assholes," Sean breathed, his head swiveling to take in the scene.

Maggie didn't budge. She couldn't. Somebody had come in after she'd left for McGurk's and draped dead rats over her furniture. On her turntable, her microwave, her good stuffed chair. Her bed. One was lying with its dead rat head on her goose down pillow. Another hung by its neck from the slowly turning ceiling fan.

There was the thick scent of mutilation in the air, and the click of unbalanced fan blades. Shadows on the floor. Maggie sucked in a breath, cold sober, and tried to control the shakes.

She closed her eyes, seeing other shadows. Other destruction. Then she looked again to find only rats.

It goaded her into action.

"What a cliché," she drawled.

Dropping her bag and purse by the door, she stepped

over rat carcasses and stalked toward the kitchen. Sean remained in the doorway, unable to take his eyes off the hanging rat that turned in a slow, obscene circle over his head.

"What did you expect them to leave?" he demanded. "Ferrets?"

Maggie pulled out two oven mitts and tossed one across the room to Sean. "Muskrats. Weasels. Wolverines. Something with more imagination."

In her loft. Her one last refuge on earth. Where her animals hid from surprises and comforted her in her sleep. Where, when he felt like it, Sean made love to her.

Maggie spun on him, furious.

"And you came to see me tonight, again, why?" she snapped.

Sean went white. His eyes met hers dead-on in fine outrage. He gaped. Maggie shrugged and tossed him a garbage bag.

"You have to admit," she said, trying so damn hard to keep her voice from shaking as badly as her hands as the bile built up in her throat like compressed lava, "the timing does look a weensy bit coincidental."

One by one, she picked up each rat and dumped it into her bag with a dull thump.

"I swear—!"

Maggie waved him off, forgetting that she had a rat in her hand. "I believe you."

And then, without a word, she bent back to the job. Sean slapped on his mitt and helped, both of them working in total silence. She should get new locks, Maggie thought, and then almost burst out laughing. She was dealing with cops. They didn't need to worry 'bout no stinking locks.

She found Ming curled like a donut beneath the couch and Wheezer quivering in the bathroom. She settled them both and bagged every rat she could find. She handed her trash bag to Sean so he could take it out to the Dumpster. She almost locked the door when he left. She didn't.

No matter what Sean was or did, Maggie couldn't lock

the door against him. She might not be able to trust or talk to him, but she needed him. She had always needed him. More, she knew, than he needed her.

Which made her shake and sweat even worse.

So the minute Sean had turned down the hallway toward the back stairs, Maggie walked over to her mantel and picked up one of her latest collection of hideous porcelain animals. A pink-and-white pig. She lifted it, looked it in its tiny black eyes, and swallowed. Than she smashed it into smithereens onto the tiles in front of her fireplace.

Smash!

She picked up another. A gray-and-green elephant with a palm tree in its trunk.

Smash!

A pug dog with sunglasses.

Smash!

The sound was so thoroughly satisfying in the echoing wood-and-brick space that she kept it up. Shards peppered her shins. The real animals skidded back into hiding. Her porcelain once again disappeared into dust.

"I always wondered what those were for," Sean said, obviously back.

Maggie didn't answer. She had ten left.

"I also wondered how you vented your rage. I'm glad to see you're being constructive. Those things are grotesque."

"I have no rage," Maggie said in perfect, calm tones as she hurled a purple hippo into atoms. "I'm a little disappointed."

Which would probably account for the tears soaking her shirt.

"Of course you're in a rage. Who wouldn't be?"

"Me." Smash! "I'm Little Zen, remember?"

He stepped closer. "Don't be ridiculous, Maggie. You have every right—"

"No!" she interrupted, pointing at him with a black-and-white cow wearing a cowboy hat. "No. I don't."

She smashed it.

"Why?" Sean asked.

She refused to face him. "Because then I'd be like *him*."

She managed to smash one more animal before Sean caught her. "No," he disagreed, his voice just as calm, infinitely more gentle. "You'd only be like him if you hurt somebody else. You only hurt *you*, Mags."

Maggie yanked free. "I—"

Smash!

"don't—"

Smash!

"feel—"

Smash!"

"—rage!"

Sean took a step closer. "Even when somebody tried to set you up for murder?"

Smash!

"Even then."

"Even when that asshole burned his baby?"

Smash! Smash!

"Even then."

"I think you're afraid of the wrong thing, Maggie," he said, hands on her shoulders. Not restraining. Supporting. "You have more right to be mad than anybody in this city. Go ahead and be mad."

Maggie smashed the last dog and knew it wouldn't be enough.

So she turned to Sean, who would only be there when he wanted. Who couldn't keep his hands off other women. Who knew her better than anyone on the earth and failed to hold it against her. And because he knew her, he smiled and held open his arms.

"Rage can be a great aphrodisiac, ya know," he offered.

Maggie couldn't stop crying. She couldn't get close to her bed, either. So the two of them scrubbed her loft with Lysol and swept the porcelain remains into a dustpan. Then, when Maggie couldn't stand on her feet anymore, Sean tucked her against his shoulder and let her fall asleep with him on her pull-out couch, her face puffy and red, and her

head hammering with the unaccustomed tears that still pud-
dled on her neck.

It was deep into the morning hours when Sean carefully
disentangled himself from Maggie and climbed off the pull-
out bed. The kitchen light was still on, and the cat was
curled up at Maggie's feet. Wheezer hadn't been seen again
since that first porcelain atrocity had gone powder on the
floor.

Even so, Sean tiptoed carefully across the hardwood
floor that gleamed softly in the small light. He took a second to look at the now-empty mantelpiece and shook his
head. Then, skirting the furniture with the ease of long
practice, he padded to the door.

He didn't go through it, though. Instead, after he'd
climbed that one step off the living room, he turned to catch
a glimpse of Maggie where she lay sprawled and silent on
the tumbled sheets.

Brave Maggie.

Passionate, loyal, driven Maggie.

His best friend and greatest challenge.

He tiptoed back and bent over her. "I'm sorry," he whispered, and dropped a quick kiss atop her tumbled hair.

The look on Sean's face never changed as he turned
away from her and walked over to retrieve her nursing bag.
Then padding back across the floor, he opened the door to
the bathroom. He gave Maggie one last look. Then, shutting
himself in, he sat on the toilet and laid the heavy bag on
his knees. And while Maggie slept off the first crying jag
Sean had seen from her in over ten years, he carefully read
through every piece of evidence she'd collected.

The next morning Sean woke Maggie with a smile, a cup
of coffee, and a couple of codeine. Maggie took them all,
then took ten minutes to manage the climb off the couch.

After that, it was only a matter of minutes before she made it into the shower and warm water therapy.

She was standing there, head down, hands on the wall, when she saw the flash. Her eyes popped open. She turned her head just in time to be blinded by another flash.

"What the fuck are you doing?" she growled.

"Evidence," Sean said without heat. "In case you need it."

"Nobody is going to see naked pictures of me for any reason, Delaney," she said. "Now get the hell out."

"We're due at Internal Affairs in fifteen minutes."

Maggie saw the bruises and scrapes when she was in the shower. She saw her face when she got out. Not too bad, really, considering all the insults it had suffered. Another layer of camouflage, a little more Neosporin, and she could go on. After all, she'd been sore before.

Besides, she had two interviews to make. And one to look forward to. She wasn't naive enough to believe she should anticipate her time with IA.

By the time she walked back out of the downtown police station an hour later, Maggie wished that, just once, she could be wrong.

Sean had introduced her to the second-in-command, Lieutenant Ames. Clean desk, no pictures, as if the guy didn't have a life other than tormenting his friends. A twenty-year veteran with pockmarked mocha skin, military hair, and indifferent eyes, Ames offered her a seat and a hearing. Sean sat quietly by, and Maggie told her story. And discovered what it was like to be a civilian facing these hard-faced men.

For the first time in her life, Maggie found herself subjected to an experience she'd only heard about. She was patronized by the police.

Hell, Ames did everything but pat her on the head and tell her not to worry her little self about it. So Maggie picked up her evidence and walked back out the door without waiting for Sean. Then she went home to stand under another shower, this time to wash off the insult she'd just suffered.

Please, God, she thought as she scrubbed. *Let Betty Wilson be better than this.*

Betty Wilson was, in fact, better. The epitome of a grade-school teacher, she was tidy, bright, and concise. A brunette Peter Pan with wire-rim glasses who lived with her husband and two children in a charming brick house in lower white-collar Glendale. Betty met Maggie and Susan at her carved-oak and stained-glass front door and offered iced tea and a seat on her chintz couch.

Maggie didn't get to either right away. Making a quick survey of the simple classic lines of good cherrywood furniture and pastel decor, she found her attention snagged by the front wall and its grouping of four hangings. Two watercolors and two photos.

The watercolors were small, intimate. Beautifully painted and definitely evocative. One was the head of a small girl. Blond and smiling and pixielike. Sweet and whimsical and sentimental, all in a very few brushstrokes. The other was darker, angrier, more unsettling. A storm catching at some trees, all swirling energy and loss of light.

Seeing the two pictures side by side, Maggie recognized them without knowing how. The best and worst of her friend Montana Bob.

"Those are Daddy's," Betty confirmed. "He was quite good."

"He was *very* good," Maggie agreed, finally taking note of the two photos. The first was a woman, Betty's older double, with soft eyes and a tiny brunette frame. The second was a standard professional black-and-white headshot. A handsome, strong-jawed young man with piercing pale eyes and a 'Nam mustache posed in the kind of precise, military-style posture endemic to law enforcement professionals.

Maggie recognized the eyes, but barely. After all, she'd

only known Bob's shell. She'd never had the chance to
enjoy the hard brain and sharp talent that had once resided
within.

And the last time she'd seen those blue eyes, they had
begged her to save herself. Because he had already been
lost.

"I'm sorry," was all Maggie could think to say.

Betty nodded. "We were so excited when he got that
apartment. For a while there, he was so . . . so Dad again.
He was trying so hard to come back. I mean, my father
held four service awards and a medal of valor from the
Bureau. That's something to say, isn't it?"

"It is. You got to see him those last few weeks?"

They were still standing there, the three of them, as if
gathered at a wake.

Betty nodded. "Sure. We wanted him to come here. This
was his house, you know. His and Mother's. But he
wouldn't . . . he was afraid he'd hurt the children if he . . .
if . . . He only began to slide after Mother died. He said she
kept him together. That she was his heart."

Maggie and Susan nodded in tandem.

"I saw him every other week when I took him up to the
VA for his doctors' appointments. He was adamant about
his schedule."

Maggie faced her square on. "And he took his medicine."

"I watched him do it." Her fleeting smile was wistful.
"He wanted accountability. He said that without it, he'd
slide. It was what he'd needed from the FBI. Why it had
taken him so long to fail."

"Do you remember the last time you watched your father
take his medicine?" Maggie asked. "By the time the incident happened, his Haldol level was zero. That would mean
he would have stopped some time before. So," she said,
remembering that awful apartment, "would the state of his
living quarters. He'd been building up that paranoia for a
while."

"Five days," Betty insisted. "The last time I saw him

was five days before he died. We refilled his prescription, and he took it with his chocolate shake at Steak 'n Shake. I saw him."

Maggie's heart rate notched up. Five days wasn't enough time to produce the dramatic results Maggie had seen. Especially if Bob had been religious about his medicine, as he'd claimed. As Betty insisted.

"Did you see any of his medicines when you cleaned out his apartment?"

Betty stopped, as if surprised. "I don't know," she admitted. "I just scooped stuff up in handfuls and dumped it in the box. The police should have seen it, though. They were here looking through his things. And the death investigator. To make sure that they didn't overlook anything."

It showed how far Maggie had come that her first thought was that what they didn't want to overlook was potentially damning evidence. Next she'd start suspecting them of planting bugs in Betty's walls to catch her conversations.

"Could we look at what you have, please?" she asked. "Maybe we'll see something they missed. After all, none of them really knew Bob like you and I did."

Betty smiled a survivor's smile, a survivor of a psych patient. Too knowing, too sad, too regretful.

And then she just walked on out to get the boxes and the iced tea she'd prepared for her interview with a nurse and a reporter.

Maggie finally sat down.

"You think somebody switched his drugs?" Susan asked, settling in next to her.

Maggie couldn't take her eyes off that tortured forest of trees across the room. "I don't know. But he sure as hell wasn't taking any Haldol. Which, if Betty's right, is impossible."

Susan sucked in a breath. "Wow. This is getting weird."

Maggie stared at her. "A growing pile of dead people isn't enough for you?"

Susan's grin was wry. "I guess not. By the way, we got

our first call from national press this morning. Be prepared."

Maggie didn't bother to answer. If she was lucky, she'd pull her answers out of the boxes Betty Wilson had culled from Bob's apartment. If not, she'd figure out something else.

"Here we go," Betty announced, settling two big cardboard boxes down on the Hepplewhite coffee table.

Trying not to betray her impatience, Maggie began to pull things out. Newspaper clippings she remembered, circled and starred and cursed at in big red letters. These about national policy, foreign intrigue, and Timothy McVeigh. No matter who was going to take over the world, Montana Bob had not liked Timothy McVeigh.

Maggie found the kind of clothing she remembered Bob wearing. Nice, but worn, tattered in places. Empty of surprises. She found a few books, mostly mysteries, and the kind of shaving equipment a careful man keeps. A man who remembers shaving as a ritual. Maybe he'd kept the symbols of his sanity to remind him, she thought.

What she did not find were pill bottles. Of any kind. Or cocaine. In any manner.

She also didn't find any reference to local news in the clippings she held. Any indication that Bob had concentrated his anxieties closer to home. She certainly didn't find enough clippings to account for the wallpapering she'd seen when she'd walked into that fetid little apartment.

Which meant that somebody might well have cleaned house after all.

But then she did find surprises. Or rather, Susan did.

"Look," the reporter said, eyes too bright for the even tone of her voice, as she held up, in order, two cameras—one the size of a credit card—and three tape recorders of varying sizes.

"Bob owned these?" Maggie asked Betty.

Betty's smile was fond. "He felt he needed them. He had the money for it. Agency pension, vet benefits, savings. He insisted we control it, which we did. But we made sure he had the things he felt he had to have ... since he ... since he wouldn't come home."

Maggie knew a lot of street guys. She knew some who had nowhere else to go, and she knew some who couldn't remember how to get there, and she knew the ones who simply couldn't come inside. Bob had definitely been one of the last. It was why she'd been so surprised by his apartment.

But she knew Betty had never understood. That Betty blamed herself for the fact that her father had wandered the downtown streets while she lived in his comfortable house in the county. And Maggie knew there was nothing she could say now that would take that away or make it better.

"Did the police ask you about these things?" Maggie asked, lifting the cameras.

Betty nodded. "Yeah. I told them the same thing."

"What about film?" Maggie asked, not seeing any. "Tape, maybe."

Betty shook her head. "Daddy didn't have any film or tape. We never bought him that. The police said that they didn't find any film or tape either. That Daddy probably just ... oh, you know, imagined he was working again."

Maggie nodded absently, still balancing that tiny little camera on her hands.

Bob *had* been crazy. Who would have thought that somebody who monitored foreign invasions from beneath an underpass would have enough sense to record it?

But if that somebody had been a decorated FBI agent?

Suddenly Maggie couldn't breathe quite correctly, because she remembered the last thing he'd said.

Get my stash.

Get my stash where my heart lived.

Could he really have left her something more than names on a wall? Could he have retained enough of his mind to remember to hide his evidence from the people he thought were following him?

Maggie looked down at the camera in her hand and prayed.

She had no proof that he'd been murdered. No proof that somebody had tampered with his medication and loaded him with a killing dose of cocaine in an effort to discredit him. But what if there really had been more to worry about than somebody believing the ravings of a madman? What if Bob had actually managed to collect something to be afraid of?

Bob, the top FBI agent. Bob, who might not have totally lost the rituals of his career amid his madness.

"Betty, if I asked you to tell me where your father's heart lived, what would you say?"

Betty blinked, then blinked again. She looked around, as if searching. Then, she shook her head.

"I don't know. Here? After all, Mother was his heart." Then, she smiled. "But then, so was the Bureau, I think."

"Did he leave anything with you to keep for him?"

"Well, sure, but he was always doing that. You know, warnings and things."

Maggie struggled to stay calm. "Could I see it, please?"

"Well, I threw most of it out. He'd write poems about attacks and warnings about invasions, you know. You know what he was like."

Maggie kept still. "Anything you might have, though, would help. And, if you can, anyplace he'd feel safe hiding something."

"What do you mean where his heart lived?" Susan demanded the minute Betty walked from the room.

"Something Bob said to me right before he died," Maggie admitted, her attention on the evidence-gathering tools in her hands. "He said for me to get his stash where his heart lived. And he'd been talking about the people he thought were killing him."

Susan went very still. "Holy shit. You think he might not have been as crazy as we think and actually left us something?"

Maggie shook her head. "I don't know. But since we don't have any easy slam dunk with any pill bottles, I hope to hell so."

And she hoped it wasn't as disjointed as the notes on his newspaper articles, or nobody but her would believe the evidence they did find.

Betty appeared, walking more slowly, her eyes damp, as she considered the crumpled notebook pages in her hand. Her last legacy of a father who had loved her enough to paint her in pastel colors. She handed them over, and Maggie and Susan divided them up.

Maggie got vitriol about Oklahoma City and the U.N. invasion of El Salvador and the CIA's involvement in the World Trade Center. Her heart slid all over again. She kept relying on a paranoid schizophrenic, and that was even more stupid than relying on Sean.

"Well, I can't argue with him," Susan mused with a half smile. "Dogs do dig and snakes do suck."

Maggie snapped back to attention. "What about a dog and a snake?"

Susan handed over the sheet, torn from a lined notebook, printed more carefully than anything Maggie had held.

The Dog digs?
The Snake sucks?
I wish they'd write it instead,
And I might know.
I might know.
How it happened to the father
And the morrisman when I
heard, heard, heard them
whispering
over their beers where they wouldn't
see
me.

Maggie sat very still, reading the poem over and over. Knowing that there was something there. Something that made her heart stutter and her chest constrict. Something . . .

She knew the others were watching her. She knew she

looked stupid, mouthing the words of the poem as if fitting them into her mouth would reveal their secrets. She knew . . .

"Jesus."

Her heart slammed into action in her chest, because she couldn't believe it might be that simple.

"What?" Susan asked, avid.

Maggie looked up, trying very hard to sound calm. "Not digs," she said. "Dij. Digoxin. Sucks. Succinylcholine. Oh, my God."

Both Betty and Susan were looking on in confusion.

Maggie faced them. "May I have this, Mrs. Wilson?"

"Of course. Does it mean something?"

"I think it means that your father might have gathered real evidence of a series of murders that happened in town. If I can have this, I think I can help prove it."

Betty was looking even more uncomfortable. "What do you mean?"

Maggie struggled to sit still. "I mean that I think your father overheard some people talking about murders that had been committed in St. Louis by medical professionals. He was always down at the Toe Tag, where the hospital people hang out. But nobody really paid attention to a homeless guy, ya know? The thing is, I think he started investigating, just as if he were still in the Bureau. And I think he found proof. He was trying to tell me that when he died." She pulled in a breath, finally giving Montana Bob the due she'd denied him. "I think that one of those people he was investigating was afraid somebody'd take him seriously, and they murdered him."

"Jesus," Susan breathed. "You mean it?"

Maggie waved the page. "The snake is Snake Pilson. One of the people on Bob's list. Snake died while in our hospital, but there's no evidence of foul play. The drug succinylcholine is used to paralyze patients. For inserting airways, or controlling head injury patients. That kind of thing. But if it's administered to a patient, he has to be immediately put on life support. If not . . ."

Susan nodded, eyes avid.

"Succinylcholine—" Maggie continued, "—more commonly called succs, would never be tested for postmortem unless there was a specific request. The same for digoxin. Called dij in hospitals. It's a heart drug that can stop a heart on a dime if misdosed. A drug there would be no reason to give an eighteen-year-old gunshot victim in the ED. And unless there was a reason to look, nobody would test for it. Trust me. Nobody looked."

"The dog?"

"Big Dawg Dwayne Carver. A gangbanger who died in the ED. I saw that one myself, and never questioned it."

Susan's eyes grew impossibly bigger. "And the father—"

"Urban McGinley?"

"Holy Mother of God."

Maggie looked again at the poem. *The morrisman.* That one she didn't get. Except that it itched at her, yet another rock unseen in the current.

Morrisman, morrisman . . .

"You think my father was murdered," Betty suddenly said, as if cementing the concept.

Maggie looked up and saw that Betty was just assimilating the most important fact to her. The fact from which Maggie had started all those weeks ago.

She reached over and took hold of Betty's hand. "Yes, ma'am. I do."

"And nobody suspected?"

It was much quicker to skate around the truth. "No, ma'am."

Betty got to her feet. "Then take the poem. Take it all. Do anything you need to find out the truth. I'll help any way I can."

Maggie followed, to face her eye-to-eye. "You can help most by not talking to anybody about this. And I mean no one, Mrs. Wilson, until I tell you it's okay."

"But why—?"

"Please. Just trust me."

"Trust you?" Betty's eyes grew brilliant with tears. That same soft blue as her father's. "You're the only one who believed in my dad. Of course I'll trust you. Just let me know what to do."

"I promise. And thank you."

"What happens now?" Susan asked Maggie.

Maggie checked her watch. "I have to call my friends in the MEs' Offices. Then I have to go to work."

Susan's eyebrows lifted. "You're still working?"

Maggie's smile was dry. "Until Legal says otherwise."

Susan's smile was positively delighted. "Well, after this, don't count on it."

Maggie didn't. But it didn't matter. She finally had something. Something concrete. Something she hoped would be indisputable. Because if an eighteen-year-old was found to have a toxic level of unprescribed digoxin in his system, even Dr. Winnifred Sweet Harrison could no longer deny the fact that in the bistate area of St. Louis, people were being murdered by the very people who should have protected them.

Maggie knew that should have made her feel better.

It just made her feel sad.

CHAPTER 15

In the end, Maggie didn't get to make her calls before heading into work. She and Susan wasted two hours searching through Betty Wilson's house in the hopes that Bob had actually left evidence there where his heart had lived and died. But he hadn't.

Evidently Bob had decided to be more inventive than that. If Bob had, indeed, left evidence, and not delusions. So Maggie put Susan in charge of checking out all the homeless angles to see if maybe Bob might have left a stash in any of the places he'd squatted, or with any of the people he'd known and relied on at the end of his life. Maggie headed into the ED, where she was scheduled to pick up the eight hours she'd be off tomorrow training with the SWAT team at the local high school.

She had to wait for her early-lunch break to call Dr. Harrison. Which was okay, because having to call Dr. Harrison put her off her food, anyway.

"Was not one visit *and* a mention in the local newspaper enough for you?" the city ME demanded frostily.

If Maggie hadn't been familiar with Dr. Harrison, she might have supposed the ME to be upset by the mention in a local gossip column. Maggie knew, however, that Dr. Harrison cherished her hard-won reputation.

"Obviously not," Maggie answered. "I thought you

might like some additional information about the names I gave you."

"I wouldn't want a winning lottery ticket from you."

Maggie didn't bother to get upset. "I have good reason to believe that Snake Pilson was killed with succinylcholine."

"You do." Amazing how only two words could be so loaded with disdain.

"And Dwayne Carver with digoxin."

There was the minutest of pauses. "Where did you get this information?"

"Someone who was observing the situation before I was."

"You mean the paranoid schiz with the roadkill tacked to his walls."

Well, so much for discretion. "Montana Bob, yes. Who, before his illness, was a multiply decorated Special Agent with the FBI."

"I know that. You think I'm an idiot?"

"I think we actually might be able to find some good evidence. But this was the first I could pull out. Will you look?"

Maggie waited with new patience. Finally, she heard a curious growling sound on the other side.

"I'll let you know."

And then, the medical examiner hung up.

Leaving Maggie with nothing to do except her job until Susan talked to the homeless guys.

"How could you?" she heard from the doorway.

Maggie turned, phone still in hand, to see Jeannie Mars standing in the doorway, hands in classic position of outrage on her hips. On anybody else it would have seemed normal. On Jeannie it looked almost ludicrous.

"How could I what?" Maggie asked quietly and hung up the phone.

"Turn on your friends. I think you deserve what you get for that."

Slowly Maggie got to her feet. "I don't get it, Jeannie,"

she said. "You don't even believe in abortion. How can you countenance what's been going on here? And, contrary to what our great white supervisor thinks, you know damn well people are dying when they're not supposed to."

Jeannie went pale, then red. She struggled mightily to control herself. Maggie could see she'd brought another one of her migraines on herself. Which meant that someone had been hurt too badly to help, and Jeannie couldn't stand it.

"I came to get you because we have an accident coming in," was what she finally said, her voice corpse-cold. "A critical child and a belligerent adult. The belligerent adult, obviously intoxicated, slammed into the side of the car carrying the critical child, whose parents are dead at the scene."

She was already turning away before Maggie could say anything.

"Jeannie . . ."

Jeannie spun on her heel. "I'm to tell you that you're to be allowed nowhere near the drunk."

And then, with a sour little smile that betrayed the delicious irony of that statement, Jeannie walked out.

Fuck me, Maggie thought, climbing to her feet and grabbing her stethoscope. One of these days I'm gonna be able to do my job without it meaning anything else.

Maggie heard the drunk long before he showed up next door. He was screaming, cursing, howling, and moaning, all, it seemed, in the same breath.

"What are you do-o-o-o-o-o-i-ing? Get away from me! Get the *fuck* away from me! Get those fuckin' things off my wrists!"

"And guess who he is?" the surgical resident asked Maggie as the two of them inserted an intercranial pressure probe into the skull of the comatose four-year-old. "Sam fucking Mardick."

Maggie looked up, her stomach in sudden turmoil. "The CEO of Mardick, Inc.?"

"The very selfsame."

The glances exchanged betrayed the fact that with a

name like Mardick in St. Louis, there was no way this
drunk was going to pay for his sins.

Not without some help.

Maggie was frantic to be in that other room. To keep
that worthless, rich drunk from dying.

But she knew she was already checkmated. Not by the
ban from Sam's room. By the life of Mary Patricia Kelly,
whose eyes were big and brown, and whose four-year-old
brain was in a perilous state.

Besides, if Maggie went in to help Sam, somebody
would just figure a way to have her kill him instead.

"Is the room ready in ICU?" the resident asked.

Maggie sighed. "Supposed to be, but they haven't called.
I'll try again."

She had just stepped out into the hallway, when she
heard the shoe drop in the other room.

"Shit! Help in here! He's seizing . . . oh, fuck, call a
code!"

Maggie tried to run in. Shara the supervisor was already
standing in the doorway, a look of outrage on her face. As
if wondering how Maggie could have killed her patient
from another room.

Maggie turned back to finish her phone call.

She was just hanging up after browbeating the ICU
nurse into accepting Mary Patricia, when one of the city
paramedics came skidding through the door.

"Goddamn, did we screw up!" he panted, waving something shiny in Maggie's face. "That Mardick guy still down
here?"

"What do you mean?" Maggie asked. "He just coded."

It was the paramedic's turn to go white. "Fuck us all.
The guy isn't drunk. He's a diabetic. We better shove some
sugar in him."

Which was when Maggie finally had the chance to focus
on what was dangling from the medic's hand. A Medalert
bracelet. The kind diabetics wear.

"Shit, fuck, fire," she breathed and spun for the room.

"He's diabetic!" she yelled at the top of her lungs. "Mr. Mardick is a diabetic!"

There was a sudden, sick silence in the room.

It was one of the most classic mistakes in medicine. Nobody looked more drunk than a patient suffering from acute hypoglycemia, or low blood sugar, one of the most dangerous crises in diabetes. The biggest problem with that was that without immediate treatment, hypoglycemia resulted in seizure, brain damage, and cardiac arrest.

Which was the exact hat trick Mr. Mardick was scoring now.

The differential diagnosis would be easy. IV-push a couple of amps of pure glucose in him, and he'd come out of it. If he'd still been a little more alert, he could have presented what they called one of the medical miracles, used all the time to astound medical and nursing students. The drooling and babbling hypoglycemic given an IV-push amp of glucose, would suddenly sit up and ask with perfect coherence what the matter was. Then, politely, beg everyone's pardon for the upset.

Mr. Mardick was too far under for that.

Too, too far under too fast for simple hypoglycemia, Maggie suddenly realized as she saw the terror register on at least three faces.

"What exactly do we need to treat him with?" she demanded into the silence.

Jeannie looked stricken. She looked around, too. "What did you—?" was all she had time to ask.

"Well, let's give him a little sugar, children," Allen piped up.

The team made one ashen look around. Then they reacted like cockroaches in a high beam, scattering in every direction and shouting in at least three languages as they tried to reverse the deadly effects of assisted hypoglycemia.

"*That* is what I'm talking about," Maggie said ninety minutes later as she and Jeannie stood out in the hallway preparing paperwork to send a now very polite and thankful

Mr. Mardick upstairs. A Mr. Mardick whose ETOH level was zero.

"I didn't even get to the picnic," Sam was saying in a soft, bemused voice inside the room. "I really wanted to see the softball."

Jeannie looked ashamed. "It was just . . ."

"A mistake," Maggie said. "Well, how many of those do you guys have to make before it's too many? Who decides how big an asshole you have to be before you don't deserve to live anymore? Which one of you makes the decision, by the way, or do you vote?"

"Me?" Jeannie demanded. "You think *I* did that? You think it's some kind of secret society with a handshake and decoder ring? Sit down at the Toe Tag for a few sessions and really listen for once. You'll find out what it is. It's just . . . oh, I don't know . . . people talking. Some people doing. Nothing organized. Believe me. If it were organized, I would have done something a long time ago. But when people like Big Dawg Dwayne Carver can be kept from hurting any more babies, then I can't say I mourn them too much."

"And Montana Bob? And Mr. Mardick in there? What are they? Collateral damage? Jeannie, even if you're not involved, you know. And you can stop it before it gets more out of hand. Before more diabetics die for looking drunk."

The worst part was that Maggie knew that Jeannie was the biggest-hearted woman in four states. She wouldn't have suffered those crippling migraines if she hadn't been. Jeannie didn't treat her patients, she adopted them. She just let someone else kill some because they were predators.

Maggie imagined it could seem so guiltless that way.

Maggie was turning away when Jeannie caught hold of her sleeve. "Maggie—?"

Maggie faced her. Jeannie flushed, looked away, suddenly uncomfortable. Maggie wondered if she was going to defend herself again, or for the first time admit that they'd gone too far. That they'd gone too far the first time they'd seen someone die who shouldn't have and turned their backs.

Finally, Jeannie let go. Looked up. "I don't mind you saying that stuff to me. But be careful who else you say it to. Just . . . be careful."

Maggie's smile was sad as she looked around at the dismay that was betrayed in the faces around her. The stunned disbelief on one or two. Maybe they'd finally at least hesitate before condemning another person to death.

"Of course I'll be careful," she said. "Besides, for a while my whole life will be here and the SWAT team. Here, I can watch out for myself, and there everybody watches out for each other."

"You're sure about that?"

"Of course not. That would be risking fate. But I do trust my guys on the team, and for now that's enough."

Maggie was trotting down the darkened steps at Northwest Public High School when she found out how wrong she was. The team had spent the afternoon practicing the possible evacuation of a high school massacre, à la Columbine. To reflect reality, the student body had reenacted all the terror and pandemonium of the real moment. Lights had been turned off, sirens and alarms on. Escape lighting strobed like lightning. Kids ran in rivers from the school, screaming. Kids clustered in darkened closets, screaming. Kids littered the floor of the library and cafeteria, screaming.

Maggie had had just about enough. Between the flashing, whooping fire alarms and the wailing, shrilling kids, she was developing a blinding headache. Then, to cap it all off, actual alarms went off. Tornado alarms. A big weather front had decided to slam through the area four hours early, which meant that all the noise and flashing lights inside were suddenly matched by even louder noise and real lightning outside.

At least it called quits to the exercise.

"Evacuation exercise canceled," boomed a voice over the loudspeaker. "Please follow tornado procedures and proceed in an orderly fashion to the lower level."

Orderly fashion seemed to involve pounding feet, more shrill voices, and even more pandemonium. Especially since somebody hadn't thought to turn off all the inside alarms, or turn on the lights.

"Okay," Maggie announced, herding about a hundred kids before her down the third-floor stairs. "Let's not get any real blood on us trying to get out of here."

Maggie's troupe of kids were the "dead and injured" from the library, made up in moulage to resemble gunshot victims. Caught in the stuttering harsh lights, they looked like the escape of the living dead.

Half a flight ahead of her, Paxton pulled off his helmet and made use of his surprisingly nice baritone.

"We-e-e-e're . . . *off* to see the Wizard . . ."

After a moment of startled silence, the kids laughed and joined in. Then they settled right into line.

Maggie just shook her head and sang along.

Maggie didn't waste any anxiety on the tornado threat. Like any good St. Louisan, she took it all with a healthy grain of salt. If she panicked at every tornado siren she heard in this town, she'd need superglue to get her eyes closed. She paid attention instead to getting everybody safely downstairs in the uncertain light.

She was laughing, singing along with all the munchkins as they marched down the huge central staircase that ran down all four floors of the high school. The sound echoed among the alarms, the lightning, the thunder. Maggie watched where she was going like a good girl, so she didn't stumble into the person ahead of her.

She forgot to look where she'd been.

The shove came from behind her. Maggie had her hand on the railing, waiting for one of the kids to hop two stairs to keep up with his friend. She'd just reached up to pull off her helmet and balaclava and give in to the heat. After all, the test was over. Exercise complete.

Then somebody shoved her against the railing. The air slammed out of her body. Her balance went. She swore somebody lifted her, just like a sack of oats, and over she went. A kaleidoscope of jerky, exaggerated expressions whirled by in the stuttering, harsh light. Hands reaching out. Screams. Flashing, spinning windows and air.

Again. Flying when she had no wings.

Nothing but her natural balance kept Maggie from landing right on her head two stories down. Instead she landed on her side.

She heard a pop and a crack and felt the unnatural wash of endorphins temporarily steal the pain. She lay there, half on her back, her arm bent beneath her, her breathing completely stopped by the jolt. And then, she saw him.

Saw him in the lightning, the bleak, strobing lights. He wore fatigues and a helmet. The deep shadows stole the contours of his face. Interchangeable Warrior Descending a Staircase.

Maggie couldn't see his weapon. If she could see his weapon, she would know who it was. Who thought to finish what an impatient car in Soulard had started.

Because she'd been pushed. She knew it now. She knew that somebody on her team had deliberately reached out to hurt her.

Somebody from her team.

Then, in a flash, the lights went on and the sirens stopped. Silence and light, snatching away the shadows and the threat. And that fast, the stairs were empty. Maggie lay there, wide-eyed and struggling to breathe, but no one leaned over the stairwell to endanger her.

"What is this problem you have with stairs, O'Brien?" she heard close to her head.

Paxton. Always Paxton finding her at the bottom of stairs in an untidy lump.

"Maggie?" he persisted, leaning closer.

Maggie struggled to smile. "Pax?" Her diaphragm kicked into gear and she sucked in a short breath. Her ribs protested. Her shoulder was coming to life.

"Yeah, hon."

"I think I just saw the Wizard."

His laugh was sharp and hard, a breath of relief.

"I also think . . . I dislocated my shoulder."

The endorphins were leaking away, letting her know she was going to live, at least long enough to hurt like hell.

"Yeah," he said. "I'd say you dislocated your shoulder good. Anything else?"

"Everything . . . else . . ."

"How the hell did you fall over a waist-high banister, you idiot?" Paul demanded, ashen-faced. Another disembodied face hovering in the stark light.

They must have called the rest of the team in. Maggie's earpiece had fallen out, so she couldn't tell what else was going on. She could hear disorder at the basement stairs. Kids still fleeing the tornado. Thudding of jump boots and murmured voices. Her team, surrounding her. Helping her.

At least most of them.

"I don't know," she said with the voice she had left. "I don't . . . you know . . . I can't breathe . . . very well . . ."

Time began to get really unpredictable. Things happened, Maggie knew. She heard snatches of oaths, and more sirens, and felt the squeeze of somebody's hand on her good one. More endorphins, she decided benignly, so that she didn't know how she howled, too, when they lifted her onto the backboard and strapped her onto the gurney.

She had a feeling she was responsible for at least a few oaths, too. To her friends. To her team. To the kids lined up, looking like the ghosts in *Sixth Sense* in their bloody chests and faces as she passed by, the unbloodied injured. She even thought to wave like the Rose Bowl Queen. But somebody had her good hand, and they'd strapped her down.

Everything began to shift back into focus when an hour after arriving in the ED somebody else finally rolled her off the backboard, arm still lying at an odd angle from her shoulder. Portable stat spine films had been taken and were negative. Trauma scale was okay, neuro scale okay, except that she was acting goofy. Well, Allen sang out for all concerned, no goofier than usual.

Maggie was stripped down and the bruises marked that were left by the various implements of destruction she'd carried in her medic vest. Everything else was x-rayed and prodded and cataloged. At the end of another hour, she was left with an injury tally that consisted of her shoulder, a broken rib, a pneumothorax, which was already being decompressed with a chest tube, and a small, nondepressed linear skull fracture they found beneath a two-inch scalp laceration they hadn't seen bleeding into her hair, which would be treated with a plastic surgeon and antibiotics.

Not a bad tally, really. Without her flak jacket to diffuse the force of the impact, she could have well lost a spleen, if not a liver.

For her shoulder, they thought, a little visit to OR. Tough to flip her on her stomach and hang a water-filled bucket in her hand to pull the joint back into place in the ED when her right lung was hooked up to a drainage system. Which meant it was time for a little sedation, didn't she think?

She did.

But not yet.

There was something she had to figure out first. Maggie knew it was something important, except that she couldn't pay attention for the pain in her shoulder. Her head hurt and her chest hurt, and sedation sounded wonderful.

But nobody had asked her what had happened.

Nobody asked how she'd ended up on her head in a high school hallway.

As if they already knew.

As if they'd expected it.

From her team.

She hurt so much, but that got through to her. That was what was wrong. What she had to figure out.

"Where's my team?" Maggie asked, suddenly frantic.

It was Allen who answered. Allen who stood over her, his hand on the IV line they'd inserted into her left arm.

Allen, who was watching her with suddenly bleak eyes.

"Where's my team?" she asked again, focusing on him finally.

"They'll be here in a minute, Mags. In a minute."

His voice was suddenly so quiet. So un-Allen. The drama was dead in his voice; his hands were still.

He looked so forlorn, and Maggie had only once in her life seen Allen forlorn. It had been the night he'd held a boy who'd committed suicide rather than tell his parents he was gay. *Waste,* Allen had whispered into the sweet blond hair of that boy. *Waste, waste, waste.*

And he looked that way now.

"Allen?"

"I didn't know," he was saying, almost to himself as he injected something into her line. "You're allergic to penicillin. You never told us."

"Why—?"

Something was wrong. With her. With her muscles. With Allen's eyes, which were suddenly so bright, so painful.

"I'm sorry, Maggie. Oh, honey, I'm so sorry. But you would have hurt us all. Everybody."

Maggie couldn't breathe. She couldn't move. He'd shot her up with succinylcholine, and it was paralyzing her. She was agape, her eyes wide open, watching her own death at the hands of one of her best friends, and she couldn't move.

Somebody had tossed her down a staircase so that Allen could put a final stop to her. Allen, who was stroking her hair, as if she were a child, and crying.

And he didn't know that it was too late. That she'd already shared her information.

He didn't know, and she couldn't tell him.

"I wish you could understand," he was saying, his hand so soft against her frozen head, his eyes on hers. "That moment when you know it's just too much. When you've just pronounced another baby dead, and you know you can't do it anymore. You just can't stand it when you hear that drunk down the hall demanding to be taken care of.

When you're sitting in the bar and someone else—someone else who's held those dead babies—lifts a drink to whoever killed that son of a bitch. And you know that it was you. You know that *you* finally made a difference."

Maggie should have felt panic. Her chest was rigid, screaming for air that was never going to get there. Her heart was slamming against her ribs like a bird seeking flight. The edges of her field of vision sparkled like the transporter from *Star Trek*, and Allen was wavering. She was dying, and he was going to make sure with a honking dose of penicillin, so that nobody thought to look for the succs in her system that stopped her from objecting.

She was dying before her very eyes, and there wasn't a damn thing she could do about it.

Maggie felt the tears slide down her temples into her hair. She felt the drop of Allen's tears as they fell on her.

She couldn't move. She couldn't so much as moan.

But she didn't feel panic.

She felt tired.

She felt so damned tired. She'd tried so hard, and it had been for nothing. Because Allen was right. It wasn't just him doing this to her. It was everyone. Everyone she'd trusted and loved and fought for. Everyone who had nodded at this atrocity and then hurt her when she'd tried to stop it.

It was Sean, and it was Jeannie and Zen and Allen himself, who was telling himself it was enough to hold Maggie as she died.

And suddenly Maggie couldn't remember why the hell she'd fought so hard, her whole life, to be worthy of all these people. These people who were, after all, no better than Tommy, trying to fit the world to their expectations and failing.

Maggie watched Allen uncap another syringe and wondered why she should fight. For her friends? Her family? Her team? They'd all walked away. All the stars by which she'd guided her life, the church on which she'd built her beliefs. Gone, tumbled and scattered and worthless.

Everything she'd fought for her entire life became pointless at this last minute before she died.

"It's Versed, honey," Allen was saying. "You at least
deserve Versed."

So she wouldn't know. A sedative and amnesic, the first
two steps to capital punishment's lethal injection. It was
already weighing her, stealing the biological terror of an-
oxia. Soothing the futility and sapping away the light.

And she didn't have the will left to fight. She had nothing left at all. No pride. No righteous indignation. No regret. She was just tired. Tired and alone, and knowing that
she didn't want to fight Allen just to face him when she woke
up.

Maybe now people would stop telling her how proud
Tommy would have been of her.

Which was, oddly enough, when she remembered what
morrisman meant. Just as the Versed was melting her brain.

Oh, Tommy.

She knew. Every damn bit of information she'd gleaned
suddenly fell into perfect place, and Maggie understood just
what she'd uncovered in her mad dash to justice. She understood because somebody had shoved her over the stairs
just to get her into the hospital, because she knew what
morrisman meant, because she saw the breadth of her own
betrayal in Allen's eyes.

She'd been such an idiot.

And now she was going to be dead.

Fitting, somehow.

But she'd been right. She didn't want to survive to this.
She didn't want to understand just what had happened to
Montana Bob and Snake Pilson and her.

But she did.

She understood it all.

Right before she died.

CHAPTER 16

She couldn't prove any of it.

It was Maggie's first coherent thought.

She knew everything, but it didn't make any difference if she couldn't prove it.

Her second thought was *My God, I'm not dead.*

No one could possibly be more surprised than she.

Actually, for a long time, she wasn't so sure. She seemed to be able to think and breathe okay, but she couldn't move, couldn't speak, couldn't open her eyes, and couldn't get away from the incessant beeping and buzzing of the kind of monitors and machines that infested hospital ICUs like mating cicadas. That was hell, wasn't it? Wasn't she in hell?

Then she got her eyes open and was sure of it. She was in ICU and Tommy was bent over her. Tommy with a black eye and a split lip.

Okay, so bad news *and* good news. Maybe somebody had already been meting out punishment.

But Maggie couldn't take her gaze away from her father's face, because finally, she knew who the morrisman was, and her relationship with her father would never be the same again.

As if it had ever been anything to crow about before.

"Okay," Tommy said, brusquely, clearing his throat. "I'll go now."

Then, without another word, as if he'd truly been worried about her, Tommy clapped her on the arm and walked out of the room.

And Maggie lay there staring at a blank ceiling.

"Maggie?"

She blinked and tried to turn her head, but it hurt. No, everything hurt. She didn't think she liked that at all.

Considering the alternative, though, she thought she could handle it.

The alternative.

Hadn't she wanted to be dead? Hadn't that been one of her last coherent thoughts?

Was anything different now?

"Sean?"

Sean jumped up as if he'd just seen her come back from the dead. "*Jesus*, Maggie," he all but shouted.

He grabbed her hand and patted her sore face and huffed a couple of times, as if he were completely beyond words.

Sean Delaney, beyond words.

Maggie decided she still hadn't made up her mind whether she was dead or not. Whether she wanted to be.

Then she really got a good look at him. He looked like hell. Bedraggled, bearded, and begrimed. He looked as if he'd been dragged backward down an alley. And he was wearing his shoulder holster.

"You're not dead?" she asked him.

"Of course not. And neither are you," he said, patting away at her as if he were keeping her in place. "Although how the hell you managed to avoid it, I sure as hell don't know."

"Why are you here?"

His smile was, at best, wobbly. He reached over to swipe the hair off her forehead, and she saw that his hands were shaking. "What do you *mean*, why am I here? Where else would I be?"

Tears. Maggie swore she saw tears in those famous Delaney eyes, and she couldn't believe it.

Sean, who breezed through life as if it were his personal arcade game. With tears in his eyes.

"What's the matter?" Maggie asked.

His face screwed up. "What's the *matter*? Are you kidding? What the hell do you *think* is the matter, dammit? Do you know what I've been through? Do you know what it's like to find you in the next thing to cardiac arrest and not be able to do *anything*?"

He was serious. Sean, who would no more profess a real emotion than quit the force. Whatever else she thought, Maggie was suddenly happier she wasn't dead.

"Yes, as a matter of fact," she told him, because she had to. Because maybe this time he'd understand. "I do know."

"I'm sorry, Mags," he said, his eyes glistening, his hand so tight around hers it hurt. "I'm sorry I've put you through this."

And he meant it. Which made difficult breathing even harder, and unaccustomed tears burn her own eyes. "I'm sorry I put you through this, too."

And then, knowing that neither of them could handle much more right now, Maggie cleared her throat. "So how come I didn't die?" she asked. "I sure thought I was going to."

Sean straightened, sniffed a little, and grinned. "Allen. He saw you crashing and yelled for help. Why the hell don't you have your allergies on file? Nobody knew you were allergic to penicillin."

Maggie felt brand-new tears. So Allen hadn't been able to go through with it after all.

Maggie closed her eyes, feeling so tired again. Poor Big Zen. No wonder she hadn't wanted to help. Zen believed in her duty almost as strongly as she believed in her God. But she believed in her children more.

Maggie wondered how much Sean knew about what Allen had almost done. Wondered how much he knew about everything. If he knew as much as she did.

But at least Allen hadn't been able to kill her.

"What happened to Tommy?"

This time Sean beamed. "You. Just about the time everybody showed up to get you out of anaphylactic shock, you suddenly came to like a banshee. Nobody's sure as hell gonna give you Versed again, honey. You took out three techs, flattened Allen, and cold-cocked Tommy O'Brien. The entire force is impressed."

"Are the staff okay?"

Sean shrugged. "The techs are fine. Allen claimed he was traumatized and went home."

Not surprising.

"Maggie?"

She managed to shake her head without it falling off onto the floor. "I just wish I'd remember doing it."

"All I know," Sean told her, "was that by the time I got there you were screaming something about changing your mind, and spitting at Allen. They finally gave you propyphol to settle you down."

"Ah," she nodded. "Milk of Amnesia. No wonder I don't remember. And they fixed my shoulder?"

"In surgery. After they reinserted your chest tube for the third time. You were pretty feisty."

"Well, I knew . . . somebody . . . was trying to kill me. Somebody on the steps."

A faceless cop caught in the lightning, like someone's worst nightmare.

"Well, nobody's gonna hurt you now. I'm here, and the SWAT team has devised a schedule so you have somebody outside your door twenty-four/seven. Just in case you've made anybody else mad."

Madder than Allen. Madder than Tommy, madder than whoever had killed three innocent people and put Maggie's name on it.

Somebody who might even be angrier than whichever member of her team had pushed her over the stairs.

Her *team.*

Maggie must have reacted more strongly than she'd thought, because Sean started patting again. "All but one of them, honey. Your lieutenant said to tell you when you woke up that your other team paramedic—uh, Jazz?—has resigned from the team. The lieutenant wanted me to assure you that the team will take care of him."

Sean met her gaze straight on, and Maggie didn't mistake his meaning. Jazz might have tried to kill her, but the rest of her team had dug him out and thrown him away for what he'd done. And then stood watch to keep her safe. No matter what she'd done.

Jazz. Who saved souls for Christ.

Unless they were imperfect souls, evidently.

But she'd been wrong. She hadn't lost everyone she'd trusted. Her team *had* taken care of her.

And Sean, whatever he knew, whatever he was doing, was here watching over her.

In that case, Maggie was glad she'd decided not to die after all.

Even though she couldn't remember making the decision.

But she didn't want to deal with that right now. She didn't want to face Sean, who held her hand even as he kept things from her, or the future, which she was going to have to step into at any moment. She didn't want to face what she had to do and who she had to hurt.

She didn't want to admit the truth that no matter how hard she tried, she might never really stop this.

Mostly, she didn't want to face Tommy.

She'd do that later. When she felt better. When her head didn't hurt and she could breathe without a tube pulling at her side.

For just a little while, Maggie thought she'd bask in the fact that she'd been wrong. That, no matter what, there were people out there she could rely on. And that, somehow, whatever his involvement, she could believe right now that Sean was one.

But she'd deal with that when she felt better. Right now, she was going back to sleep.

So she closed her eyes and let Sean hold her hand. "Tell the lieu thank you, Sean. And thank you, too."

Sean just squeezed her hand and held on. Maggie felt tears dribble down into her hair and thought how silly it was to be crying. After all, things were beginning to look up.

At least until she got out of here and followed up on the morrisman and Montana Bob.

Down at the Salvation Army on Washington Avenue, Susan Jacobsmeyer walked the line of men waiting for their noon meal. She was wearing jeans and a T-shirt, her hair scraped out of her eyes and her tennis shoes the ones she did her gardening in. There was no point dressing up here. These guys didn't respond to tailored clothes and salon-dyed hair. These guys responded to a human touch and a smile and a pack of cigarettes.

She offered all three.

It didn't do any good.

She'd trolled every homeless shelter, every hangout she knew. She'd already been here once, seeking somebody who might have had contact with Montana Bob. Everybody knew him. Nobody knew anything about him.

"Kinda kept to himself," one old black guy offered the by-now familiar litany. "Didn't trust nobody."

Another grizzled white head up the line nodded. A guy wearing plaid flannel and a ski cap in ninety-degree weather. "Shared his stuff, but didn't want nothin' from nobody."

"Did he ever talk about what he was doing?" she asked. "Something that might have upset him?"

That got her a chorus of laughter. "Lady, *everything* upset him. Fluoride in the water, black helicopters, Martha Stewart."

A couple of other guys nodded. "Fuckin' *hated* Martha Stewart."

"Do you remember seeing him with a camera? Maybe a tape recorder?"

"Knew he had 'em. Don't know what he did with 'em."

"He didn't leave anything with you guys? Anything he considered evidence, something important to him?"

Another round of laughter. "Honey," a skinny, tattooed guy in scrubs assured her, "he didn't trust us, neither. Took my picture when I was trolling in the trash behind the stadium one day. Said it was proof that I was in the CIA. Shit. Like I'd be eatin' here if I was in the goddam CIA ... pardon, ma'am."

Susan grinned. "Watch your fuckin' mouth."

Everybody got a kick out of that.

They were her friends within minutes. They still had nothing to tell her. Just like everybody else. She should be gone. She wanted to get over to the hospital and see if she could talk to Maggie. She needed to find out exactly how she'd ended up in the ICU, what could be done about it.

She needed some fresh ideas.

"So you wouldn't have known Montana Bob well enough to know if he stuck to a particular pattern? Someplace he always went? Someplace he always stayed, a place he might hide something important to him?"

For a minute, she got stony silence.

"I'm not trying to steal anything. You want, any of you can come with me and look. But there's a question about whether somebody murdered a homeless guy and got away with it because he was homeless. I'm trying to make sure it doesn't end that way, ya know? And I think Bob hoarded something that might help me prove that he was murdered."

There wasn't a guy on that line who didn't appreciate how perilous his existence was. Stony silence dissolved into hard consideration.

"Bob had no patterns," one guy offered. "Said that it prevented ambush."

Several nods.

"Except for the fifteenth of the month," another said.

Susan's antennae went up. "Fifteenth of the month?"

"Yeah," another guy offered with a wave of his finger. "The day his disability check came in. Bob always left lunch early. Didn't say why."

"Do you know where he went?"

A chorus of headshaking, which dislodged enough flakes to coat a Christmas tree.

"Just said he had an appointment at one. Every fifteenth."

"And he cleaned himself up."

Another nod. A big grin. "Like he was goin' on a date."

"Seeing his daughter?" Susan ventured.

"Nah. He never dressed up for her. She was by a few times. Nice lady. But he never dressed up for her. Only on the fifteenth. Washed his hair and everything."

"But you never knew where he went."

"Wouldn't say. Wanted to prevent—"

"Ambush. Yeah, I know."

Fifteenth of every month. It was the first solid lead Susan had been given. An appointment important enough for Bob to get dressed up for. A date, maybe. And not with his daughter.

She wondered, though, if his daughter might know with whom.

"Thanks, you guys. I really appreciate it."

"Let us know," the guy in the ski cap said. A guy with soft brown eyes and a Parkinson's tremor to his right hand.

Susan smiled and touched his arm. "The minute I do."

Big Zen came to see Maggie as darkness fell. Maggie saw the pain in those soft eyes and tried to sit up. Zen waved her back down and sat on the edge of the bed.

"Do you know where he is?" she asked softly enough that Paul, this evening's guard, didn't hear out in the hallway.

Maggie could at least reach Big Zen's hand. She felt the solid gold band Zen had never removed, even twenty-five years after her William had died.

"I'm sorry, Zen. I'm so sorry."

Just like Allen. It made Maggie wince.

Zen glared. "*You're* sorry? After what that boy did? He

told me. Called me. Then . . . just left. Somewhere."

"He didn't," Maggie insisted. "He stopped before anything happened, Zen."

But Zen was still thinking of that bright little boy who had become a murderer. "I never thought . . . he just feels things so hard, ya know? He was with his daddy that night. Held him in his arms when he died. Sounds melodramatic, but it changed my baby. Changed him in ways I couldn't get to. I thought bein' a doctor, helpin' people would be enough. But now this . . ."

"It has to stop, Zen."

Zen huffed in impatience. "You think I don't know that? You think I'd let somethin' like that go on if I knew about it? I just started suspecting . . . oh, I don't know. But it's not that easy, girl. It's just . . ."

"Frustrated people talking over beer. I heard."

Jeannie was the next one to show up sometime the following day, looking pinched and white and defiant, as if it were all Maggie's fault.

"I told you."

"Yes, you did."

Jeannie looked around, but Paul was back in the hall chatting up one of the nurses.

"There's nothing anybody can do," Jeannie insisted.

"They can stop," Maggie said.

Jeannie glared. "Will you?"

"You mean they will if I do?"

Jeannie nodded, her forehead tight with the pain behind her eyes.

"Answer a few questions first," Maggie said.

Another nod, this one wary.

"How did they manage to substitute drugs so that I ended up killing my own patients?"

Eerily enough, Jeannie smiled. A satisfied, job-well-done smile that Maggie never thought to see on those gentle features. "God, Maggie, you're such an innocent sometimes. There's nothing easier in the world than handing you what you think you expect. Just 'cause it says lidocaine doesn't mean it *is* lidocaine. Anybody can make that switch."

Maggie supposed she should have felt furious. Betrayed. Oddly enough, she felt relief. At least she wasn't crazy. Negligent. Homicidal. Those people had died at her hand, but not through her fault. Just as she'd tried so hard to tell people.

"How many?" she asked. "How many are involved?"

"How many know?" Jeannie retorted. "Or act? A far different number, and I'm not going to tell you. Besides, there's nothing you can really prove."

"I can prove that somebody got into my hospital file and changed the data on my medical allergies. Given enough time, I can probably even figure out who."

Jeannie paled a little, but said nothing.

"Do you know where Allen is?" Maggie asked.

"Yes."

"Tell him to get in touch with his mother."

Jeannie all but sneered. "You don't want the son of a bitch to fry?"

"I just want the son of a bitch to call his mother."

Jeannie stared at her, for those few moments, the old Jeannie. Vulnerable, sincere, dedicated. Maggie missed her already.

"Okay, then," Jeannie said, standing, her hands smoothing the skirt of her uniform much as Maggie had seen nuns iron their habits. Distance back in place. Shields up. "Since you agree to quit, so will . . . everything."

Maggie didn't bother to tell her that she hadn't actually agreed to anything. In any event, she didn't have time. As Jeannie turned, she ran right into an arriving Susan Jacobsmeyer.

Jeannie spun right around. "What is *she* doing here?"

She even sounded like a nun, Maggie thought with a shrug. She hoped like hell that Susan was wise enough to take the hint.

"Follow-up," the reporter immediately chimed in. "Our Ms. O'Brien here is the scandal du jour. The paper decided that since I was the one who started the story, I got to follow it, all the way from heroic savior through innuendo of patient abuse to dramatic injury. By the way, Ms. O'Brien, you might want to know that there's a veritable feeding frenzy of press outside the door downstairs."

"I should probably run like hell," Maggie groused.

"I can say you're recovering?" Susan asked, well aware that Jeannie still stood behind her, and Paul behind Jeannie.

"You can."

"Can I say how you were injured?"

"I figure everybody knew that. I fell over a railing while trying to herd a gaggle of high school students down the stairs."

"A gaggle. I thought they came in pods, like aliens. I also heard there was a crazy guy involved. Like, you might not have fallen on your own."

"That's for my lieutenant to say. All I have to say is, 'I'm feeling *much* better now.' "

"And that you didn't kill anybody."

"Sure. That, too."

"Mind if I follow up some more?"

Maggie managed a shrug. "You'll do it anyway."

Susan's smile was brilliant. "So I will."

She left, taking a couple minutes to make eyes at Paul on the way by. Which might mean she thought she could get more info from him, or she'd bought into Maggie's story about his mythic size.

Jeannie stayed behind for just a minute, her face deliberately turned from Maggie. "Allen stopped on his own. I thought you should know."

"I do, Jeannie. Thanks."

Jeannie nodded, her movements stiff and silent.

"Make sure he calls Zen. She's worried."

Jeannie turned, her eyes sharp, as if she still didn't believe that that was all Maggie wanted. Then she nodded again and left. Maggie closed her eyes and hoped she was finished for the day.

It wasn't the fact that she could well be vulnerable to another attack that made Maggie so impatient with her inactivity. It was the fact that, tied down to a chest tube and IVs, she couldn't escape the people who sought her.

Like now.

"I'm sure you know that we're too short-staffed to cover for you while you're in here," Shara said, her hands fluttering before her as if seeking those Precious Moments nurses to comfort her.

"I'm sure I do."

Shara nodded, her tightly curled hair not moving a millimeter. "You won't be able to return for at least four weeks. At least four weeks."

"I have sick leave accrued."

Shara waved her off like a plane on approach. "I need the staff. I'm sure there will be another position somewhere in the hospital available by the time you return to us."

"But not in the ED."

Shara stopped making any attempt at eye contact. "Most probably not."

Which would probably fit right in with Maggie's plans. If, that is, she still had a job out at Chesterfield Fire. If she still wanted it after they'd jettisoned her so fast. If she still wanted them.

"Thanks for letting me know."

Fortunately for Maggie, the phone rang, and Shara saw her escape clear.

"Don't say a word," Susan said in Maggie's ear. "I don't want to give myself away."

Maggie laughed, and then thought better of it. She felt, suddenly, like she should be talking on a shoe.

"Thanks for asking. I'm fine. And nobody's here right now. So talk away."

"I found out that Montana Bob used to have a date after

lunch on the fifteenth of every month. A date he got gussied up for. Any ideas?"

"Have you asked his daughter?"

"Not home. I left a message."

"Nobody knows where he went?"

"Nope. He was a secretive little shit."

"Well, it's a cinch we can't follow him. I have a feeling his daughter knows."

"Okay. Everything else okay?"

Maggie huffed again, all the laugh she could get out, even with her lung fully reinflated. That damn tube was coming out today, but until then, it still pulled.

"No. I want you to do some digging for me."

"What have you had a chance to dig up in there?"

"Morrisman."

She heard the silence, suddenly taut.

Maggie sucked in what breath she could and pushed herself right over the edge. "I want you to find out for me if Jimmy Morris is still alive."

"Jimmy . . . Jimmy Morris! The guy your father was kicked off the force for beating up? The one he really didn't beat up?"

"The guy my father rolled over like a tame lapdog for rather than face an investigation. Yeah. That Jimmy Morris. The one his rookie beat to a pulp."

"Which landed Jimmy Morris in the hospital . . ."

"Kinda like being pushed over a railing, ya know?" .

Maggie got another stricken silence for that as Susan worked out the particulars.

"Holy shit. You mean you think that Morris was supposed to be one of the victims?"

"Yeah. I think he was."

"But that would mean that your father . . ."

"The first confirmed murder I have happened twelve months ago. My dad was only kicked off the force nine months ago. The arithmetic isn't promising."

"There's more, isn't there?"

There was more Maggie could share, certainly. "I always

thought that the murderers used chance to get the victims close enough to the hospital to be murdered. You know, the next time a certain gangbanger gets popped, we take our chance. But after what happened to me, I'm beginning to wonder. Jimmy Morris was arrested for suspicion of raping a ten-year-old. Everybody in the city knew he'd been let out earlier that year because of a technicality for a similar crime."

"Twelve-year-old at a bus stop. And he'd just gotten out of prison from doing his dime on multiple rape charges just before that."

Maggie nodded to herself, all of it so clear to her now. "I've had a chance to do a lot of thinking while I've been here. And heard some stuff. I think that the murders started out just the way I thought. Somebody suddenly overwhelmed." Allen, maybe, a dead teenager in his arms. "Why, we'll probably never know. That last small straw that nobody can remember. Next bad guy he sees, next person who spits on him, he hauls out the syringe. But I think it got talked about. And talked about some more. And I think, in time, it went from murders of convenience to murders of contrivance. Conspiracy of the moment, ya know?"

"And you think your father was involved?"

Maggie closed her eyes. "Eventually. Yes. I also think he'd do anything to protect what he thought was a righteous action."

"So Tommy threw himself on his sword for the cause?"

Maggie shook her head. "Maybe."

Probably. She should have guessed when she saw how delighted he'd been by the whole situation. How protective.

"Do you realize what this means?"

"Sure. Not only do I get to help arrest my friends, I get to arrest my own father."

"First we have to prove it."

"First we have to figure out where Montana Bob went the fifteenth of every month."

CHAPTER 17

The chest tube was out. Maggie's IV was out. Her bouts
of dizziness were minimal, and her stomach stayed in one
place when she walked to the bathroom. She was just waiting for the neurosurgeon to give his blessing, and she could
check out before more bad news found her.

She was too late.

Dr. Harrison swept in like a rain cloud and sat herself
down on the one good chair in the room like a deportment
instructor.

"You look like hell."

And that was just her idea of a pleasant greeting.

"Strong talk for a woman who can move faster than a
cripple with sore lungs," Maggie said, figuring she'd blame
the drugs for her attitude.

Dr. Harrison almost smiled, then reconsidered. "Do you
know that the hospital press office is overrun? You're quite
the story."

"I know that nobody will let me watch news or read a
paper. They said it would be counterproductive to healing.
What's the latest? Am I an angel of death or a mad psy-
chokiller?"

Dr. Harrison considered Maggie a moment. "I don't
know," she said. "What are you?"

Maggie felt suddenly worse. "I'm trying to prove that
homicides have been committed."

"Well, then, you have your wish. Big Dawg Dwayne Carver was, indeed, murdered. With a massive dose of digoxin." She shrugged. "Not that it would have made a lot of difference. He would have bled out all on his own in another five minutes."

Maggie knew that her eyes were wide. Her mouth was certainly open. "Then what's the problem? Bob was right."

"The problem is that I've also managed to prove that Levon Repton was murdered with a massive overdose of insulin, and that Rodney Culpepper was given a massive dose of heparin, so that he bled to death."

All over Maggie's hands and shoes and pants. She remembered.

"Guess what they all had in common?" Dr. Harrison asked briskly.

"I asked you to look into them," Maggie said.

"You took care of them."

Maggie forgot to close her mouth.

Dr. Harrison was actually looking uncomfortable. "I'm afraid that someone in my office—who does not work for me anymore—mentioned it in the wrong place."

Probably the same person who'd first mentioned it to all the police. Mort Gorman, Maggie's favorite death investigator.

Well, at least he didn't have a job either.

Then Maggie got the real message. Her stomach hit her knees. "Which means that the press have it."

The ME looked even more uncomfortable. "Which means that the prosecuting attorney also has it."

Maggie wondered if she needed that chest tube reinserted. Suddenly she couldn't breathe again, and she was sweaty and cold.

"You've got to be kidding me. *I* came to *you* with my suspicions."

"It's a matter of public trust," Dr. Harrison insisted dryly. "If the prosecuting attorney has this information and doesn't look into it, the press would wonder why."

"God forbid the prosecuting attorney gets a bad reputation. What am I supposed to do?"

"Get a lawyer and lie low."

Maggie laughed. She actually laughed. And she'd been feeling so much better.

Dear God.

"What about Montana Bob?" Maggie asked. "Did you find anything on Bob?"

"I still have tissue. We'll see."

Dr. Harrison got to her feet and smoothed her skirt. Not like a nun, Maggie thought. Like a queen. She was tempted to ask her to say "Off with their heads" just to see what it sounded like.

Maggie wanted to be prepared.

Prepared.

Jesus. In all her permutations, she really hadn't considered this one. Not seriously.

She'd set out to catch a killer, and might end up only catching herself.

"Thank you for coming by, Dr. Harrison," she said. "I do appreciate the warning."

"If you did murder those people," the woman answered very quietly, "I'll personally make sure you hang."

"It's lethal injection now," Maggie answered instinctively. Knowing far better than Dr. Harrison of which she spoke. "And you won't have to worry about dirtying your hands with any syringes on my account."

She hoped.

She had to get hold of Susan Jacobsmeyer.

Which was sad. Here she was surrounded by some of the best forensic talent in the state, and she had to rely on a reporter who was trying to work her way up off the features page.

"Mrs. Wilson," Susan Jacobsmeyer said with a smile, as Montana Bob's daughter opened her door in Glendale.

Betty Wilson shared her quiet smile. "Hello, Ms. Jacobsmeyer. I thought you'd be by. Won't you come in?"

"No time. I have to get back to the paper. I do have one question, though. An important question."

"Of course."

"On the fifteenth of every month, the day his disability checks came in, your father went to meet someone. From what I've heard, he cleaned himself up for it. Was he seeing someone? A lady, perhaps?"

For a second, Betty Wilson looked confused. Then thoughtful. "He got dressed up?"

"According to the people who knew him at Sal Army. They said it wasn't to see you, though. That this was different."

That quickly, Betty Wilson's face changed. Understanding and a wistful satisfaction lit her eyes. "Of course. Of course he was seeing someone. I should have known. That's why he had me get the flowers."

"Do you know who?"

Betty's smile was sweet. "Yes, as a matter of fact. I do."

Maggie got a lawyer. For a minute, she thought of getting the lawyer who had worked out Tommy's deal nine months earlier. But then, she figured he'd be needing him again himself, soon.

She hoped.

What a thing to hope.

Sean broke her out of the hospital in time to get her animals fed for the day and put to bed right alongside her. Sean stayed too, taking up the other side of her bed to share warmth and silence with her, which gave Maggie her first good night's sleep since she'd been injured. And in the morning, he made her breakfast and told her to stay put until he got back off work.

He'd been taken off suspension. Maggie didn't ask details. Sean didn't offer. He just smiled, kissed her as if she'd break like one of her ugly porcelain animals, and left, his utility belt creaking and jangling like a horse's harness.

Maggie popped a couple of Darvocet and climbed gingerly out of bed. With both Wheezer and Ming as attendants, she limped over to her desk, where her computer awaited her. She hadn't heard from Jacobsmeyer yet, and she needed some answers. She had the most terrible feeling that time was running out.

She should have known. She'd no sooner gotten into the *St. Louis Post-Dispatch* archives than her phone rang.

"Pick it up," Tommy's voice commanded on her answering machine.

Ah, fatherly concern.

Maggie picked up the phone as she typed MORRIS, JAMES 'JIMMY' into the question heading.

"How's your eye?" she asked her father.

He laughed. He would. "I taught you a great left hook, girl. You took out three of my own guards."

"I'm so proud."

"Don't be a bitch. It was your own fault, and you know it."

"I'm feeling much better, Dad. But thanks for asking."

She was sore and bruised and trying to anchor the phone on her left shoulder while she typed one-handed, since her right arm was still strapped to her waist. If she took too deep a breath, somebody stabbed a knife in her ribs. And her poor, abused hip had taken yet another hit. Other than that, she was just fine.

Then she started getting hits on Jimmy Morris. The original story of how rape suspect Jimmy Morris had shown up at his arraignment with a face that looked like ground meat. How the arresting officers had claimed that the suspect had resisted arrest. The questions. The complaints. The sudden resignation of Officer of the Year Thomas "Tommy" O'Brien.

Blah-blah-blah. Maggie had lived through that part. It was the follow-up she was interested in.

"You're an O'Brien," her father scoffed at her. "Of course you're better. I raised you tough."

Kind of like roughing something up with sandpaper,

Maggie guessed. Or chewing on leather to make it flexible.

Oh, she probably shouldn't talk to her father when she had drugs on board. They seriously sapped her self-control.

"What did you want, Tommy? Besides a real concern for my welfare."

"It *is* a real concern for your welfare. You think I want some hotshot hurting you again? You've pissed some people really bad, little girl."

"I know."

CONVICTED RAPIST FOUND DEAD IN CELL.

Oh, God. She'd expected it, but she really hadn't wanted it.

Maggie scanned the article and found just what she thought she would. Delayed justice for a handful of little girls.

Jimmy Morris, after plea-bargaining down to one count of felony rape, had been found hanging in his cell at the Potosi State Correctional Center no more than four months after his arrest.

Suicide, the report said. Maggie didn't think so. She thought that somebody had finally played out what her father set up four months earlier.

Her father, who was on the phone.

God, she was so tempted to say something. Something sharp and unforgiving. Something she'd wanted to say her whole life.

But there was much more at stake now than her own self-respect. Her bid for freedom.

"Maggie? You listening to me?"

"Yeah, Tommy. Don't I always listen to you?"

She got a sharp bark of laughter for that. "Shit, you never listen to me, girl. But listen this time. It killed me to see you like that, in that hospital bed. I'm glad you decided to back away, for your own sake."

Not for your own? she almost asked.

"Uh-huh," she said instead.

"I promise—and you know I can—I'll try and corral

everybody. It's a bad thing that's happened, but it won't happen anymore."

"Thanks, Tommy."

No surviving family members listed for Jimmy Morris. Nobody close enough to the victim to protest his untimely death. Just a non-involved public, who would see the "convicted rapist" part and feel themselves a little safer, a little holier, because their justice system had seen one more violent offender taken off the streets.

And Tommy.

Whom Maggie was going to have to face with this sooner or later.

She almost puked the Darvocet all over her computer.

"Uh, Tommy, I have to go now. Okay?"

"Okay, little girl. You get some rest. I'll come see you soon, okay?"

Maggie squeezed her eyes shut against the reflexive terror. "Yeah."

"Oh, and Maggie?"

"Yeah."

"There is enough evidence to convict you of those murders, you know. If the prosecuting attorney really wanted to do it."

If you don't behave.

Maggie had thought she couldn't feel any worse.

Silly her.

"Don't bother coming by, Tommy. But thanks all the same for the warning."

And she hung up.

She didn't know how long she sat there staring at Jimmy Morris's obituary and thinking about the proof she needed to save herself. To stop this. To convict her friends of murder.

Thinking of the walls closing in on her, both literally and figuratively. She still had friends. Maggie knew that. Friends might prevent anybody else pushing her over a balcony, but they couldn't save her from concrete proof that she'd killed at least three patients.

Because she had.

No matter who had put the digoxin into a bristoject marked lidocaine.

She didn't even hear the phone ring again until she got yelled at over her answering machine.

"Tell this blockhead to let me into your building!"

Susan Jacobsmeyer.

What blockhead?

"Susan?" Maggie asked, yanking up the receiver. "What blockhead?"

"There's a police unit down here that thinks I'm harassing you. Like the uplink trucks down the block."

Maggie closed her eyes again. Maybe she should just get back into bed.

Or under it.

"Let me talk to him."

"Maggie? It's Paul. You sure you want to see her?"

"Yeah, Paul. She's actually helping me on getting some information for my defense."

"That's bullshit, you know."

She smiled. "I know. Thanks, honey."

Susan was banging on the door by the time Maggie hung up. It took Maggie considerably longer to let her in.

"Get on your Hardy Boys disguise," Susan said in greeting as she shot into the room. "We're going to in-ves-ti-gate."

"Right now I feel much more like Miss Marple."

"You look much more like the corpse in act one. Jeez, have you seen your face?"

"It's called raccoon eyes. Typical."

"Very attractive. But it's gonna be hard to sneak you by the press."

Maggie peeked out the window to see that, indeed, the narrow streets of Soulard were beginning to fill up with camera trucks.

"Good God. Isn't there a war going on somewhere they'd rather cover?"

"Probably, but I bet the amenities aren't as good."

"Are you sure we have to go out there?"

"I am."

"Why?"

There was enough of a silence that Maggie pulled her attention back from the beehive of activity on her street. Susan was smiling. Susan wasn't just smiling. She was gloating.

"Because I know where Montana Bob went on the fifteenth. I think I may know where our evidence is."

Maggie straightened so fast her head spun. "Well, why the hell didn't you say so?"

It took them twenty minutes to work out an escape route. Paul helped by shoving a hooded and covered Susan out the front door into a car for the press to follow while Maggie crept out the back. Susan met her half an hour later, and the two of them sped east toward I-70.

It took fifteen minutes to get where they were going. When they did, Maggie found herself facing an angel. And not just any angel. The Drunken Angel. Maggie's favorite monument in Calvary Cemetery, which she'd visited often in her earlier years, since most of her family was buried there.

Usually carved in bird-stained marble, the winged seraph lay draped over a large rectangular tombstone, a posy hanging from her hand, as if caught in a moment of intense grief. Except to irreverent teenagers, who thought it looked more like the morning after a bad prom date.

And one of the angels had draped herself over the tomb of Montana Bob.

"Oh, Susan," Maggie said, standing before it. "I just don't think I'm in any shape to dig anybody up today."

"The flowers," Susan said easily. "Look at the flowers."

In fact, before the left side of the big granite slab, which evidently belonged to Bob's beloved wife, named Mary Ellen, was an inground vase. Right now, the only flowers evident were a few very faded plastic roses that wilted almost as drunkenly as the angel.

"Flowers."

Susan huffed in impatience. "You *are* on drugs."

Without another word, she knelt to the side of the graves, one soft and groomed, the other still a raw wound, and reached to lift the vase out of the marble stand that held it.

Maggie took a second to pat the fresh grave. She wished she could tell Bob how sorry she was that she hadn't believed him. That she hadn't been able to save him. That he'd had to suffer his demons at all.

Useless guilt, just like his daughter's.

"I'm right!" Susan squealed, then turned, as if expecting spies.

Maggie almost smiled. Paranoia must be contagious. Even from a three-month-old grave.

Susan pulled her arm from the cavity, and came away with a plastic bag.

A bag that held tiny spools of recorded tape. Pictures. A small, precise little notebook, the kind an agent might carry to record his evidence, his thoughts, his suspicions.

Left right there, where his heart lived. With his Mary Ellen.

"Holy Mother of God," Maggie whispered.

She'd searched for it. She'd hoped for it. She hadn't really believed it existed. Maggie followed Susan back to the car like an acolyte behind the monstrance, knowing for certain that what had passed for her life was utterly changed.

Because of a bag.

Because of what the bag held. A last gift from a friend who had once given her flowers.

The minute the car doors were closed and the air-conditioning on, Susan opened the bag. Maggie was surprised by the panic that washed through her.

She remembered Zen talking once about going into labor. How she'd waited breathlessly for nine months to have her baby, but that when the time had come, she'd frozen. She'd changed her mind. Because she knew that in another twelve hours, her life would never be the same.

At least Zen got a baby out of it. Maggie was afraid she was about to lose everything else she held dear.

"Do you know any of these people?" Susan asked.

Maggie looked over to see that Susan had fanned some of the photographs across her lap. All black-and-white, professionally crisp. Clear. Unquestionably identifiable.

"Oh," was all Maggie could say at first, her hand reaching instinctively out toward Allen's intense face. "Oh, no."

"You don't?" Susan asked, surprised.

Maggie closed her eyes. "I do."

And set aside her paralysis. Opening her eyes, she reached for the rest of the shots. They had all been taken at the Toe Tag. Nobody could mistake that decor, or the extras in the background. Each with a different date and reference to a tape number.

No names, though. Bob probably hadn't known all the names.

Maggie did.

"We need to listen to the tapes," she said, flipping through Bob's notebook.

She found no more than she'd expected from an FBI agent. A record of every tape, every photo, every occasion Bob had collected evidence, all in small, precise print, as if Bob's discipline had temporarily kept the madness away, like fires in the night.

Susan, meanwhile, was pulling a minirecorder from her glove compartment. Without hesitation, she chose a tape and popped it in.

Two voices, male. Background bar noise.

"At least you didn't have to shoot him."

"Nah. You can always rely on gangbangers to do the deed if you piss 'em off enough. You sure nobody'll know?"

"After all those holes in him? Even Tommy's kid didn't catch on that Big Dawg didn't die of that bleed."

"And another one bites the dust."

"And another one . . ."

They swung into the old song, chortling and, Maggie thought, high-fiving. She wanted to be sick.

"Who is it?"

Maggie thought she knew. She couldn't prove it, though. Bob hadn't known names, so his notes of the tape recording mentioned only date, time, and a transcript of the conversation.

And names of the victims. Twenty of them, starting sixteen months ago.

Twenty.

And that only included the ones before Montana Bob.

Susan played another tape, and another. More incriminating voices, more laughter. More toasting. One voice Maggie knew better than most, another she dreaded hearing. Enough here to put anybody away.

After hearing a bit of each tape, Susan dropped the tape recorder back into her lap. "There's no way we can prove who these people are."

"We have pictures."

"Yeah, but no definite link between the two."

Maggie looked at that picture of Allen and wanted to cry. He looked so sincere. So serious and angry. She thought of the names she thought she knew, the people she'd trusted.

"I think there's a way."

Maggie made one phone call, and they left the cemetery for the Tower Grove South neighborhood of the city. One of the older, row house areas of the city, where streets were pockmarked by blight, and residents struggled to maintain property values. Gangs harried and harassed, and neighbors tried their best to stick together.

It was where, against all odds, Big Zen had raised her four children into responsible adulthood.

Maggie and Susan pulled up to her faded redbrick row house and climbed out of the car. The neighborhood was quiet right now, too early for the gangbangers to be out or the workers to be home. Except shift workers, like Zen. Maggie opened the gate to the small, sparse yard and walked up to the green concrete porch.

"You're sure about this?" Susan asked.

Maggie nodded. "After spending thirty years as a dispatcher, nobody in the world would question Zen's ability to recognize a voice. At least of any of the police. And we need to know who the cops are before we take this to anybody. We need to know who's safe out there."

Zen met them at the door, her face calmer than when she'd visited Maggie. Allen had contacted her again, then. Maggie would ask later, after the reporter had gone.

"I didn't know you was gonna be so much trouble when I introduced you," Zen greeted Susan.

Susan's smile was almost apologetic. "Nice to see you again, ma'am."

Zen sighed. "Zen. Just Zen. Come on in."

Zen's house contained two stories, each with three connecting rooms. Maggie and Susan followed Zen through a spotlessly clean living room and bedroom, into a weary linoleum-and-Formica kitchen, where Jesus hung on the surgically clean white wall along with a sampler made by little hands that said *Mothers are God's Gift*.

Zen pulled out three brown plastic-covered kitchen chairs and carried over a pitcher of iced tea. In summer, no home in St. Louis was complete without a pitcher of iced tea.

"You need me to listen to something?" she asked, adding mismatched plastic glasses.

"We were hoping you could identify some voices for us," Maggie said, as Susan set up the tape recorder.

Zen just nodded and poured. The tape spun.

Zen heard the first conversation and stopped. For a moment, she stared at the machine, as if it were a cockroach that had climbed up on her clean kitchen table. As it went on, though, she closed her eyes and slumped down onto her chair.

"I don't know the one," she said quietly, her voice tired, "but I know Bob Walker. Third District. And Vandever of the Sixth."

John Vandever. The rookie Tommy had sacrificed his career for.

Opening her eyes, Zen deliberately finished pouring the tea and handing it around. Maggie made the note. Susan changed tapes.

"Big Bill Williams," Zen said. "Homicide."

Another note, another tape.

Zen's eyes weren't opening anymore. She just sat there, looking smaller and smaller as she heard men and women abet murder. "That boy, Jazz," she said in a dispirited voice. "The medic on your team. I don't recognize the other one. Do you?"

Maggie, getting sicker by the minute herself, nodded. "Yeah. He's my partner out on the ambulance in West County."

At least it explained how Mrs. Quinn had died from the lidocaine she'd once liked so much.

Zen shook her head and took a look over at Jesus, as if he could explain things.

And then with the next tape, Zen's head came up and she stared at Maggie, stricken. "You know who that is."

"*Come on*," he said, his voice wheedling, "*we can get Big Dawg in a situation where they can act. Talk to his rival OG. Tell him Big Dawg is planning on a drive-by. He'll act, I promise. You'll have Big Dawg on a hospital gurney in a day.*"

"*Do you think digoxin has been used too many times?*" he asked on another tape. "*Somebody might guess.*"

"*Like Maggie?*" somebody said.

"*She's my kid. She'll never say anything.*"

Tommy.

"*The guy's a fuckin' pedophile. A priest, and he's diddling kids. You think he should get away with it? I'm telling you, if we just give him the chance, that kid's dad'll put that priest right where he should be.*"

Always there, a whisper in the background, a siren; urging, cajoling, planning, praising. Tommy, whom nobody evidently noticed, was orchestrating everything behind the scenes. Tommy, on his throne down at the Toe Tag, planning murder.

Maggie should have known. She should have figured it out right away, especially when she first realized that the murders had been happening since long before he quit the force. It was the fact that had been niggling at her. The one she'd ignored, because, she decided, it was much simpler that way.

But Tommy would have never let anything like this get by him. He never would have missed all the fun. Or left it in anybody else's hands.

Everybody Maggie heard on these tapes had felt righteous because they hadn't planned a thing. They'd just reacted. Street preachers stomping out sin.

They'd reacted because Tommy had planned for them to.

Those murders might have begun as spontaneous acts of agony. They had become Tommy's personal handiwork.

"What are you gonna do?" Zen asked, shaken.

This time, Maggie didn't smile. "I'm going to turn this over to the prosecuting attorney."

But they weren't finished.

She'd thought the worst betrayal she could feel was to hear her own father's voice on that tape. It turned out that that wasn't true.

The worst betrayal came two tapes later.

" . . . *whatever we do, we have to make sure Maggie O'Brien stays clear of this. She's too damn smart, no matter what anybody says.*"

"*You'll take care of her?*"

"*Happy to. Anything for the cause.*"

"Oh, sweet Jesus," Zen breathed in distress, her huge eyes on Maggie. "Baby, that's wrong. That just can't be."

"Can't be what?" Susan asked.

Maggie didn't say a word. She couldn't. Her stomach was somewhere in her throat.

"It's Sean," Zen said. "It's Sean Delaney."

Maggie couldn't take her eyes off that deadly little tape

recorder. "You didn't hear anybody you recognized from the PA's Office?" she asked, her voice flat.

Zen laid a hand on hers. "No, honey. Nobody."

Maggie nodded and lurched to her feet. "Then it's time we did something about this."

"Maggie? Are you sure?"

Maggie looked at her old mentor and smiled. But her smile was dismal. "I never had a choice, Zen. You know that. Warn Allen."

Because, of course, though they hadn't said it, his voice had been all over those tapes, too.

At least she hadn't heard Carmen. Or anybody else from her SWAT team but Jazz.

At least there was something left.

Zen climbed to her feet as well and reached up to take Maggie's face in her hands. "I couldn't be prouder of you if I was your mama. You know that."

Whatever else, Maggie had Zen back.

Maggie matched her tear for tear. She gave her a kiss and a hug, and she headed out the door.

"I never did ask," Susan said in an obvious attempt for light subject matter as they walked back out the front door. "Among those six wives of Tommy O'Brien, I never found out what happened to your mother."

"My mother?" Maggie asked, stepping out into the hot, shadeless sun. "Oh, she's been dead a long time."

Hanging from the clicking, unbalanced ceiling fan in their apartment, the end of a three-year suicide that had begun when Tommy had thrown her out. It had taken Susie the Slut that long to admit that she couldn't live without a man, no matter what kind of man he was.

Maggie had thought she'd learned that lesson well.

She guessed not well enough, considering how she felt right now.

Which made it only inevitable, she guessed, that when they climbed back into the car, it was to find Sean already there.

"Drive," he said to Susan.

"What?" she asked, turning.

"Drive."

And then he pulled a gun.

CHAPTER 18

Susan froze, halfway inside the car.

"I said drive," Sean repeated coldly.

Maggie spun in her seat so fast she almost stopped breathing. "What the hell do you think you're doing?"

Sean pointed the gun at Susan. "I'm not going to say it again."

He wasn't grinning. He was grim and sweating and silent. Susan dropped into her seat. Maggie blinked a couple of times as if it would help her focus better.

It didn't. A sense of unreality swamped her.

She should have felt something. Fear, anger, outrage. Disbelief. But she felt nothing, a huge, terrifying emptiness that froze her in place. Just like she'd felt when she'd fallen and the endorphins had kept the pain away for those first few moments. Too many disasters, and she was overwhelmed.

She couldn't feel.

She couldn't think.

She couldn't assimilate the fact that it was Sean in the back seat in T-shirt and jeans threatening Susan with his backup Colt.

"Don't be absurd," Maggie snapped instinctively. "You're not going to hurt anybody. Let us out of here."

Sean gave Maggie a calm, level look as he nuzzled his Colt snug against Susan's ear. "Fine," he said. "By now the warrant is out for your arrest for the murders of three of your patients. And Big Bill Williams put himself at the head of the line to serve it. You know Big Bill?"

Big Bill Williams from the tape, who had admitted, among other things, to have shot Sancho Martinez in what they'd all thought had been a drive-by.

Maggie felt what little blood that was left in her face, fade. "You know everything, don't you?"

"Of course I know everything. Now, if you don't want to meet with an unfortunate 'resisting arrest' accident from Big Bill, you might want to convince your friend to take us where I want to go."

"That gun does a fine job all on its own," Susan assured him. "Where to?"

"East—40 East."

Which either meant downtown or across the Mississippi into Illinois. East St. Louis, almost a no-man's-land of gutted buildings and decaying economy, where a car—to say nothing of a body—could be lost for months.

Maggie wanted to say something. She wanted to demand answers. She couldn't.

She must be having a relapse again. She couldn't think. Her head was going to split open, and her side was on fire. She wanted to lie down. She wanted to close her eyes and disappear.

Nothing could be worse than this.

Oh, she shouldn't even think that. Every time she did, she found out what worse could be.

But Sean. Bright, irreverent, loyal Sean.

Sean, who had told her he'd almost died when she had.

Something was wrong with this.

Something was very wrong.

But she couldn't think well enough anymore to figure out what.

"Breathe, Maggie," Sean said without looking away from the road.

Reflexively, she did. Her side hurt worse, but her dizziness dissipated. Her sense of unreality didn't.

"You want to tell us what's going on?" Susan asked, obviously not as stricken by the turn of events as Maggie.

"No. There'll be no talking."

"Just setting the ground rules."

"Those are the ground rules."

They reached 40 and headed east, past Union Station, past city hall and the ball stadium and the Gateway Arch. Swinging out over the river, where it glittered like pewter in the stark sunlight, past the arcing riverfront water fountain on the eastern riverbank, and toward a brick skyline of decline and desperation. Maggie's heart slammed into her throat, and she fought for another breath. Jesus, it was easier breathing with a tube in her chest.

Susan didn't speak. Sean didn't speak, simply pointed toward the highway split toward the Highway 55/70 north sign, which Susan followed. Maggie wheezed quietly on her side of the car, the plastic bag that had started all this lying in her lap like a sacrificial offering.

"Pull off here," Sean instructed as they reached the Route 203 exit. "Take a right."

They'd passed the outskirts of the city. Along the north side of the highway sprawled the Gateway International Raceway, its parking lot empty on a weekday afternoon. To the south, marshlands encroached and weeds littered empty fields.

Empty fields.

They were heading to one, now, Maggie bet.

She still couldn't believe it. No matter what was on the tape. No matter what Sean was doing.

It wasn't Sean.

She swore it wasn't.

"Okay, turn left."

A deserted road that led to nowhere. They'd been on it a couple minutes when Maggie saw the dark sedan parked under a lone cottonwood tree just off the road.

"Stop here and get out."

Doors opened. Heat rushed in. So tight now she felt every ache in her body, Maggie gingerly climbed from the car. She probably shouldn't have been surprised when she felt Sean's hand beneath her arm to help her. Susan just laughed, as if that put the icing on the cake.

Somebody else was opening the sedan as they closed Susan's car.

With the slamming doors still echoing in Maggie's ears, Sean whirled on her, his face furious. "What the hell were you thinking?" he demanded, waving the pistol like a baton. "Did you want to get yourself killed?"

Since he'd been the one with a gun and she hadn't said a word, Maggie wasn't sure how to answer. So she just stared at him. Her knees were sagging, and the light was beginning to flicker.

"Damn it, Maggie," Sean snapped, grabbing her at the waist. "Don't pass out on me now."

Without any ceremony, he sat her right down in the scorched grass and dirt and shoved her head between her knees.

"And the Lord said," he murmured in her ear.

"Not applicable," she snapped. "I don't have a penis, and I'm certainly not feeling amorous."

"Sadly enough"—he sighed—"neither am I."

Maggie sat a moment longer, her face down, the blood seeping back into her brain. She could hear the breeze scratch through the dry grass and a distant plane circling Parks Airfield to their south. She could smell dust and motor oil and a hot radiator. Beneath her sandals a column of ants marched industriously by, not noticing the drama unfolding above their heads.

Life, it seemed, went on. It was just a little hard to keep that in mind with all those sudden surprises tumbling around like sharp rocks in Maggie's brain.

"She okay?" asked the man approaching from the sedan.

Maggie's head came up so fast she almost took out Sean's chin.

She should have known.

Ames. The superior son of a bitch who had patronized her in the Internal Affairs office.

"She's fine," she said, glaring at him, the rocks tumbling faster.

Finally, the final one clunked into place, and Maggie spun on her best friend. "You're working with IA."

Sean flushed. "That's what I brought you here to tell you."

Susan blinked. Then she howled. "You threatened us with a gun to get us here to tell us you're one of the *good* guys?"

Sean spun on her. "I threatened you with a gun to make sure you shut up long enough that you weren't overheard saying something stupid like 'Now we have all the evidence we need right here to put everyone away.' "

"Well, what's wrong with that?" Susan demanded.

"What's wrong with that," Sean explained very patiently, "is that you're not dealing with amateurs. You're dealing with people who have technology available to them. People who have become paranoid enough to protect themselves in any way they could."

Susan's eyes grew very large. "They bugged my car?"

"And Maggie's apartment."

"The rats," Maggie breathed, sick at the thought all over again. Rats, slowly twirling from her ceiling fan.

Sean nodded. "The rats. It's probably the real reason they left them all there, as camouflage. I didn't know until later."

She kept staring at him, trying so hard to work it all out through the haze of drugs, injury, and astonishment.

And betrayal.

Maggie blinked again, as if that could help.

The pattern finally appeared. "You've been working with IA all along," she breathed, as if that could help the truth sink in any better. "You knew even more than I did about the people who've been dying, and you told me I was imagining things. You've been doing the same goddamn investigation I have."

Sean wasn't smiling. "I'm sorry, Mags."

Maggie climbed to her feet, stunned. Furious. She

should have known. She should have damn well known.

"You're sorry an awful lot," she said as if no one else were there to hear her. "Why didn't you tell me?"

"We wouldn't let him," said Ames.

Ames, the pockmarked veteran Maggie had spilled her guts to. The man who had patted her head and sent her home. "You wouldn't let him."

Ames stroked his tie, as if it gave him comfort. "We were pretty sure Tommy O'Brien was involved. We didn't know how much. You are his daughter."

Maggie turned again on Sean. "You didn't think you could trust me?"

Sean had the immense courage never to look away. "We're talking about Tommy, Mags. We couldn't take the chance."

Maggie felt as if she'd been slapped. Humiliated, diminished. That naked, needy little girl again.

Because he was right. She would never have told Tommy to help him. To finally gain approval or reprieve. She would have ended up telling him in anger. Taunting him with it the very next time he'd hurt her. The next time he'd hurt any of her friends.

They were right not to trust her, and that hurt worst of all.

Maggie conceded first and looked away. Looked down to where insects busily occupied themselves in a deserted wasteland of grass and trash. Then, because she couldn't hold herself up, she just sat back down.

Sean was back on his knees next to her. "What did I ask you, Maggie? Leave it to IA, I said. Leave it to the police. Why the hell do you think I told you that?"

"I don't know, Sean," she said quietly. "Why did you?"

"Because I knew how far this had gone, and I knew where it was heading. I wanted you safe! I did every fucking thing I could think of to keep you safe."

Maggie still couldn't look away, as, finally, she understood everything. Every little decision. Every lie and evasion.

"Even pretend you were screwing underage cheerleaders, I hope."

"Of course even that, damn it. I had to get you angry enough not to ask questions about my suspension, didn't I?"

But she knew now. She knew better.

"Of course. And if I'd backed off, like you say you wanted, how much evidence would you have pulled together over in IA, Sean?"

Susan was watching back and forth like a tennis match. The breeze came again, rustling now through the cottonwood. It didn't help. The sun beat down on their heads and shimmered off the ground.

Neither Ames nor Sean could quite face her.

"How much?"

"Not anything specific enough for indictments," Ames admitted stiffly, both hands now worrying at his tie. "Names, overheard conversations, the deaths. And, of course, The List. No hows or whos. It's a hell of a tough case to prove, you know."

Maggie nodded, still very still. "Oh, yes. I do. And I imagine that without access to hospital records, you wouldn't have had any luck at all. After all, until the last ten months or so, the police really didn't get personally involved with making sure the victims reached the hospital to be killed. And besides, the murders were medical, and who would know how to kill somebody in a hospital better than a nurse? Isn't that right?"

Sean stood, shoved his hands in his pockets. If he rattled his keys, Maggie would pull his own gun on him.

"You sat back," she accused, her voice soft with the hurt of it, "and waited for me to collect your evidence for you. Didn't you, Sean?"

"Maggie—"

"I should have figured it out, really. I mean, how stupid could I be not to know that you wouldn't just blow me off the way you have been? You knew all along I'd never leave this alone."

"I told you to go to IA," he insisted.

"After I had most of the leads already lined up. After I had most of the information that could get you your indictment."

Finally, Sean faced her, and Maggie saw what his deception had cost him. She knew damn well that whatever else Sean Delaney was, he was an honest cop. He was a good cop. He was a good friend. And this time he'd been caught dead astride both those demands. He'd tried to protect Maggie from herself and from the case, while trying his best to help solve it within the restrictions placed by his bosses.

Maggie knew that no matter what she did, she couldn't punish Sean any more than he would himself.

But that didn't mean she could forgive him. Not now. Not soon.

So she turned away and looked out over the weeds. "We have all the evidence you'll need," she said.

"What evidence?" Ames demanded.

"Montana Bob's evidence."

"That head case?" Ames retorted, smacking the side of Sean's car as if it were an unruly child. "Don't be an idiot. He couldn't tie his own goddamn shoes, much less convict a killer."

"He was the one who led us in the right direction," Sean reminded his boss.

Maggie looked up and laughed, a dry, unpleasant sound. "You mean to tell me that Bob came to you first?"

Even Ames looked a little sheepish. "He kept dogging us. Insisting we check out these coincidences. These voices he overheard at the Toe Tag."

"And you didn't believe him."

"He was crazy, Mags," Sean insisted. "Who'd believe a crazy guy hearing voices?"

"Until you started overhearing the same conversations." Maggie shook her head. "I don't suppose he told you he had evidence."

"Of course he did," Ames huffed. "So what?"

"You all should have listened to him," she said. "As a paranoid schiz, he was a better cop than the cops."

"Bullshit."

"We have the evidence he collected, remember. Photos, notes, and audio evidence linking enough of the deaths to get convictions. Damn good stuff, I might add."

"But that's not . . ."

Maggie chased an ant across the dust with her finger. "I have the medical records that tie them together. Zen can identify the police and one paramedic on those tapes, and I can identify some of the medical people. There are some county people I didn't recognize, but you can follow that up. Dr. Harrison also has definitely concluded that at least three people on my list were given lethal dosages of drugs. Which means you can go to the prosecuting attorney's office with it, because nobody in that office is either mentioned or implicated."

Maggie felt Sean's hand on her hair and almost pulled away. "It was why it took us so long," he said. "We had no way to get proof. I got close, but not close enough. I'm sure Tommy didn't trust me."

Maggie managed a short, dry laugh at that. "Oh, I'm sure he didn't. I wonder who was stupid enough to think he would."

"I was," Ames said, and Maggie heard him lighting up a cigarette.

Maggie just shook her head. "With a batting average like that, Lieutenant, if you played ball for me, I'd bench your sorry ass."

"What happens now?" Susan asked.

Sean straightened, as if slipping back into his uniform. "I borrow your car to go to the prosecuting attorney with what we have, and Ames drives you two somewhere safe 'til this is wrapped up."

"No," Maggie said, straightening. "I'm going with you."

"Maggie—"

She was implacable. "I found the evidence. I was the only one who listened to Montana Bob. I owe it to him to deliver this. Besides, I find myself in need of clearing my name for murder."

"And Tommy?"

Maggie looked back down, this time to the bag in her lap.

"Tommy," she echoed bleakly.

It was almost too much, after all. Sapping her strength and battering her courage. *I don't suppose I could just stay here*, she wanted to ask. *Never get up from where the ants are scaling my toes and the sun will eventually wither me to an apple dolly, never to have to face the most terrible moment of my life.*

Tommy would never understand. He would see her act as treason. Tommy would know with the conviction of a warrior that he was right, that his cause was just. That his was the only way. Tommy wouldn't understand the fact that his only daughter had turned on him. His disappointing daughter, the only chance he'd had, after six wives, to re-create himself. And she refused to be re-created.

Well, she'd worked her entire life for the moment she could stand up to her father.

This was the goal she'd sought through every day, every nightmare, every sweaty, exhausted, overwhelmed second she'd fought for her place in the hospital, on the ambulance, on the SWAT team.

To be different from Tommy O'Brien.

To be better.

No matter how hard she'd worked for it, she'd never anticipated how much it would hurt.

"You have the evidence you need against Tommy," she said. "He was the instigator. Oh, not right away, I think. But later, when he realized that he could control what was going on. You can hear him in the background, like that voice that tells you to do what you want to do instead of what you should do. Tommy urged every one of them on." She paused a moment, gathering strength. "He also took that dive for beating up Jimmy Morris to protect the program so that nobody would know that he'd done it just to get Jimmy into the hospital so he'd be killed. But then, he managed it some other way."

"What?" Susan asked.

"You didn't have time to check," Maggie said. "Jimmy Morris died in prison four months ago. Hanged. Which means that if I have anything to say about it, Tommy's going to prison, too."

Sean truly looked worried. "Are you sure?"

Maggie sucked in a breath and faced him. "There has to be somebody out there I can protect from him."

Sean didn't so much as smile. He just kept his hand on her shoulder, keeping her close. Maggie heard Susan rustle behind her.

"That is not for publication," Maggie snapped.

"I know," the reporter admitted, then paused. "But it's killing me."

"Console yourself with that front-page spread."

Then, sore, battered, exhausted, and so sick she wanted to lie down in the grass in a little ball and just stare at the ground, Maggie gathered what was left of her strength and went into battle. With Sean's help, she lurched back to her feet and handed him the bag of evidence.

"Okay, let's go get this done before Tommy finds out. You want to stop by the hospital on the way to the prosecuting attorney's? That's where the bag with the rest of my notes and evidence is."

"The hospital?"

She grinned. "My locker."

Sean just shook his head. Obviously, he'd been looking for it. "Afterward, I think. We need to get this stuff to a safe place, and I don't want to run the risk of meeting up with anybody before we do."

Maggie nodded and turned for the car.

"One more thing, Mags," he said. "So you know."

Maggie braced herself all over again.

"Allen is meeting us down there."

Maggie's smile was sad, but she nodded. "I knew he would."

She hadn't. She'd hoped. But no matter what else had gone wrong with him, he was still Big Zen's son.

Five minutes later, the field was empty once again, with another cigarette butt to add to the litter.

In the end, it was easier than Maggie thought. Once he knew for sure that the prosecuting attorney's office was clean, Ames called to set up a meeting. Maggie and Sean walked in to be greeted by not only damn near the entire legal prosecuting staff, but Ames, the captain of Homicide, Dr. Harrison and, finally, Allen, who had turned himself in wearing a bright orange silk jumpsuit and sequined knit cap and tennis shoes.

For the first time since she could remember, Maggie burst out laughing. "Never let it be said that you'd go quietly, Allen," she greeted him with a big hug.

"Well," he admitted with a generous wave, "I thought I should get myself acclimated to my new environment, ya know? What do you think, darling, does prison chic do it for me?"

She reached up and patted his gaunt cheek. "You'll make it the next trend, Allen. I swear."

Allen patted back, his hand hesitant and betrayed by a fine tremor. "You cannot forgive me, my saintly little stormtrooper. It would be too much."

"I can forgive whoever I damn well please, my very decorative beauty queen. And I can forgive anybody who finds he can't kill me after all."

"I'll make you proud."

"Make Zen proud. That's tougher."

They smiled like kids and, without a word, turned back to business.

After that, it only took half an hour. Allen was escorted away to meet his lawyer, and Maggie and Sean left to clean out her locker at the hospital.

By the time she walked onto the ED worklane half an hour later, Maggie was exhausted. One more job, she thought, and then it was over. She would have closure. Broken from her friends, finally severed from her father. Ready to go home and rest.

"There you are."

Not quite yet, it seemed.

Maggie turned from her open locker to see Tommy standing about ten feet away. Decked out in his razor-pressed security uniform, his face taut, his hands fisted against his side, he looked like Judgment at its most terrible.

Maggie knew she shouldn't have sent Sean off for a trash bag. Who the hell cared if she saved the drug manuals and trauma scale cards she'd hoarded in her locker? She didn't want to deal with Tommy alone.

But, it seemed, that was just what she was about to do.

The two of them stood there a moment, gunslingers faced off across the length of a dusty street, all the townsfolk walking about their business as if they didn't notice.

They noticed. Maggie saw them. Some looked triumphant, some frightened. All looked apprehensive. The only surprises trauma staff liked came on ambulance carts.

"Yes, Tommy," Maggie said, shutting her locker. "Here I am."

It was about five feet from the locker wall to the heart of the worklane, where a full load of patients was keeping the staff hopping. The radios crackled, dissonant alarms buzzed, and staff bounced along the halls like random ions.

But amid the usual chaos, Tommy stood perfectly still. Maggie found herself walking toward him, just wanting to get it over.

He knew, of course. She could see it in his eyes. The disbelief, the rage. Maggie O'Brien had turned on her own father, the great Tommy "The Terminator" O'Brien. To Tommy, it was an incomprehensible act.

Just what she had thought it, until only a little while ago.

"What would you like me to say, Tommy?" she asked as she reached him.

"I'd like you to tell me why you did this."

Maggie didn't even have to consider. "Because innocent people were being murdered."

"Bullshit," he snapped, and turned to walk away.

Maggie stayed where she was.

"You won't admit it," he amended, waving his hand behind him. "You think you're so fucking righteous, when you're no *fucking* different than any one of us."

Maggie didn't say a word. She stayed right where she was. Better to let him get it out of his system once and for all. Then she could finish and leave, and it would be over.

But Tommy didn't finish. Tommy didn't walk out the door, as Maggie thought he would. He reached the edge of the pressure mat that controlled the automatic doors and turned.

Which was when Maggie realized what he really had in mind.

He had a gun in his hand. His Beretta nine millimeter, with an eleven-round clip. And he was pointing it right at her.

"Come here," he snapped.

The activity on the worklane screeched to a halt. Somebody gasped. Somebody else yelled "Gun!"

"Shut up," Tommy commanded, his quiet cop voice unignorable. "I said come here."

Maggie walked toward him. She saw the stunned disbelief on the faces of her co-workers where they'd frozen in place. She smelled the usual miasma of blood, exhaust, and Betadine. She felt sweat break out across her back, because she better than anyone else knew where this was headed.

Tommy was setting her up.

He was forcing her to the ultimate challenge.

"What do you want, Tommy?" she asked quietly, already in negotiator mode.

His smile was vicious. "I want you to finally admit it. You're no better than I am. In fact, you're worse. You're a lying whore who doesn't even have any guts. You're nothin'."

Maggie stopped some five feet away. Directly in the line of fire. Solidly in Tommy's line of sight, so he couldn't terrify anybody else. Because nobody else had ever seen this face of Tommy.

"This isn't making things any better," Maggie said, her free hand to her side, all her fingers open.

Empty hands. Non-threatening hands.

She wasn't well enough for this. Hell, she'd never be well enough, but right now her heart was doing triple time, and she was beginning to shake.

Tommy laughed. "You think there's a better answer to this? You turned me in to the prosecuting attorney's office. My own kid. The kid I had such hopes for. How many times do you have to disappoint me?"

"I don't know, Tommy. But this isn't the way to settle it."

His smile never wavered. His eyes damn near glowed. "Oh yes it is." With one hand, he reached into his pocket and pulled out another gun. The Smith & Wesson .357, with enough of a kick to redislocate Maggie's shoulder, and an impact that could knock a hole the size of a fist in Tommy's chest.

Never taking his gaze or the gun from Maggie, he bent to slide the pistol across the floor to her feet.

"Pick it up."

Maggie shook her head. "No."

"Pick it up, Maggie. You don't know what I'll do if you don't."

"Yes, I do, Tommy. I've seen variations on this theme since I was three."

His eyes narrowed. "You haven't seen this one. If you don't shoot me first, I'll begin shooting everyone in this department. One by one."

Maggie heard the sudden rustle of movement behind her. She saw mouths sag and bodies go rigid. She ignored them. She was smiling at her father.

"No you won't," she said softly. "No matter what you've done to criminals, in all your life, you have never deliberately hurt an innocent. You won't hurt any of these people."

"I won't?"

"No, Tommy. They haven't done anything to you. You won't do anything to them. Now, would everyone please vacate the hall? Evacuate the department as quickly and quietly as you can, please. This is between my father and me. I'm sure you understand."

"You sure, Maggie?" she heard behind her.

"I'm sure. Tommy's not going to hurt you."

The color rose on Tommy's face. His stance grew more rigid. Maggie knew that he couldn't argue, because she'd told the truth. It was part of Tommy's code. Montana Bob he could hurt because Montana Bob had been a threat. These people weren't.

"No," Tommy said. "You can only go as far as the rooms. I'll give you that. No farther. And tell them to lock these doors"—he motioned to the frosted doors behind him—"or I shoot her. One joint at a time."

Somebody must have believed him. Maggie heard the locks engage. She heard the quick shuffle of feet and the sighing of doors. And she saw what Tommy couldn't, that they were trying to empty the rooms behind him.

Now all she had to do was talk him out of this.

Go into hostage mode. Play the Stockholm Syndrome against him.

Her father.

Her *father*.

But then, rule one of being a successful hostage was getting the hostage taker to see you as a person. If she hadn't been able to accomplish that in the last twenty-six years, Maggie didn't see any chance of doing it now.

Her *father*.

She took in a breath, struggling to stay calm. To stop shaking and sweating like a junkie with a bad jones.

"You know that the SWAT team's been called by now,

Tommy," she said. "There isn't that much time left. Please. You still have a way out."

"Not until you admit that I'm right. Not until you show me yourself that you aren't any better than I am."

"I'm not . . ."

"You hate me. I make you furious. You think I'm wrong. That I'm a murderer. Well, show me, little girl. Show me your stuff. Stop me before I kill again."

An elephant, she thought desperately. Just one orange elephant holding an umbrella over its head. A lime green donkey with a flower in its teeth. Please, God, she needed to smash something safe so she didn't pick up that gun.

She needed a backloader and a crane to get all the stupid porcelain ornaments into her apartment she'd need to smash after this.

Please, don't let him do this.

Don't let *me* do this.

"Are you mad yet, Maggie?" her father asked in that siren's voice of his. "After all that work, all that secrecy, you could have just come to me. I would have told you. And now, you want nothing more than to just get even with me. For once in your life. Stand up to me. You have the way to do it right there."

Maggie saw a door crack just past Tommy's shoulder. Saw a foot clad in familiar tennis shoes. God, she wanted to shout, to warn the person.

Tommy heard. He knew. His eyes grew sly. His smile broadened.

"No, Tommy," she said, trying to take slow breaths. Trying not to let him see that sweat was soaking the back of her T-shirt. "I won't do that. You don't want me to do that. Not here."

"I don't?" he asked, then seemed to consider. "You're sure there's nothing that would make you pick up that gun."

"I'm not going to shoot you, Tommy. I walked away from guns ten years ago, and I'm not picking one up now."

Especially since it was Tommy who told her to.

She was better than that.

She was better than Tommy.

She was shaking so hard her teeth were rattling.

Maggie could hear frantic voices beyond the closed patient room doors, the grumble of cart wheels skidding along the back halls. She heard feet pounding and the incessant beeping of suddenly disconnected monitors. She hoped like hell nobody was hurt in all this.

Especially her.

Or even, she thought, struggling for breath, Tommy.

It wouldn't prove anything.

"Ya know, you're right," he suddenly admitted, chuckling. "I have to admit. I never have hurt anybody who didn't deserve it."

Maggie didn't know how to answer. The words were right. The expression was wrong. The .357 was still resting against the tip of her sandals, and Tommy hadn't lowered his Beretta.

"I could shoot *you*," he said to her.

"You could," she answered. "But then you'd lose, wouldn't you?"

He nodded, as if considering. "Yes, I guess I would. So I'll have to do the next best thing."

And without hesitation, he whipped around and fired his gun.

The door that had been opening shattered in a spray of glass. The foot that had made a move out of it stuttered a little, and then slid. Maggie saw the jeans, saw the T-shirt, saw the blood that had bloomed on its abdomen. She saw the surprise on Sean's eyes.

He tried to smile, but his knees gave out, and he just crumpled to the floor.

"Sean!" she yelled, running for him.

Tommy grabbed her by the arm and swung her back around.

"All right," he said in a jovial voice. "If you don't shoot me first, I won't let you go until he's dead. Now, what do you think?"

CHAPTER 19

The 911 call reached the city police dispatcher at 17:24. A possible hostage situation at the Blymore Memorial Hospital Emergency Department with multiple hostages. The watch commander and two squad cars were immediately dispatched, with the SWAT captain and lieutenant put on notice of a possible intervention.

The lieutenant decided not to wait for further orders. Not only was the call at a hospital, but the hospital was no more than a mile away. At least half his team could get there within fifteen minutes. He pulled Pax from the break room and told the dispatcher to page a 1040 for the rest of his team.

"Shit," Pax huffed as he skidded into the office. "A hospital. It's the only goddamn place in town we haven't practiced."

The lieu grabbed his stuff and headed for the door. "We were too busy making sure we had the high schools and casinos covered. Why don't you radio the watch commander and tell him to get maintenance to meet us at the security office with the hospital plans? We can stage there, unless there's a problem."

By the time they reached Blymore, the ambulance entrance was clogged with flashing units, and patients and staff loitered across the blacktop. The watch commander was using his people to herd the crowd to the far side of the hospital and set up a second perimeter. He met the SWAT lieutenant in the doorway.

"I don't guess the hostage situation has miraculously resolved itself, has it?" the lieutenant asked as he finished strapping on his vest.

"It has not," the watch commander answered, following inside. "One perpetrator, who's evidently closed off that hall there." He pointed toward the far end of the short triage hall where the frosted doors onto worklane one remained closed. "The other two halls have been cleared along with surrounding departments, and some of the rooms on this lane. I've managed to insert a couple of guys in lab coats behind the doors on worklane one to scope things out. Plans are on their way up."

The lieutenant nodded. "Check out one of the other worklanes for layout, Pax, and let me know. Get me a throw phone, and maybe we can talk to this person. Do you know anything about the perp? Male or female?"

"Definitely male," the watch commander said. "It gets worse."

The lieutenant plopped his helmet on his head and grimaced. "Of course it does. How?"

"Even though most of the staff and patients left in the hall are tucked behind closed doors, there is one hostage in the hallway. Maggie O'Brien."

Both the lieutenant and Pax skidded to a halt.

"Maggie?" the lieutenant echoed. "What the hell is she doing here?"

"Facing off with her father, evidently."

There was a moment of dead silence.

"Oh, shit," Pax breathed. "Tommy."

The watch commander nodded. "Tommy."

"Get me John in here now to negotiate."

It was then they heard the gunshot.

Calm.

She needed calm.

She couldn't find it. Maggie's heart slammed against her ribs, and her chest closed. She couldn't see very well. She couldn't breathe. She was drowning, and she couldn't fight her way free.

She wanted to kill her father.

She wanted to *kill* him.

And he knew it.

He was smiling.

Maggie thought she'd vomit.

Instead, she turned toward where Sean had slumped, his legs caught in the half-open door.

"Get him into the hallway," Tommy said.

"I will not," she answered. "He's going to get help."

"No," Tommy said. "He isn't. Not 'til we're finished. I told you."

Maggie whipped around on him, her voice barely recognizable. "You can't mean this, Tommy. You *can't*."

"Oh, but I do. If you don't pull him out here, I'll start shooting out his joints. His right knee first. Then, his left elbow, I think. You believe me, don't you, Maggie?"

Maggie believed him. But she still couldn't move. She couldn't do this. She couldn't keep her control anymore. She couldn't keep her hands off that gun.

She couldn't save Sean if she did, and she couldn't save herself if she didn't.

She bent over Sean and did her best to grab him with her free hand.

"I'm sorry," she whispered.

"You didn't . . . shoot me," he assured her, that wide grin of his just a little shaky as he pushed with his feet to help her.

She got him just outside the door and laid him out. Grabbing a pile of linen, she propped his head up a little.

"Okay?" she asked.

His grin broadened. "I'm at your mercy. How'd you know it was me, Tommy?"

"Who else would give a damn about her right now?"

"More people than you think, actually."

"That's enough," Tommy snapped. "Get back here where that gun is, Maggie."

Control, she prayed. Calm.

She'd done this before. As a SWAT team member. As a daughter. She could get through it.

Please.

Maggie turned back to her father and walked over to where the .357 lay, her hand once again held out at her side. The classic position of surrender.

But Tommy knew that Maggie wasn't surrendering. His smile grew.

"You can't tell me you're not mad now, little girl," he said.

He was sweating hard, his hand not quite steady. His eyes seemed dilated, as if he were sexually excited. Maggie was having so much trouble facing him. Facing the man who'd taken her to ball games and precinct barbecues. Who'd only wanted her to be like him.

Who still held her self-assurance in his beefy hands.

A pink Pekingese waving a flag. Smash against her fireplace. Smash! Smash! Smash!

Maggie saw red. She actually saw red. And here she'd always thought that kind of thing had only been literary license. She was shaking again, with Sean lying alongside her, her father before her and that deadly, seductive gun at her feet. And she saw it through a real red haze.

"I'm not going to shoot you," she managed through a dry, tight throat.

Bargain with him. Placate him. Understand him.

It was what she'd done before. It was what she'd been trained to do with hostage takers just like him.

It was what she was supposed to do.

It wasn't what she wanted to do. She wanted to scream at him like a harpy, take her nails to his eyes, her teeth to his throat. She wanted, finally, *finally*, to make him stop.

"But you're angry, aren't you? You're furious. You want to kill me. Just like you wanted to kill that guy who toasted his son. You *want* that so bad, you're sweating with it.

Don't tell me you're not, because I can see it."

"Is that what's going to make you feel better, Tommy?" she asked, still as quietly as possible, statue quiet, so that his attention stayed with her.

In a moment, she'd move. Just a little. A step or two. So she could distract Tommy long enough to get Sean through that broken door.

One-handed. With ribs that were already screaming at her.

Uh-huh.

"Is it?" she repeated. "To hear that I'm as human as anybody else? Okay. I'm human. I have the same feelings as anybody else. But I can't pick up that gun just so you'll feel self-righteous."

"You will," he insisted on a hiss. "Just like everybody else, because you want to. You *want* to, right down there at the bottom of your gut. It's why they did it, you know. Not 'cause it was right. Because they *wanted* those people dead. They wanted to feel better, if only for a little while. They wanted to pretend they were *strong*."

"Is that what you told them, when you whispered in their ears? That they'd feel better? That it was their right? That it was only fair? Is that what you taught your rookie?"

She had to stop. Jesus, she wasn't helping a thing. Maggie knew damn well how to negotiate a situation like this, and yet she simply couldn't tell Tommy that she understood. That she sympathized. She couldn't do whatever it took to get him out alive, agree to anything, be anything.

Not anymore.

Not with Tommy.

"It was only fair, little girl. It was their turn. It was *our* turn, and don't you forget it. But I don't think you will forget it, because it's *your* turn, now. It's your turn to do what you've always wanted to do, and you'll tell yourself that you did it to save Delaney's life. And, in a way, you'll be right, won't you? 'Cause I'm not moving 'til he's dead, and I'm not going to let you move, either. And there's only one way to stop me, little girl."

"You'd die just to prove you're right?" she asked.

He shrugged. "What's the difference? You've already condemned me to hell. I'm a cop. You think I'm going to like prison?"

"Something you might have thought about before you started all this."

"Something you're going to think about after you shoot me. After you pick up that gun, the one you've been toeing for the last five minutes, and aim it. Right at me, little girl, right at my chest, because that's what you want to do. It's what you're aching to do, and you know it."

But Maggie shook her head. Took another tiny step to her rear, away from Sean. "I can't do that, Tommy."

"Not even for the man who saved you from me?"

Maggie looked over. She shouldn't have. Sean was ashen, panting. She didn't see much blood, but that didn't make any difference. The bullet wound was in his right upper quadrant. Spleen, liver, diaphragm, maybe intestines. Any or all. She could see him bleeding to death before her, and his hands weren't even red.

Tommy couldn't ask this of her.

No one could.

But Sean smiled. He turned his head toward Tommy and grinned. "Don't get *me* involved," he said, his voice high and breathy. "I'll kill myself before I let her pick up that gun."

"Don't be an idiot," Tommy snapped at him. "You're gonna die."

"You're killing *her*," Sean said. "Don't you see?"

Tommy turned his head away.

"Do *not* pick up . . . that gun, Mags," Sean said, and all the humor was gone. "I couldn't live with . . . that."

No person in the world could have given Maggie a greater gift.

But she wasn't at all sure she could accept.

She wasn't sure if she could live with his death on her head.

So she was just going to have to get out of this as fast as possible.

Without that gun.

Without becoming Tommy.

Maggie was turning back to Tommy when the loud-speaker clicked. "Tommy," came the voice of her uncle John, "we'd like to throw in a phone so we can talk. You know we're all out here."

Oddly enough, Tommy smiled, as if he had not only expected this, but anticipated it.

"I can get the phone if you want," Maggie told him. "They won't stop talking 'til you answer, and that loud-speaker's going to end up driving you nuts."

"Get it."

Maggie saw Flower lean a hand out through the gap in the glass of the door from room four. She walked over to retrieve the phone he held, smiling at him in reassurance. He surreptitiously offered her a pistol. She shook her head and made it a point to look down at Sean, where he lay almost at her feet. Then she looked back up and let her eyes stray around toward where she'd stood. Flower nodded. Maggie felt a flicker of hope as she walked away without once meeting Sean's eyes.

She handed the phone to Tommy and walked back toward where the gun lay, but stopped farther away, a little toward his right. Farther from Sean. Farther from Flower where he hid behind that door.

"I'll say this once, John," Tommy said into the phone, "and only once. The only person I'm talking to is Maggie, and she's already in here. When we're finished, we'll come out. Do you understand?"

Maggie heard her uncle John object, his voice as carefully calm as hers. She heard him try his damnedest.

"Anybody so much as sneezes in one of those rooms," Tommy said, "you try and force your way in before I'm finished, and I'll start shooting. And you won't want my body count, my friend."

Then Tommy turned off the phone and threw it so hard

it splintered against the far wall. Maggie flinched at the sound of it cracking into the tile.

"Now," her father said, his eyes deadly calm and composed. Flat. Purposeful. "Your choice, Maggie."

"That's not going to stop them, Tommy. You know that. They'll page you again, and then they'll start playing with the lights and then they'll toss a flash-bang in if they have to. They can't let these people stay at risk."

"And they can't negotiate with me. I know all the tricks. So make your choice."

Make her choice.

Which was no choice at all.

"Fuck it, anyway," the lieutenant snapped.

John didn't so much as blink. "You didn't really expect anything different, did you?"

The lieutenant sighed, rubbed his hands over his face. "No. But it would be nice to be surprised for once."

Flower's voice could be heard over the earpieces. "C1, I have an ID on the third person in the hall. Sergeant Delaney. It appears he's taken a small caliber wound to the abdomen."

"Shit," the lieu snapped. "Can't Delaney just once stay out of the way of stray bullets?"

"I doubt this one was stray," John admitted. "Tommy's hated Sean since the kid was fifteen and roundhoused him for hurting Maggie."

"It just gets better and better, doesn't it? And me without any medics left on my team."

John actually smiled. "I think that might be the one thing we don't have to worry about here. Everybody in the hospital is on alert."

"Well, what do we do now?"

John rubbed his hand through his hair. "Tommy won't talk, I can guarantee it. And I'm not sure how long Maggie can hold out. Nobody's more important to her than Delaney, you know."

"What does Tommy want from her, anyway?"

John's smile grew sad. "The same thing he's always wanted from her. Control. We need to get in there before he gets it."

"What do you suggest?"

John sighed. "If it were just Tommy and Maggie in there, I wouldn't be too worried. Tommy's not going to shoot Maggie, and Maggie damn well isn't picking up a gun. But Sean changes things."

"Can she talk him out?"

"I don't know. I simply don't know."

"In that case, I think we need to get our special ordnance people into that room with the broken door and be ready to flash-bang him out of that hall."

"Maintenance has discontinued oxygen down here, so the incendiary won't be a problem. But we need to be able to get to Delaney fast."

This time the lieutenant smiled. "It's what we're trained to do, isn't it, John?"

"C1," Flower said, his voice as quiet as possible, "I can see the situation from here. Maggie is trying to move the perpetrator away from the downed officer. If she distracts him enough, we might be able to get to him without injury."

The lieutenant engaged his mike. "Hold there. I'm coming to evaluate. We're going to try and get more team in that room. Copy?"

"Ten-four."

"You're going to have to do this with surgical precision," John warned.

The lieutenant just shook his head. "This wasn't what this was supposed to be for."

And then he walked out of the security office and rejoined the rest of his team.

It wasn't working.

Maggie saw Tommy smile and knew that he'd figured

out her plan. Deliberately, he stepped back so he could keep Sean in his line of sight.

Sean, who was struggling to keep his eyes open. To keep Maggie from making that terrible decision. Sean, who was dying before her eyes rather than see her finally surrender to her father.

She had to do something.

She had to act.

She didn't have any more time.

She looked at that gun, that deadly, powerful, *easy* gun. She thought about what it would feel like in her hand, fitting against her palm like a lover's caress, promising power. Promising decision and finality.

Tommy gone.

Tommy out of her life. Finally.

Tommy triumphant.

Maggie sucked in a short, stabbing breath and struggled against the tears, because if Tommy won against her, then he won against them all. Most of all, he won against Sean, who had spent his life protecting her from her own father.

"Come on, Maggie," her father said, the disdain in his voice softened to velvet, as if he knew she'd rather sharpen herself on his disdain. "Come on and pick it up. Let yourself be mad. Be furious. Be so sure of yourself that you don't have any choice but to do it."

That gun, lying there.

That gun he'd given to Cheri the Cheerleader and Susie the Slut and Brenda the Barfly. That gun that was the symbol of his ultimate control.

Maggie focused on it, but she couldn't see it. She could only see herself opening the door to her apartment after school. Calling to her mother. Seeing the shadow on the floor. Twirling, twirling. As slow as a dance, with the fan blade clicking in syncopation and one shoe toppled to the floor in counterpoint.

So Maggie closed her eyes, because she didn't want to see anymore.

"He's dying, Maggie. He's lying there dying because

you don't have the guts to do it. You don't have the balls, little girl, do you? Not like your friends, even that skinny fag of a doctor of yours. Even he has more guts than you with all your SWAT crap and your rebellion. You're nothing. You're less than fucking nothing, and I've just proved it. And your friend is gonna die because of it."

Sean.

Maggie could hear him, even with her eyes closed. Small, painful pants of air. Anxious little movements of his body as he sought to escape the pain, as he struggled to find a way to save his strength.

Dying.

And there wasn't time for her uncle John or her lieutenant to save him.

Only her.

She had to give Tommy what he wanted.

She had to save Sean, even at the cost of her pride and sense of self-worth. She had to act.

"Worthless," Tommy murmured like a lover. "Worthless, sneaky little whore who spreads her legs for the likes of that asshole on the floor. Worthless, the both of you, and I just proved it."

And Maggie snapped.

Her eyes flew open. She straightened so hard she was trembling. She met her father's disdain with a sudden flash of her own.

No more.

She simply wouldn't take any more.

And because she wouldn't, she gave Tommy a truth even she hadn't admitted to since she'd been seven years old and walked in on her mother's suicide.

"You want to know if I get mad, Tommy?" she asked, stepping forward, stepping over that gun on the ground. "All right, Tommy, yes. I get mad. I get in rages even you wouldn't recognize. I get so furious I have to break anything I can get my hands on, and I do that so often that I have to shop for cheap breakables to have on hand just so I can smash them against the floor. Or against the wall. Or against my own head. I puke everything up in my stomach and then cook more so I can puke that up, too. And thank God for Sean, because if he weren't there when I was mad, I'd fuck the first five men I saw, just to work off my anger, and I'd probably break their backs doing it. Instead, I take it all out on Sean. And then I get down on my knees and hand scrub my loft until I could do surgery on the floor, because it's the only place I've been able to do penance since the last time you took me to church."

She stepped up closer, right up to Tommy, up to that nine mil he held to her sternum, and she told him the rest, panting, tears staining her shirt, her hand as tight as pain at her side. "Yes, Tommy, I get mad. I get really mad. And when I'm mad I do some crazy shit. But I'll tell you what I don't do. What I've never done, and what I will never do. I've never, not once, hurt another person, just so I feel better. So I feel more in control. I may have wanted Jimmy Krebs to die for what he did, but this is important, Tommy. I would never, *never* have done it myself. And God knows I've had the chance. But it's not my job, Tommy. It's not yours, I don't care what the hell you'd like to think. So no, Tommy, I'm not like you. And I'm not going to be like you, or I would end up betraying not only myself, but my mother and my friends and most of all, Sean."

"That's bullshit!" he raged, shoving the gun right against her sternum as if he could push her off with it. "You think your precious friends believe you? Your friends who've been killing people?"

"My friends," she retorted, her voice a quiet that was terrible. Then she shook her head and leaned into the gun. "My friends are your friends. At least they were. And those friends are good people, Tommy. The best. They're the ones who risk death every goddamn day to help people they don't even know. They're the ones who face the worst in all of us and keep smiling. Keep trying. A few of them succumbed to a terrible temptation, Tommy. I know, because I heard the tapes Montana Bob made, and I know that there weren't more than a handful who actually acted.

Those few are going to have to pay for it in ways you can't even imagine. And the ones who just let it happen will suffer even more."

Now, Maggie was the one poking, her finger in his chest, her eyes shards of fury. "But you, Tommy," she snarled. "*You* were the temptation. *You* were the one who coldly, calmly took advantage of your friends' anguish and frustration to convince them to commit the acts *you* wanted to commit. And they listened to you because they trusted you. They looked up to you. They *honored* you, because you were a good cop. But you weren't a good cop, Tommy. You were an incubus, sucking out their souls for the sake of a little revenge. Well, Tommy, it's time you paid for all the hurt you've caused. You're going to prison, Tommy, and I'm going to be there to make sure of it. But in the meantime, if you're gonna shoot me, then please just get it the fuck over with, because I'm going over to help Sean."

For a second, Tommy just stood there. Maggie just stood there. The tiles echoed with breathing and nothing more. And then, slowly, softly, as if the effort was great, the clap of hands.

Sean.

"Bravo, Mags," he said on a whisper. "Oh, bravo. I think I waited . . . my . . . entire life . . . to hear that. Although I don't think . . . that's really . . . in the . . . hostage negotiator's handbook . . ."

Maggie, suddenly, wanted to grin. To laugh. To dance with Sean in her arms. She simply stepped back, away from the barrel of Tommy's gun.

"Don't move!" Tommy screamed at her. "You stupid bitch! You think this is over?"

Maggie didn't even answer him.

"You can't do this to me!"

Maggie was already on her knees beside Sean. She looked up at those words and caught the look in Tommy's eyes.

And realized what this was all about.

Fear.

A flash of it in his eyes like heat lightning. Not heard, so discounted, if it hadn't been seen.

It took Maggie's breath away, because suddenly she knew just how much her own father had betrayed her. He hadn't only wanted her surrender, he'd wanted her assistance. He'd been standing there trying to get his own daughter to help him commit suicide by cop, so he didn't have to face up to what he'd done.

For a moment Maggie just stared at him.

"You know, Tommy," she said softly, sadly, "I've called you many things in my lifetime. But I never thought I'd have to call you a coward."

And then she just turned back to Sean.

Stunned, Tommy lowered his gun. Maggie got to her feet and opened the door to room four so that Flower could help her get Sean to safety.

"Drop the weapon, Sarge," she heard behind her.

"Maggie!"

It was her father's voice. A voice she'd never heard. Pleading. She ignored it.

Doors opened. Boots sounded on the hallway floor. The team had arrived.

Flower had just dumped Sean onto the cart when Maggie heard the sudden clatter of movement behind her. A yell of "Gun!"

Maggie spun for the hallway. She saw the team flatten, the guns raise, her father turning with the .357 in his hand to challenge Paul. She ran to stop him.

Uncle John got there first. With one shot from his service weapon, he caught Tommy dead center in his right hand. The .357 tumbled to the floor and skidded right back to Maggie's feet. Tommy turned on his friend with a howl of rage, his bleeding hand held out like an accusation.

John just stood before him in full gear, his gun down, his great brown eyes distressed. "Maggie's right," he said in softly scathing tones. "I never thought you were a coward."

Tommy looked around him. He saw what Maggie saw,

and it broke him. She saw it in the sag of his shoulders, in
the sudden pallor of his skin. In the way, suddenly, he
didn't seem so big.

All those cop eyes he'd counted on to worship him now
looked at him with the same disdain he'd accorded the
lesser people in his life.

Tommy "The Terminator" O'Brien was no more.

But Maggie didn't have time for that. She had to save
Sean's life, and she wasn't sure she was going to be able
to do it.

"Call for a trauma team!" she yelled as she ran back into
the room.

More doors, more feet, the rumble of equipment. But
Maggie wasn't paying any attention. Sean's eyes were
closed. He looked, she thought in terrible premonition, like
Montana Bob, splayed out on that cart: diminished and
small and not quite human anymore, and Maggie was terrified she'd taken too long.

And she didn't have Allen here to save him.

"Sean!" she yelled as she ran to him. "Sean, dammit!"

But he didn't answer.

So she did what she did best. She went into Little Zen
mode, as if none of this mattered, and she did her job. But
this time, she did it with tears streaming down her face.

Epilogue

It was summer again. The heat was back, the thick, stifling humidity that sapped energy and patience, and weighted the air like regret. There were fights and murders and an infinite variety of injuries to be seen at local EDs.

Only the cicadas had gone. Now the nights were filled with more normal sounds of planes and boom cars and thunder. The days stretched out hot and still and heavy.

Which meant that Maggie was still busy. Busy at the Blymore ED where she still worked, and on the SWAT team, where she was now the senior medic.

To that end, she was pulling her car up to another perimeter line and shutting off the engine.

The team had gotten the 1040 call forty minutes ago, and it had taken her that long to break away from the shift at Blymore ED and drive to the far southwestern edge of St. Louis County, where the woods lay lush along the hills by the Meramec River, and subdivisions had gated entries and swimming pools. The team had a hostage situation. Woman holding an entire day care hostage in her basement. From the look of things, the day care was situated in a Ramada with Porsches.

Maggie was already assessing the well-landscaped scene where cops clustered at the brick driveway and the West County ambulance screeched to a stop alongside the Viewer 2 uplink truck a block away.

Tucking up her hair, she plucked her kerchief and sweat-band from the lap of a newly decorated Ted. Since Maggie and Sean had returned from Sean's recuperative trip to Hawaii the winter before, Ted had taken to sporting a bright Hawaiian print shirt, pukka shells, and a big white plantation hat. Kinda like pulling up to a situation with McGarrett in the other seat. Maggie dropped a kiss on his blankly smiling face and hopped out of the car.

"I saw you making time with that stranger," Paul greeted her, his Remington slung over his shoulder and his helmet in his hand.

Maggie grinned. "I'm too much woman just for Delaney."

"You won't get an argument out of me." He held her medic vest while Maggie slid into the bulletproof under-version. "Where is Delaney, anyway? Usually he shows up at these gigs whether we want him to or not."

Maggie accepted the thirty-pound medic vest and Velcroed it closed. "He's pouting over the fact that he hasn't made the team yet."

Two new women had joined the team, which meant Maggie finally had someone to share her tiny locker room. Still, Sean couldn't get his shooting scores high enough, and it rankled him. He had, however, regained his stripes, his position in Homicide, and his shotgun-shell Christmas tree.

"Besides," Maggie said, "Allen is premiering the Potosi Players tonight. Sean went out to help. And, if you're interested in joining us, Susan is covering the event."

Susan, who had made it off the features page with a splash. The good news was that she'd won several news awards. The bad news—for Susan, at least—was that her story had broken at the same time as a war.

As for Allen, he would be spending the better part of his active years behind bars. Maggie visited him at least once a week, bringing Zen along. And, as was Allen's wont, he'd vowed to make the best of his time there. Not only had he personally reorganized the infirmary, he'd raised enough money to paint the common rooms in primary colors, and claimed a starring role in not only the new prison softball team, but their theater troupe. And nobody but Zen and Maggie, and on some days Sean, saw the price Allen was paying for what he'd done.

Tommy was at Potosi, too, but Maggie didn't visit him. Neither of them seemed to mind much. Tommy was too busy protecting himself from the mopes he'd arrested and too obsessed by the fact that Allen wielded more power than he. Maggie was just glad finally to be able to spend her days free of tension.

Bad tension, anyway.

Tommy tension.

She much preferred the kind that waited for her behind the closed thousand-dollar doors she and Paul were approaching.

It had been such a long year. Holes had been left in the structures of all their lives. People missing, more changed utterly. Prison sentences handed out to a handful of medical people, another of police, people Maggie had loved, some she'd loathed, some she just felt sorry for.

Jeannie Mars, who had protected the guilty with her silence, had lost her job and license. She worked now on the riverboats where her husband gambled. Lieutenant Ames, who had supervised the Internal Affairs investigation with such casual incompetency, was walking a beat in North City. John Vandever, the rookie who had beaten Jimmy Morris into the hospital for Tommy, had turned state's evidence against the man who had protected his job. After the trials, John had moved to the coast to work in construction.

The impact on the St. Louis area had been greater in the whole than in the parts. Trust lost, notoriety overcome, questions raised that would never have answers.

Maggie hadn't known how right she'd been when she'd told her father that the people who had stood by would suffer. She saw it every day, as the people who had once stood by in silence now quietly offered work and commitment as their personal penances.

Oddly enough, The List survived. But a list that was now carefully monitored, like a leaky valve in a boiler room. The hospital now provided stress and trauma counseling, and maybe someday the cost of working the front lines could effectively be kept at a minimum.

Someday. Not yet.

Maggie had been wrong about one thing. She hadn't been shunned. She hadn't so much as been bad-mouthed. Not after Tommy's final diatribe. Not after all those people had found out what they'd really been involved in.

It wasn't perfect. It hadn't gone back to what it was before. It never would. There would always be holes in Maggie's life as well, places she didn't want to revisit. But Maggie could live with it. She had her team still, her work again, and Sean always.

He'd moved in for good in November, and she'd finally forgiven him completely in January. Someday, maybe they'd get up the courage to marry. Until then, they lived their lives as best they could.

"So, what's the score, Lieu?" she asked as she joined the team at the command van.

Paxton was already there, and Flower and Kim, the gas guy. Uncle John, it seemed, was already in the van setting up negotiations.

"We have another Maggie O'Brien special," Flower announced.

Maggie came to a halt. "Aw, c'mon, Flower. You can't pin every bent twig on me."

"I think I can pin this one. She asked for you by name."

Maggie looked over at the lieutenant, who shrugged. "I'm afraid so. John's inside waiting for you."

"Who is she?"

"A woman named Anne Evergreen. You know her?"

Maggie stopped fiddling with her earpiece. "Aspen Annie? Sure. I used to see her all the time when I still worked the ambulance. She thinks she's a tree."

"Well," the lieu said, "she's holding five saplings hostage in there."

"With what?" Maggie laughed. "Annie's strictly deciduous."

The lieutenant scowled. "A chain saw."

"Whoa. She's definitely gone old growth on me."

Flower held open the door to the van, and Uncle John waved her in, his negotiating frown firmly in place.

"Okay," Maggie relented. Stepping inside, she dropped her favorite uncle a kiss. "Give me the headset. And prepare to lob in some pinecones. Annie absolutely *hates* pinecones."

Flower moaned. "I *knew* it . . ."

Maggie laughed and set her helmet down. God was good. She was glad to be home.

Turn the page for an excerpt
from Eileen Dreyer's next book

HEAD GAMES

Available in hardcover
from St. Martin's Press!

No man becomes depraved in a single day.

JUVENAL

Prologue

There is comfort in ritual.

There is order.

There is the security of knowing that our most precious needs can be protected by enclosing them within the high, strong walls of familiarity and precision.

Kenny understood this. He recognized the need for ritual, the joy of it. He cherished the keen anticipation of each deliberate act. Kenny practiced his rituals as carefully as a priest performs high mass.

One of the keystones of Kenny's ritual was the ten o'clock news. Kenny watched the news the way other people read obituaries. Once he knew his name wasn't going to be mentioned, he could get on with planning the next day's work.

But not just the ten o'clock news. The ten o'clock news on Channel 7. Kenny preferred to get his news from Channel 7, because it tended to carry the most lurid stories. Kenny liked to hear the breathless outrage in anchorwoman Donna Kirkland's soft voice when she said words like *startling* and *gruesome*, almost as if she derived sexual pleasure from them. He liked the way her plump little lips wrapped around the vowels and her eyes widened at the words. But that wasn't something he figured he should dwell on when he had his new friend with him, as he did tonight.

Flower. Her name was Flower. It was such a wonderful

name, Kenny thought, turning to her. She was such a wonderful person, comforting and quiet.

"Ten o'clock is the only time to watch news," he told her as he settled himself back down on the nubby brown-plaid couch and wrapped his arm around her shoulder. "By now, anything that's going to happen has happened. No big surprises, ya know?"

Flower agreed with him. She always did.

"Today," Donna Kirkland intoned with barely suppressed delight on TV, "a grisly discovery in Forest Park . . ."

Grisly. Another word she seemed to get off on. Kenny found himself getting hard. Reaching over to retrieve his beer from the end table, he took a long swig. Beer went well with the news. Beer went well with everything, but Kenny especially liked it with the news.

So he smiled. He had his beer, Flower was here with him, and there was murder on television. And to make it all perfect, Donnatheanchor—Kenny always thought of her as that: Donnatheanchor, as if it were her entire name—was excited by it.

". . . two park rangers found the partially clothed body of a woman in the woods while clearing brush."

On the TV the camera panned over the obligatory stand of dead trees silhouetted against a gray sky. Caught clustered in a fold of land like cattle sheltering against the wind stood about a half dozen uniformed officers bent almost double, an ambulance cart, and a couple of fat guys in down vests and baseball caps.

"Now they'll get the official report from the homicide officer," Kenny said with some disgust. "You'd think they'd change the format just a little."

"Jamie?" Donnatheanchor called out to the reporter. "Have there been any official statements?"

A slick twenty-something guy showed up, standing in front of the downtown police station. "Well, Donna," he said, frowning, "identification has not been made. We spoke with a representative of the Medical Examiner's office a few minutes ago."

"*Not* homicide?" Kenny objected.

The TV now showed the inside of some generic government office. A woman stood quietly listening to a question being asked off camera. Kenny saw her and forgot all about the homicide officer he'd expected. He forgot the story entirely.

His heart suddenly raced. He felt the surprise right there in his throat. Squinting, he leaned closer. He opened his mouth to say something and then didn't remember to say it. He thought maybe he'd stopped breathing.

"My God," he whispered, stunned.

She was petite, small-boned, and trim. Short, neat auburn hair. Bright brown eyes with laugh lines and lots of experience stamped on almost pretty features, small hands tucked in the pockets of a serviceable gray suit jacket.

Older, much older, it seemed to Kenny. But then, so was he.

"My God," he breathed again, shaking his head. "It's *her*. Why didn't I know?"

"The Medical Examiner believes the victim to have been at the site for about four days," she was saying with appropriate solemnity. "We won't know the cause of death until the autopsy has been performed in the morning."

Kenny always remembered her smiling. But he remembered this look even better. Her sad look. Kenny remembered her looking at him this way, like she wanted to say something or do something that could make it all different.

Maybe that was why he suddenly recognized her. He'd finally seen her sad look. The look he'd always thought was all his.

Forgetting his beer, forgetting his friend Flower, he focused on the TV, so excited he could hardly think.

"Molly Burke is a death investigator for the city of St. Louis," Jamie the reporter said as he appeared again on the screen.

"Molly . . ." Kenny's laugh was sudden. "Oh my god, Molly. Yes, of course!"

He turned to Flower, truly thrilled. "You don't understand," he said. "I knew her. I *know* her. I wondered for so long what became of her, and now to realize that she's been right here, that I've *seen* her! I wasn't sure . . . I mean, you hope, ya know . . . but . . . well, I've just got to let her know I'm back."

Kenny turned to the TV, but he was too late. Donna-theanchor had moved on to recap the top news story, which charted the various government agencies that were temporarily shut down in the wake of the latest congressional budget deadlock. Molly was gone and wouldn't come back. But Kenny knew where she was, and he knew just what to do about it.

For a few moments, he just sat there alongside Flower and considered his good luck. Kenny had never been the kind of person who had good luck. And even on the rare occasions he did get it, usually he didn't know what to do with it.

Well, he knew this time. He knew because for more than twenty years he'd been anticipating what he'd do if this very moment ever came. He'd been practicing hard in his head so that it would be perfect.

Twenty long years. And now he would finally get to act out his most precious dreams.

Tilting the long-neck Busch up to finish it, he set the bottle down and stood up.

"Time for lights out," he said to Flower. "I'm going to have a busy day tomorrow."

His friend Flower smiled back. But then, she always smiled. So Kenny smiled as well, because tonight he was happy, too. Then, with the exquisite care he showed all his friends, he lifted her head off her shoulders and put it back in the refrigerator where it belonged. Then, turning off the lights, he went to bed.

i am   nobody

nuthing

she says so

Join top authors for the ultimate cruise experience. Spend 7 days in the Western Caribbean aboard the luxurious *Carnival Elation*. Start in Galveston, TX, and visit Progreso, Cozumel and Belize. Enjoy all this with a ship full of authors, entertainers and book lovers on the **"Get Caught Reading at Sea Cruise"** October 17 - 24, 2004.

PRICES STARTING AT $749 PER PERSON WITH COUPON!

Mail in this coupon with proof of purchase* to receive $250 per person off the regular **"Get Caught Reading at Sea Cruise"** price. One coupon per person required to receive $250 discount. For further details call **1-877-ADV-NTGE** or visit **www.GetCaughtReadingatSea.com**

*proof of purchase is original sales receipt for this book with purchase circled.

Carnival
The Most Popular Cruise Line in the World!

GET $250 OFF

Name (Please Print)

Address _____ Apt. No.

City _____ State _____ Zip

E-Mail Address

See Following Page For Terms & Conditions.

For booking form and complete information go to www.getcaughtreadingatsea.com or call 1-877-ADV-NTGE

Carnival Elation

7 Day Exotic Western Caribbean Itinerary

DAY	PORT	ARRIVE	DEPART
Sun	Galveston		4:00 P.M.
Mon	"Fun Day" at Sea		
Tue	Progreso/Merida	8:00 A.M.	4:00 P.M.
Wed	Cozumel	9:00 A.M.	5:00 P.M.
Thu	Belize	8:00 A.M.	6:00 P.M.
Fri	"Fun Day" at Sea		
Sat	"Fun Day" at Sea		
Sun	Galveston	8:00 A.M.	

TERMS AND CONDITIONS

PAYMENT SCHEDULE:
50% due upon booking
Full and final payment due by July 26, 2004
Acceptable forms of payment are Visa, MasterCard, American Express, Discover and checks. The cardholder must be one of the passengers traveling. A fee of $25 will apply for all returned checks. Check payments must be made payable to **Advantage International, LLC** and sent to: **Advantage International, LLC, 195 North Harbor Drive, Suite 4206, Chicago, IL 60601**

CHANGE/CANCELLATION:
Notice of change/cancellation must be made in writing to Advantage International, LLC.

Change:
Changes in cabin category may be requested and can result in increased rate and penalties. A name change is permitted 60 days or more prior to departure and will incur a penalty of $50 per name change. Deviation from the group schedule and package is a cancellation.

Cancellation:

181 days or more prior to departure	$250 per person
121 - 180 days prior to departure	50% of the package price
61 - 120 days prior to departure	75% of the package price
60 days or less prior to departure	100% of the package price (nonrefundable)

US and Canadian citizens are required to present a valid passport or the original birth certificate and state-issued photo ID (driver's license). All other nationalities must contact the consulate of the various ports that are visited for verification of documentation.

<u>We strongly recommend trip cancellation insurance!</u>

For further details call 1-877-ADV-NTGE or visit www.GetCaughtReadingatSea.com

- -

For booking form and complete information
go to **www.getcaughtreadingatsea.com** or call **1-877-ADV-NTGE**

Complete coupon and booking form and mail both to:
**Advantage International, LLC,
195 North Harbor Drive, Suite 4206, Chicago, IL 60601**